HUNTER
AND
FOX

A SHIFTED WORLD NOVEL

HUNTER
AND
FOX

PHILIPPA BALLANTINE

an imprint of **Prometheus Books**
Amherst, NY

Published 2012 by Pyr®, an imprint of Prometheus Books

Cover illustration © 2012 Cynthia Shepperd
Cover design by Grace M. Conti-Zilsberger

Inquiries should be addressed to

Pyr
59 John Glenn Drive
Amherst, New York 14228–2119
VOICE: 716–691–0133
FAX: 716–691–0137
WWW.PYRSF.COM

16 15 14 13 12   5 4 3 2 1

Library of Congress Cataloging-in-Publication Data

Ballantine, Philippa, 1971–
    Hunter and fox : a shifted world novel / by Philippa Ballantine.
        p. cm.
    First published: London : Gollancz, an imprint of the Orion Publishing Group, 2006.
    ISBN 978–1–61614–623–8 (pbk.)
    ISBN 978–1–61614–624–5 (ebook)
    1. Good and evil—Fiction. 2. Imaginary places—Fiction. I. Title.
PR9639.4.B39H86 2012
823'.92—dc23

                                                                    2012004776

Printed in the United States of America

For all the strong women who have passed through my life.
Gone but not forgotten: Ruth, Dorothy, Jean, and Mavis.
Because of your example, I never gave up. I hope somehow you know that.

CONTENTS

ACKNOWLEDGMENTS

Thanks first to Lou Anders, the editor who took a chance on this strange land and tormented woman. I am delighted to have a chance to work with him. To Laurie McLean, my agent, whose eye was first caught by this story, and who never gave up on it. To Gabrielle Harbowy, whom it is a delight to work with again. I love how the world turns but friends still find each other. Finally, and most certainly not least of all, to my husband Tee Morris, who is my strength and inspiration and travels with me through all these worlds hand in hand.

CHAPTER ONE

TALES TO TELL

To hunt a man was not meant to be an easy thing—however, it had become a fixture in the life of Talyn the Dark.

Her fingers clenched in the razor-sharp hair of her mount. The creature resembled a great war horse but possessed a heart that was as tumultuous as the Chaosland beneath its hooves. Talyn was aware her thoughts should have been full of guilt, but they were as empty and barren as the scene she looked out over.

How many mothers and fathers had she killed? How many promises of vengeance had she heard? More than it was possible to count. Generations had grown and come to claim revenge for some ancestor or other, yet none had ever succeeded. It was immutable proof that there was no justice in the world, no higher power to hold her accountable. No hope for redemption.

Between her thighs, Syris the nykur tossed his green shaggy head—the sound of his saberlike teeth sliding against each other set her nerves on edge. No one had ever tamed a nykur before, which made Talyn even more feared by the general population. Yet even she had not dared to put a bridle on him.

By knee pressure alone she guided the creature down from the rough granite foothills toward the village. Above, a storm was gathering; purple-gray clouds were running across this half-tamed landscape that reeked of salt and bitterness. The howling winds full of stinging sand tugged her dark hair free. She pushed it impatiently out of her equally dark eyes and focused on the ragged little settlement where her prey awaited. The village, ramshackle and nearly abandoned, rattled under the assault from the oncoming storm like a child's toy shaken by an unkind hand. Talyn had not timed her visit with the weather in mind, but it was appropriate, considering her mission.

The rider and mount passed under a lightning-blasted tree hung with totems that clacked and clattered in the gale. The yellow skull of a dead cat twisted mournfully as the wind straight off the Chaoslands whistled through its eye sockets. The Bone Lord could not protect the village from the Caisah's bounty hunter.

These people knew why she was here. They scattered before her like chaff, rushing to the perceived safety of their homes. Parents tugged their children closer as she passed their doorways.

Talyn's forefinger idly traced the engraved swirls and flourishes on the flintlock pistol that rested against her leg as her gaze slid from house to house. The ebb and flow of time and possibilities ran through her Vaerli senses in ways none of these villagers could possibly understand. The yester-thoughts in this place murmured of full harvests and joyous celebrations, but the future-thoughts uttered dire warnings of silence and death. The human-shared human willpower, the malkin that held this place static in a world of chaos, was fraying and disappearing. Talyn rode in, not as the soldier of destruction but merely as one of its scouts.

Shifting in her saddle, she smiled bitterly. The racing heart of her prey sounded loud in her ears; he had nowhere to hide. The Hunter dipped into the stream of time and found her prey in the crippled house farthest from the road. His footprints in the gray earth led to the door, the ripple of before-time telling her he had only just fled there.

A woman came out of the house, thin arms crossed in front of her, a hard look tinged with weariness in her eyes. Like everyone else, she must have recognized the small woman with the golden-brown skin and dark eyes atop the green beast, even if Talyn hadn't been wearing the black chainmail and the scarlet cape of her master. The Caisah used his Hunter to maintain control at the dusty edges of his empire, and everywhere she went, fear followed.

The tension in the air finally reached the nykur, and Syris surged back on his hind legs, twisting under her like a mini tornado. The Hunter held her place atop him easily by tightening her knees and leaning forward. Her black eyes never left the woman in the doorway. After the nykur returned to his hooves, prancing and snapping, Talyn slipped off his back and walked the scant distance to the doorway.

Being shorter than the other woman, the Hunter was forced to look up. Talyn, though, was not the one who flinched.

This woman was his wife. The Hunter could read that easily enough. The foolish creature felt she had to put up some sort of show. It might be pointless, but he was the father of her children and that still meant something to her.

Why Esthelon the carter had drawn the Caisah's attention was unknown.

He was a very small target, hardly worthy of Talyn. She didn't try to understand her master's motives; she only obeyed and was rewarded.

Esthelon had been crouching behind the door, sheltered by son, daughter, and wife. Silence lingered for a moment, and then he made a run for the low scrub behind the house. Talyn stepped into his path, moving so fast in the before-time that to him she must have appeared a blur. In slow motion the tired, dirty man pulled a dagger from his coat, aiming for where he presumed her heart to be while panic contorted his features.

Always there was an instant where Talyn was tempted by the before-time. The knife moved in a silvered arc, and it would have been very easy to move into it or even just watch its descent, but the Caisah's oath held her faster than any death wish she harbored.

So instead Talyn stepped inside his guard, dragged his arm down, and buried the knife in his chest. Time snapped back when the man fell to his knees, and Talyn was there, standing above another bloody corpse.

In a Vaerli there should have been some reckoning, some empathic link between her and her victim. None came. That inkling of compassion had been lost a long time ago.

The children didn't know that. They dashed past their mother, whose face had slipped into her hands. The little boy threw himself on the cooling shell that had only recently been his father, but the bright-eyed girl stood staring up at her. The rest of the world faded to insignificance. It was only the two of them in it.

Her little dirt-smeared face glowed with sudden shock and hatred, and she spat out one word. "Talyn."

It was a curse in their tribal language—a demon of death, whom they believed claimed the lives of the innocent. Every Chaos storm was heralded by its arrival, and they locked themselves away praying to whichever Scion of Right they followed to protect them.

It was an appropriate name, and she had taken it on with no sense of fear. After all, her own had been stripped from her—gone along with the person she might have been before the Harrowing had killed most of her race and scattered the remainder.

Talyn nodded to the little girl, respecting her anger but expecting little from it. Then she pushed the sobbing brother from the corpse. The Caisah was not a trusting man—he needed evidence. Striding to her mount, she flung the remains over Syris' back, and then mounted up behind them.

She turned Syris quickly and did not look down into the eyes of the grieving. It wasn't that she feared them—it was just always the same. She couldn't face the dire repetition of it. Talyn rode out of the village and no one moved to stop her.

Returning to the road, she kept Syris to a slower pace than he might have liked; neither of them had any real reason to hurry back to V'nae Rae where the Caisah waited for his bounty. They had just climbed to the top of the first peak a mere mile from the village when Syris arched his neck and pranced sideways. She heard a distant and deep rumbling.

Only these two things gave her a moment's warning before the landscape tilted. Luckily both she and her mount had plenty of experience with the vagaries of living in a constantly changing landscape. The skree slope buckled, but the nykur danced lightly atop the shattered rock, keeping his footing as well as any mountain goat.

It was only a momentary change, a perfectly expected shift as the Chaosland to each side of the road pushed upward, yearning toward becoming a mountain. By next week its aspirations would be realized.

This was what the world had been like before the arrival of the peoples, when it had been just the Vaerli and the Kindred. Now there was stability and control—concepts that Talyn still bristled against.

Still, that was not the only surprise the Chaoslands would throw at her today. An abrupt pain stabbed through Talyn, as though a needle of steel was passing from one side of her head to the other. It was so unexpected that she almost cried out. Instead she gripped Syris' mane and clenched her teeth against the agony. For the briefest moment she feared a Kindred was walking in her shadow, but those guardians of the land had long ago abandoned the Vaerli. No, Talyn decided, it had to be the Second Gift—a power that some called Kin Sense.

Lifting herself in the saddle, she scanned the landscape for signs of life with a flutter in her belly that might have been fear or excitement. Nothing. The gray of the skree slope was empty, and the only noise was the wind blowing over the sharp edges of rock.

The Caisah was indeed cruel, taking all other Vaerli Gifts but leaving this one. Thanks to the curse he'd placed on her people, to touch another

Vaerli would result in both their deaths. However, Vaerli could still sense others of their kind. It was a little twist of the knife—something that her master excelled at. That moment of searing pain had to be a before-time echo of a Vaerli somewhere nearby meeting death all alone. There was no other explanation that made sense. Despite all the time that had passed and distance between them, Talyn dipped her head in a moment's contemplation. She would not have named it a prayer.

"Where does a story start?"

Looking out into the gathered audience, full of dirty, unhappy faces, Finnbarr the Fox didn't really expect an answer.

It was how he had been taught: begin each talespinning with a question to make the audience consider. This was the one he always used. It was his mark. But the crowd tonight barely looked up, more interested in their beers or the tavern's hollow-eyed wenches.

Finn did not lose faith, though. He'd been doing this for years, and he did not earn his living by giving up. His teachers, the legendary Talespinners of Elraban Island, had instilled in him a love of the story, and it didn't matter how few listened. Just one made it worthwhile.

Tonight he felt the familiar cloud of melancholy sweeping through him, and after that uncomfortable truths came bubbling up. Sometimes the tales chose themselves, his teachers had warned.

A few of the audience lifted their eyes to the tall man with the crop of unruly red-gold hair in the corner of the darkened inn. He read it in them; they wanted some relief from the misery of their lives. But he would give them something else altogether—the truth.

Hooking a chair closer with his foot, he brushed his hair from his eyes as best he could, and began. "The story starts in you." He easily gave away the answer it had taken him twelve years to learn. "I've traveled through all of Conhaero, walked with Blood Witches, dined with high Praetors, and scrabbled for scraps with the lowliest street urchin." They laughed at the image. "And yet every time I tell this story the Caisah seems somewhat displeased."

He barely heard the ripple of consternation pass through his audience—

the story was already taking him. It wouldn't matter if a garrison of Rutilian guards broke through the door at that very instant—only by killing him could they have stopped the story.

So Finn told them the tale of life before the Caisah, in the time just after the Vaerli had summoned the various races to Conhaero from the White Void. "It was a golden time," he whispered to them. They had to shift their chairs closer to the stage to catch his words, and many of them did.

Finn's voice dropped into the cant of talespinning, reaching out to find the vulnerable places in the people's hearts. If he disturbed them with mention of the Caisah, he now took hold of them and washed that fear away.

He told of the Kindred who then were unafraid to walk the earth, and the Vaerli who were their allies. Finn murmured of how though the newcomers to Conhaero had been torn loose from their gods in the White Void, they had found among their own ranks scions who had led them to this land. Even now, they could still appear to their believers. "The Lady of Wings herself has been seen only a few miles from this place," he continued in a reverent tone.

The patrons shifted and looked about them as if she might appear at the back of the inn somewhere.

He took that belief and wove it tighter about his audience. "The time when the new peoples had arrived had been one of peace and prosperity, before the Harrowing of the Vaerli and the iron grip of the Caisah."

As a talespinner he recognized their weaknesses. At the fringes of the civilized world, with their backs to the dangers of the Chaoslands, the people here were hardest pressed by their overlord's taxes. He hoped mentioning this time of plenty would make them think.

He almost had them, but Finn couldn't quite help himself. Foolishly he kept on and told the tale of the rise of the Caisah. It was an amateur mistake; one that he should never have made. The listeners did not want to hear of his powerful magic, his immortality, and his crushing of those who had stood against him. By trying to raise their sympathies for the Vaerli he had gone too far. They did not care what had happened to that blighted race nearly three hundred years ago—it made no difference to their everyday lives.

Finn might empathize with those scattered and torn people going into lonely exile—but they did not. He'd had his one chance when he mentioned taxes but now he had lost them.

Recognizing this, he bowed to the audience. "This is a tale of warning by Finnbarr the Fox, for what the Caisah has done to the Vaerli could happen to any of us at any time."

He might as well have been conversing with himself, for they had already turned back to their beer and talk of the next harvest. It was not what they had wanted, a cruel medicine to people who had been expecting something diverting. They didn't want to hear stories of sorrow about a people they'd been taught to despise.

Finn slipped off the stage and made for the narrow room that was the meager price for such a grand telling. He caught the innkeeper's eye and got the distinct impression that he thought it was too much rather than too little. It had been his wife who hired Finn, and the storyteller could only hope that would not cause her any trouble.

Flopping down on the thin mattress, and hearing the distant sound of music striking up, he contemplated the dark ceiling. Once he would have been angry and lashed them with the rage of a talespinner, making them crawl back to their beds nursing fears and guilt. But anger was a short-lived fuel, and he'd long ago run out.

Instead, he unwound the tatty skein of wool from around his right wrist and threaded it through his fingers. It was an ancient child's game, but it had become more than that to him.

He wove the patterns, the ones his fingers alone seemed to know, and felt the narrowing of the world around him. All existence focused on that space between the threads and the things it showed him beyond.

The blackness resolved itself into grayness and then, as always, he looked into the eyes of the child. They were blue eyes, the color of the sky just before the sun left, and set in a boy's face that somehow hovered between sorrow and delight. It was this communion, Finn knew, that brought the only joy to the child's life. But then, it was the same for him.

When he had first found the design in the thread he'd been a boy himself, but while he had aged somehow the other had not. Time, it seemed, ran differently between their worlds.

"You've been gone weeks." The child's brow furrowed, he looked closer, observing the changes in Finn's face. "Is it longer for you?" There was a hint of accusation in his voice.

"I'm sorry, Ysel," Finn said, his hands trembling between the thread. "Sometimes I can't find the pattern or something intrudes."

"I know you try," Ysel whispered, "but when I can't speak to you I get worried."

The boy could only be ten at the most, and Finn knew he lived in frightened solitude. Ysel had let slip once that his protectors were trying to hide him from something, but what exactly that might be he had not divulged.

Finn narrowed his eyes and tried to get the dim background of the boy's world to resolve into something he could put a name to. The storyteller couldn't be positive but it appeared to be the same room as always, even though it was a mere blur of color behind the boy's shoulder. If he could just identify a feature then he might be able to work out a location.

Ysel was always strangely reluctant to part with details. Finn could understand that, for while he'd known Ysel all his life the other had only known him barely a year.

The talespinner tried to comfort the boy, but it was hard when all the contact they had was the space between the threads. He could not touch his shoulder or wipe away his tears. "No need to worry about me, Ysel," Finn replied. "I'm in a decent-enough place, and actually got paid for my telling this time."

Ysel shot him a doubtful look. "I've dreamed, Finn. Men are coming for you, and I see darkness all around."

A chill descended on Finn. The boy was never wrong. Once he had avoided lynching only because of Ysel's warning—he would be foolish to ignore this now.

Not getting a reaction obviously unnerved Ysel. "Men in armor, red like blood." His eyes were wide as if he was seeing them at that very moment.

It could only be the Rutilian Guard; the Caisah's enforcers.

"You should go," Ysel repeated.

How could Finn tell the boy he was tired of running, tired of being ignored? He was too young to understand what the end of a road felt like. So Finn smiled. "I will, of course."

"I'll speak to you afterwards?"

"Certainly, I will see you soon." The thread unraveled in his fingers, and Ysel's anxious face went with it.

Finn sighed, for he had already heard the heavy footfalls down the hall. Apparently he wasn't going to get the chance to find out if he would have waited for them or if some shred of self-preservation still lingered.

The rickety door smashed to the floor with the first kick, and the hallway beyond was full of guards. They were indeed the familiar Rutilian.

"Stop, traitor!" The guard captain's sword was already half out of its scabbard, as his men pressed eagerly behind him. The Caisah was getting a little thin on enemies, and there was competition amongst his soldiers to find them.

Suddenly filled with desperation, Finn ran at the wall, sure that it could only be made of daub. He'd made such escapes before.

Luck was not with him this time. The inn was made of stouter stuff; all he did was bruise his shoulder. Dropping to the floor, he cursed the blind scions who had made him so ill-starred. Capricious creatures, but they would not let him die there at the end of an enthusiastic guard's sword. Whatever his powers were, they diminished him in the eyes of his attackers.

He is too small, too insignificant to bother with, those powers whispered. *The Caisah has no interest in such little creatures.*

They gave him a sound beating instead. Lashing out with fist and foot, they reminded him not to speak that tale. He rolled into a ball, taking the blows, but feeling them more on his spirit than his flesh.

They spat on him and then departed, joking amongst themselves— already eager for beer and women. Finn was left where he lay, shaking with anger and frustration. His fingernails bit deeply into his palms and his teeth ground against each other. He demanded his little powers to be more. They did not obey, only capable of making him inconsequential. He raged, but the melancholy lengthened into his familiar foe, depression. He lay tucked up near the wall for a long time.

Until a kind hand on his back told him that he wasn't alone. Finn looked up into the worried face of the innkeeper's wife. "Let me help you, lad."

She guided him until he was seated unsteadily on the edge of the bed. He wiped a hand through his hair and tried to find his composure.

Sitting next to him, she shook her head. "You should never have spoken that story. What a crazy thing to do . . . unless you have some sort of death wish?"

He didn't even know her name, and here she was offering advice. She was right. It was a certain kind of madness to go about telling old tales that only got him beaten.

She was staring at Finn, trying to see beyond the blood on his face and the faraway stare. Perhaps she thought he was crazy. It wasn't that he was; he was just determined to change things, to make people listen. And to make them listen, he had to cause a stir.

And where was the best place to cause one of those? Finn asked himself—not disallowing any kind of answer.

He began to grin. "Thank you for your concern, but those guards might have done me a favor. They've cleared my head rather nicely."

She frowned and hastily got off the bed with a snort. "More like done it in, I suspect."

"Oh no, they've made me realize that I have been aiming too small—too small by half. What I really need to do is go to Perilous and Fair, and tell my story there."

Now she was using a look surely reserved for the most drunken of her patrons. "You really want to get yourself killed, don't you?"

Finn considered that for a moment while sucking the inside of his cheek. Was that what he was doing? He rejected the idea quickly. The urge to tell his tales was deeper than that. "You know he had all the Vaerli talespinners disposed of, so if we don't tell their stories, who will?"

She was shaking her head and making for the door. "They're a cursed people, young man; no one wants to hear their story—not even them."

"When people hear it, they'll know the Caisah is wrong. They might do something about it," Finn replied eagerly.

His benefactor was already gone, shutting the door and clomping down the hallway. Surely she considered him dead already. Finn smiled to himself. He wasn't yet. Not by half.

CHAPTER TWO

TO THE PERILOUS CITY

It was a journey that everyone said you had to make at least once. Perilous and Fair was a city like no other, a many-walled, many-towered glory on the Umber River, with the distant blue mountains acting as a magnificent backdrop.

Its crowning glory was the Caisah's Citadel, which stood at the center of the city. He knew it to be a labyrinth of white stone with a thousand rooms surrounded by the music of water. The waterfalls had been pleasing to the original owners—the Vaerli; ironically it appeared their destroyer enjoyed the very same thing.

The city was the jewel in the Caisah's empire, so it was not idly named. The attachment of Perilous to Fair, however, only served to draw more people to it. Danger always added spice to beauty—the storyteller knew that very well.

Finn paused for a moment among the throngs of other people right before the Phoenix Gate. Craning his head back, he saw the two magical birds, both carved into the gates of lapis lazuli and taller than five men on each other's shoulders. The crowds streamed around him, the citizens no longer moved by the beauty but used to visitors needing to stop and gape.

Even the walls were a marvel. The thick, brightly colored mosaics depicted animals and plants, even creatures of Chaos. They appeared to scamper up the curved walls, making them more alive than something of brick and mortar had a right to be. Bright gems picked them out with consummate skill. They were no creation of the Caisah—his buildings were stern and utilitarian. The images belonged to the lost world of the Vaerli and the time when they had lived in Conhaero.

Finn adjusted his slight pack over one shoulder and walked up the slope and into the gates. As he went, he tried to imagine how it would have looked back then. Surely there would have been Kindred flocking through the very gate he now passed under. The land beyond could have been any shape at all, rather than the mountains that the Caisah held constant.

For a while Finn let himself be carried around the streets by the eddies of humanity, not looking for anyone, or anything, in particular. He just enjoyed soaking up the sounds and smells of the place. This was where the road ended, at the Caisah's front door.

Every trader in the world came here, by water or foot, so there were stranger and more exotic sights within the walls than anywhere else. Sailors, reeking after months on ship, climbed the short distance from the riverside port to the city itself, excited by what it had to offer. Desert traders mounted on grumbling camels passed Finn by. The smell of musty beasts mingled with exotic spices, while on every available street corner came the calls of pamphleteers.

One shoved a thin sheet of paper into Finn's unsuspecting hand. By the time he had turned to reject the offering, the crowd had pushed him farther in. Turning it over, he half-expected it to be a diatribe against the Caisah—a call to arms perhaps. Disappointingly it wasn't, just a cheap offer of accommodation. The citizens of Perilous were wealthy indeed if they could afford to give away paper. He would be sure to keep his eye out for genuine rabble-rousing publishers.

Still, it would be hard work in such a pulsing throng. The colors and textures whirled around him, while his talespinner's mind tried to catalogue each one. Surely there were a hundred stories to be found in this street alone.

The only thing that could spoil this moment were his own black moods, which descended from anywhere—even from the square of bright blue sky framed by the castle's walls. Finn's chest tightened and a wave of unrealized panic washed over him, until suddenly even this vista wasn't enough. His eyes dimmed, and a thousand demeaning voices emerged from his own subconscious. He jerked his head, drawing a shuddering breath, and briskly walked away as if he could somehow outrun his fears.

While Finn was thinking and worrying, his feet had found their own way to the great Waterfall Gates of Iilthor, the heart of Perilous and Fair. The inner sanctum of the Citadel was nestled into a red outcrop of rock and the gates themselves were surrounded on each side by the graceful curves of two waterfalls. It should have been a beautiful spot, but he who lived behind the gates made it one of the most feared. Beyond was solely the Caisah's domain and death came to those uninvited. The crowds of people unconsciously veered away from the gates. They even skirted the Citadel's shadow nervously.

Finn found a quiet spot and tucked himself into a corner where he was unlikely to be noticed. At this entrance there were guards—taller and sterner-looking than in the provinces—but there was no other sign of defenses. A master of Chaos perhaps felt no need for such displays, and three hundred years of domination had taught his subjects fear.

Finn fished out a piece of dried bread from his pack and chewed on it, all the while watching the comings and goings from the gate.

After three hours, though, he'd confirmed his suspicions: there were none. No carts came laden with food, and no footsore messengers approached the guards. The center of castle was as isolated as its lord was; more importantly, there was no way he could squirrel himself in amongst deliveries as heroes did in the tales he spun.

The bread was long gone and his throat was ready for a drink of some kind. Before he could lever himself out of his corner, everything abruptly changed. A few muted cries of alarm reached him but were quickly cut off, until all that remained was silence. Into that, she arrived. Finnbarr the Fox got his second look at Talyn the Dark. She would not recall the first, nor, he hoped, this one.

The crowd shifted around her, none meeting her eye. All were anxious to get out of the way—nykur were not renowned for their forbearance. So that was what people saw, rather than Talyn herself—the great terrifying bulk of the green beast. They didn't look farther, or try to meet the hollow eyes of its rider. They did not want to draw her attention in any way.

Finn noticed things because he was making an effort to take her measure. Taller than the rest of the crowd, he got an excellent view of the Hunter perched high on the back of the nykur with its slashing teeth and curved claws. She looked like a child on such a huge beast, but the glint of blade and pistol broke that illusion. Also, there was the body of some poor man strapped before her saddle—her hunt had obviously been a successful one.

Sliding down from the creature's back, she paused a moment to whisper something into its curled green ear. A shudder ran down its back and its teeth clashed like bright swords. Talyn the Dark strode to the guards, talking so softly that again Finn could not hear what was said.

She didn't seem like a danger—but he knew she was. He had experience to remind him. She had always needed just herself, and while that was sad, he envied her for it somehow.

Talyn was the Caisah's creature, even more completely than the dreaded Rutilian Guard, or the relentless Swoop. It was a foul bargain she'd made for her life, when all of her people were outcasts.

She turned, and he saw her properly as he hadn't since their last parting. Being Vaerli, nothing had changed about her; she was still dark-eyed and golden-skinned, and there was no wrinkle or scar on her face to show that any time had passed at all.

Finn could not see her features properly from this distance, but he didn't need to. His recollection of her storm-cloud eyes was clear and he knew that even now they would be flicking over the press of people on the street. In such a way she judged who was a danger and who were merely sheep beneath her notice.

She was not just a person to Finn. She was a life-changing event. He saw her as lovely when all others only saw her as frightening.

Dark of eye, dark of will, dark of power
Pass me by until another hour

That was the incantation meant to keep the Hunter at bay. It was paltry and ridiculous when faced with her. And even knowing what she was, Finn had no desire for her to pass him by.

As if summoned, she was looking directly at him through the press of people. All sound suddenly ceased. Pity clutched at Finn's heart; there was such infinite sadness inside Talyn the Dark. The Vaerli lived through days beyond measure, and in her look was every moment of that tortured existence.

He did not think she would recall him with one glance, but a small part of him longed for her to cross to him. Though what she would do after that was uncertain—their last parting had not been amicable.

Talyn did not move; her face was a calm study, no expression or emotion bent it. She turned away suddenly and Finn was left feeling oddly upset. He watched her unload her terrible burden before leading the nykur into the Citadel, and found he was able to move only after she was gone from sight.

She was not the reason he was here, Finn reminded himself forcibly. Shaking himself, he hitched his pack once more over his back and left the corner. His odd gift ensured that no guard noticed him depart.

It had also allowed him to observe much, where others would have been prompted to move along by the guards. He might well have to trust his undefined skills to get him in under their notice. Still, a well-traveled storyteller was not without friends, and he knew of places where he could find those who would help him. Finn could only hope their greeting was more than a chilling glance.

Perilous and Fair they called it, and for most who saw it, it brought hope and delight to their hearts. To Talyn, though, it was the greatest symbol of defeat; her people's only city, the single constant in a world that changed so quickly. They had called it V'nae Rae, and it had been truly special. Only four places were of any significance to the wandering Vaerli: two lost, one haunted, and this last trampled beneath enemy feet. If her heart wasn't already dead, it would have broken every time she came back here.

The yester-time made it worse. Her eyes deceived her. At every corner she could see the ghosts of times past. Childhood friends lurked in the shadows, long-dead relatives waved from beside fountains, and memory burned her in every street.

It hurt because it was *his* home now. As she reported her arrival and handed off her bounty to the captain of the guards, her eyes drifted to the crowd. She was used to the downcast eyes and the acceleration of footsteps—what she wasn't used to was a man staring. Looking closer, Talyn realized that something of familiarity lingered about him. His red-gold hair and tallness marked him as one of the tribes of Manesto. His stance was empty of deference and full of something else she could not name . . .

A wave of unreality swept through her as if she might faint. Balancing on her toes, she managed to avoid falling, but the sensation did not pass. The Void pressed close; it was the brightness of the between-worlds itself. Memory of it lingered in her peoples' blood from the time of the Great Conflagration, and it was forever their greatest fear.

Straightening, Talyn turned away from the man, not acknowledging his existence. Fear—like every other emotion—was lost to the Vaerli now. If the White Void was opened once more it would, as foretold, signal another great destruction. She could only pray such a time would come and swallow the Caisah with it.

Still, the moment echoed inside her as she walked within the gates and found a quiet stall for Syris; one where he would not attack horses or be approached by foolish stable boys. Occasionally one would attempt to prove his manhood, and it always ended badly.

She untangled a matted portion of his mane, accepting the cut fingertips, and sighed into his ear. "Thank you."

The nykur's hide ran with a shiver. He too felt the gaze of the Caisah, and Syris liked neither V'nae Rae, nor her master.

"It's all right, boy." She patted the thick green fur of his flank as the lie settled inside her.

However, a nykur could taste untruths, and the great shaggy head turned, regarding her with a dark intelligent eye. Many years and many times they had both ridden here. It was always the same. Both wished only to be away.

Talyn left the stable, making for her room with the pistol tucked under one arm and her blade in her left hand. The small bare room on the second floor had been hers for her entire service to the Caisah. Talyn had chosen it because it was one of the few rooms in the Citadel that was not shadowed by yester-time shades.

She dropped the pistol on the bed with disdain; it was the Caisah's weapon. Pistols had been unknown to the Vaerli but developed by the Manesto in recent years—though where the Caisah had found such knowledge was not known. What Talyn knew was that the weapon made her shiver. She had instructed the gunsmith to carve Vaerli symbols on it in an effort to halt that reaction, but it mattered little. Whatever of her people's nature remained inside her, it abhorred the gun and everything it stood for.

It was illegal for a Vaerli to carry weapons; she was the only sorry exception to that rule. Whenever possible she tried to share the fate of her people, and so carried no weapons while in V'nae Rae. Talyn had few rebellions against her fate, but at least she did not have to carry his weapon when not needed.

Under the narrow bed was a silver box worked with the Vaerli's flowing letter-magic, *pae atuae*. The box, like the blade it contained, had been her mother's, so Talyn would never take them into the Caisah's presence. To do so would sully a pure memory of one whom she'd loved.

Her own magics had been taken like everyone else's at the Harrowing. Not for hundreds of years had the pure sounds of music-magic, *maie atuae*, passed her lips. She raised one hand to her throat as if she could still feel them there.

What was the matter with her? A stolen glance across a cobblestone road, and her memories would not lie still.

Talyn placed the blade within the box, and the letter-magics rang like broken bells when she closed the lid, telling her that the protection spell was activated.

She washed the dirt of the road off and braided her hair back from her face. He had once said he did not like her unkempt in his presence. Talyn would give him no excuse to withhold the bounty price.

She walked expressionless down the corridor and four flights of steps to the Caisah's wing. Two swordsmen, most of their faces covered by shining helmets, with shields held at attention, stood guard outside the thick bronze doors. Talyn hardly noticed. As she walked to the door, the guard on the right eased his stance, but the other sprang forward. On closer inspection, she found she did not know his name—so he had to be new.

He stepped forward. "State your name and business!"

The older guard tugged on his arm. "It's Talyn, the Caisah's Hunter, you fool," he hissed.

The other flinched when Talyn raised her arm, yet when she opened her hand it had no weapon, only the spiraling tattoo that marked all of the warriors of the Caisah's Swoop. It was identification enough; she had no desire to prove her place as Hunter. The Swoop was her master's bodyguard, and though she was never called upon to do their duties, she held high rank in their number. She occasionally even prayed at their temple—though more out of a desire to find a place of peace rather than real belief.

The newcomer's heartbeat fluttered at his neck, but Talyn had no interest in killing anyone unless it was for her bounty. Still, she wouldn't reassure any of the Caisah's men. Let him think she would come for him out of the shadows one night. Instead she gave him a little smile; the faintest curling of her lips, a slight revelation of teeth.

"You may pass," he said, blinking abrupt sweat out of his eyes.

So Talyn the Dark went into the Caisah's inner sanctum to claim her reward.

The suite was smaller than many would have thought, the smooth white walls only broken by large murals of different parts of Conhaero: from the

Blood Witches' caves, to the waters of the heated south. It was another outrage, for the Vaerli would never have been able to paint their world.

At the end of the hall the Caisah sat on a simple-enough chair; only the triple-headed serpent carved on its legs marked it apart from others in the room. It was where he held audiences and ruled the world. Talyn's boots echoed on the marble, and the skin between her shoulder blades itched the closer she got, but she did not flinch under his gaze.

Naturally there were others present: the chamberlain, the Lord of the Purse, Holder of the Keys, the sycophants, and the cortege of mistresses. The Caisah was not like other men except in this one area. His conquests extended not only to this herd of beauties but also to any woman who caught his passing fancy. This moment's queen hen was Kelanim, the First Mistress of his Court. She was glaring at Talyn over her fluttering fan with green eyes that inspired sighing odes from the court talespinners.

Despite their unparalleled beauty, the mistresses were a sad lot, really. The usual way to power for such a woman was to give their master sons— but the Caisah had never fathered any bastards. The terrible torture he had inflicted on one long-ago mistress for attempting to claim a pregnancy as his, said he knew he could not. The horrors the woman had endured were still remembered in legend—even after a century.

Talyn could smell the constant anger and fear that hovered around the harem. It was not a life she envied. Most of the flock were fragile and foolish, but not the First Mistress.

Kelanim was the beauty of the age, as everyone said; and if that had been all, the Hunter would not have given her a second thought. However, she sensed there was more lingering behind those renowned emerald eyes. For some reason the First Mistress had decided that Talyn was a threat—though she had never shared the Caisah's bed. It was unknown what bitter words she poured into his ear when Talyn was not around.

Kelanim tossed her mane of scarlet hair and whispered to one of her fellow mistresses behind the fan.

The Hunter gave her an askew smile and let her eyes rake over the exuberance of lace and satin she was wearing. Some deep part of her enjoyed rattling the cage of the jeweled beauty, but she only ever addressed the Caisah.

Once they locked eyes, the rest of the Court faded to insignificance.

The Caisah of Conhaero, Master of Chaos watched her with a faintly puzzled look, as if this time he hadn't expected her to return. It was always like that. For her part Talyn looked directly back, examining him minutely for any change since their last meeting. She never saw any.

His skin was similar to that of a Vaerli, but his eyes were like none of her kin. They stood out bright blue against the golden tan of his face. The faintly curled black hair was perfectly oiled as always and exactly the same length. The Caisah was a paragon of lean male beauty. He was older than Talyn. Even though that was impossible. Even though no Manesto ever outlived a Vaerli. He was unnatural, but he could also be charming in his way.

One day, Talyn reminded herself, that beautiful neck would find itself at the sharp edge of her blade—maybe not this century, but sometime before she died.

He stood easily, for all the world like a man of twenty, and walked toward her—not letting her dictate where they met. His clothes were always simple but cut to show his broad shoulders and fine leg, a simple cambric shirt of cream and soft leather trousers. His mistresses parted like a flock of disturbed birds before him. Kelanim gave way last of all.

He took Talyn's hand when they drew level, and smiled. "I see once again you have not failed me."

The Court fluttered around him, sharp eyes looking for any sign of his displeasure or delight. The mistresses as always unconsciously straightened, adjusting cleavage with efficient gestures.

"It was a simple matter, my lord," Talyn said, dropping her eyes and letting her voice fade into calmness, "and the bounty a simple man."

"Is that a note of admonishment?" He chuckled. "I believe you are wondering why I sent my Hunter after a man like that. You think perhaps he was not worthy of you?"

"It is not my place to question such things," she replied softly.

He made no comment, instead wandering to the window to look out at something, or perhaps nothing. He did not invite her to join him, so Talyn could not tell.

She felt a raven in the midst of peacocks, as uncomfortable in the Court as any place in her world. He ruled here, and her status was merely that of a slave to his sycophants. It was easy to admit it chafed her.

Despite herself, as always, she pondered the Caisah. He had become the sole reason for her existence, his missions her only goals, and yet she did not even know his name.

After so many centuries, he was still a mystery; why he did things or why he needed her at all were unknown.

Truth be told, they both had been studying each other for too long. It was an odd little battle, but one Talyn had to win.

She did hate him for all his beauty and power. He was evil, the killer of her people. If she had thought for one moment that he could die by a blade, she would have tried then and there. Too many Vaerli had already attempted that and failed horribly.

"Dear Talyn the Dark," he said softly, and went back to his chair, "you give me the greatest amusement." His eyes flickered to a place she could not follow. "Do you recall how you first came to enter my service?"

How many hundreds of times had he asked that? Each time, she gave him the same response. "You saved me." This was in some ways true.

She had grown, become a woman, and wanted to die. When she found her brother's Wyrde in the tiny village near the coast, it had seemed right. The carved symbols told her everything she needed to know.

Two joined circles with a wavy line about them. *This one has given up.*

A spiraling line carved deeply—the symbol for the burning death.

Ignoring the increasing pain, they had found each other. Byre was a man now—so different to the bright-faced boy he'd been on that terrible day of the Vaerli destruction. Without words they accepted death, and reveled in the fact it would be with each other. It was the same fairly often with their people—to die in a loved one's embrace somehow became more attractive than living apart.

The pain passed through them like a wave beating against a shore, but it was a welcome pain in that instant. If they hurried they would at least feel the embrace of the other before the conflagration claimed them. They would at last be free.

It was not to be. The guards surrounded them. The Caisah's Swoop came between them and drove them apart. Talyn could still recall the final glimpse of her brother's dark head. A pit of great sorrow had claimed her, and she cried out. It was the last time she allowed such a weakness.

The Swoop had brought her to the Caisah. Why he had claimed her and offered a glimmer of hope, she had never been able to find out, and he never explained the reasons for his actions.

She hadn't sought out her brother again, and there was at least the comforting knowledge deep within her that he was alive somewhere.

The Caisah made a steeple out of his fingers and peered with empty eyes over them at her. "Yes, I saved you, and our little game continues."

They had many little games, tricks within tricks, each searching for a break in concentration. It was not a game she would have chosen to play, but it was all she had. The only pity was, he knew it.

"Well," he whispered, breaking his gaze with her, "you will want your reward, then."

Talyn turned and deliberately smiled at Kelanim, knowing full well that the mistress was not allowed into the Puzzle Room.

Each time she had to stop herself from appearing too eager, even if they both knew she was. Nevertheless, Talyn followed the Caisah through the ochre door. The arched and polished ceiling reflected the nearly complete puzzle which in golden glory covered the floor. The only decoration in the room, apart from the puzzle itself, was an old-looking eagle sculpture that hovered over the far window.

The puzzle represented three hundred years of work for Talyn, and each piece was someone's death or lost freedom. Her parents would have been horrified, disgusted even, at what their daughter had become. However, the shadows had swallowed them long ago, so they did not have to live in a world of her limited choices.

Now, looking down at the hundreds of tiny pieces, Talyn could feel the vague fluttering of disquiet in the pit of her stomach. Each piece represented so much anger—so much loss. None of that showed on her face, though.

Instead, dropping down to one knee she examined the leading, incomplete edge with an intensity she reserved only for this room—this task. Thin gold sheets made up the puzzle, each inscribed in swirls of silver that ran like water across it. They might have been words, a picture, or even a map; that was the most frustrating thing about it—only when the last piece was finally in place would the secret be revealed.

The Caisah lightly touched her shoulder and passed her the piece she had earned. Her eagle-sharp eyes quickly found the ragged edge where it would go, and she dropped it into place. Always, there was a moment where she half expected something to happen, but nothing followed except silence.

"When the puzzle is complete you will have your answer," the Caisah repeated as he always did.

It felt like she was trapped in this room forever, with him and with the inscrutable puzzle. It was the same scene played again and again, the only difference being that each time a grand fear grew larger in her mind—the fear that it was all in vain.

Talyn ground her teeth, swallowing back those fears. This was the only hope for her people who were out there dying all alone, robbed of their birthright, and worse than strangers in their homeland. Killing the Caisah had been tried many times, and now this was the only way. The only hope.

Talyn did not cry, or tear her hair, or even say a word to the Caisah. Instead she rose to her feet and went to the door. She could still feel the puzzle against her back, as aware of it as the sun in the sky.

"Your escape is not going to be that easy, my Hunter." The Caisah's voice drew her back. "I have no new bounty for you just yet, but there are still duties I expect of you."

Talyn held her sigh in. Sometimes it came to this. The Caisah liked to display her on the odd occasion, preferably to rebellious lords who needed to be reminded of the creature their mighty master held on a tight leash. She had railed against such humiliation in the early days, attempting little rebellions such as wearing her ugliest clothes or not bathing for days beforehand. Those times were long gone. She was worn down to a nub, and the effort it took was no longer worth it. With as much dignity as she could muster, Talyn bowed.

The Caisah was not done with her quite yet. "The Lady Kelanim will assist you with finding something suitable, since I know your wardrobe is . . . minimal."

He guided her out into the main chamber, one hand hovering inches from the small of her back; she could feel it like a poised knife. Kelanim snapped her fan closed and glided over, eyes brimming with delight.

"The Caisah has told me you will need to be outfitted." Her voice was like poisoned honey. "The ball is a masquerade event, but I believe you alone will be unmasked."

He chuckled behind her. "What would be the point of hooding the hawk? No one would know it among doves."

Talyn would never have called the Court of the Caisah doves, neither was she pleased to be singled out in this way. Despite all her years of discomfort, she let out the smallest of displeased sighs.

The Caisah leapt on it immediately. "Come now, my Hunter. These celebrations are special events—four hundred years since I saved Conhaero. That is worth marking, I would think."

She hardly needed to be reminded, but had been desperately hoping to be away on a bounty.

"There will be music and dancing, and games of all sorts to mark the occasion. Everyone from Praetors to clan lords will be arriving. I would have you there for all of them."

"As always, I obey," Talyn replied evenly. "May I go now?"

He was stroking Kelanim's perfect face, but his words were for her. "Won't you stay here the night?"

It was her preferred custom to sleep beyond the walls of the Citadel. The voices of the lost troubled her inside: the whisperings and echoes of laughter, the cries from yester-times.

"It disturbs me . . . what you have done," was all Talyn would say to him.

"Done? I have changed nothing in it! If you have any objection to the stability of the place then I suggest you discuss it with one of your elders."

That was a barbed jibe, even for him, and anger that usually simmered now bubbled to the surface in Talyn. "V'nae Rae was given to us by the Kindred; its permanence a symbol of the pact between us. It should never have been yours."

Kelanim was forgotten and suddenly the Caisah was standing directly behind her. She could feel his breath ruffle the hair on top of her head. "I have taken many things that are not mine, Talyn. It is something I thought you had learned to accept." His words were like sharp needles in her back.

Talyn let the habit of disinterest roll over her, smothering the power of her own anger. "I thought so, too," she said and headed for the door.

As always the Caisah snatched the last word. "You will stay within Perilous for the duration of the celebrations."

So she would be his dragon in a gilded cage, and all the worse for knowing she helped make it.

CHAPTER THREE

THROUGH PAIN AND FIRE

The blow came from behind, so quick that even if Byreniko had been paying attention, he would not have been able to avoid it. He was on the ground spitting blood before even seeing his assailant. The taste of dust was hardly new, though.

"Vaerli scum," the surprisingly wiry and dirty man yelled, drawing the attention of others in the market. Ever since the loss of the Third Gift, people often took a perverse delight in knocking Vaerli to the ground, especially in seething little towns like this one. Many leagues from the baleful eye of the Caisah at V'nae Rae, they practiced the same bloody sports that he favored. Byreniko wouldn't be the first Vaerli to end up in the arena in a distant rural town. If they were especially perverse they might throw another of his kin in, too—some people liked to watch the Harrowing consume Vaerli in flames while consuming their lunch in the stands.

He got to his feet quickly before a mob could gather and looked about for an escape route. On closer examination, this had not been one of his better ideas. Though he longed to wade in and give as had been given to him, his saner part prevailed.

Carefully not turning his back on his persecutors, Byre tried to edge his way to the outskirts of the market. It wasn't easy; eyes were turned in his direction and his steps were dogged with a raft of whispers, like a boat's wake behind him. Old women hissed at him from the shelter of bright stalls, and some of the fruit sellers were preparing to lob their ripest wares in his direction.

Before the Harrowing there might not have been cheers for the Vaerli, but at least there was not this loathing. He knew all too well the reason for the change; Talyn the Hunter had made his people feared as well as hated. He was only grateful that they didn't know how close he was to the Caisah's hound, or things could be a lot uglier.

He found himself jogging, darting between the stalls, and hearing the rising tide of anger behind him. A tremendous bang made him leap back, just as the water seller's largest jug on the right of his head exploded in shards. One caught him under the eye, the pain sharp and sudden. Someone had a pistol back there. Though that was surprising, he wasn't about to look back and investigate.

The market was disintegrating into two camps: those trying to catch him, and those trying to get out of their way. Things were thrown at him and everywhere there was screaming and shouting. Desperately Byre shoved a gold seller's stall onto its side and leapt over it toward the edge of the market.

His ears were full of the sounds of feet and yelling. A weaver merchant grinned at him as he ran past. Byre caught only a glimpse of his face because then the world turned white. All the woven baskets, packed with birds, burst open in a cloud of wing-flapping and mad cooing. Feathers seemed to be everywhere.

In the chaos his arm was yanked, then he found himself inside the warmth and darkness of a covered wagon. The lustrous eyes of a Mohl tribeswoman peered at him over a scarlet scarf. The contrast between her beautiful dark skin and the brightness of the cloth had him dazzled for a minute. She dropped the scarf and held a finger to her full lips in a commanding gesture.

Byre didn't need any instruction; he found he was holding his breath already.

The sound of the pursuit traveled on past.

"*Asthro.* Thank you, lady." He dipped his head. "I owe you my life."

She smiled enigmatically and beckoned him deeper into the wagon. In the manner of her people, his rescuer offered him a seat on a pile of marvelous tapestry cushions, and a tiny glass of sweet tea. Such hospitality after sudden danger made his head spin.

Byre drank. He knew that she could not exchange words with a stranger, but once they had drunk together they would be strangers no more.

Tucking her fabulously bright scarf about her, she set down her glass. "I am the Sofai of Mohl."

"I am called Byreniko."

She smiled again, a flash of white in the close darkness of the wagon. "Not your true name, I think."

"Near enough. Since the Harrowing none of my people have true names."
The Sofai nodded. "Just so."

Byre shifted awkwardly. "Thank you for helping me, honored one—not many would have dared to do that."

She offered him a slice of candied orange peel from an embossed brass bowl. "Hospitality is everything to my people. The Vaerli invited us to this world, so we still owe them guest right. We do not forget—even if others have."

Byre nibbled at the edge of the orange; it was tart and sweet, and the best thing he'd eaten for months. He glanced at his savior out of the corner of one eye because he knew staring was considered the height of rudeness to her people. He thought her young to be a Sofai—prophetesses of the Mohl were usually old women who worked long years to attain their power.

Her voice was warm as the tea, thick with an accent that curled the edges of every word. "You have questions?"

Byre paused and licked his lips. He was ill used to sharing—the fall of his people had seen to that—but this woman had saved him, and there was comfort in her dark eyes. "Two nights ago, I dreamed."

The faintest of lines creased her brow. "The Vaerli never dream."

"Seldom," Byre corrected her, "but when we do, we know it means something."

"And what did you dream of in this important dream?"

"Fire and pain . . ."

All around him burned. All of his own flesh was gone, all he could hear were whispers in the brightness. He could not understand the words, which bothered him greatly. And something hovered at the edge of his vision—a presence that somehow felt friendly. He called out to it and demanded to know why he was there. The only answer came in a whisper. "Achelon."

The Sofai repeated the word, rolling it round in her mouth with a curious expression on her face.

"Do you know what it means, honored one?" Byre leaned forward. "I came to this town because it has the largest library on the coast—but the doors were locked against me. The officials take the Caisah's edicts very seriously."

She nodded sagely, but he noticed her fingers picked at the edge of her robe like a nervous child. "I have heard it in my own dreams; it is a name none now speak above the earth. It is the city of Choana."

The World Builders, like the Blood Witches, were not accommodating of visitors. Even before the Harrowing, no Vaerli or any of the twelve tribes had gone there.

Though he was afraid as soon as she had spoken the words, he knew he must go. The Sofai must have read it in his face, for she leaned across and touched his hand. "If you must dare the Choana, then I will draw the sands for you."

It was the greatest of honors. He was not of the Mohl tribe, or even of the Manesto, but he did not refuse it. For a minute he remembered the Seers of his own people and wished there was one to guide him. It was an empty, foolish wish.

At his nod of consent she drew the bottle of sands from where it lay under her clothes, near her skin. It was the finest Mohl glass, spun and twisted so that the various tubes containing the different colored sands were bound tightly together. She took his hand, placed it on her warm shoulder and then, humming to herself, she picked up the bottle. Spinning it between the palms of her hands, she let the sands pour out according to their own rules, mixing and gathering on the table below in a tracery of chaos. The wagon was suddenly full of the scent of warm spices that tickled Byre's nose. The Sofai with great reverence put the bottle down and turned her eyes to the patterns.

"I see darkness around you—closer than your own shadow and deeper. But you shall break free of it, if you seek the fire instead. You must go to the Great Cleft in the earth—only there is peace to be found. The future is . . ." she whispered and paused, shaking her head. "Dim. I see change and pain, but more . . . there is someone within the flames. It knows you, it watches . . ."

The sands suddenly ignited, and the table was flared with fire. The Sofai slumped forward and would have fallen into the flame if Byre had not caught her. He leapt about, beating the fire down with one of the cushions before noticing that her head scarf was charring. He tore it off and tossed it outside with a curse.

The Sofai was stirring. He helped her sit up and found a last drip of the now-cool tea to pour through her lips. He was holding her as close as a lover and, suddenly realizing that himself, Byre blushed. It was more human contact than he had experienced for months.

She smiled shyly and murmured, "Thank you," before levering herself away from the table. "I am all right."

They both examined the sadly scarred tabletop.

"That was my grandmother's marriage table," she whispered.

"I'm sorry."

"No, no." She took his hand again. "It was not your fault. Something stood between the seeing and me. I pushed too far. But I did see the Great Cleft in Achelon—you are right to go there."

Byre looked away, unable to meet her eyes. "In truth, I am afraid—not for the journey, but for the taste of hope. I have been wandering for so long with nothing to sustain me. My people are broken, and our Gifts stolen, and I fear this dream is just a cruel joke of the Caisah's."

"It cannot be," she replied confidently. "I saw that you would be here. I was told to aid you, so there must be something else at work here."

The Mohl, unlike the other tribes of the Manesto, did not have any scion like the Brother of the Green or the Rainbow Mistress. He knew there were many tales about this strangeness. Some said they'd traversed the White Void without having one, while others whispered that they had in fact killed him as soon as they arrived in Conhaero. Whichever was the case, Byre was unsure what she was putting her faith in.

"Then I will go to the World Builders, I will find an answer to the flame. I have been doing nothing for three hundred years. I don't even know . . ." he stopped suddenly, the revelation choking his throat.

"Why you continue?" The Sofai lightly touched the back of his hand. "So many Vaerli have gone—but something is stronger in you."

"I was almost too young to remember the time before the Harrowing. I wasn't even raised by my own people. I am the least of my kind."

She laughed, low and soft. "And how can you judge that, pray, when you have met so few?"

Unbidden, he chuckled too. "I suppose that is true."

Rising, the Sofai opened the camphor chest at the end of the wagon. "I see you have lost your stick, Byreniko. You cannot go through the world without a weapon."

"Mine was taken at the city gates. Apparently it's not enough to ban us from carrying swords."

He found a smooth fighting stick pressed into his hands, bound with silver. He looked closer, and could see the World Tree of his people etched upon it. He also recognized heart oak and the hand of a master in its making.

"As you can see," she said, "I did indeed foresee your coming."

"It is too much. I will be the best-equipped Vaerli in the world."

"Not quite," he heard her murmur.

He knew of whom she spoke. Ducking his head, Byre accepted the gift. "I have nothing to give you in return, honored lady . . ."

Taking him to the entrance, she dared a look outside. Once ascertaining the way was clear, the Sofai turned her deep brown eyes upon him. "You have nothing now, Byreniko of the Vaerli, but I feel next time we meet there will be enough for you to offer."

Not quite knowing what to say, but feeling his skin heat under her gaze, Byre tucked the stick under his arm and darted from the wagon.

The Sofai sighed to herself and glanced back over her shoulder to the ruination of her grandmother's table. The paths she had seen there were imprinted on her mind as the fire had so nearly been on her face. She had not dared to tell the Vaerli what she had seen, lest his courage fail him. Many betrayals lay ahead of him, and hers was only the first.

Up close, the twelve open mouths of the goddess seemed larger. Pelanor stood trembling in the thin shift and awaited the moment of transformation. She could feel the cool wind of death flowing from those mouths—one of which she was about to throw herself into. Afterwards there would be no collar of pain or fear about her heart; she would be free of all mortal concerns.

She risked a quick glance out of the corner of her eye to where Alvick stood at her side. He wore a matching shift of white but also the torc of the *gewalt*.

The only other person in the narrow chamber was the priestess, dressed in a sheer robe of deepest red. She held the long knife *nehmer*, the life giver, straight before her, and her face was as impassive as that slice of steel.

She gestured sharply toward the primus mouth, where the chaos was thickest, and Pelanor and Alvick stepped forward despite the chill in their bones. Pelanor held out her hand, and he took it before stepping in farther and folding her into his arms. She inhaled the strong clean scent of him, burying it into her memory, while holding tight to his friendship and goodness.

Quickly the priestess bound them together, intoning the words to twine their souls, while the thick cord of the Making cut into their skin. "Two lives end, one greater begins. Now all strength comes from love and power from blood."

Pelanor looked into Alvick's eye, feeling his breath mingle with hers, his heart racing to the same beat. An overwhelming peace stole over her. It was not such a bad thing to share death and blood with someone you loved.

Together then, they chanted her last living words. *Almore sun lethe merya. We go together.*

No more time remained. The priestess' blade descended—faster than thought, surer than fate. Pelanor's body arched as the blade drove through her but only grazed the chest of Alvick. Her death and his blood—just as it had always been for the Phaerkorn. He kissed her then and took in her last mortal gasp. The priestess cried out, a wordless joyful sound, before she shoved them roughly into the last mouth of the goddess.

They tumbled together. Pelanor had lost her breath, never to take it again. Her skin was cool, but her faith was all around. Alvick never let her go; he bound her to the edge of the living world, holding her back from the beyond by the barest threads. It was the most magnificent kind of love. She arched against him in rapture while taking his first Given, the honor of his blood, into her mouth. His flesh opened under her teeth willingly and the last mouth of the goddess gave them her boon. Tumbling through a rainbow of darkness, they became the eternal couple. Pelanor's heritage as a Blood Witch was secured. She had passed the test and so had Alvick. His love for her was found strong enough to hold her back from the gate of death.

The goddess had accepted their gifts. She was the center of destruction and life and she now held them in her grasp forever.

How long they spent within her darkness could not be measured, but when finally Pelanor felt cool marble underneath her knees and heard Alvick gasping next to her she knew the material world had claimed them again.

The descent into faith had not been easy. Her transformed body was trembling and seemed hardly hers to command. She felt Alvick's hand slip from hers, but the link between them was still there. His blood was hers now.

The priestess's voice had changed, warm and loving, where before it had been cold and clinical. "Welcome back to the world, beloved of the goddess." Gentle hands lifted Pelanor and Alvick up to stand bewildered in the light of their success.

The new Blood Witch found that her newly sharpened eyes could pick out a dark figure at the end of the temple. She did not know the name of this person, but she knew his purpose. He smelt of earth and fire. A Vaerli had come to the temple and surprisingly he would provide her first blood price.

The priestess beckoned him forward and he came, with the lightness of foot his people still possessed. Yet he looked tired, weighed down with the burden of the Harrowing, and Pelanor felt, even in her now-cold heart, sorry for him.

He did not give his name, as was custom, instead presenting a box inlaid with silver and Vaerli magic. Opening it, the priestess took out three scrolls and ran her eye over them. "And these are most precious to you?" she asked quickly.

A flicker of pain passed over the man's face. "Three songs of our ancient folk, lost and gone. We can no longer read the language. Even so, they are more precious to us than gold."

The priestess paused but heard truth in his words. "It is acceptable," she said. Then, stepping back, she gestured to Pelanor. "Give this one the name of the blood, and it shall be done."

The Vaerli's head drooped, and his voice when it came was low and sad. "Talyn the Dark." He glanced up, looking directly into the face of the newest Phaerkorn. "To save us all, and prevent another innocent life being lost, kill her. If you can . . . make it swift."

A mighty blood price. Pelanor's heart raced—a truly heroic one. By doing it, she would assure her place in the rolls of the Blessed and earn Vaerli gratitude for her people. Alvick's hand slipped into hers and he was grinning at her.

Pelanor laughed aloud into the high reaches of the temple.

CHAPTER FOUR

THE FISH THAT SANG

Finn knew there were many evils in the world that the Caisah ruled, but looking around at the prosperous faces of the inhabitants of Perilous it was hard to see any. In a city whose streets bulged with traders, the only visible danger was that of being run over by a cart or wagon. They seemed to be everywhere, laden with spices, barrels, huge rolls of lush fabric, or baaing sheep. The scents alternately delighted and repulsed him. In this one city there was as much diversity as he'd seen in all his travels. The tribes of Manesto outnumbered the others ten to one. In his short trip from the Gates to the port itself he did see a group of cloaked and hooded Phaerkorn. Blood Witches abhorred the light, but he did catch a glimpse of a pale face under a hood. They were among the first wave of settlers from the White Void, but others had followed. He also saw a number of the tall and elegantly dark-skinned Mohl. They had high cheekbones and liquid eyes that marked them out as gazelle among sheep.

As he walked the last few streets to his destination, a small efficient figure lingering near a corner in a long silver cloak and dark gray shirt caught his eye. The deep eyes, when they glanced up, caught at his before moving on. Finn's thoughts immediately went to Talyn the Dark, but this was a man with grizzled hair and his face was no mask of indifference—his anger was there for any to see. The Vaerli turned away from him, retreating into a private world of pain.

Finn could only wonder why a Vaerli would be here. They could sense one another, and even this far from the Citadel he would know another was near—perhaps that it was even Talyn.

Walking on, Finn made a conscious effort not to look back. His destination was not far now and his pace quickened. The streets did not feel as friendly as they had only moments before, and the back of his neck was itching.

In many ways the Singing Fish was like any other inn on the edge of the port, yet it was special in ways few other places in Conhaero could claim to be. The Caisah's eye did not reach here. It was a freak of the Vaerli magic, a gap in the Chaos, and hence a gap in their enemy's power. The oddly shaped inn walls had been built to the exact shape and breadth of the discrepancy.

Finn went into it with a smile on his face, even though he knew inside would be full of the bitter smell of too much beer and too many people. Once beyond the door he saw that indeed nothing had changed.

He nudged his way to the bar and caught the publican's attention with the subtle lift of one finger. As was custom, in addition to his own pint of beer, he also ordered a shot of whiskey for the small altar to Brother of the Green that stood behind the counter. He was not the scion of Finn's tribe, but he was the traditional protector of public houses. It didn't do to offend him in a place like the Singing Fish.

The publican smiled and poured the small offering over the pottery representation. Finn raised his glass and turned to survey the crowd. He didn't know any of those around him, but it was full of the atmosphere he liked. It was a touch of freedom. People spoke easily here. Perhaps this was how it had felt before the Caisah's coming, when the Vaerli ruled.

"By the Crone's whiskers, Finnbarr the Fox!" His name struck him between the shoulder blades, and he jerked around half expecting to find a pack of guards blocking the door. Instead he saw three familiar and welcome figures.

Varlesh rushed over and embraced him, smothering him against his rough jerkin, and clapping him so hard on the back that he coughed and spluttered. When he finally released Finn, he yelled right in his face, "Boyo, you look like you were dragged through a blackberry bush backward."

Finn smiled into the older man's broad, honest face. "Well, so would you if you'd been running from the Rutilian Guard for so many weeks."

Equo, dressed in black as usual with his graying hair pulled back into a ponytail, grinned thinly. "We had heard rumors about that."

Their third, Si, who usually said so little, chimed in, "But you still came."

"Just lucky I guess. Here, sit down everyone, have a beer."

"I gather you won't be paying, though." Varlesh caught the barmaid's eye. "Let's take our drinks to a corner. Even here there are ears."

They found a dimly lit corner in the folds of the inn, and sat. Finn, Varlesh, and Equo drank, but Si remained quiet while scanning the inn with his piercing blue eyes.

"Don't mind him." Varlesh chortled, wiping foam from his beard. "He's always a bit paranoid."

"I'm getting that way, myself," Finn replied.

"Well, you shouldn't be surprised," Equo whispered, "since you've been going through the whole kingdom telling the story of the Vaerli—what did you expect?"

"Truthfully . . . I thought I might meet Talyn the Dark." Seeing their shocked faces, he gave a short laugh. "I don't know what I was hoping for. Maybe just that they would understand a little."

Varlesh leaned back in his chair and waved his hand dismissively. "The teaming masses? Why bother, boyo? They don't care. The Vaerli are nothing to them. They're nothing to themselves either."

"The truth still matters," Finn said firmly his eyes drifting to where Si was looking. Their quiet companion made him nervous—always on edge, always looking for trouble.

Equo and Varlesh exchanged a glance, but they knew him better than to quibble.

"Well, you've come to the place where there is a definite scarcity of that curious commodity," Equo commented quietly.

They talked on for an hour or more. They recalled times when they had traveled together, drinks drunk, and moments of horrendous crisis—which at the time had been terrifying but looked back on were for some reason deeply funny. Si was the only one who did not participate. Finn had long ago learnt not to try to reach him. When he spoke it was usually to impart words that seldom made any sense.

Varlesh, though, more than made up for his friend's shortcomings. It was impossible to keep him quiet, and he only ever paused to drop some beer down the back of his throat.

"So what's your plan?" Equo finally asked when the reminiscences were all done.

Finn swallowed hard. "I guess I just want to make a difference. I want to tell the story, and see what happens."

"We all know what will happen," Varlesh growled. "You'll end up with your head decorating the gate of Perilous, like a hundred fools before you."

"But you try, too," Finn pointed out, dropping his voice to a mere whisper. "That's why you meet here, and I know about your links with—"

"Nothing," Equo hissed quickly. "You don't know anything about anything or anyone!"

Si was watching Finn now, his heavy forehead beetling over eyes that made the storyteller squirm in his seat.

Finn fairly jumped when Varlesh grabbed his arm and growled, "Maybe we do the odd thing, but we always meet carefully, only ever in small groups. We certainly don't go about telling dangerous tales in every bar." Sitting back, he pulled a pipe out of his coat and filled it with great care.

"We think before we act," Equo added.

The rational part of Finn's brain knew they were right, but there was another stronger part of him, perhaps the bit that helped him find the boy in the pattern, which drove him on. "All I know is that I must speak up—in the very lap of the Caisah if necessary."

Varlesh shook his head, Equo sighed, but only Si said anything. "The truth does still matter."

Whatever his two companions may have thought, once Si spoke, their attitude changed. They always listened to what few words he threw out and, since Finn himself had only heard the other speak without being spoken to one other time, he was inclined to listen as well.

Varlesh pulled his pipe momentarily out and downed a hefty gulp of ale. When he lowered it, he stared over the rim at Finn. "There are ways into the Citadel—ways that don't mean barging through the front door."

"I am sure that wasn't your plan," Equo muttered.

Finn ignored him.

"It would be churlish of us to not help—especially if you're so set on it," Varlesh went on. "There are those still in the city who know ways to get around your particular problem. If you will only wait a few days, we can sort something out for you."

Finn's mind drifted to other plans that could well occupy his time.

"You're not thinking of something even more foolish, are you?" Si asked warily.

The talespinner spread his hands and grinned. "There are always the celebrations to take in."

"I get suspicious when you give up that easily." Varlesh slammed his mug down on the table. "Too crafty by half, you are."

Though Finn could feel Si's eyes fixed on him from under his hood, he shrugged. "Comes with the training I'm afraid."

Varlesh rolled his eyes skyward before sliding a small bag of coin across the table to him. "That should at least get you a decent room. If you get caught, you better not mention our names."

"I won't get into any trouble," Finn promised. "I have a knack for these things."

"Mind you don't," Varlesh's eyes narrowed. "There are more important things happening in the world than your foolishness."

Equo slid the last of his ale over to Varlesh, who downed it easily. "We'll be in touch in a couple of days, then." And with that they departed hastily.

Finn tucked the purse into his pocket and glanced around the bar. The place was full to capacity, as many wanted to see the games and events the Caisah would be staging in the next week. Finn sidled up to a few conversations and managed to get the information he needed. Tomorrow night would be the grand event; a masque ball where all of Conhaero's elite would wine and dine and laugh far too loudly. The gossip was that the Caisah's Hunter would be there—perhaps with the heads of her enemies hanging around her waist. Talyn the Dark had a fierce reputation and obviously liked to keep it that way. She brought men to her bed only in the provinces. She kept whatever desires she had mostly in check.

Finn couldn't help thinking about her. Like the fairy captives in his own tales, some part of him longed for her despite everything.

With a little bow to the locals he went to organize his accommodation upstairs. Finn felt an urgent need to wash the dirt of the road off and rest a little before any more adventures.

The pretty maid led him to a room that was small but better than he had enjoyed for months. Dropping his meager pack down on the bed, he did what he had been desperate to try since setting foot in the city. He took out the simple bit of string and, sitting himself cross-legged next to the bag, began to weave the patterns.

His mind dipped and ranged far ahead with the sway of the thread, seeking out the boy, trying to find his fate. Something different was in the way. Finn felt a resistance, a tugging at the threads. It felt distinctly like someone was thrusting their fingers into the pattern and trying to pull it away from him. Finn hissed and struggled back, seeking the pattern desperately.

A moment of fierce resistance, and then he felt it snap back. Finn was once more able to weave. Ysel's face appeared, pale in the dark with the shadow of a bruise down one side. Suddenly Finn felt his inability to reach the boy, to protect him.

"What's happened?"

Ysel looked at him sullenly, but didn't reply. "Where were you?"

"I couldn't find you in the pattern. I'm sorry, I tried. What's happened?"

The boy's lower lip trembled. "Soldiers came to the house."

"What did they want?"

Ysel touched his cheek lightly. "They were looking for something . . . I don't know what. Anji argued with them, and I thought they wouldn't listen to her, but they went away after a while."

The boy had never mentioned a name before. Even though Finn had surmised he must have had a guardian of some sort, this was the first time he'd revealed she was a woman. The talespinner knew better than to press—when he'd tried before, the boy had somehow made the pattern tear apart.

Instead, Finn told him about breaking into the Caisah's ball. He tried to make it sound like an adventure, but with little risk.

Ysel's expression said he didn't really believe that. It was easy to forget he was just a young boy, because he was so very serious. He never gave the impression of running and playing or doing anything remotely childlike.

"You'll be careful," Ysel insisted, the same admonishment he always gave. "Dances can be dangerous."

Finn gave a short laugh but realized the boy wasn't joking.

"And don't let the Caisah see you. For if you do—" Ysel stopped and glanced over his shoulder.

He tried to soothe the boy. "I will try, Ysel, but it will be his party—"

The threads in Finn's fingers began to shake and the pattern hummed. They started to pull apart. Finn tried desperately to hold them, but they had become elusive as puffs of smoke and unraveled before him.

The boy's wide eyes disappeared into the void between threads, and Finn was left swearing impotently to himself.

He never knew when his strange gifts would desert him. It was a good choice not to rely on them to get him inside the Citadel. His three friends could be trusted with that. Still, he couldn't shake the memory of Talyn's dark and tragic eyes. Two people were depending on him now and he was not one to take responsibility lightly.

Rolling over, Finn let dreams take him where they would.

Byreniko slept and dreamed once more. This time the voice of the Sofai accompanied him and like dark honey it drowned his senses. She was speaking in a language he could not grasp, though it sounded like an incantation, and his mind's eye followed it down into the darkness of the earth.

Byre had no sense of his own body, but he could hear breathing, long and slow in the shadows. Fear gripped him and almost tipped him into panic. He knew instinctively whatever he could not see would swallow him whole. He was Vaerli, so there should have been nothing in Conhaero that could wake such fear in him. Yet here he was, broken by the unknown. It wanted him. It demanded all that he was. Nothingness waited.

He woke with a shout in the back of the wagon. Ungro, the driver who had picked him up two days previously, glanced over his shoulder. His craggy face registered surprise as his lone passenger had up until now offered very little conversation.

Byre raked his hair out of his eyes. "Sorry, bad dream."

"Had those myself, out here. It'd give anyone the jitters," the driver replied before turning back and, with a flick of his reins, urging the carthorses onward.

Waggoners out here were far less inclined to hatred of Vaerli—in fact, they often tried to find one before setting off into the Chaoslands. They thought it was good luck, imagining it might protect them and their cargo.

Byre wasn't sure how much protection he truly was, but at least it was a way to get south fast. The guild of Waggoners used the seed-magic of their tribe to give their beasts incredible endurance. Managing to get a ride on one halved the time it would normally take, since the carthorses could run two days straight if allowed, and with a second person on board the Waggoner could let them.

It would not take long to reach the jungles of the south. Already Byre could feel the back of his neck getting sweaty. Propping himself up amongst the stout wooden boxes in the wagon, he flicked the awning up a little and watched the world roll away from the road. The whole of the country was wonderfully golden and his Vaerli eyes ate it up. The horwey trees, growing on pure chaos, were tall and stately here. More adaptive than humanity, the trees would alter with their surrounds; low tough succulents if desert came, or flat tough mats if mountains appeared. The seasons were turning as well, coming toward a winter that in time would bring snow. He loved the change. It reminded him that things could be different and with each cycle there was at least hope.

He'd been just a child when the Harrowing happened. Though he could remember it clearly, he could not recall ever having the full use of the Gifts like his older sister had. The Vaerli children took a long time to grow into their powers, and he had been many years away from that time.

It perhaps made everything a little easier. He had, unlike the majority of his people, only felt the pull of suicide once in all the Harrowed Time. That moment still burned in his memory—but it had not been despair that had driven him there, only a desire to see his kin again.

"You're the quietest Vaerli I've ever had in my wagon," the driver said and spat the last of his magra leaf out onto the road, "and that's saying something!"

Motivated by curiosity, Byre slipped over the seat and sat next to him. "So you've seen a few, then?"

"More than you, I would say." Ungro shot him a glance out of the corner of his eye as if afraid how his humor would be taken.

Byre grinned in response. "And what are they like?'

"Well," the driver replied with a shrug, reached into his coat pocket, pulled out more magra and stuffed a wad against his gum, "they say the Vaerli used to keep to themselves. Course, they can't do that no more, so if folks are fair to them they'll talk well enough. Not much choice now, I guess."

"I suppose." Byre stared at his hands for a minute, not quite knowing what to ask but still desperate for information.

"One thing a lot of them mention is that Talyn the Dark. You know, the Caisah's Hunter?"

That hurt. Byre could feel the steel of longing run through him. He hadn't heard her name in a very long time, yet he missed her like the sun. "What do they say?"

"The usual. How she's outcast and not one of them anymore. They get this funny look on their face as well, sort of like they've eaten something nasty." The driver flicked his reins. "Not that I'm blaming them, with her working for him that made the Harrowing."

"You seem to know a lot about my people. Most in Conhaero no longer care."

"They're good company mainly, and they tell a lot of stories. I've heard that there is even some talespinner that travels around collecting them. Course, he probably wants to save them before the Vaerli are all gone."

"He'd best hurry, then," Byre whispered.

Conversation ran out after that. They both sat still, listening to the relentless hammer of hooves on the road and watching the sun set. It was a peaceful and companionable silence, until the first riders came at them from the shelter of those golden trees.

Another Vaerli might have frozen, paralyzed by the loss of Gifts, but Byre had never known them. He had always had to rely on his own skill and strength. Quickly sliding his stick out from under the seat, he glanced at Ungro. "Can we outrun them?"

The driver shook his head, pulling out his blunderbuss and laying it across his knees. "Old Clopper can run for sure, but the rest are tired. We won't be able to for long."

Byre's sharp eyes picked out a section of cliff only a mile or so ahead. "Can we at least make it to that outcrop?"

The driver squinted against the horizon. "Can't see what you mean, but if you say it's there, I believe you!" Ungro flicked the reins, and with a snort the carthorses broke into a thundering gallop. Stoutly built as the cart was, it began to heave alarmingly. Still, this would not be the first time it needed to outrun bandits.

The five riders let out a whoop. Byre ran down the length of the rocking wagon and peered out the back. It was hard to tell yet who they were, but certainly they wanted something badly enough to risk a Waggoner's blunderbuss.

Byre could only wish for some arrows, but it was as illegal to sell those to Vaerli as to sell a sword. He would have to rely on his stick and whatever natural abilities still remained.

With a crunch the wagon lurched off the road and onto the rocky path he had pointed out.

"It'd be good to see you use some of that Vaerli magic," Ungro yelled over his shoulder.

It didn't matter how much people knew that the Gifts were gone, they still expected the legends to be true. The before-time was something he had only heard about as a child.

The wagon lurched again as the driver turned in a tight circle. Byre leapt off the back and ran quickly around to the front just as Ungro's blunderbuss roared. Byre had seen him pack it with wickedly sharp rocks that very morning. One of their pursuers screamed horribly, fell back in his stirrups and was carried away by his terrified mount.

His companions, apparently unconcerned, rode on, yelling and waving their rusty blades above their heads.

Ungro swore loudly and pulled two wickedly curved knives out from under the seat. "Bastards, you'll not have nothing from me!" It was an almost-convincing act. Bandits could not afford to leave witnesses to an attack on the Caisah's wagons; the penalty for that was drawing and quartering.

The leader rode in hard, seeking to knock the apparently vulnerable Byre off his feet and onto the rocks. The Vaerli stood still until the horse was almost upon him, then with a cry and wave he lunged forward. Bandit horses were not war-trained and this one, unused to sudden noise, twisted aside with its eyes rolling madly. Their attackers were no great horsemen and while the bandit struggled to turn his mount, Byre lunged forward with his stick. The silver knuckle of the oak staff snapped against the bandit's shoulder, twisting him out of the saddle to land with a thump on the ground.

Before Byre could attack again, the other riders were upon him. He turned and leapt up among the rocks, forcing them to dismount or risk ruining their horses. One raced past the shouting Ungro and fired an arrow at him. With a thunk the driver was pinned to his seat through the shoulder. He roared in rage at the bandits' audacity. "Bloody cowards!"

But the bandits still appeared to find Byre the greater risk. That was yet another problem with being Vaerli, and Talyn was responsible for this perception. But they wouldn't waste arrows on him, believing the folktale that none would be able to touch him, so perhaps the Hunter did him some good as well.

Byre balanced lightly on his feet while his eyes darted between the three advancing bandits.

His enemies taunted him. "Vaerli scum. We'll dice you up good and take your head for trophy."

A Vaerli must be buried with all his parts or risk the damnation of Chaos, and they knew it. One laughed as he swung at the cornered Vaerli. Byre caught the blade on his upraised stick and with a twist of his body downed the man with a swift riposte to the head.

The two remaining enemies circled more warily while getting on either side of him. He waited calmly, his stick above his head, feet lightly placed in the guard position. One struck at his legs; he simply jumped back with a speed that would have done the Seventh Gift justice. Then, deftly changing the stick to his left hand, Byre caught the other brigand by surprise, thumping his stick with real force into his elbow. The man howled and dropped to the ground, screaming that his arm was broken.

Spinning around to face the last uninjured bandit, Byre deliberately left his guard down, his head seemingly exposed. His enraged opponent took the bait. When he lunged, the Vaerli stepped nimbly back on his left foot and swung heavily out with his stick, catching the bandit directly in the face. He elicited a most satisfactory howl of outraged pain and dropped his sword.

A life on the run had taught Byre how to look after himself, but it had also taught him realism. His odds of surviving so many opponents without a sword were slim.

Indeed, the one he had knocked down was already getting up. The stick was meant for defense, to allow time to run, but he had nowhere to go—even the horses had fled.

They rushed him as a group this time, taking the knocks and bruises he dealt out and bearing him to the ground. Swords gave way to knives and though he struggled, he was no match for three men. One caught at his hair, dragging his head back to feel the kiss of steel. "This will teach you," he hissed.

But exactly what lesson that would be, was suddenly lost.

The men screamed all at once, a dreadful chorus of surprised pain. The blades rattled to the ground and Byre was able to scramble out from under his attackers. The earth itself had grabbed hold of them. For an instant he couldn't hear anything but the sound of bones breaking and stones rumbling. It was a dreadful cacophony as the bandits were pulled into the soil, still crying out in horror. Byre watched in frozen shock.

When the Kindred emerged, he didn't know what to say; in his childhood he had seen only one, and that memory was dim and colored by childish fears.

The two creatures, seething with the fires of the earth, slid through stone and turned their burning eyes on him. Immediately, he felt their immense sadness weigh upon him.

"Thank you," he managed to gasp out of a tight throat.

There is no need to thank. The great curved head bent toward him with the intensity that a bird of prey might examine a mouse. That regard almost unmade him.

Dropping his gaze, Byre scooped up his fallen stick, not quite understanding why the Kindred had come to his aid. The pact had been broken between his people and theirs, even before the Harrowing.

Made by Kindred, but broken by Vaerli. The second Kindred's eyes ran with blue flame. He heard Byre's thoughts more easily than if he had spoken. It might have even been a form of humor, but Byre had no real way of telling.

Lost one, the same creature was suddenly in front of him though he had not seen it move, its voice almost a purr. He felt the heat of it near to his face. *Son of Ellyria Dragonsoul, we do not forget. You are the last of innocence and must be protected, because no sin weighs you.*

Byre laughed at that, thinking of all the dreadful things he had merely done to survive. He could have almost cried.

You are on the path. You and yours have called us forth; already one of our kind has risked much for your line—just as we have this day. Without a face and expression to judge, it was impossible to tell what emotion was attached to that statement—joy or irritation.

Byre did not know the words to bind or to summon. He had none of that lost knowledge, yet standing in the warmth of the Kindred he wished for them.

Things can never be as they were. The blue-flamed Kindred reached out to him, but stopped a hair's breadth from his skin. *You must follow your flame-dream, youngest. Go to the World Builders.*

Dimly, Byre heard Ungro finally labor down from the wagon, followed by the rasp of his indrawn breath. As if a mere mortal gaze disturbed them, the Kindred began to retreat into the earth. The stone slid aside, while their flame dimmed before disappearing entirely.

Byre stood transfixed, but their final words lingered in his mind.

We will be watching.

CHAPTER FIVE
PAINTING A PREDATOR

The Lady Kelanim was taking particular joy in her discomfort. Watching her out of the corner of one eye, Talyn could only glower as the mistress swept across the room dragging fine dresses behind her. She was presently engaged in pulling out every dress she owned and scattering them around her large bedchamber. A flock of chambermaids were trailing in her wake, busy trying to keep them from being stepped on while managing to hide their horror.

Kelanim seemed to be more interested in holding the fripperies up to the Hunter than offering them to Talyn—not that she minded that.

It was galling, though, how she also reveled in every opportunity to stick her with a subtle jibe. "This gown is divine. I wore it at the midwinter festival. It would almost be your color, but you can see it is totally unsuitable. Your shoulders are far too wide, they would snap the sleeves."

Talyn did not rise to the insult. She had earned every muscle in her body in defense of her people. While Kelanim delved deeper into her cupboards, the Hunter roamed the room, idly flicking through the trinkets of the mistress's life: a thick gold bangle, screeds of lace underthings, and a positive mountain of makeup. A pile of papers caught her roving attention. They appeared to be religious images devoted to the Scion of Right, but when viewed from other angles they were something else entirely. Talyn's lips twitched. Some of the poses were almost physically impossible and deeply amusing.

Kelanim sailed over, her emerald eyes honing in on anything that her rival might find of interest. Her smile was like a dagger. "I would have thought this was more my area than yours . . ."

She was making sure Talyn knew all about her relationship with the Caisah.

The Vaerli let her finger linger on the picture. "Why would you think that my people never have sex, Kelanim? Do you think we had no joy in life? Or perhaps that we grew from the ground like vegetables?"

Something flickered across that dazzling face, and for an instant Talyn wondered if the mistress knew of her dalliances beyond V'nae Rae, but then those beautiful eyes turned icy. "Of course not, but it seems there is no other way for you now."

Talyn smiled back as gently as she could. "Once there were many ways for us. In fact, some Vaerli were masters of the sex-magics, the *kahi atuae.*"

"I have heard of this," Kelanim said stepping closer with a rustle of silk, her breath near to Talyn's skin, "but I had not believed it was true."

She was probing for power. She would take any chance to keep the Caisah interested. The Vaerli glanced into the before-time and saw the parting of ways that lay in this discussion. After a moment she took half a step back. "But I am not one of those masters."

"Certainly not." Kelanim's voice trembled a little as she turned back to the dresses. "Our Caisah has taken all such pagan powers."

The mistress decided quickly after that, and found a suitable dress near the back of her wardrobe.

"It is last season's fashion, but the sleeves will hide your brawn while white will suit you well enough. I will send my seamstress to adjust it for you this evening."

With that Talyn was bundled out of the room like so much dirty laundry. It was no great loss to her to be expelled from that den of female intrigue.

While retreating to her own quarters, the Hunter passed through one of the tranquil garden courtyards. Few lingered in such places; the carved figures on the walls spoke of long-gone Vaerli, and it unsettled the Manesto even if they didn't acknowledge it. Talyn thought it was small-enough justice.

It was cool here even in summer, while the reflecting pool practically begged to be lingered by.

Glancing over her shoulder assured Talyn she was alone. It surprised her how Kelanim's words had stung; she'd thought herself well past caring what she looked like. And yet here out of the glare of the mistress' attention she allowed herself to look at what centuries of servitude had made her.

Staring into the water, she could see her mother reflected back, only hardened by life. Kelanim was right. Underneath the light shirt she could feel the rigidity of muscles honed by sword and shield. Hardly any feminine softness remained; her breasts bound as they were gave little away. If the Harrowing had never happened, then this would not be her body or her face. Her voice would have been all that was required of her. Life would have been the *maie atuae*. She had not been able to sing since that awful day.

It was so foolish to let Kelanim's words affect her. Talyn slapped the water, shattering her reflection, and turned away.

She had not seen Syris since they rode in, and knowing full well the dangers of that, her trail turned toward the stables. At least she was properly attired for this particular journey. The stable boys, used to seeing her there, looked up and smiled. For them it meant they did not have to deal with Syris.

The nykur had the largest stall farthest from the rest of the horses, since the smell of meat unsettled his stable mates. While they liked barley and hay, he liked blood and flesh.

Talyn climbed up and hung her arms over the top of the high gate to the stall. Syris glared at her with his dark eyes and pawed the thickly laid straw with one hoof. It was meant to be a chastisement.

He was no horse, so she took his threats seriously. Still, she laughed and wiggled her fingers, daring him. He lunged, wicked teeth at the ready, but she was quicker—pulling back beyond the reach of his teeth and instead grabbing hold of his mane. He tugged and shook his head, but she held on.

Finally, the nykur reluctantly let her stroke him. His mane bit and cut her fingers like rough grass, but the loss of a little blood was nothing to her.

She let the nykur lick it delicately away with his barbed tongue. Such little rituals were a pleasant distraction from ridiculous talk of dances and dresses.

Talyn was not so distracted that she did not hear the lurching steps of Faustin, Chief of the Horse, behind her. Hopping down from the gate, she gave the old man one of her rare smiles. Faustin was one of only two people she really smiled for in V'nae Rae these days. He was short like her, so neither had to look up at the other.

His nut-brown face, wrinkled and off-center from an ancient encounter with Syris, lifted to see her too. "You planning on feeding that old devil your fingertips again?" His voice was gruff but laced with genuine affection.

"Not today, I think the Caisah wants me to have them for his dance."

Unlike most people in the Citadel, the Chief of the Horse did not wince when the master was mentioned. He was rarely at the stables and as long as he did not interfere with the running of Faustin's little empire, he was of no consequence. It was the reason that Talyn liked the chief so much.

Faustin leaned against the gate and watched Syris prance and snarl. "Still likes his bit of flesh does the old devil, though he's had none from my boys this week."

Talyn always found it curious how Faustin still admired and loved the nykur; his voice was never touched with anger or bitterness. "Not like he had from you."

The chief smiled in a distant, melancholy way. "That was a long time ago—not that I have forgotten the feeling of his teeth in my flesh, mind. He stopped me from getting around properly ever after."

Unlike her friend, Talyn could only faintly remember the unscarred, jaunty lad Faustin had been before Syris knocked him down and tore into him. In those early days he had not been worth saving a memory of. "Don't you hate him?"

"Hate?" Faustin looked at her with genuine puzzlement. "A fine beast like that? Never. He was just doing what instinct told him to. It was me who made the mistake." He peered more closely at her. "You've asked me this before."

Talyn sighed. "I am sure I have explained how my memory gift works. Haven't I?"

"Aye, that you have. Must be a shame though—living so long and remembering only little bits."

"Sometimes I think it is the greatest gift. That of forgetting." She smiled bitterly.

Faustin was beckoning over a wide-eyed stablehand who was carrying a small bucket. It smelt of blood, and he handed it quickly over to his chief before scampering back to the safety of the horses. Syris sidled closer to the gate, pressing his great clear eye against the gap and clashing his teeth together. It was a frightening sound, yet not necessarily always a sign of aggression.

Faustin offered the bucket to Talyn, but she gestured it away. It would be good for the nykur to be fed by another besides her. The chief began sliding the tastiest morsels of liver and tongue through the special gap to the hungry beast. He was careful to keep his fingers well beyond the grasp of those teeth. Sometimes he even dared a pat on the remarkably soft nose. Talyn winced every time he did, but Syris did not even flinch. When Talyn had seen the stableboys try that, she had witnessed a few lose a finger or two.

Perhaps the nykur had taken all his aggression out on Faustin when he was a lad, for he was meek as a lamb now—at least as long as the treats kept coming. Once they were finished, Syris snorted and retreated to the back of the stall.

Faustin laughed. "The devil in him! I can never get a pat once the meat is finished. You'd think he didn't want to go soft on me."

"He likes you, but he doesn't want to become your pet."

"Ah well, I can respect that." The old man looked faintly sad, though. "It must be a great thing to ride out on him." He glanced down thoughtfully at his twisted leg.

"The first time I got on his back he nearly killed me," Talyn said. "I'd gone down to the river where he was lurking, and I lay down on the bank."

The chief stared at her as if she was mad. "And he didn't trample you to death? I would have thought first chance he got . . ."

"Well, they might be as swift as water and as deadly as fire, but they have one real weakness. The nykur are very curious. So he climbs out of the water and comes over to nudge me. He's trying to work out what I am. That is when I leap up and onto his back."

Faustin slapped his good knee and lent forward in delight. "Now that I would pay gold to have seen. I guess you must have survived."

Getting into the unexpected joy of telling a tale, Talyn threw her hands in the air. "I thought I wasn't going to! He flung me around until all my body ached, trying to reach me with his teeth or break my spine. Finally, he threw himself down to roll on me."

Safely behind the gate, Syris could be heard scraping his hooves on the ground beneath the straw, perhaps reliving the trial himself. Faustin barked a laugh. "I can just see the old devil. You must have had to move pretty sprightly."

"I jumped out of his way, and when he got up I leapt back on. He made such sounds of anger that the very earth churned. The villagers all ran from their houses in fright. They came to see though, just as he charged into the water to be rid of me by drowning."

Faustin looked puzzled.

"There are tricks we Vaerli know, some that even the Harrowing did not remove. He was not going to get rid of me that way and in time he came to realize that."

"Perhaps that if he stuck with you there would always be liver and sweetbreads."

Talyn knew that was the polite way of phrasing it. In truth Syris knew that there would always be fighting and chaos around her.

"Still," she said, getting up and watching the nykur through the gate, "I know he didn't really expect to be shut up here for so long."

Faustin was staring at Syris with unguarded desire, his face for a moment reflecting a young man's longing.

Talyn knew then what had really happened. "You tried to ride him too."

His blue eyes gleamed. "That I did. I was young and so foolish and brave. I can't be sure, but he seemed to understand me. He looked at me with that dark eye of his, and before I knew it I was grabbing his mane and mounting." He rubbed his thumb and forefinger together thoughtfully, perhaps recalling the cut of the knife-bladed hair on his hands. "It was a glorious feeling, for a while at least. I thought he liked me."

Talyn lightly touched his shoulder. "He did, otherwise he would have killed you."

"Well, as it turned out, the old devil changed my life for the better. With a crippled leg I got a lot more serious about horses. Now, here I am Chief. Funny how life finds a path for you even when it seems darkest."

Talyn left the stable hearing those words settle deep inside her. They were words of hope that were not what she was used to, but the old chief could be right. Things felt very dark at the moment, no end in sight, so perhaps it was a sign.

The masque would start with the full moon the next day, but there were other festivities that the Caisah insisted she accompany him to. Luckily only the masque would require her to dress appropriately.

Today it was the battle games, the letting of blood to appease the lust of the Caisah. She would have to sit at his shoulder and watch, something that always turned her stomach. Her battles were for the freedom of the Vaerli. These sports were for baser reasons.

Returning to her quarters, Talyn read several Rutilian Guard reports and tried not to think much on the upcoming few days. Trouble was brewing in the east again. Rebellions were as common as sunrise out there, but the reports showed that the rebels were being smarter this time, gathering their forces in secret. It was a forgone conclusion that there would be bloodshed on the coast before the month was out.

Midday arrived. Talyn washed and strapped on her mother's sword. The honor-guards were waiting at the Gates in formation around the Caisah's palanquin. Kelanim was preening on the steps, dressed in a swath of emerald green to match her eyes with her hair piled up in auburn waves. She didn't even nod at Talyn, but her lips tightened fractionally.

It wasn't a good day for the Mistress; there were rumors that her position was not as secure as it had once been. Lately the courtesan Nanthrian had been taking the Caisah's eye and there lingered the possibility that she might also take Kelanim's place. Talyn couldn't decide how she felt about that. At least she knew the current favorite's ways.

With Kelanim being chosen to ride to the games with the Caisah, it seemed her place was safe—at least for now.

The crowd of courtiers arrived, a noisy whirlwind of people and dogs, with the quiet center of the Caisah. Talyn waited on the fringes, neither moving forward nor shying away. He was arrayed in blood-red robes studded with gold, and his hair was oiled so that every curl gleamed. He was beautiful like the sun. Such beauty would move any woman, while the cloak of power he wore only made him more desirable.

The Caisah turned and looked straight at her, as if he had heard her thoughts. It was not impossible.

Talyn dropped her eyes before he did and thought on what that dangerous man had done to her people. It calmed her nerves.

With a slight smile the Caisah held out his hand to Kelanim. As always he spared no compliments. It should be enough for her that she was in his presence. They were about to get in the palanquin, when he turned as if it was almost an afterthought. Holding out his other hand, he spoke softly. "The hawk will ride with the master."

Talyn felt as though she was rooted to the spot. She could think of nowhere she would less like to be than trapped in a confined space with the Caisah and his calculating mistress. As always, she could not refuse.

His fingers locked tightly around hers and pulled her into the shadows of the palanquin. Kelanim could not contain her rage. Her face went white and her full lips disappeared into a tight line. She sat next to the Caisah glaring with fiery eyes at Talyn. He liked it that way. He moved everything in his world to conflict—from warring tribes to bickering women.

It might be amusing in someone who was not so powerful. Talyn let her fingertips rest lightly on the pommel of her sword. This day she'd had too many misgivings to leave it behind.

Outside, beyond the ring of protective guards, she could hear the cheering of the people. Today was a good day to be one of the Caisah's citizens. They would have games, and there would be largess given at the Gates, beer and bread for all of those who had need of it.

"Do you wish it was you going into the arena, my Hunter?" The Caisah leaned forward, the light from outside outlining his face in stark and beautiful planes.

The question was sudden and took her by surprise. The before-time never told her anything about him.

"If I did, my lord, you would soon run out of gladiators."

He chuckled at that. "Yes indeed, for none stands above my hawk." Stroking Kelanim's arm distractedly, he went on in a softer tone. "I hear from my lady that she has found a suitable dress for you."

"It will suffice." Talyn made a show of looking out at the waving and cheering throng.

"You will be spectacular in white, Talyn, and all will see that my hawk is not only deadly with her sword but with her beauty too."

She could not tell if Kelanim had mentioned the color to him. The Caisah had many ways of knowing things, but she was positive he dropped such hints in their conversations to unnerve her.

He was looking at her with such an expression that for a moment she quite forgot who he was. "I am not beautiful. I do not need to be," Talyn whispered back.

Abruptly Kelanim lurched out of her quietness. "Why don't you just bed her and be done with it!" she screamed with such venom that even the nearest guards outside turned and looked.

The air inside the palanquin grew suddenly hot and seemed to buzz with energy. But the Caisah did not deign to use his power. Instead, he backhanded his mistress so hard that her head banged loudly against the paneling. Talyn waited for him to dole out some to her as well, but he did not move in her direction. He made no words of reproach or explanation for his behavior. It was as if Kelanim were of no more consequence than an irritating fly. He waved to the masses instead.

Talyn shared a look with the mistress who was rubbing her cheek, eyes full of tears. Kelanim might feel sorry for herself, but the Hunter knew she wouldn't complain. Her lust for power was too strong. She would not retaliate as was right.

No Vaerli man would have done such a thing. The Gift of Knowing would have made him share the pain and anger along with his victim. The Caisah had no such concerns.

Talyn wondered how she would react if he ever did such a thing to her. She had the dire suspicion that she would accept it just like Kelanim. They were as bad as each other.

They spent the rest of the ride to the arena in silence; he watching Talyn, she staring back, and Kelanim glaring at them both.

Once they reached their destination and stepped down, the Caisah and his mistress smiled and waved. The sun was high and beating down fiercely, but the people gathered at the arena gate seemed unconcerned. Only the glazed eyes behind the guards' helmets told of their discomfort.

The Caisah and Kelanim went quickly into the shade of the entrance while Talyn trailed in their wake. People's eyes skidded off her. They had no wish to see the dark Hunter on this day of celebration.

In the days of her people this had been the edge of Chaos, a marshy area filled with birds and beautiful flowering plants. The first thing the Caisah had done was to drain the area and build this great hulking edifice. Where he had got the idea was impossible to judge, but there was nothing as huge as this sunken arena in the rest of Conhaero. Wide cut steps surrounded the circular front area and were packed to capacity with excited people. Interest was so high that guards had to be brought in to keep those unlucky latecomers out— and it was not just the townsfolk, either. As Talyn followed the Caisah's procession down to their seats, she could see every nation and tribe of Conhaero represented in the crowd. They were surrounded by the murmur of different languages and dialects.

Street sellers of all descriptions were running back and forth selling warm nuts, hot spicy breads, and tawdry foldout broadsheets on the games. Even those who could not read could at least enjoy the lurid images and take them home to show those not lucky enough to get in.

The area set aside for the Caisah's entourage was sheltered from the beating sun by a huge draping of Imperial scarlet, and the Court settled under it with much chatter. Talyn took a seat to his left and just a little behind. The beaming Kelanim took hers to his right, his attack apparently already forgotten. The Rutilian Guard took their places around the Caisah and his guests and then snapped to attention with their bright spears.

The Caisah sat quietly. His eyes fixed on the empty sand arena. It was smooth and clean—for the moment. About him the Court was excited with the prospect of blood.

Talyn shifted uncomfortably in her seat and examined the crowd. Better to look there than try to be entertained by the Court. Ordinary people fascinated her. She had little contact with them apart from when she was hunting, and they shied from her at other times. Yet here she was—literally within feet of them. She could smell their food, hear their conversations, and almost sense their normality.

A little family was seated just below the Caisah's area, and she found herself straining to hear the flow of everyday family life. The child was fractious in the heat so the parents were distractedly trying to calm its frazzled nerves. The mother was dawdling it on her knee, while the father chuckled the chubby chin.

Talyn felt a familiar clench within her, a deep longing that most women would have been easily able to identify. By rights there should have been children in her life, perhaps a daughter to raise in the tradition of music-magic. But the Harrowing made that impossible. No child had ever been born of a union with a non-Vaerli and to try anything else was suicide.

That was numbered among her many burdens. Every day was a hundred bitter losses, but this was perhaps the greatest. Talyn shot a look across at the Caisah, worried that he had heard that too, but for once he did not glance her way. It was strange how they shared so many things: immortality, people's fear, and the lack of children.

When she looked back to the crowd someone else caught her attention. It was the man from outside the Gates, the one who had stared at her the other day, and there he was staring again. This time there was no odd sensation apart from the gaze itself.

Most people gawped at the Caisah, yet all of his attention was fixed on Talyn while the hint of a smile played about his mouth.

He was handsome, yet not in the Caisah's overbearing way. Something about his expression implied great kindness. His red-gold hair was longer than most wore it at Court and the wind whipped it around his eyes, which were the most incredible shade of blue, like a peerless day in the Chaoslands.

If she had met him there she would have smiled and offered him more than that, too. However, this was V'nae Rae and that look was verging on the over-familiar.

The gladiators entered the arena and the crowd leapt to its feet with a roar of delight. People waved colored flags and screamed the name of their favored fighter. By the time they had subsided into their seats once more, the man was gone.

No time remained to search him out, for the Caisah was accepting the gladiatorial salute and the games began.

It had been many years since Talyn had been to the arena, and she found herself not having to feign interest. These were the best of the fighters from schools throughout the Caisah's world, so there were no easily completed matches between old hand and doomed new recruit. She watched with a discerning eye.

The Caisah, for once disdaining his cool and calm demeanor, yelled with the crowd, and dispensed justice when it was asked for. Kelanim also bounced up and down in her seat. If she was feigning interest for her lover's sake then it was masterfully done. The guard about the Caisah took their cue from their master, cheering and slapping each other on the back if their preferred fighter triumphed.

She had only a moment's warning. Talyn looked up, feeling a slight chill in the air. The faintest of dark clouds had appeared in what had been a perfect blue sky. The Blood Witch dropped among them like an ill-wind and panic erupted.

She was small, of a same height as Talyn, wearing a cloak of shadows with dark skin and eyes that gleamed red even in the heat of midday. Strangely, she also seemed very young, but she was obviously not without power. Those eyes narrowed and everyone suddenly felt it too.

The wave of fear she spun about her hit even the Caisah's guards. Talyn sensed the edge of spell-made terror, but it washed past her. Apparently the Vaerli immunity still held. The area under the awning was abruptly full of screaming people scrambling to get away from thousands of personal terrors and demons. The guards dropped their spears and ran with the crowd—heedless of honor or training.

Strangely, Kelanim was not one of the stampeding hordes. The mistress was huddled at the base of a pillar with her expensive dress bundled in her hand. Though her face was terrified, she had not left her master. Talyn couldn't help feeling a moment of admiration for the woman. Bravery was a rare thing among the courtesans.

Still, it was the Hunter alone who stood in the way of the Phaerkorn; she was the only thing between the creature and the Caisah. Drawing her sword, she let the screams and the chaos fade away.

She had faced weavers of magic before. The people who had come through the White Void had brought many with them, but she had never faced a Phaerkorn before. Though Talyn had no experience with a Blood Witch, she did not make the mistake of underestimating the girl. They were few in number, yet their powers were legendary. Rumor had it they felt no pain or fear and were capable of physical marvels.

Talyn glanced behind her but saw the Caisah had not moved, nor was the air any warmer than normal. He smiled and spread his hands, as if to make obvious how vulnerable he was. He was watching her, not using his own power, sitting back to observe his hawk and see if she defended him. He probably thought it fit right in with the other gladiatorial combat of the day.

Not wanting to satisfy his blood lust, Talyn spoke instead of moving. "Go home, little Witch. You have stumbled in on the wrong party."

Her lips parted until her pointed teeth could be seen, but made no reply. She moved faster than any other previous opponent, but Talyn dropped into the before-time. Blocking the girl's rush, she twisted her leg about the Witch's and flipped her off course.

Her attacker landed nimbly and sprang again. This time she drew a narrow silver blade. Three times Talyn caught her in the before-time and turned her aside without having to use her sword. She rebelled at spilling blood for the Caisah merely as entertainment. People had a right to hate him, after all.

The Witch would not give up. With a lithe movement she swung around the awning pole and cast something at Talyn. The Hunter could do nothing in the before-time against spells; her master had not given her the song-magics back. The darkness wrapped itself around her eyes.

She took a step back, letting her other senses take over while her eyes were bound. She sheathed her sword and took up the watchful guard position.

The air burst with heat all around and the blackness dissolved with it. Talyn shook her head. The Witch was gone, but dead or not she couldn't tell.

"I dismissed her." The Caisah, who hadn't even risen from his seat, shook his head in dismay. "I grew tired of it all."

"Did you arrange this?" Talyn asked in what she hoped was a steady voice.

He stared at her hard while remaining silent. The guards shook off their panic first. Pale with embarrassment, they began to restore order. The Court straggled back, laughing nervously, unsure if the interlude had been part of the games. The Caisah chose not to give them a sign. Instead, he waved for the last of the afternoon's combatants to take the stage.

Only when the gladiators and the crowd had returned to their previous activities did he lean across to her and whisper, "You'd best hope your next bounty is not a Phaerkorn, my hawk. I was not quite sure how that was going to end."

He still had not answered her question, and left Talyn with the distinct impression she had been tested and found wanting.

CHAPTER SIX

UNLUCKY SIGNS

Finn wasn't there when the Phaerkorn attacked—he had long ago had his fill of blood and sand—but he was nearly trampled by people fleeing.

He heard the screaming which heralded the approach of the mob, but not from inside the arena. He was wandering in the markets just outside the gate to the arena, and saw the sellers, who had seen this sort of thing before, nimbly leap up onto the stalls. Taking his cue from them, Finn clambered quickly onto a nearby wagon.

The panicked crowd poured out from the gates. They passed around the stalls, the roads surrounding the arena being thankfully wide. Behind could be felt the trailing edge of some magical horror that had caused this whole thing. Only Phaerkorn were trained in such befuddlements. Finn had studied his myths well but had never encountered the actual effect before. It was impressive and definitely terrifying this close up.

For a while it was utter chaos, but then it became apparent that the mob had outrun the source and the effects dissipated quickly. Everyone abruptly stopped running and stood about baffled—like people waking from a terrifying nightmare. Many people were sobbing and plenty of others looked abashed.

Finn hopped down to help with a couple of wounded who had not been as lucky as he. Surprisingly, most avoided serious injury, but a few bruises and cuts were being nursed. An old lady had been pushed into a stack of barrels, and as Finn pulled her out all she could mutter was, "I had a good seat." Her voice was full of accusation as if he had a part in the whole thing. He dusted her down, and she quickly found her anxious family.

With a few well-placed questions, he was able to ascertain that he had been right. A Phaerkorn had attacked the Caisah himself right in the middle of the arena. The crowd milled around without a purpose until a Rutilian guard appeared on the balcony overlooking the main gate. "The assassin has been dealt with. The Caisah has commanded the games not be disrupted."

They cheered at that and eagerly turned around to go in once more. The crowd would not miss out on the last of the games.

Finn swallowed his disappointment. The Caisah knew how to entertain his people, and they ate it up. The storyteller would not go with them; instead he found himself an inn. Seated in something once more resembling civilization, he sipped a cider and tried to make sense of the day he'd had.

He had used his minor power to avoid detection and got into the games early. He still wasn't sure if the Caisah's guards were hunting him here or not, but he'd risked it for a chance to see her again. Talyn. In the aftermath of the panic, he acknowledged it was like poking a dragon with a stick. No one actually stared at the Hunter, and the way her eyes had narrowed indicated she certainly wasn't used to it.

He wanted her to remember him even if it wasn't for their encounter of years gone by. He certainly hadn't been able to forget and thought of it often. Like now. It might have been his imagination, a wish fulfillment, but he could have sworn that he had seen softness in the Hunter that night. Near tears were in her eyes. He was not quite prideful enough to think his lovemaking had put them there.

Taking a deep draught of cider, Finn put himself in her place back then. It was an easy thing for a talespinner to do. Vaerli with the Second Gift would have been wrapped in each other's thoughts—closer than any other being could imagine sharing with another. To have such closeness and then have it denied would be a great loss. He felt terrible sorrow for her, but back then he hadn't understood.

Finn laughed into the dregs of his drink. Surely he was the only person in all of Conhaero who had sympathy for the Hunter. He could also imagine what the dreaded Talyn the Dark would do with these emotions.

It had been easy to get into the games, but getting into the masque could be far more difficult. Since coming to Perilous, he had felt the weight of despair lift, and he now viewed spitting in the eye of the Caisah as a worthy challenge—if he got to see Talyn, that would be icing on an already-tasty cake.

"There you are!" Varlesh plumped himself down in the opposite seat, breaking the direction of Finn's thoughts. At first his visitor appeared to be alone, but a glance out the inn's window showed Si and Equo helping pick up some poor basket seller's wares.

"Pure One's backside," Varlesh swore easily, before crooking a finger at the serving girl for his own pint, "that's quite a ruckus."

"I had nothing to do with it," Finn insisted.

"Well you might not, but things seem to happen around you, boyo. Not your fault, mind, but it is a disturbing fact."

Before his friend could fully dissect his fault, Finn changed the subject. "Have you found a way into the Citadel yet?"

Varlesh accepted his beer with relish, and Finn had to wait until he had gulped down the top half. He leaned over and pressed a tiny piece of paper into the talespinner's hand. "The good thing about an old city is that there's always a back door or two. So we got you this for your night out." Varlesh drew an exquisitely painted and carved full head mask out from inside his coat.

Finn took it in his hands. It was black and red with feathers around the top, beautiful in a reptilian way. He looked sideways at his friend. "Where did you get this?"

Downing the last of his beer, Varlesh wiped his mouth on his sleeve. "Picked it up on our travels. Now, be careful with it. The folk I got it from said it was old—maybe even Vaerli."

"Thank you, Varlesh." Finn clasped his hand as he made to get up. "You've all been good friends to me, despite everything I've put you through."

He flicked some coins onto the table, enough to cover both their drinks, and left before they could try to dissuade him.

Varlesh stared after Finn for a moment. Then he downed the dregs of his beer and went outside. The crowds of Perilous had already swallowed his friend up, but Si and Equo were there waiting for him. They tipped their hats to the woman they'd been assisting and wandered over to join him.

"Is he really going?" Equo asked, brushing stray strands of willow from his cloak.

"Course he is," Varlesh replied gruffly, "but if he thinks it has anything to do with the Caisah and not that she-devil of a Hunter then he's lying to himself."

"Nothing we can do about it?" Equo shrugged.

"Not a thing," Varlesh muttered. "The Crone's whiskers, he's always had a pining for that creature. It'll get him killed someday, for sure."

Equo slapped Varlesh on the back a couple of times, and then both of them turned toward the food market in search of their dinner.

Si stood there a moment longer, looking back the way Finn had gone. "But not today." He smiled. "Most definitely not today."

Oriconion was where Ungro's route ended. Byre peered out cautiously from the back of the wagon, rubbing gingerly his newly acquired bruises. He smelt salt and fish, and heard water lapping against the shore. This small seaside town had a reputation that far exceeded its appearance. He had heard tell that it was the most rebellious town in the Caisah's empire. The Vaerli thought he just might like it here.

They had made good time reaching the port, but he would still have to find his own way farther south. He would have little time here to explore.

The wagon creaked as Ungro got down. He hobbled around to the back. The gruff man's arm was wrapped and hanging in a sling. Byre might not know much of the ways of the Vaerli, but he knew well how to do a field dressing.

Ungro couldn't meet his eyes, though. "I'm grateful to you for saving my life, lad, and for patching me up, but I hope you don't take offence if I stay at a different establishment than you." He looked embarrassed about his own cowardice, but Byre understood. Traveling with Vaerli when all they wielded was a stick was one thing, but seeing them converse with the stark elements of the earth itself was another story.

"Let no one say that Ungro is a mean man." The driver dipped into the hanging purse at his waist and held out a few bronze coins to Byre.

"No, there is really no need for thanks."

The driver closed Byre's fingers on the money. "You're a good lad, but don't be foolish. This run is a well-paying one, and you saved the cargo and me with it." He clapped him on the back before taking Old Clopper by the bridle and leading his team up the street.

Byre hopped down as the wagon rolled off. Barely had his feet touched the ground when a familiar sensation ran up his spine. He felt immediately that he was not the only Vaerli in the area. It was an odd discomfort, like a burning tingle at the tips of his fingers. She was very close but not near enough to cause deep pain.

Closing his eyes, he concentrated on the sensation and felt along the connection. It was Nyree the Seer-to-be. They were family in a distant sort of way. His mother had been a second cousin to hers, and he remembered being awed by her as a little boy. An aura of expectancy hung about her shoulders, and she followed Putorae the Born Seer everywhere with a mysterious look on her face—as if she could already see into the future. She had not yet taken the marks of her profession back then. Later there would be no chance to.

He would have liked to talk, to find what had been happening to her in this town. Instead, he decided to find the message she would have left, most likely near the city gate. After the sheer horror of the Harrowing had subsided, the Vaerli still needed to communicate. So they reverted back to the Wyrde, a system of tracking signals that had previously only been used for hunting. Now it was the only way left to communicate. The Wyrde remained a code only the Vaerli could read.

Backtracking a little, he circled around the town gates, trying to look as inconspicuous as possible. He found Nyree's Wyrde marked on the back of the nearest shop. Her small precise knife cuts into the wood were typical of the would-be Seer's neatness.

A circle sharply bisected with two lines. *This one does not want to meet.*

That was good, Nyree was still hanging on.

A series of intersecting slashes. *Unsafe town. Get out quickly.*

A semicircle with a suspended dot. *Rutilian Guard active.*

That was bad. The Rutilian were the enforcers for the Caisah, making sure no Vaerli had an edged weapon of a certain length or was out on the street at night. Often, though, they carried vigilance much further, killing Vaerli merely for sport.

Checking over his shoulder, Byre used his eating knife to quickly cut his moniker in below Nyree's. Now others would know he was alive.

Then he slipped away, determined to find a wagon heading south as quickly as possible. His stomach was rumbling, though; the last food he'd had was Ungro's morsel of bread the night before. No matter how bad the situation, he still needed to eat. As long as he was out of the town by nightfall, he should be all right.

Byre looked around. All he could see were wagons and guards—no sign of immediate danger. That was the trouble with some Vaerli; they became overly paranoid. Most times he had seen that Wyrde, it had come to nothing.

Not quite knowing where to find sustenance, Byre took a different direction to the one Ungro had. After an hour or so of aimless wandering he soon worked out that there was something very different about this town. A high wall divided it, and the only people he saw on this side of it were the tribes of Manesto. He couldn't have stuck out much more if he had painted himself purple.

The looks Byre got walking the street were even more unfriendly than usual. It wasn't illegal to be a Vaerli, but being here he wondered if perhaps things had changed in the last few days. At the market where he stopped to buy some sweetbreads he had to try three places before finding one that would serve him. Most of the sellers turned their backs and pretended he wasn't even there.

Not daring a public inn, Byre tried to find himself a quiet corner. Finally, he settled on wedging himself in a doorway behind an abandoned stall. He was still on edge since his last problems in a market.

"Spare a coin, young sir?"

The old woman was crumpled in the corner as if someone had abandoned her there. Byre had thought her a pile of old rags, but on closer inspection, both impressions could be correct. One eye was filmed over, though with illness or injury was hard to tell, and her dark face was a maze of lines and wrinkles. She held out a mangled hand but somehow managed not to make it seem like a plea.

He dipped into his flimsy pouch and pressed what little he could find into her palm. She hid it away so quickly she might have had the Seventh Gift. In return, she grinned and magically produced a small satchel of dried figs that she wordlessly offered to him.

Byre sat down next to her and offered the sweetbreads to her.

"Not at my age, son. Meat does horrible thing to my digestion." She stared at him and then barked a laugh.

He laughed with her. "Forgive me asking, but are you of the Mohl tribe?"

"You're a sharp one." She popped a fig into her mouth and began to suck on it with great relish.

"Seems I am lucky in my travels to meet so many of your tribe."

The old woman gave him a piercing look.

"What is going on with this town?" Byre tried another tack. "I saw the wall, and I seem to be the only person not of the tribes of Manesto here."

"Powder keg this place is," she whispered. "The Portree, one of the lesser peoples to come through the White Void, proud folk they are. Always fighting. Always seeking to be free of the Caisah."

"And for that the Caisah had to put up a wall?"

The woman nodded. "Said it was for everyone's safety. Keep them in line. But the Portree still have their ships." Her eyes narrowed on him. "You shouldn't be here, young Vaerli."

Byre looked at her sharply. How could she know how young or old he was? Past a certain age all Vaerli looked much the same.

She chuckled and poked him. "It's your walk, son. You ain't got none of that Vaerli swagger. All the old ones have it."

Byre looked down at his fingers. "I wasn't raised by my people. My sister found me a family in the provinces who didn't mind caring for a Vaerli child."

"Must be brave folk."

"Were brave folk," Byre corrected her.

The old woman nodded. "Hard times, hard times indeed." She reached out and patted his hand. "But don't you worry, there is something else at work here." Her voice was younger, stretching toward youth somehow.

Byre darted a look at her, but she had dropped her head to concentrate on her dwindling supply of figs.

"Tell me," he went on carefully, "have you ever met the Sofai of your tribe?"

"Me?" She pointed at her thin chest. "When would I have done that?" She patted him on the shoulder, and her touch was light as a sparrow's. "You best be off and find that wagon south you need. Do not linger here." And with that she tucked away her figs, nestled down into her mass of cloth, and went to sleep.

Getting to his feet, Byre looked down at her, but now she seemed just like any old lady. Shaking his head, he turned to do as she had suggested. He didn't like this place, and he didn't like the feeling that somehow something was following him. Fate or destiny, he didn't believe in either of those.

Evening was pulling in and unless he found a wagon heading in the right direction soon he'd be forced to find shelter for the night. The cluster of inns Ungro had headed for was his best chance, though it was very close to the brooding presence of the wall. He lingered there, chatting to the drivers, but they were only late arrivals. Few were setting out until the next morning and none in the direction he wanted.

Recalling his promise to Ungro, Byre turned away from the inns, becoming resigned to the fact that he would have to sleep in this ill-fortuned town. So preoccupied with this stroke of bad luck was he that he didn't notice the group of Rutilian Guard lingering by the town fountain. The first thing he heard was low chuckles.

Byre certainly didn't want to be drawing their attention, but curiosity got the better of him. He tried to see what so amused the Caisah's own. He thought they might be drinking ale, or telling lewd jokes, but frantic splashing cured him of that supposition. The Rutilians were far too busy with their sport to notice when he stopped in the middle of the square and stared.

A tall blond-haired Rutilian with his helmet in one hand was towering over the far smaller form of a dark-skinned, sloe-eyed woman standing drenched in the fountain. She had a beautiful purple turban on her head, and tucked among the flamboyant orange of her dress was a small child. She managed not to look scared, but the way she turned away from the guards said she was not comfortable.

One of the trio poked her in the shoulder. "What you doing this side of the fence, little bird?"

She dropped her eyes, and her voice was low with a slight tremor to it. "I have trade on this side. I was allowed to cross."

"Well," the third man, broad of shoulder and still wearing the intimidating helm, spoke. "It's nearly dark, and your kind shouldn't be about."

The blond pushed closer until he was almost standing on her toes. "You Portree whores should be back where you belong. Or were you touting for business?"

The woman blazed at that. Her face tightened with anger before she whipped out a long-bladed knife and pointed it directly at the offending man's crotch.

Byre couldn't see things getting better from there, so he decided he really should say something. "I am sure there are plenty of whores elsewhere in this fine town. Why not leave this one be?"

The woman shot him a look as angry as the one she'd just used on the guard.

"Not that you're a whore . . ." Byre stammered, feeling his rescue attempt coming apart at the seams.

The guards laughed.

"Find your own slut," said the blond, giving Byre a little shove.

His swarthy companion looked a little harder though. "You're a Vaerli . . ."

Byre felt their attention shift away from the woman, which was good for her, but could be deadly for him. He flicked his fingers at her, and hoped she would realize now was a good time to melt into the shadows. "Yes I am," he replied with a lift of his chin.

The petty amusement in their faces slowly drained away. Though everyone knew his people had no power left, there was still residual racial fear.

"Boy, show us," growled the smaller guard, shouldering himself forward, "you're not carrying any bladed weapons."

Byre let out a little sigh. It was always the same. He might be nearly three hundred years old, but for some reason Rutilians always insisted on acting as if he was an infant.

"Of course he isn't," the blond one sneered. "Without their powers, the Vaerli are all cowards."

That shouldn't have bothered him. It shouldn't have made any difference after all these years. The woman, who was sliding as quietly as she could out of the fountain, shared a look with him. He could see she was smiling.

"Damn right." One reached forward and shoved at him.

It was enough.

Byre had trained too long and in too many disciplines to let it all go to waste. Moving his weight to his right foot, he slid aside from the touch and smashed the butt of his cane up against the guard's elbow. The satisfying sound of crunching bone was accompanied by his opponent's surprised scream as he dropped to the ground in agony.

Byre didn't make the mistake of being overly gentle. Experience had taught him that once these things got started they moved quickly, and he didn't want to face three opponents at once as he had recently.

The blond one, who looked to have more battle training, did not leap in. He shoved the woman and she tumbled backwards once more into the fountain. No one wanted an angry mother with a knife at their back.

While their downed companion howled in pain, the other two drew their swords and spread out. These were no desperate bandits. They had experience slaying people, probably some of those had been Vaerli.

They came at Byre together, with both swords only a heartbeat apart. Catching the first one, he deflected it aside and whirled behind to parry the other. Mid-turn he swapped his stick to the other hand so that he caught the second attacker by surprise. His blow slipped up and under the defense, smashing into the man's temple. He dropped like a stone, but Byre was not quick enough dodging out of the way of the blond guard's riposte. The tip of the sword glanced across the top of his shoulder.

Stepping over his comrades, the tall guard smirked. "Not invincible without those Gifts of yours, are you? I should tell you how many of your kind we've killed. How many we captured. How they screamed and begged for death."

Byre ignored his boasts and the pain in his shoulder. He waited calmly in the high guard position, cane held above his head, weight balanced through his feet.

His opponent lingered just beyond striking range with his sword before him. "I've probably seen more of your kin than you have!"

Such a jibe might have provoked him once, but that was at least a hundred years in the past. Since then he'd learnt patience and acceptance.

The Rutilian attacked swiftly. Drawing a long curved knife he tried to get within the spiraling curve of Byre's swinging cane. He was fast too, catching all the blows the Vaerli aimed at knee and head.

Byre drew back, his brow furrowing. He had to admit the Seventh Gift would have been useful at this point, that or an actual blade.

Behind him, he could hear the spluttering woman and her indignantly wailing child climbing once again out of the fountain. Around the square the darkness was beginning to come alive; there was the sound of shoes on the pavement and the feeling of held breaths all about them. The guard knew they were drawing a crowd. He darted glances over his shoulder.

Byre closed and with a lunge managed to sweep his opponent off his feet. He lay there looking up at Byre with white-faced fear.

The dripping woman stepped down next to the Vaerli. "You should go now," she said softly.

He looked up as figures emerged from the darkness, dark faces, solemn and angry, all of them, he guessed, Portree.

"We work on this side of the wall," the woman went on, "but each night we must go back. My kin will see me home safe." She stepped over the wide-eyed guard and made her way toward the crowd. "You should not linger here. People will have seen a Vaerli fight."

He followed her gaze up to the windows of the surrounding houses. He moved away but lingered just beyond the corner of the house to listen.

They had forgotten the guard as if he didn't exist. They offered him no words, but no violence either. The woman spoke to her quiet kinfolk. "You see it is happening. The Vaerli are rising. Now it is time for us to do the same."

Byre heard their murmurs of assent, the sound of their retreat, and a chill settled over him. They had been expecting him. The Sofai had spread the word before him like an unfurled carpet.

Byre didn't like the feeling that fate was dogging his footsteps, and yet since the dreaming had begun, it appeared he could not avoid it.

CHAPTER SEVEN

THE CHAINED HAWK

Talyn tried to maintain her calm, but being dressed like a Manesto sacrificial heifer was humiliating in every way she could imagine. Still, when Kelanim's maids invaded her small room to begin the process she managed silence. It was not their fault, and they would only be whipped if the task was not done.

Besides, they were frightened enough. Dressing the Caisah's Hunter must be perceived as a dangerous assignment.

A pair of huffing servants lugged a great steel bath up the stairs, followed by a trail of grumbling maids with bucketfuls of steaming water. It was scented with rose and jasmine, and Talyn could at least appreciate the luxury of taking a bath. She stripped off her clothes and climbed in with a sigh. Weeks tracking bounties didn't afford many opportunities to wash.

The maids unbraided her hair from its long confinement and cleaned it as gently as possible. Talyn relaxed into the pampering and, closing her eyes, let them wash her body.

One maid couldn't help herself. "There are no marks," she whispered into her companion's ear.

But Talyn heard—and smiled. They would expect her body to be covered in scars and bruises, but a Vaerli was not subject to such effects for long.

Eventually the maids dried her hair and combed through sweet-scented oil to make it gleam. Climbing out of the bath, she let them dry her with thick towels and begin to build the image the Caisah had commanded. They were not done with scenting her. Rose oil was applied against each pulse point before she was laced into the dress.

At first they were tentative but, with her silence and compliance, they gained confidence. Tugging and pulling her more vigorously, they worked her body into the shape demanded. Her long dark hair they curled with hot irons from the fire and swept up in a thick pile on the top of her head. They held the weight of it in place with many tiny, diamond pins.

The fashion was for pale skin so they tried at first to disguise hers with powder, but when she remarked that the Caisah wouldn't like her to not look like herself, they quickly removed it. Instead they settled for reddening her lips with ochre and coloring her eyelids with malachite green. They even filed back her nails and placed over their broken ragged forms ones carved from ivory, which they then painted with eggshell gloss. Last they fastened a bright choker of moonstones around her neck, similar to the collars the Caisah's hounds wore.

Looking in the mirror, Talyn couldn't decide if she liked what she saw or not.

The youngest maid with wide blue eyes couldn't help herself. "You look beautiful," she blurted out.

Talyn regarded her in the mirror, watching as she turned red and endured the nudges of her companions. "Thank you," she replied coolly. Now if the inside only matched the outside.

The maids scuttled off, no doubt to tell tales in the kitchens about how they had survived an encounter with the Caisah's Hunter.

"Not that I look like a Hunter," Talyn remarked to her reflection before turning and going down to face the real humiliation.

The night could not be more lovely, warm and languid like the Court itself. They lingered outside the Grand Ballroom in more splendor than usual. All were masked and cloaked. Every inch of expensive cloth must have been stripped from the city, hundreds of wild birds must have given their lives for the feathers that adorned the women, and seamstress must have gone blind sewing the sea of beads on all the dresses.

As she walked down among them, the only one with a bare face, Talyn could feel their eyes on her. Peering out from behind fantastical masks, all of the looks were cold and calculating. She had never felt more naked. It seemed the anonymity gave them courage to examine her minutely.

She immediately knew the Caisah. He'd dressed as the scion, the King of Fire. He turned toward her. His head was framed with a corona of gold and copper spires replicating the sun. The mask covered only from his mouth up, and she could have identified those lips anywhere. Every time they opened she listened. He was bare-chested, the smooth expanse painted with gold dust, while around his hips he wore the *dulma*, the ancient Manesto short wrap long since fallen from fashion. She could not guarantee it was not a garment he had worn as a child, so little did they know of where the Caisah came from.

He liked to show his body, perfect and young as it was. The smooth hairless chest and well-formed legs were those of a man in the prime of his life. Such a display of agelessness could only have been designed.

His costume said much, and it was not likely that any of the Court missed its significance either. Not content with ruling all on the earth, he aspired to be something even more godlike. On anyone else, it would have been sacrilege.

Talyn paused, not sure what to do. It was a masque, and she knew she was not supposed to be able to tell who the Caisah was. And while the rest of the Court was good at playing these sorts of games, she was not. Nor did she feel comfortable talking to anyone else. The games of courtiers had never been her games.

"Impressive, isn't he." Kelanim's voice was unmistakable, and when Talyn turned she thought the same could have been said of the Mistress.

She had never seen such a sight, the beautifully crafted cat mask in hammered silver and the brilliant blue dress covered with a sea of sapphires, all of which was more than a poor farmer could hope to make in his lifetime. Her tiny waist and heaving bosom were every male's fantasy.

It helped, actually. Before, Talyn had thought she was hideously overdressed, but on seeing the Caisah's mistress she realized she was practically demure. Stifling a smile, she replied easily, "The King of Fire is always most impressive."

"You're thinking about taking him to your bed." Kelanim stepped closer, forcing Talyn to look up.

She was not intimidated. "If I knew who such a fine figure of a man was . . . I might."

Kelanim's breath hissed over her teeth at Talyn's admission. The cat leaned closer. "You are out of your depth here. This is my hunting ground. Do your part, which is to stand there and frighten the Praetors. Nothing more." With that, the enraged Kelanim sailed off toward where the ballroom doors were opening.

It irked Talyn, but the mistress was right. If she did try to play the game that way, she would not win—and perhaps the Caisah only tolerated her because she did not.

She stood there silent as the murmuring crowd followed after the Caisah.

"Do you need an escort, milady?"

Talyn did not recognize the voice. But, turning, she found with some surprise someone addressing her directly. She hadn't expected the question to be for her. The man's clothes were dark and unremarkable, so he was probably one of the lower gentry, a minor Praetor's son. But it was the mask he wore which surprised her.

Talyn had to bite back an exclamation. The curved fanged face was a Vaerli ceremonial headdress, a representation of Morleth, the first Named Kindred. She had seen many such masks used in the remembrance plays. It swallowed up the man's head so that only his eyes and mouth were visible.

"Did I startle you?" he asked mildly.

It was nothing. He was just another foolish Manesto lord and had probably picked up the headdress at a market or in some dusty attic without knowing its significance. Once, it would have been unforgivable for any hand but Vaerli to touch such a sacred object.

Stuffing down any comments, she instead tried to smile pleasantly, as was her part. "I am never startled."

He bowed a little, so she could not tell if he smiled or not. "Then you should not be surprised to be offered an escort. Such beauty should never go unaccompanied!"

Talyn held in a sigh. It was obvious he was merely another young upstart, probably in from the country, trying to make an impression by approaching the Caisah's Hunter. Still, she had not had any other offers and she did feel very much at sea.

He loomed over her, tall and broad of chest. Most of the time Talyn forgot completely how small she was when compared with the rest of the world, but at close quarters she could admit a desire to be a little taller. It never daunted her in anything. It was just she was sure that at this moment he was gloating a little.

She took the young man's arm and let herself be led into the column of people filing into the ballroom. Her unnamed partner was examining her.

Turning her head slightly up, she glared at the boy—it was usually enough to put people in their place. Something about the vast darkness of Vaerli eyes inevitably caused a retreat.

The lips beneath the mask were indeed smiling, but he remained silent.

They moved forward another few feet in the press of people and Talyn found herself concentrating very hard on the backs of those in front of them.

Finally she marshaled her thoughts. "I don't know where you come from, boy, but it is rude to stare."

"I was not staring," he replied softly so that only her ear would catch his words. "I was merely dazzled by your beauty."

On that line she choked; several people half turned their heads toward her. She couldn't help retorting under her breath, "I am old enough to be your grandmother's grandmother's grandmother."

Her self-appointed partner leaned in conspiratorially. "Ah, but I know your taste runs to younger men."

It was not said with any malice, but a spear of shock ran through Talyn. What did he know? She had never felt any shame in her rare dalliances with men. She lived and breathed, therefore she had needs like any other creature; still, she had always kept them quiet. The eyes of the Court and the Caisah were sharp, and she wanted no perceived weakness to reach them.

Steadying her breathing, she was at a loss to know what to say.

He touched the back of her hand, and there seemed to be real concern in his voice. "I hope I have not offended you, milady. I was merely saying that to you we must all be boys."

So perhaps he meant nothing by it, but either way she was very much out of her depth. Talyn knew very well that when it came to trading subtlety and barbs she was unskilled.

The ballroom, seen intermittently through the press of people, was magnificently lit by hundreds of candles twinkling in cut-glass candelabras. The gold leaf gleamed on the rising pillars, and the musicians high above in the gallery were playing a sweet tune.

The man at her side caught his breath, and she smiled with satisfaction. Whatever backcountry praetorium he came from was obviously not equipped with such grandeur. Through the milling, scurrying multitude the Caisah and his mistress could be seen within a circle of admirers. Their outfits fooled no one, though certainly they would all be pretending as hard as possible.

"Do you think the Caisah will require your presence all night, milady?" her escort asked her, softly leaning over slightly so that no others might hear.

"Hopefully not," Talyn replied. She could feel the tenseness of his arm under all that finery.

"Then may I ask for a dance later?"

"You don't even know if the Caisah's Hunter can dance . . ."

"All Vaerli can dance and sing like scions. I will find you later." With that he drifted off and was lost to her.

That was certainly the strangest conversation she had been part of for many years; not many bothered to learn anything about her people.

"Talyn." The Caisah was at her side when she turned. It was obvious that he had been standing there for some time. Those storm-cloud eyes were narrowed and his lips unsmiling. He used her name so infrequently that she did not like the sound of it now.

"Whom were you speaking with?" His voice was smooth enough, but the tense lines of his body said far more.

"No one of consequence."

He turned slightly, seeking out her former escort in the throng, and when he turned back, calm seemed to have been restored. Taking her hand, he led her back into his circle.

Half a dozen vassal lords and Praetors of various regions of Conhaero were dutifully impressed with meeting the Caisah's Hunter. They all smiled pleasantly and nodded, but Talyn could see something strange in their eyes—disappointment. Without her armor, sword, or pistol they did not recognize her as dangerous.

It was a sad state of affairs. Once, anyone would have deferred to a Vaerli; now, her people had diminished so much as to become almost invisible. All these sycophants saw was a short, attractive woman. They didn't feel her power without the trappings the Caisah had given her.

Kelanim saw how they treated the Hunter even if their master chose not to. She could not hide all of a satisfied smirk behind a fluttering fan.

Talyn gave her a hard look and reminded herself that the mistress would be dust while she remained. The thought was not as comforting as it been in the past.

So she stood there silent, even her usefulness as an object of interest gone. Eventually when the conversation flowed to other things, she was able to slip away and make a circuit of the ballroom. It certainly was a lovely spectacle: the flashing jewels, a thousand hues of swirling dress, and everywhere laughter. They were laughing in the home of her people and their merry feet were treading all over the bones of her ancestors.

Talyn stood still and found that she was looking for the tall shape of her escort. It was not that she was curious. It was just that she knew so few here and did not care to know those she did. He at least had shown an interest in Talyn the Dark, most despised of the Vaerli.

She thought she caught a glimpse of him moving between the circles of people chatting at the fringes of the dance. But no matter how she stared, his distant figure grew no closer, and the more she concentrated the harder it seemed to spot him.

"Talyn." Once again the Caisah had come up on her without warning, but this time he was free of his entourage. That implied he had ordered them not to follow. He took her hand from her side and led her out on the dance floor. Out of the corner of one eye Talyn saw Kelanim twitch her fan faster.

The Caisah gestured out to the musicians. "The Vigoura," he commanded.

It was a lively dance, and Talyn had not performed it for decades. They circled each other, hands on hips, eyes never leaving each other, feet stamping to the beat.

No one else dared enter the floor uninvited while their lord danced with his hawk. He caught her up by the waist, pushing her up and above his head, before letting her slide down his length to the floor once more. It was a dance of eroticism, usually danced at weddings and fertility rites—hardly suitable for dancing with her. She could feel every one of his mistresses' eyes boring into her, and every member of the gentry watching each step just as minutely.

Talyn took his hand and they turned. "What are you doing?"

The Caisah caught and held her again. "I saw you talking with that man."

She stepped away with the beat of the music, only her fingertips touching his. "I don't quite get your meaning."

Another swirl of the rhythm, and he propelled her into the air before letting her once again down, pressed against him. "All this time I thought you were mine, my Hunter. But now I hear whispers that your eyes travel elsewhere while you are not at Perilous."

Her throat caught as she spun away trying to find an answer, a dissembly that would soothe his strange jealousy.

They circled again, eyes locked. "I think you should be reminded you are mine." The Caisah's voice was a low rumble barely heard above the music.

The dance was ending with the drums rattling out the last pounding rhythms. The Caisah grasped her waist and pulled her taut against him. His face was inches from hers, while their breath came rapidly against each other's cheek. If he kissed her now Talyn wasn't sure what she'd do, for she had no blade.

Whatever whim had stirred him departed abruptly. Before she could react, the Caisah had dropped her back on her feet and stalked from the dance floor. Talyn, after a second, followed.

She retreated from the whispers and stares, knowing she was acting like a beaten dog. The Caisah had disappeared entirely. Deprived of their sport, the rest of the masked observers reluctantly took to the floor.

Taking a small glass of chilled juice, Talyn slipped through the outside door and to the relative quiet of the balcony. Angrily, she discovered she was shaking.

What thoughts were in the Caisah's head? Had one stranger's meager attentions changed something in their set relationship? After being sure that she would give in to any sexual advances he made, Talyn was now uncertain.

He knew something of her actions beyond V'nae Rae. Even a few hours' ease from the rigors of her life was too much, it seemed. Perhaps she'd been lucky for her dalliances to pass unnoticed for so long.

Talyn rubbed her arms, abruptly aware that they were bruised and sore where he had grabbed her. If she had needed another demonstration of his power, this was it. They would fade quickly, yet the point had been made.

"Am I disturbing you?" Her young escort stood poised to leave if she spoke the word. His masked face was doubly hidden in the shadows.

Taking a sip from her glass, Talyn considered for a moment before replying. "It is dangerous for you, I'm afraid."

The tall form stood straighter and, taking a sudden step closer, shut the balcony door behind him. "If you don't mind the company, I'll dare it."

They stood for a while, each with their own thoughts, looking out over the moonlit beauty of V'nae Rae. He was a good-enough companion: bearing her silence, and not asking any questions about what the whole of the Court had just seen.

Finally, though, Talyn finished her drink and watched him cautiously out of the corner of her eye. Dipping into the before-time, she endeavored to see what he might do, but there was nothing.

So she spoke instead. "Won't you tell me your name?"

A smile flickered at the edge of his mouth. "Now, what would be the fun in that? Besides, this is a masque, there are no names tonight. Not even for the Caisah."

Talyn managed to keep the names she'd have liked to call her enemy to herself.

"Why don't you tell me a story instead? How about a tale of V'nae Rae? You must know it as no other does."

And because he had been kind to her, and because it was indeed a beautiful night, she did.

Talyn pointed to the outer curtain wall where the *pae atuae* could still be seen gleaming against the stone in silver and white. "When the Vaerli ruled here, those walls would have been lined with the *maie shara* on a full moon like tonight. They would be calling to the Kindred with such pure voices that any who heard them would weep with the beauty of it. The magics they sang strengthened the pact with the realms of Chaos and allowed Perilous to remain."

"*Maie shara*," he whispered. "The artists of song who weave magic with it. What a wonder it would be to hear them . . ."

It was shock that made Talyn blurt out something she'd never mentioned to anyone before. "I was meant to be one of them—before the Harrowing."

"Indeed." He actually sighed. "The Harrowing has another victim, then, for it would have been an honor to hear you sing. I'm sure you have an exquisite voice."

She couldn't read his face, no intent of his stained the before-time, but suddenly she felt as though they had met. Surely no one of five minutes' acquaintance could look at her so boldly.

"I really am a fool." Talyn stepped closer to examine what little of his face showed beneath the mask. "It was you at the Gates and then at the games. Who are you? Why are you following me?" He had certainly looked like no well-to-do gentry at either of those previous times.

He cocked his head. "Perhaps I can help you recall."

Reaching out, he took her face in his hands. Talyn did not move. Then he bent and kissed her. It was not the gentle enquiring kiss of a new love. It was tongue and teeth with the ragged breath of full-blown passion. It was the kiss of someone who already knew her, and had felt her lips before.

He let her loose and stroked her cheek. "Now must I die for my impertinence, Talyn the Dark?"

She swallowed. "Twice tonight I have been accosted by men and not asked for it, but perhaps this night all sins are forgiven. I shall let you keep breathing."

He laughed and bowed a fraction. "Then I shall escape while your graciousness remains. Perhaps next time you will really recall where we have met and who I am." He turned and slipped out the door.

What a strange night. Talyn turned away and tried to think rationally. She had not looked for all this, and it certainly did not figure in her plans. She was simply not used to such turmoil—at least not recently. With bounties there was always a beginning and an end. It was always very simple a matter between her and the hunted. Tonight was quite different. Yet somehow her spirits were lifted. She did not daunt at least one person in this world, and perhaps that meant that a spark of her old self still remained. It was a comforting thought that she held onto.

Of all the foolish things he had ever done, Finn knew going out onto that balcony had topped them all. He shut the door behind him as quickly as he could, and stepped away, letting his minor power hide him amongst all the lords and ladies. He did not know if it would cloak him from Talyn, but at this stage it was all he had.

Walking away, he did not hear her follow. It was a good thing, too. She would probably recover herself soon enough and, though not carrying a weapon tonight, she could still kill him in a hundred other ways.

His purpose in coming here had not been to kiss the Caisah's Hunter, but seeing her out on the balcony like that, he had taken a chance. Finn had seethed with anger when the Caisah had mauled her on the dance floor. The emotion on her face afterwards was there for everyone to see: despair and loathing. The talk around him had been worse—he only hoped she had not heard it.

"The Caisah's Hunter?" one pale-faced lady had sniffed. "More like his whore."

He had ground his teeth at that. Couldn't they understand how trapped she was? How tormented? If there was one thing Finn understood it was human emotion, so he couldn't be angry with them for long because they were blinded by fear of Talyn the Dark. They had never lain in her arms, kissed the soft small of her back, or all the secret curves of her body usually hidden by armor.

"Focus," Finn whispered as he wove deeper into the crowd. Sometimes he wondered if he enjoyed tormenting himself. Depressive darkness always hovered at the edge of his vision and he was its maker. Tonight, though, he had to remember why he was here.

He could always judge the mood of a place, and right now the air thick with perfume was ripe for the weaving of stories. The ballroom, packed with drunken people and more than a little loosened by the anonymity of the masks, was perfect for his purposes.

It could still be his last talespinning, but desperation had driven him here. The people of the inns and the streets, whom he had spent years trying to foment into rebellion, were not falling into line with his plans. They cried at all the appropriate moments, thought when goaded, but still did nothing.

What was needed was a leader, someone who would dare to begin an uprising. Previous rebellions had failed because of the lack of a really charismatic figurehead. Looking around, Finn could only hope that there was some hard-done-by member of the gentry he could reach here. Surely there was someone who had felt the touch of the Caisah's cruelty and was ready to make a move. If there was, then his talespinning would reach someone and it wouldn't matter what happened to Finn—he would have passed the torch of rebellion on to another. Once lit it would spread. Or so he hoped.

A lull in the music was his signal. With a well-considered flourish, Finn leapt onto the table where a huge lavender cake was displayed. It was the center of the milling crowd, and it would do as well as any stage. He had only seconds to speak before the guards realized what was happening. If he did not have them in his thrall quickly then the whole effort would be in vain.

They cheered and raised their glasses, thinking he was one of them and well into his cups, and probably expecting him to topple off the table at any moment. At this late stage in the festivities they were looking for some variety in their entertainment, and he meant to give it to them.

Always start with a bang, Finn reminded himself. Taking a well-measured breath, he began.

"In between chaos and order, against destruction and death, the Vaerli stand."

The crowd paused. Even those who had not seen him mount the tabletop were turned in his direction. His voice, trained by years of dedication to his craft, traveled right to the back of the ballroom, cutting across the faint strains of the musicians tuning for another song. Finn used all his body to speak, his breath perfectly timed from his diaphragm as his teacher Muyesth had schooled him, and every note of his tale was colored with emotion. From the first words out of his mouth he knew that he had them. At the doorways, even the guards were not moving.

"The leader of the Vaerli, Ellyria Dragonsoul, was tested by the Kindred. Through fire and pain she had to travel to earn the right to stand before the red hot core whence all Chaos comes."

A slight movement in the crowd caught his eye. Entranced already by his words, the lords and ladies only swayed slightly to allow Talyn to pass. She took her spot near the front—but did not move to stop him. He could have sworn there was a ghost of a smile on her lips.

He was too much of a master to falter at that.

"The Vaerli came to Conhaero through the White Void which had been opened up just for them by the Kindred. In the nature of their kind, the Kindred did not make anything easy for Ellyria and her people.

"After finding places in the changing landscape for her people to live, Ellyria set out to find the Kindred who called to her through shadow and fire. Many years she had to travel, looking in every boiling lake and deep cavern of the earth. The journey exacted a terrible price on her, for the Vaerli were new to the world and did not yet possess the Gifts. She grew old and tired looking for the voices that led her into all the wilds of this new land.

"Finally she came to the lake of molten fire at the edge of the world, beyond which lay only the raw stuff of chaos. Despite her age and struggles the Kindred would not yet aid her in any way.

"Three times they called from within the lava boiling from the depths of the world. They called for her to jump into the flames and speak to them in their own realm. Ellyria may have aged, but she did not yet wish to let go her grip on life.

"The first time she demanded, 'Show me your face.'

"The lava leapt forth and burned away a portion of her own face, including her peerless eyes.

"Howling, she again denied them. 'I cannot walk where you walk.' At this refusal the fire sprung forth and burned one leg to a withered stump.

"Again they called and this time, she had nothing left of herself to lose. Crawling on her knees, clawing her way forward with her fingernails, she finally entered the lake of fire.

"Though her body should have been burned away totally, the lava scourged her but did not consume. The pain was more than any creature before or since has endured, but Ellyria did not call out. She let the pain have her and passed beyond it to the other side where the body is lost and only the pureness of spirit exists."

Finn paused for breath, only a beat but enough to judge his audience. They were silent, entranced. Even Talyn, who surely already knew this tale, did not stir. He went on quickly before his thrall wavered.

"The Kindred stood before her wreathed in flame and power. Though they were fearsome to look at Ellyria did not bend to them.

"'Why have you called me here?' she asked, though she could not even tell if she still had lips.

"'You are to be blessed.' The swirling eyes of the Kindred seemed to pierce her through. 'You and your people will be given great Gifts and great burdens.'

"Ellyria knew the way of things and that such generosity usually came with a price, so she was cautious. 'Why?'

"The air grew hot around her. 'You of all the people in the White Void have been called to us to join us in the great task. You will become part Chaos and receive the Gifts we offer in order that you may be equal to the task.'

"Ellyria felt the weight of those words enter her and knew this could be the making or the unmaking of her kind. Yet she was strong and stepped forth boldly. 'We will take up the task.'

"'Be warned,' the Kindred whispered, 'if you fail, if you fall at your task, there will be no safety in this world or any other.'

"'I swear we shall not fail you,' Ellyria promised in her arrogance.

"'Very well then.' The Kindred caught her up once more, bringing her into their fire. Into her eye they burned seven stars to equal the seven Gifts they had to give.

"And from this came the Pact that all Vaerli sing to this day.

They gave us Gifts mighty Kindred, for we are held most high.
First given; earth sense, no place would ever be strange.
Second was empathy, another's feelings would exchange.
Third found was the strength of flesh, to pain and not to die.

Fourth; the giving Seers could see the future through their eye.
Fifth was the gift memory control, so it would never derange.
Sixth; both gift and curse, to travel and yet to never change,
Last gift, the Seventh, time mastery, though for others it might fly.

Ellyria's Pact was made, the Chaos Kindred bound.
But Gifts are not given easily, and for everything
There is a price for Vaerli and for Kin who stray.

Beware the Void they called with frightening sound,
Cursed you will be if it comes and you cannot sing.
Hold fast your word, and flame may be held at bay."

He knew in the Vaerli tongue it sounded better, yet he hoped the message still reached them.

The room grew suddenly warm and the slightest of stirrings in Finn's audience told him he did not have long before the Caisah returned. He'd been lucky to get this far.

He went on quickly, for a moment losing his careful pacing. "But it is we who must not forget. The Pact was broken and the Harrowing has all but destroyed the Vaerli. The time of reckoning is coming, and without rebellion against the Caisah the world of Conhaero is in danger from chaos and destruction."

His ending words were not enough. Just before leaping off the table, he swept back and bowed to his audience. "This is a tale of warning by Finnbarr the Fox. Ignore it at your peril."

He could actually see the top of the Fire Lord's costume over the heads of the crowd and recalled Ysel's warning. Despite his yearning to come face-to-face with the tyrant, he suspected it would be the last thing he would ever see.

Letting himself fall backwards off the table, Finn called on his minor powers with all of his strength. He promised not to think of them as little if they would only help. Even though he had been prepared to risk his life for this telling, he would still prefer to walk away. Would the Caisah call on Talyn to slay this upstart talespinner? Would she obey?

As it was, he would never find out.

The world dipped, wavering even as he waited crouched at the far side of the table. He could hear the Caisah's footsteps only a yard from his position, but he did not look up—concentrating instead on his powers.

"Search the grounds." The Caisah's voice was full of outrage, and the room was so warm that sweat began to pour down Finn's neck and back. "Find that rebel and bring him to me immediately!" The guards' armor clattered as they hurried to obey.

The ballroom broke into chaos as all thoughts of mindless pleasure were abandoned. Taking a deep breath, still keeping his eyes averted, Finn rose to his feet and joined his erstwhile audience escaping the ballroom. Surely Talyn could see him even if the Caisah could not. His cloak of insignificance had never fooled Vaerli. However, there came no shout of alarm or heavy hand on his shoulder.

Even when he stood breathing heavily on the streets outside the Waterfall Gates of Iilthor he still couldn't really believe it. The Caisah had looked right past him, like just another person. It raised his spirits. Their tyrant was not all-powerful if even a minor talespinner had been able to dupe him.

With a spring in his step, Finn turned downhill to his inn. He had gotten away with kissing the Caisah's Hunter and had repeated a seditious tale in front of the whole Court. All in all, it wasn't bad for a night's work.

CHAPTER EIGHT

A FEATHER
IN THE WIND

They caught up with Byre not far from Oriconion. He had considered leaving the Road and heading into the Chaoslands, but he was not trained in the ways of his people. It would have been a quick way to suicide, so he stuck to the Road hoping to find a wagon.

Byre's luck, such that it was, did not hold; no before-time flash warned him, only the sound of pounding hooves. So he ran, but this was open country and with nowhere to go the Rutilians simply rode him down. He managed to get a few satisfactory whacks in with his stick, but their greater numbers overwhelmed him.

Knocking him to the ground, they set about kicking and punching with great enthusiasm. Rolling into a ball, he tried to protect his head and let his mind wander away from his body even when he recognized the tune of a rib snapping.

When they had finally worked themselves into a state of exhaustion, they pulled him to his feet and tied his hands behind his back with never a word spoken.

Gasping at the pain, Byre dimly made out two figures standing watching the whole affair. The Kindred wore their ethereal form, and their red eyes were fixed in an impassive stare. This time, though, there was no help. No eruption from the earth itself came to save him.

Byre didn't understand.

The guards threw him over the back of a horse—as if he was no more important than a sack of wheat—and set off at a canter. The Vaerli was able to gather from their conversation that the whole of Oriconion had risen up, but from their coarse jests Byre realized it wasn't the first time it had happened. They didn't seem particularly worried.

In a very short space of time they had ridden to Fort Harsen, but Byre got to observe little of the outside. Most of what he caught, as he dropped in and out of unconsciousness, was the dusty road and the cobblestones of the keep. His head rattled about and his whole body ached, yet he sensed there was far worse to come.

He had no chance to get his bearings before they dragged him down to the well-equipped dungeon area. Already there was a considerable resident population. Byre glimpsed wild eyes and grasping hands beyond the bars, and the smell of fear and defecation made him gag. The sounds were a kaleidoscope of panic: soft sobbing, frantic wailing, and hoarse ragged shouting.

Byre was desperately afraid, himself, for he had heard the tales of the Caisah's punishers. His adoptive parents had made him listen, hoping to instill in him such a deep fear that he would never get himself into a situation where he met them. They would have been sorely disappointed today.

Though the prison was stuffed to overflowing, there was still enough room for one more. He even got a cell all to himself. They quickly manacled him to the wall and shut the barred door behind them.

He hung there for a while, enough time for his aches to subside. His people's remaining two Gifts, which the Caisah had not been able to strip them of, healed his bruises and gave him a little more hope than most of these wretches. Byre was no fool. He could be made to feel as much pain as any of them.

The door opened, and he was grateful to be on his feet to meet his captor. He was surprised though, for it was a woman that entered. Her brown hair was tugged back in a ponytail and a thin bead of sweat rolled down her forehead. Dressed in workday pants and shirt, she looked vaguely dirty and harassed, as if she was part of a hard-done-by workforce. She was unremarkable in every way. That was, until she looked directly at him. Her eyes were a startling shade of green and drilled right through him.

Striding toward him with a sigh, she backhanded him. Byre's head rocked back, his jaw snapping with the impact.

The woman was smiling now. "My name is Flyyit, what is yours?"

Tasting blood in his mouth he replied carefully, "Byreniko."

Her eyebrow rose at how easily he had given it away, but it was not his real name so it was nothing. A stooped figure had arrived at the door and Flyyit gestured him in. With a lurch, Byre saw this newcomer was laden with a tray of instruments whose purpose he need not guess. The newcomer placed it just beyond the range of the manacles and, with a little bow, left.

For a moment, looking at those dreadful implements, Byre felt utterly beyond himself—as if he had stepped into an awful nightmare. He could work out exactly how he had got here though, that was the worst bit. If only he'd paid attention to the Wyrde.

Flyyit was arranging the tools on the tray with all the professional efficiency of a dressmaker at her silks. Her voice was light and chatty. "I have never had the pleasure of working with one of the Vaerli."

"I'm glad to hear it."

He might as well have saved his breath, because she didn't acknowledge his presence. "I understand those two remaining Gifts of yours will make you resilient to damage. You might think that will help you, but in fact I think soon enough you'll be wishing you weren't Vaerli."

Byre swallowed and strained against the manacles. "What do you want to know?" he asked, trying to buy himself some time.

Flyyit was tying on a thick leather apron. She waited until she was finished before turning to face him. "Know? Nothing. You are Vaerli—that is all I need to know. The Caisah has given the word that should any of your people be anything but compliant, they are to be tortured as warning to the others. Your pain is all I want from you."

He gabbled a few incomprehensible sentences, trying to slow her approach, but she was nothing if not dedicated.

She worked him with pincers and red-hot irons at first, before pausing to examine her work and watch his body heal. Byre took long, shuddering breaths through tortured lips, while the smell of his own flesh burning dissipated into the cold room.

Then she got out her knives.

The world narrowed to incredible simplicities: the application of pain, and the blessed relief when it stopped. Byre did not cry out despite it all. His blood boiled and his flesh screamed, but only gasps came out of his throat.

Flyyit paused, mainly to wipe her brow and take some water. She eyed Byre speculatively even as his body healed. "Why do you not scream? People have told me it releases some of the pain."

Byre smiled, though his jaw was still half broken. "Have you not heard the story of Ellyria?" His voice came out slightly slurred. "The Kindred tested and tormented the first Vaerli. She went through the fire and said nothing. What can you do to me that my kind has not already suffered?"

She smiled at that and strode across the room. Her kiss forced open broken lips and jaw and nearly shattered his fragile control. Flyyit pulled back, grinning. "Foolish, very foolish to lay down such a challenge like that. Believe me, I am only getting warmed up. I like to find the most effective places lightly at first. Men are like a lute to me, but I think I have found your sweet spots."

While he was still reeling, she unchained him from the wall and knocked him roughly down. Then she manacled his neck to a ring set in the stone floor. Gasping for breath, Byre was only just able to turn his head, as she bound his arms at his sides and against the flagstone.

He could feel a change in the atmosphere: a ripple that he knew signaled only one thing. The two Kindred in etheric form were watching him again, red eyes narrowed.

Flyyit had picked up a heavy mallet. She rested it near his head before bending down to stroke his wet hair out of his eyes. "I have a theory."

"How nice," he whispered into the dust.

"If I break your arm and tie it tightly enough so that your body cannot heal it properly, I believe the pain will be . . . exquisite."

She got to her feet and took up the mallet.

Byre squeezed his jaw tight. The first blow made the world explode into brightness, but—terribly—not unconsciousness.

"Impressive," Flyyit muttered behind him, winding herself up for another blow.

Byre tasted blood in his mouth once again, but this time it was because he had bitten through his own lip. He prayed for darkness and death, though what gods might be listening he could not imagine. The Vaerli had never owned any before.

Through the pain, he kept his eyes locked on the impassive Kindred who watched his agonies and yet did nothing. They had helped him before and now, when he was at his greatest need, they did not move in his defense.

As Flyyit worked and sweated over this most unsatisfactory of victims, she could only take some small measure of victory. The Vaerli, when she paused, could be heard whispering against the stone, "Why? Why?" over and over again, while his eyes remained locked on the corner of the room. She gave him no answer and instead set herself to the task at hand.

If there was one place of peace remaining in V'nae Rae, it was the temple to the Lady of Wings. As Talyn knelt in the stone coolness of it she tried to let the turmoil of the previous night pass over her.

The tall vaulted ceilings with their vast honeycomb of nests running right up to the ceiling echoed with only the sound of birds. Though it was a temple to a Scion of Right, Talyn felt herself calm in such a place. Everything was blue-gray and serene. Even the occasional bird dropping was hastily swept away by a small army of acolytes.

Talyn sat at the far end of the temple near to the only other decoration required in such a place, an image of the Lady herself. The simple statue showed her with wings outspread, a beatific smile on her face, as she prepared to lift into sky and transform into a bird. Above the image in letters deep, yet blurred with time, were words of praise.

O Lady, exalted creature of the air, thou art the hawk in the sky, avenger of man, and the judge of all words.

If only that were still true. The Lady was the scion of the Refae clan of Manesto. It was she who had found the way through the White Void for them. So perhaps Talyn rightly should have harbored some resentment toward her.

The Lady's Swoop had always been a force for good in the days before the Caisah. It was not their fault that—like all of Conhaero—they had to bow to him.

Few birds remained in the roosts. They were a symbol that most people obeyed, but when called upon the Swoop could be a dreadful enemy indeed. Still, looking up into the beautiful gold eyes of a sleepy owl, Talyn could only find peace here.

She heard the sound of boots against stone. Talyn kept her head bent in the hope that whoever it was would pass on by. All chance of that vanished when she glanced out of the corner of her eye and saw Azrul smiling back at her.

"Thought I might find you here." The Commander of the Swoop tugged her honey-brown hair out of its braid and pulled herself up to perch by the statue of her Lady. She sat there, grinning at the Hunter and swinging her winged helmet in one hand. "I only just got back and already I hear you have been causing quite a stir."

The number of people who would have greeted Talyn the Dark with such familiarity could be easily counted on the fingers of one hand, and yet despite that the Hunter could not dislike the young commander. It was not just that she was an efficient and capable officer. It was the ease with which she did everything. Her brown eyes were honest and unfettered by any dark motivations. Talyn had more than once found herself close to unburdening on the young commander.

"I'm sure you have heard many things," the Hunter replied, getting up and giving Azrul a chilly look, "but not even half of them are true."

"You mean not even the bit where the Caisah nearly kissed you?"

"That, however, could be," Talyn admitted with a shrug. "He only did it to show everyone I am his. At least, that is what I am hoping it was."

Azrul examined her toes. Any mention of the Caisah always made her flinch, so it made for difficult conversations. Deftly, she managed to move the subject from their lord and master. "And what about this suicidal talespinner? I've heard so much already . . ."

Talyn stared at her blankly. "It was a good story, that is all."

"More than that." Azrul took her arm without any sign of fear and guided her into one of the side chapels of the hall. "The whole city is buzzing. They are talking of rebellion and how the loss of the Vaerli might have condemned us all. It must have been a real tale!"

Talyn looked up at the lanky commander. "I cannot comment on the truthfulness of it, as it is merely a myth among my people, but his telling of it was . . ." she paused to choose her words carefully, "very moving."

Azrul sighed and leaned back against the stone of the chapel for a moment, closing her eyes. "I wish I had been there. I could do with something to take my mind off all of this." She gestured about her with something verging on desperation.

It was not the first time that Talyn had heard the Commander of the Swoop complain about the Caisah's missions. The Swoop, once the symbol of fortitude and religion, was now relegated to no more than a force of tyranny: another cog in their master's machine of domination.

For Azrul, there remained little choice. The tribes had few groups like the Swoop but, in the absence of an actual scion, they were ultimately ruled over by the leader of the Manesto. It was more than just tradition. It was a binding of the highest magic, and once this link had kept the tribes together in the maelstrom of the White Void. It was only Azrul's misfortune that had born her into a generation where that leader was the Caisah.

Talyn opened her mouth to find some platitudes, but instead found herself screaming in agony. It had been so long since she had shared the Second Gift that she quite forgot herself. The pain of the other swept over her, bringing her to her knees and making the world flair white. Dimly she heard Azrul's voice, her hand touching her shoulder, but she could do nothing but scream mindlessly. Against the back of her eyelids Talyn saw a knife flash, and a woman's hand wielding a huge mallet. The word *why* battered against her head as if someone was shouting it directly into her ear. All around was such fear and pain that for those moments Talyn's own body dissolved away. She wore another's skin and shared his fear and horror.

When it subsided she found herself sobbing on the floor, while Azrul held her hand and patted her back. She had not cried in centuries, but she did now. Talyn screamed his name, his secret deepest name, and it was not just the pain that made her do that, but also the knowledge that she was powerless to help her brother. Finally, when she had spent all the tears she felt her body had ever owned, she rolled over and stared at the beautiful vaulted ceiling.

"Please forget what you have seen and heard today, Azrul," she finally said through a torn throat.

The commander sat back on her heels. "Only if you tell me what it was. If it is some affliction . . ."

"None that a healer can mend," Talyn replied, getting to her feet. She staggered, and Azrul helped her to sit on the pedestal next to the Lady of Wings. "It is my brother. Somewhere out there, he is in terrible pain. I have not felt that connection for many, many years."

Azrul frowned. "Then why now?"

"I do not know. It was not one of the Gifts returned to me by the Caisah. The Harrowing only left us the ability to sense each other, not empathize." She shook her head. "Now I do not know what to do . . ."

"For if you go to help," Azrul said softly, "you will both burn for it."

Talyn's hand clenched; her whole body knotted with frustration. "I love my brother. We were close before the Harrowing, but I do not know what sort of man he has grown to. I know nothing of his foster parents or how he has lived all these years. But I would dearly love to find out."

"He is not dying?"

"It is hard to kill a Vaerli—but he is in great pain." With horror she found she was shaking. "He could still be slain, I did not see enough to know." She turned her head in the direction he lay. The connection still vibrated like a plucked string, but the waves of agony were dimmed. It had been so sudden she did not even know how close he was. Talyn thought she had plumbed the depths of her despair, but she was obviously wrong. To know he was in danger and be unable to do anything about it was the worst torture. Every part of her wanted to find him, save him, but it would be death for both of them.

Azrul must have read it in her face, for she put her arm around the Hunter's shoulder and hugged her. "My brother was killed two years ago, a foolish fall off his horse. I loved him dearly too. If you can do anything . . ."

"What can I do?" Talyn snapped, pulling away. "I have no friends, no allies to ask for help to search for him."

"I would think you could ask me," Azrul replied quietly.

Looking down, the Hunter realized with a start that she had hurt the other woman with ill-thought words. "I would," she said more gently, "but both of us are tied to the Caisah. We are his creatures, and I fear he might well be the cause of my brother's pain. Neither of us can afford to go against him."

"Even if it means the death of your kin?"

Talyn couldn't answer that question. She had single-mindedly chased her goal without thought of the consequences, imagining that she had done the worst things possible to achieve it—but she had been wrong. To abandon her brother to death would be the very lowest.

"I must think about this," she said slowly. "There must be something I can do . . ."

Azrul nodded, more than aware of the painful choices a minion of the Caisah must often make. "May the Lady of Wings light your way." She sketched the Lady's Kiss in the air, a swooping gesture like a bird in flight from breast to lip with the fingertips.

Talyn returned the blessing, though she did not really believe in such nonsense, and quickly left the temple. Her thoughts whirled as they had not for centuries, and it was painful.

She found her way swiftly back to her room and drew the silver carved box once more from under her thin bed. Opening it quickly she removed her mother's sword with reverence and, laying it on the bed, pulled clear the maroon velvet of the lining. The *pae atuae* protected not only the weapon; underneath the padding of the box were other precious things: her stash of coin, two small carved stone figures of Kindred, some *pae atuae* poetry, and a silver ring. The money was what she'd come for but the ring drew her eye. It was unaccountably warm and heavy in her hand. She didn't even remember picking it up, though she couldn't forget where she had got it from. Some memories were impossible to shake off.

On impulse she tucked it into her pocket with the coins. Money had never really featured in her life before, but Talyn was glad now that she had considered it might one day. She had squirreled away thick gold coins, some from her bounties, others she had picked up in her many years, for a moment such as this. Though she was not one of them, she knew there were plenty of people who would work hard for gold. Hopefully she would be able to find out about Byre, and then perhaps she could do something to help him. It was not much of a plan, but it was certainly better than waiting for news of her brother's death to reach her.

Byre woke with a cry. Had it all been a horrific nightmare? The coolness of iron on his arms and legs soon put paid to that happy thought. Raising his head with as much care as he could, Byre carefully looked about, but the cell was empty. It was coming toward evening, and Flyyit had worked hard all day. She was hopefully exhausted from her efforts and would let him sleep soundly. Byre could only hope his torturer was not completely dedicated to her job.

His body ached with remembrance but the physical damage she had inflicted on him was already beginning to heal: all but one.

She had been right—the pain was incredible. Breaking his arm, she had bound it tightly at an impossible angle and all day his body had sought to set it right. The fight between the torturer and the Third Gift would have left Byre crippled if he had not used the mastery technique all Vaerli children learned. It was a way of setting aside pain, of going beyond it for a little while. It had been used since ancient times, particularly when dealing with Kindred who had no concept of pain and how much they could inflict on flesh. Tucked in a corner of his mind the agony still lingered, and it would return in greater strength soon enough.

For now at least, he would not go mad with the torture. His arm shattered and bound as it was would not slow him down should he manage to escape the cell.

And how will you manage that? The Mastery had left him deaf to other things. He was not quite as alone as he might have thought. A single flame-eyed Kindred, present still only in ethereal form, lingered in the corner of the room.

"There is always a way to escape these situations," Byre replied with firmness he really didn't feel. "Perhaps you might even want to help me as you did last time . . ."

The alien head twitched like a bird watching for prey or predator. *You really are a remarkable kin. None of your race has been able to see us in this form since the Harrowing.*

Byre shifted, cautiously trying the strength of his manacles. "If I am so remarkable, then some help would be appreciated."

The Kindred glided closer, nearer to his face so that he could actually see the far wall through its insubstantial body. *That would not serve our purpose.*

Byre knew full well the creature could use the stone around itself to fashion a useful body. He had seen them do it in defense of the wagon only a few days before. He ground his teeth in frustration. "Does it serve your purpose to watch me die in here? It will happen. She will have had her fun and then it will be over. What will you watch then? Will you let me die alone?"

The Kindred's voice almost seemed sad. *We can only watch—as Ellyria knew. But you are not alone.*

The words hung there for a moment and the peculiar intensity of the words pierced Byre through. He dredged his ancient memory for what he could recall of the Kindred. They were both danger and salvation to the Vaerli, but their thoughts were alien and unknown. Often what they did could indeed seem cruel, but there was always a reason. If only he could understand what that was.

The pain of Byre's broken and contorted body was beginning to break through his Mastery. It would not be long now before pain rendered him incapable of thought. In desperation he stretched forth his unbroken hand toward the Kindred. "Help me!"

You have all the help you need.

Then he did cry out. Flyyit would be sorry to miss his final crumbling. He sobbed and called out the secret names of those long lost to him. He saw their faces as he remembered them. Mother long dead, father long lost, but most of all his sister's fall—the person he most loved. He had hidden their memory away, stuffed them down beneath three hundred years of day-to-day existence, but now writhing on the floor of the cell he allowed it back. His Vaerli nature, so long denied, flooded through him, toe to fingertip, skin to heart. The Kindred's eyes leapt to life, full of flame and triumph.

Byreniko felt it again. He could hear them all: the lost, the angry, those near suicide, those who had stilled all thought of being Vaerli. So many feelings should have destroyed him. Instead he felt more complete than he had ever been. It was as if he had been blinded for centuries and was only now seeing.

He sought her out, and though her mind was tangled with self-loathing and despair, to feel his sister's thoughts again was very, very sweet.

His arm was still broken and trapped and he might well die very shortly, but Byre rolled so that he could see the sky outside and smiled.

"Is the Harrowing ended?" he asked the Kindred with a voice that seemed to him to be that of all of his people.

No. Nor have you yet earned the return of all Gifts, but you are the first kin to come even this far.

Byre lay still for a moment, letting the connection subside—but only enough so that he could think for himself. "But it was the Caisah who caused the Harrowing. How did you make him return even one of them?"

The Kindred was retreating, fading into the earth, leaving him with unanswered questions. *Not all kin deserve to come home, and not all Gifts are given easily. The puzzle is not finished yet.*

Byre let his head drop. The creature was gone but the Second Gift remained. He held onto that, and the pain when it returned would not be enough to break him.

CHAPTER NINE

PAYMENT IN KIND

Pelanor sat quietly on the stone floor, her eyes closed and her mind reaching out across distance to her *gewalt*. Alvick was so far away, but she could hear his blood pounding within her and taste his desire for her like sweetness on her tongue.

"You failed." The priestess' voice was soft in the darkness. "You know you cannot receive the Blood until the price is paid."

That irritated the young Witch. She had not studied hard for seven years to forget such a thing, but she showed none of these emotions when she replied. "The Caisah dismissed me. His power is one not even you could stand against, Mother."

A little dangerous to goad a priestess of the twelve-mouthed goddess, but no punishment came. She was now a full Blood Witch and not a mere acolyte.

"There will be other chances, little one," the priestess said. "The Hunter never stays too long by her master's side; there is no amusement in that for him. You must follow her in the wilds and take her there."

Again her elder was testing her. Pelanor rose. "There is no Witch alive or dead who can track a Vaerli. Their blood is immune to our magics."

Her elder remained silent, watching her out of narrowed eyes.

Then Pelanor knew this was a test, and she and her *gewalt*'s existence depended on passing it. The goddess might give the gift of the Blood, but the Council decided if she was worthy to be one of them. Although she might be nearly immortal, her vulnerability was Alvick, whom they had hustled away shortly after the ceremony.

She thought on the nature of the Hunter and the magics that surrounded her. Finally after a short silence, she lifted her head and smiled. "The link between Hunter and prey is powerful."

The priestess raised an eyebrow. "Well done, little one. You have only to wait until her prey is named . . ."

"And if I find that person then she will come to me." Pelanor folded her hands and dropped her head once more. "Then if you do not object, Mother, I will meditate until the link is made and try to think of ways I may overcome the Hunter."

"A fine idea." The priestess pressed her hand against the Witch's forehead. "You will need much preparation if you are to accomplish what no other of us has: the defeat of a Vaerli." There was no sound to mark her leaving, but the air was still suddenly.

Pelanor did not reply, instead fixing her mind on the glory that was bound to follow.

Few people looked directly at Talyn the Dark as she strode through the Lower City. Truthfully, she did not look about herself much, either. It was too distressing to see the tumble of houses leaning over the streets like drunken fools. Vaerli had never been enough in number to need a building beyond the walls of the Citadel itself. These days it seemed like the city was larger and harder to escape.

She would have also liked to ride Syris into the town, but the nykur was ill at ease in such close quarters, and she didn't need any incidents or further attention—not that she was able to move unnoticed through the streets.

A tide of rumor raced ahead of her. Children were yanked hurriedly into houses and even beggars scrambled to get out of her way. Naturally, there were others too, footpads, people who had lost kin to her bounties, these all lurked in the lower portions of the city. She could feel their regard from the shadows of the alleys, but the before-time whispered that they were too shy of death to approach.

It was not in Talyn's nature to be subtle. She had no contacts, and no shady go-between to smooth her path through the city's underbelly. So she went to the one place she knew such people could be found, the Singing Fish.

Pushing open the conveniently squeaky door of the public house, she heard the patter of conversation stop suddenly. Every eye was on her, and despite herself, she smiled. It was certainly a curious effect. Not that smiling did her any favors, either. A couple of nervous patrons leapt up and made for the back door.

Ignoring them, Talyn walked confidently up to the bar. Then, turning, she raised the full purse of gold. "You all know who I am, and you know despite everything I do, I do not lie. I need information, not on any bounty—but on my kin. Anyone who can find the location of my brother—known as Byreniko—will earn this purse . . . and my gratitude."

Most kept watching her, but a couple exchanged glances as well. Good, she had some interest at least. She went on boldly, one eye always in the before-time. "He is most likely hidden, tortured even, but I will pay well for knowledge of his whereabouts, even more to secure his release. It is a simple matter that will earn you enough to last a lifetime."

She'd caused much harm to other people's families, but hopefully the lure of gold would erase that from people's minds. Tossing the purse lightly in one hand to make it jingle attractively, she turned to make her exit. "Leave a message at the Temple of the Lady of Wings if you wish to earn more money than fomenting rebellion will ever do."

At her back, the patrons sounded like angry bees, but if there were no rescuer there then at least the rumor would spread. It was the only plan she had. It was also Byre's only hope.

The Caisah sat in the dark, and Kelanim hesitated at the doorway. She had made the mistake of interrupting his thoughts before—the bruises had taken weeks to subside from around her throat. Whatever dark shadows he battled, they put him on the edge of violence.

Just how she had come to love the Caisah, Kelanim could not say. It was certainly not as if she had expected it. Her father, an insignificant official, had been trying to gain favor at the time, and she was the only thing of any value he had. So when Kelanim was sent dry-mouthed and terrified to Perilous she had only expected to hate. In fact, she had already planned to try to escape.

But, from the moment she had seen him there was never any risk of her running away. Maybe it was his power or his fine looks, but she had never wanted to be anywhere else than at his side.

The Caisah, still not perceiving her, sighed heavily and rested his head on his hand. She longed to rush to him, soothe his brow, and ask what was making him frown. She knew there was little chance he would share.

Once only had he opened his thoughts to her. She had woken by his side just as morning broke; the dawning sun was just licking the window, and she had seen tears in his eyes. A soft touch on his hand, a look of love that even he could understand, and he'd whispered to her almost plaintively, "I was not meant to be like this; I was not made for immortality."

Even now she had no idea what he had meant. He'd immediately slammed the door to his innermost thoughts in her face. He answered no more of her questions, and if she ever spoke of that moment he would look at her blankly.

Kelanim bit her lip. It was hard to love an immortal when she wasn't one herself. She knew all too well that there had been generations of clever and beautiful women before her, and all around was temptation that he might at any moment give in to. It was not just memory she had to contend with, because the presence of Talyn the Dark lingered over everything. She and the Caisah had shared so much together that it hardly mattered if they had shared a bed or not. Both were immortal and both recalled days and decades before her time.

The mistress tightened her fists in the lush curtain fabric and held in her rage. It was almost the end of her time with him. She was smart enough to feel it. She would turn gray and go to ash, and there was nothing to be done about it. A child at least would have secured her place and bound him to her—but there was none. Everything had been tried, every witch-woman consulted, every vile preparation they recommended swallowed, but nothing of his quickened in her. She liked life too much to try to get pregnant with another man's child and pass it off as his.

Yet there was a small hope. Unclenching her fist, Kelanim stared down in wonder at the note that had been slipped beneath her door this very morning. She had no clue as to who might have written it, but there in clear bold strokes were words of hope—the only ones she had ever had. The timing of it was exquisite. It was a dangerous task the letter set her, though, and should she be discovered Kelanim was in no doubt what her fate would be. Yet there was nothing else for her. Only lonely exile in the women's apartments awaited her. No other man would marry the Caisah's cast-offs for fear of the master changing his mind. She had seen enough of these once-mistresses, and their miserable ends, to be more afraid of that than the Caisah's anger.

Gathering up her courage, Kelanim went to him, being careful to rustle the fabric of her dress and give him warning. That beautiful face turned and she could almost see the emotions flee. He stood and pulled her against him.

Fiddling with the buttons of his elaborate coat, Kelanim said as coolly as she could, "So, has Talyn left yet to hunt down that fool of a talespinner?"

He shrugged easily with his mind still far away. "Such fare is too meager for my hawk."

"Perhaps," Kelanim whispered, snuggling closer, "but there is much talk in the Citadel."

"Talk?"

"There is always talk, beloved."

His lips twitched. He had no liking of such terms of endearment, but she knew him well. The Caisah might feign indifference, yet he always had a wary eye out for stirring rebellion.

Taking his silence as a good omen, Kelanim pressed on. "They say you are losing the will to rule. That you allowed a filthy spinner of tales to mock you in your own home." She flinched, expecting him to lash out.

This time his temper held. His finger traced her cheek, cool and calculated. Kelanim worried he could feel the letter burning a hole in her pocket. Finally, he spoke. "My Hunter has had less grand prey of late, I suppose. And I cannot let such an insult go unpunished, can I?"

Catching his hand, she pressed it to her lips. "No, my lord, for you are mighty and dreadful."

He laughed then, and let her draw him back to her room. Whatever dark thoughts and powers possessed her love, for a while he laid them aside and was just a man.

It had been a close thing. Finn had been upstairs at the Singing Fish that morning when Talyn the Dark came with her incredible offer. By the time he emerged from his room the whole place was in near-riot. The inn was now full of people clamoring to hear the story.

Circling the room, Finn gathered several versions of the event, most obviously embellished. He doubted very much that Talyn had killed fifty men on her way down the street, nor did he believe that she had been dressed in nothing but boots and sword. Talespinner that he was, he admired the effort and could imagine that by nightfall there would be a hundred different accounts leaving Perilous for new life in outlying districts. The pamphleteers would be hard at work all evening.

He was sure that the Hunter had no idea what she had unleashed. Despite her great age Talyn had little contact with ordinary folk, but the talespinner had seen the power of story before.

Three years before, Finn had been wintering in a small coastal village to the north. A hapless fisherman, who thought himself a spinner of a yarn or two, bragged about a fish of gold that he had hauled in just off the bay. Now, told to his neighbor over the back fence, the story would have gotten no farther than the village; but, by broadcasting it to a heaving public house with many well into their cups, he'd brought himself nothing but misery. Scarcely a week later and the villagers were inundated with people searching for this shoal of gold-filled fish. Some got rather angry when told there was no such thing. The fisherman who had started it all ended up with his boat holed and was forced to move to another village altogether.

Telling a story wasn't as simple as it first seemed. Finn knew there was power in words that most didn't really understand. Within hours after she made her offer, the rumor had spread to practically everyone in the city—within days, it would have reached even the farthest corners of Conhaero. It would not just be a bag of gold Talyn was offering, it would be a chest, and more besides. Soon Perilous would be full of conmen, desperados, and the mentally unstable. They would be dragging every father, son, and husband they thought might pass as her brother to her doorstep. As Finn thought about it, he realized it would also make Vaerli valuable property, and it wouldn't matter to them that getting two in a room was always fatal.

It was almost comforting that Talyn had made such a mistake. It did, however, mean that his performance of last night was not the most interesting news of the day.

"Know any Vaerli hereabouts, talespinner?" A tall fellow with beefy shoulders stood very close to Finn.

Finn paused on a reply and looked around. Yes, he was right; they were all staring at him. He tried to sidle away from the gathering crowd. Though he was used to attention, this was not the kind he wanted. The gleam in their eye spoke of gold madness.

They pressed closer, blocking his way to the door. The people were being absorbed into a crowd, losing their identity and becoming bold with it. They poked him, beginning to yell, and Finn tried his best not to panic at their odor and aggressiveness. He'd seen men torn apart in a mob by normal everyday people. He heard the publican yelling for order, but no one was listening. It seemed strangely funny that a talespinner might be dismembered by a crowd so desperately wanting a story.

He was saved when Equo's spare shape interposed itself between the talespinner and the crowd.

Spreading his hands and smiling charmingly, the new arrival said jovially to the crowd, "He really isn't that good."

"Half-rate talespinner if you ask me." The top of an enormous green hat was just visible near the back. The voice was unmistakably Varlesh's.

The crowd rippled with laughter.

"He wouldn't know a Vaerli from any other beggar," Equo went on.

Finn could feel himself getting a little red.

"Much more likely to find a Vaerli out in the market," Varlesh boomed, sounding suspiciously as if he was nearing the bar.

Miraculously, the near-mob dissipated, and they became people again. Some made for the door to investigate Varlesh's claim, but the rest settled down to their seats.

Equo took a firm grip of Finn's elbow and guided him back to his compatriots. The dark-eyed Si nodded at Finn. Varlesh appeared, beer mug in hand, sat down quickly, and ordered some meat pies from the relieved barmaid.

Draining his mug with relish, the older man grinned at Finn. "You're so predictable, boyo—always in a pickle and never knowing how to get out of it. You'd think a man of words would find a way out of such messes."

"I give performances, not debates," the talespinner grumbled before taking one of the trio's hot pies, "but you seem to know how to handle a crowd."

"Experience," Equo replied affably.

Varlesh wiggled his fingers. "That and a little bit of magic."

Finn stared at him for a moment, not quite sure if they were joking or not. Something about Si's fixed look suggested more.

"Still, it's nice to see you've survived," Equo said in a lowered tone. "We really didn't expect you to. But maybe you were right. There are rumors more powerful than even the appearance of Talyn the Dark in the Singing Fish."

"Wasn't so much the story," Varlesh went on, "more the amazement that someone had the bare-faced cheek to speak the words in the Caisah's Citadel."

"You've caused a stir, Finn, and now we have to get you out!"

"Unless you really do have some fool death wish . . ."

Finn traced the rough surface of the table. Truthfully, he hadn't been thinking that far ahead. "I guess I have done what I came here to do . . ."

That admission was enough, and before he knew it the trio had him upstairs packing his meager possessions and getting out of the inn. He did resist being taken down the back stairs. "I'm not a fugitive!"

"You should be." Si touched his shoulder. "The Caisah will make a puzzle of you."

"What does he mean by that?"

The other two shared a glance.

"Don't know for sure, lad," Varlesh replied, "but the Caisah has set some mighty puny bounties recently, and from last night's performance you could well be on the list. The Pure Maid knows how we are going to get you out of the City!"

"It's possible you got your wish, Finn," Equo said. "You might just have got the attention from the Caisah you wanted."

So Finn allowed himself to be hustled out the back way and tried not to wonder if that was a surge of fear or excitement in his chest.

Everything was waiting, for Talyn the Dark: waiting to end the Harrowing, waiting for news of her brother, waiting for the Caisah to command her. She was indeed, as he called her, a hawk—pinned to his wrist, a hood over her eyes, totally unable to take action for herself. She might not be one of his mistresses, but he had her just where he wanted her.

Talyn had sweated away the day in the confines of the Citadel, unable to settle anywhere. With nothing to do but wait for her next bounty, Talyn found time weighing on her. As the day stole away, she lingered by the Great Hall and found in the air a feeling of expectancy she had never felt in the Citadel. So she buckled on her mother's blade and the Caisah's pistol and went out to see if V'nae Rae would tell her what was happening.

The night had just opened, and the air was wonderfully chill. It was a magic time. Looking down from the Southern Terrace, Talyn had to admit the beauty had not left with her people. Under the silver-blue light of the moons, the carved walls glowed. Despite herself she sighed, eyes roaming over the courtyards and towers, recalling with deep melancholy the past.

Nostalgia might be a pleasant sensation for shorter-lived races, but for every Vaerli, even those practicing *nemohira*, it was nothing but pain. There was just too much of it. The ghosts of her people were conjured up on each corner, and everywhere Talyn looked she felt nothing but the weight of time.

She'd been born here, like her mother, but now it only caused her distress. It was only in the night she would allow herself such thoughts and never while on a hunt. Memories rushed from all about to plague her: whispers of children's voices, the brazen recollection of events, and the faces she somehow still expected to see.

A'shenn, her brother had called her, after the smallest letter in their alphabet—a mocking of her size in the manner of children. Never had there been time for her to choose an adult name. The Harrowing had intervened, cutting her away from the Kindred.

The Kindred. Why was she suddenly thinking of them? Something familiar stirred in her.

Because in the quiet you feel me, Vaerli'meroth.

A thrill of fear passed through Talyn the like of which she could not remember having felt for a very long time. All she had learnt of the Kindred came rushing back.

"I feel you indeed, but walking within a Vaerli shadow is forbidden by the Pact."

The Pact is broken. Your people scattered. We have nothing between our kind anymore.

The Kindred were not to be treated idly. Even before the Pact they had been deadly and fickle, just as that foolish talespinner had said. Who knew what they had become since the Harrowing.

Talyn was frozen with sudden fear.

I feel your thoughts, Talyn called the Dark. You have forgotten that your ancestor made the alliance possible. Do you think one of my kind would hurt one of Ellyria's children?

"The line of Ellyria is broken like the Pact. How do I know what you may do?" she snapped. "Why are you in my shadow?"

The world is moving, Talyn. If your kind were whole they would feel it as we do. The balance has been disturbed and changes are coming if the Caisah wills it or not. His time of domination is ending.

She found she was holding her breath. It was too soon. The Vaerli were still crippled by the Harrowing, and if another Conflagration erupted they would be helpless.

It will not wait. We will not wait. Already others are reacting, if the Vaerli cannot. The world is beginning to ring to the sound of uprising. Will you not join them, Talyn the Dark? Shake off the bonds you have made for yourself and cast down the Caisah!

Oh, there was a moment of temptation in that—a brief second of imagining, where she could see herself attacking their ancient enemy. Then reality found her. No hope existed for the Vaerli if she died. Only the Caisah's promise and the Golden Puzzle held any hope.

Foolish child-Vaerli. You are making your own prison. The Caisah plays with you like a toy, and you only have yester-thoughts not future-thoughts. He uses this against you and laughs.

"We made the strongest of blood pacts. He cannot break it without breaking himself. Now get out of my shadow!" she yelled, making the walls of V'nae Rae ring with Vaerli anger.

You and your kind have no power to command me, Talyn the Darkest, so I will stay and watch and wait.

She slammed her fists into the unforgiving stone wall, hoping the pain would reach the Kindred, but it did not come out and she could not Name it.

"I will not let you. I will not!"

Despite herself, Talyn jumped when the pale face of the young guardsman from the Caisah's door appeared around the corner she'd been leaning against. She recognized the young man who had challenged her.

Gulping down her frustration, Talyn tried to recapture her icy mask. "Yes?"

"Forgive me," he made an unconscious half-bow. "The Caisah has a bounty for you, so your presence is required."

Thankfully the Kindred within made no comment. Talyn made her way to her room and replaced the sword lovingly in its box. Dropping the pistol, she followed the impatient heels of the guard. They passed Kelanim in the presence chamber. She was reclining on a low sofa and smiled prettily at Talyn as she passed. The Vaerli could smell sex on her, and she supposed this was why the mistress looked so very pleased with herself.

The interior of the Puzzle Room was different, seen by torch. The light flickered and bounced over the pieces, lending a liquid amber glow to the ceiling and illuminating the Caisah waiting near the window in a sinister cast.

He was dressed only in light trousers of pale linen, and his chest gleamed with sweat. Talyn didn't need an explanation as to why. It was indeed the only reason the Caisah went to bed. He never slept, but he did like to maintain the impression of something akin to humanity. The population already lived in terrible fear of him. How much more afraid would they be if they knew his eyes never shut, and he spent his nights in dark contemplation of his work?

"My Hunter, I see you are as restless as I tonight." He beckoned her closer through the red-gold reflections. "I thought I would have the pleasure of your company for many days yet, but needs must. I will avenge all insults against me."

She drew up within arm's reach of him and waited, holding her tongue for him to say the name. The world narrowed down to that.

"His name is Finnbarr the Fox." The sum of her last remaining Vaerli magic flared. Talyn was momentarily blind. Her skin prickled and her muscles twitched as the name buried itself within her. She saw the face and was not surprised to recognize it. The talespinner had been a fool to push the Caisah.

"He is not far," she whispered under her breath. "Within the city."

"Yes, that is what I am told." The Caisah's eyes were now hooded. Whatever emotions he had in such moments he always kept to himself. "He is not much prey for my worthy hawk, but he is an annoyance and thus justifies a piece of your puzzle. It should be an easy piece . . ."

He enjoys seeing you hunt, foolish Vaerli. The Kindred's voice was like salt in an open wound, but she did not flinch or reply. To show weakness before the Caisah was something she would not allow.

It was an easy piece for her to claim and she wondered at it. What could be his motivation? Was he bored with their game after all these centuries, or could it be that this Finnbarr was more of an adversary than he was letting on?

Why do you puzzle over it? You will bring him back dead or alive to your master's feet, like the hunting hound you are.

She turned on her heel, acknowledging neither the gold-cast Caisah nor the entrenched Kindred. Nothing was to be gained in doing so, and she was well used to ignoring the irrelevancies of life. For the moment she had her prey and prize to consider.

CHAPTER TEN

FROM LIGHT
TO SHADOW

It would have been better for Finn and his friends if the moons had not been as full—but they had to work with what they had. Still, Perilous was quiet. All the hustle and bustle of the day was packed away, and only the desperate or the dangerous were out on the street. Finn couldn't pinpoint exactly which of these groups he belonged to.

Lighting was sparse, with only a few lanterns hung at street corners. They moved quickly and quietly to the outermost edge of the city. The gates were shut for the night, but Finn's friends knew plenty of people who would shelter them until daylight.

He had to admit to a surge of nervousness. The houses here drooped over the streets like conspirators in some ancient plot, and he did not like being unable to see the sky. The neighborhood had a reek of urine and wine, and the lack of people responsible for either of those made it unbearably spooky. He was a talespinner, so he knew spooky intimately.

Admittedly, he shouldn't have been surprised when a figure appeared in the dim light, barely discernible from the rest of the darkness except for the length of blade that she carried before her.

"I do believe you are out after your bedtime," she said quietly.

Finn was, for the second time in less than a day, looking into the eyes of Talyn the Dark—and this time he felt the thrill of fear. He froze, knowing she already knew any move he would make and could be there before him. He was in that instant very aware of his life and its fragility. It was her only gift to her victims.

Even then, he couldn't give up; his talespinning training wouldn't let him. He smiled at her while his friends watched with undisguised horror. "You don't need to do this, Talyn. You don't really want me to die."

"You presume much," Talyn replied, though he thought he detected the faintest of blushes. It was just possible that the Caisah's Hunter did not want it revealed that he had kissed her lips . . . or even more.

"What I said was your people's story. I made them listen, even if just for a moment. If you let me go, I will continue to speak the truth and the Vaerli will be known. People will care what happens to them."

Talyn frowned but did not move.

"You don't need that butcher. He killed your people and he is doing the same to you by inches."

"Careful, boy." Varlesh kept his voice low, as if the Hunter were some frightened horse.

"It is a terrible thing I do," Talyn replied, her eyes not meeting Finn's, "but I sacrifice myself for them . . ."

She was blind—he saw it now. "And what about the innocents, Talyn? What about the orphaned children? The poor wives and husbands crying in the night? The fathers and mothers whom you rob?" He yearned to grab hold of her and give her a shake.

His words had the opposite effect of what he wanted; her sword came up and her eyes now met his with dark and deadly force.

"That's broken it," Equo stated the obvious. "Run!"

They all obeyed, knowing it would do them no good.

Talyn could have found Finn by his aura alone. With him named as her prey their bond was unbreakable, except with his death or capture.

His eyes were no longer calm and she recognized the fear in them with some relief. So he was just a man capable of feeling emotion, and not some vengeful spirit. He could be brought down and his bounty collected.

They ran—which was to be expected. The before-time blurred around her. Then her prey stopped, and Talyn dropped out in confusion.

"Wait." His voice was honeyed and tempered with the power of a tale-spinner. She was fully aware she mustn't pause for him to bind her with any spells or mind-myths.

The world reeled. In her shadow the nameless Kindred keened in the high voice of Chaos, momentarily halting her step and blinding her senses.

Talyn spasmed as it ripped its etheric form free, and tasted metal as it burned out of her throat. For a moment, conscious thought was impossible.

When her eyes cleared it was to horror. The Kindred was all around Finn in a visible nimbus of fire. Talyn's body went cold. It could not be!

The nameless Kindred cried out a name in Vaerli through Finn's throat. The cry set the walls ringing and the ground to heaving. The sword dropped from her fingers in shock, just as the Kindred fled deep within Finnbarr's shadow.

It was impossible, and yet Talyn felt its power shuttering around the four men.

Only then did the Hunter move with the speed and grace of her people, but it was far too late. The Kindred took them through the earth, and she was left touching only a cooling piece of stone.

Kneeling there for a moment, her fingers traced the spot while her mind wandered far ahead. The Kindred were her people. The Great Pact had been between them and no other. Why would one protect a Manesto? It went against everything she knew.

"I think you met your match, little flower." Talyn's chest tightened, and the world became stranger still as she heard the pet name from a voice she hadn't expected to hear ever again.

Shaking with a rush of anger and hope, she turned.

Her father was not tall even among the Vaerli, but he had always had presence. Her eyes could not drink in enough of him, the strange golden hair that marked him out from the rest of their race, the deeply set gray eyes, and the smile almost hidden beneath an immaculate mustache.

Who was crying? Why could she not breathe?

"Am I dead?" Talyn finally gasped.

His eyes were full of tears too, but he held out his hand. "Don't fear, daughter. Neither of us is."

Reality and the past were now intruding. She backed away from him. "But the Harrowing . . . how are you here? Where is the pain?"

His gaze dropped and his shoulders sagged. "I heard," he whispered softly. "They finally told me what you had become, what you have been doing since that awful day."

Talyn shut her eyes and willed him not to say such things. It had been so long since she had heard his voice, and to hear it now condemning her was unbearable.

"I read the Wyrde they had left for me, carved into the places where we used to meet. They told of my beloved daughter and never had such despair touched me—even when your mother was killed. They said that the time had come to stop your treachery to the memory of our people."

In her mind, Talyn had already considered the possibility that one of her own would find her and take her into the fire with the conflagration of the Harrowing. It was almost surprising that they had taken so long to reach the same idea.

Her father's voice continued on, wrung out with sadness and shame. "Even when I heard what you have done, I could not stand by and let you die. So I went to the Hill of Sorrow in the Salt Plains and performed the trials of Sundering, the *goroa'shan*."

Talyn's shocked exclamation burst from her body—a sudden explosion of horror and guilt. She'd not been expecting that. Only now did she see the gray hairs amongst the golden. Flinging herself into her father's arms, she hugged him tightly.

It was true, then. No flames arose to claim them, but then neither was there the taste of empathic joy. The only sensation was the feeling of his tight embrace. She couldn't feel the rush of joined minds and feelings. He had cut himself off from that, and all for her.

She cried until her body ached and her throat broke raw. He held her, stroking her hair, whispering inane and pointless words. All the time, between them was the void where none should have been.

"*Mathiel*," she finally found her voice with the endearment, "that is for criminals, evil Vaerli who must be exiled from the people. Why would you do such a terrible thing?"

He touched her hair and smiled. "You have no children, little flower, or you would not ask."

"I thought you were dead."

"Which I am, in a way. Ah, but it is good to see you again. You are so very like your mother to look at." A deep frown etched itself on his brow. In the time before the Harrowing the Vaerli married for life or until love faded; there was nothing they did not share. How that moment when the bond was broken had felt to her father, Talyn could only imagine.

"But nothing else of me is like her . . ." Bitterness crept into her words.

He did not answer but, taking her hand, held it tightly. "No time for anger now, little flower. I cannot stay long. Your brother too is in great danger; he walked my dreams this month past. I have been told where I can find him, and I hope I may be able to do him some good."

"I felt it," Talyn whispered. "If only for a little while. I . . . I didn't know what to do. Tell me this danger he is in."

"I cannot, and you know why. You are the Caisah's creature."

She kicked a stone away and tried to control her temper. Her father had not always been like this. The one she remembered had been sunny and full of laughter.

Her disappointment must have been written large, for he squeezed her hand. "We are all changed. It has been centuries of pain and anguish for each of us. Try to remember that."

It was hard, this talking about emotions, especially when empathy had once been there instead—so many ways to be misunderstood and to misunderstand.

"Then will you not help me as well?" She fought back the urge to cry again.

"I have been able to go places, see many things, since I set myself apart from our people. You must give up this bounty you seek for the Caisah."

She flung his hand away. "Give it up! I am so close now. So few pieces remain. I cannot just abandon it when I have done so much . . . hurt so many people. It would all have been for nothing."

"You were young when you started on this path, daughter. We were all lost in our pain. No one will blame you for this."

Yet she did blame herself. Talyn bit the inside of her cheek to keep those words from flying out. At least if she won out in the end, she could know she had reached her goal. To give it up would mean she'd been wrong and others had suffered needlessly for it.

His hands clenched, so obviously he didn't need to be empathic to feel her anger. "He will demand you bring back this Finnbarr, and he will probably demand you help his Swoop quell yet another rebellion in the east. Will you add to the crimes you must repent for? How many will you trample beneath you?"

It was by far easier to be angry and push him away than to take his words in. Anything else was unthinkable. Perhaps one day he would see it had all been worth it.

"I will never repent," she cried hotly. "I will pay for what I have done, but if I burn at least I will be happy knowing my people are safe. At least I will have done something!"

He flinched at that, knowing an accusation when one was thrown his way. Her father went on softly as if she were some skittish colt in need of guidance. "You know what will happen if you do this."

She was well aware, but she would not tell him of the anguished days and nights she'd spent before accepting the Caisah's offer, or how she'd cried aloud for her mother who could never come again. He would take it as weakness. Instead, she replied evenly and looked into his eyes so he would know she was as determined as he was. "No price is too high to end the Harrowing. These are our people, living in desperation and pain for hundreds of years. Wouldn't you do anything to stop all that?" Her voice cracked with the depth of her emotion.

His expression changed, a shifting from determination to endless grief. She had just told him she was prepared to risk greater pain than death itself.

His hands dropped to his sides, palms out in supplication to a world that had long since abandoned them.

It was the hardest thing in the world not to embrace him one last time, but Talyn did not. "Go now, *Mathiel*. Leave the words you must for our people. I will not be swayed. Let them send their messenger of death if they will."

He ran a tired hand through his hair. "You are like your mother in more than appearance. I hope we shall meet again, but I cannot tell if we will."

Then the darkness claimed him, and there was only the hollow where his presence had been. Terrible times she had seen, but to Talyn this was the worst of them all. Before, she had at least been able to imagine she was doing this for her people, and spun a story in her mind of her father's pride. Now there was only harsh reality.

This was the path she had chosen, and she'd known there would be no going back once she was set on it.

So, she raised her head and felt her prey sense going out. It was still there, the faint tug to the east where Finnbarr the Fox had gone. Whatever the Kindred had called him in that moment of light, he remained her prey.

The world rushed around Finn. Earth and stone and pebble flew about his head. He was wreathed in flames, his horrified yell smothered before it left his mouth.

Whatever magic Talyn had unleashed on him would be his death.

Then just as abruptly as it had started, it stopped. The heat was replaced by sudden chill, and Finn found himself along with his companions on a dusty wind-blown hillside. The men all gaped at each other.

It was Varlesh who found his voice first. "Well, that boiled my eyeballs but got us out of a very sticky situation. Good work, boyo."

"I don't think it was Finn . . ." Equo directed their gaze to the creature standing against a large boulder not two feet from them.

On first glance, it appeared part of the stone itself, an unremarkable pile of shingle and pebbles that almost looked like a small dog. Then the creature raised its head and eyes of flame looked back.

For one very long moment, even Varlesh did not say anything. The men all stared back at the strange creature.

"Well," Equo said and cleared his throat, "that would explain our abrupt departure. Kindred can travel through the earth faster than thought."

Finn was finally returning to himself, and he could not let that pass; he knew his stories. "But they have no physical form."

"They used to," Si murmured.

They eyed the silent and still creature once more.

"Doesn't look dangerous." Varlesh, regaining his composure, bent over and had a closer look. "Are you dangerous?" he boomed.

"Whatever it may be, I hardly think it's deaf," Finn commented.

The creature cocked its head, somehow managing to now look birdlike. A funny little burp, and it was suddenly on fire, burning but not consumed. Varlesh leapt back, but it remained where it sat, obviously content it had made its point. It could be dangerous if it wanted to be.

They argued for a good hour trying to decide if it was a Kindred, and if so, what had happened. Si occupied a rock close to the creature and said not a word to either side of the discussion.

In the end, the conclusion was that it had to be a Kindred, though exactly where it had come from, or how it had taken physical form, they could not decide. Outside of the ranks of the Vaerli, there were few experts. Since the Harrowing they had not taken form, and had fallen into myth. It was only known in the stories that such creatures were spirits of Chaos and the enemies of the Caisah. Even if it did look like a lady's overstuffed lapdog, that reality alone guaranteed it respect. And there was the fact that it had undoubtedly saved their lives. Though when Varlesh roared a "thank you," it did not respond.

Having that sorted out, they tried to work out exactly where they were. Equo and Finn clambered to the top of the rocky outcrop and stared up at the stars.

"There is Arleth the Strong's Sword." Equo pointed to the long line of stars rising from the horizon. "It can only been seen in the southern sky."

Finn sat back on his haunches, stunned. They had traveled almost half the known continent and were near the easterly edge. Perilous and Fair lay thousands of miles to the northwest.

He sat down on the ground with a thump. "How is that possible?"

"Mighty are the abilities of the Kindred," Equo replied, "and we best not be lulled into stupidity by this one's appearance. It is undoubtedly far more powerful than it looks."

Finn glanced over his shoulder. Si had appeared on the ridge, and his head turned toward where the sun would shortly rise. Pointing back the way they had come, Si whispered, "She follows."

Finn bowed his head, even as Equo grasped his shoulder. They might have put thousands of miles between Finn and Talyn, but he was still marked as her prey. She was coming for him.

"Looks like you got what you wanted, Finn: the attention of Talyn the Dark."

He should have been consumed by fear, maybe his life should have flashed before his eyes, but instead Finn was surrounded by calm. He had to think, though. This was certainly not the way he had planned to have Talyn back in his life, and he was certain there would be no passion in her for one she considered prey.

The sun began pulling itself above the rock-filled valley, revealing the desolation of their surroundings. Shadows still remained only around the pillars of rock. In a few weeks, this place would be something else entirely—maybe a mountain, maybe a lake. They maintained their power even in the face of the Caisah. His Road was the only constant thing, and it was paltry compared with their power. For it was now obvious where they were.

They were starkly beautiful, the Chaoslands, and though they were somewhere no sane person would hide, they could still be Finn's salvation.

Around a meager breakfast of tackbread and dried meat Varlesh had retrieved from their ill-prepared packs, they discussed what to do.

"We're not far from Oriconion. The rebellion will have started with the new moon," Varlesh said while chomping down a mouthful of bread. "We should go there."

"You mean like last time?" Finn asked archly.

None of them replied to that, but Equo let out his first smile of the day. "Nyree lives in Oriconion—unless she's become too troublesome to the Caisah."

"That sounds like a good place for you," Finn said, "but I won't put you or anyone else in danger. I will go into the Chaoslands. Maybe this creature," he gestured to their still savior, "will be able to help."

The three men exchanged glances as if deciding whether his idea was madness or brilliance.

Varlesh jerked his head, and the three of them walked away from Finn. What followed was obviously an argument. He could hear little of it, except Varlesh when he barked, "We can't just leave the lad!"

Si rested his hand on his shoulder and whispered something to his friend. Varlesh subsided into mutterings, but when they returned he spoke for them all. "All right then, but you promise me you'll keep moving and not wait 'til that black witch catches up . . ."

Finn grasped his offered hand. "You have my word. I've seen enough of her for the moment."

"He'll be fine," Equo backed him up. "In a town he'd be easy prey, and with the Kindred . . ."

"Head south, boyo. Get into the Stillness of Bayresh. It's the border to the Choana realm, and maybe the World Builders might remove the deathmark. If not, then they could slow her down a little."

No one mentioned the small fact that none had survived the Choana either. Finn let that one go without a smart remark, for he was conscious that every moment he waited here was less distance between him and Talyn.

"Take heart." Equo clasped his hand in farewell. "The Vaerli are not the only ones with magics in this world."

They said their brief goodbyes, short claps on the back and lowered eyes, and then they left. Hiking among the rocks, they quickly disappeared over the ridge. Finn was left alone, except for the stone-eyed nameless Kindred—and there seemed little joy in its company.

Flyyit was certainly a hard worker. Byre had not been asleep for more than a minute, wrapped in the warm thoughts of the Second Gift, when she returned. Her second dose of pain couldn't reach him because Byre could retreat along the empathic chain and hide amongst the safety of another's feelings. She wracked him hard until his bones shattered and flesh tore, but it was as satisfactory as dissecting dead meat.

Finally, she threw him down and observed from the corner of the cell as his body healed. Byre came back to himself slowly, but did not give a sign, instead watching her out of half-lidded eyes. She was not giving up, merely waiting for his spirit to return. It was a cruel tactic that he couldn't avoid.

Flyyit strolled to the table where the instruments of her trade were laid out. Carefully she cleaned the blood off those she had already used today and considered which other ones might be of use. She had a long curved knife in her hand, just by chance, as the door to the cell was kicked open. For a long strange moment, the Vaerli standing in the doorway and Byre's torturer stared at each other. Then Flyyit moved. Flinging the knife at the intruder's head, she turned back to the tray for another weapon. The throw was mistimed and inaccurate, and the Vaerli didn't really need to dodge it at all. By the time the torturer had turned around, it was someone else's steel that was in action.

With a surprised half-sound Flyyit grabbed at her throat, but the blood pouring from it wouldn't be stopped. She died quickly on the floor in front of her prisoner. Byre shook his head, certain that he was hallucinating.

The Vaerli kicked the twitching body of the torturer. "If I only had more time to show you the true meaning of pain," he said softly, but with venom.

Then Byre knew he must be dead, for he recognized the voice. It was one he had never thought to hear again, and even though he didn't believe the delusion it was still sweet. "Father," he whispered, a tear leaking out from the corner of his eye.

It was Retira's hand that brushed his hair. "Lie quiet."

He could feel this imagining uncouple his restraints, so he lay back and enjoyed the happiness. It was only when his father hauled him upright that the room spun. His bare feet slipped in Flyyit's blood, and he realized that he was not dead. Nor were the fires of the Harrowing touching either of them.

The true horror was that he felt nothing, no touch of empathy, no singing of recognition in his brain. It was his father, with the voice that had read him stories in the night, but the gold hair wasn't as he remembered; there were strands of gray in it.

Dreadful certainty clutched at his throat. "You went to the Hill of Sorrow."

His lips pressed together. "Not now, Byre." Retira propped him up by the door and dared a glance around the corner. "The guards change at midday." He dragged Flyyit's body farther into the cell, out of direct line of sight. "Hopefully they will not notice her immediately, and they might think the blood is yours. How are you?"

Byre could feel his body healing. It burned and itched, but it was slower than before; days of torture had robbed it of much of its reserves. Despite all the questions that crowded into his mind, Byre had little desire to stay in this prison and test the skills of Flyyit's successor.

"Not the best, but I'll manage," he replied. On closer examination, he noticed lines on his father's face.

Retira must have felt his regard. He touched his son's cheek for an instant. "You've grown, I can see that, but long discussions must wait until we are out of this place. I didn't have much time for a plan."

Byre could only remember his father as kind and gentle. The first few moments of their reunion told him a great deal about what Retira had been through and how he had changed, but he was still his father and this was a reunion he'd never expected.

"How about we just get out of here by the quickest route?"

"Sounds grand to me." His father pressed a pistol into Byre's hand. It was obviously not his, for Vaerli were forbidden them, so it meant he had not gone entirely unnoticed entering the garrison. Into the other, now healed, he handed over the stout stick that the Sofai had given Byre. His son could only guess he had retrieved it from the guards.

Staggering and leaning heavily on the stick, Byre managed to follow his father out into the corridor. They paused there for a moment and Byre's eyes locked with a bedraggled prisoner in the opposite cell. The old man held out his hands in mute supplication. Perhaps he had learnt the futility of cries. The crooked and broken hands were minus three fingers.

Byre moved toward the ring of keys on the table, but his father stayed his course. "Quick and quiet is the only way we are going to get out alive."

"I can't leave them in here."

They shared a long look and though Byre felt nothing from his father, he could read his annoyance. Perhaps in his long life he too had seen the inside of the Caisah's torture chambers. "We can only let them out," he relented. "They will have to look to themselves to get out of here."

Hard as that was, Byre understood; they stood not a chance of escape with so many. In a distant time he would have argued, but life had knocked most of the heroics out of him.

As silently as he could, Byre unlocked the cells. When that was done, fifteen men stood in the corridor assessing their situation. Three had run off mad with delight before Byre could stop them, so it might be that his compassion would yet get them killed.

Faced with their reality, his resolve melted. "Perhaps we can help these ones . . . if we stick together . . ."

He was interrupted by one of the prisoners, a lanky and grizzled man who had managed to hold onto the shreds of fine clothes. "Sorry to say, friend," he said, his voice quiet yet firm, "but we'd rather go on by ourselves."

Byre looked around, but none of the erstwhile prisoners would meet his gaze.

"We're grateful," another added, holding his hand to the spot where his eye had once been, "but you being Vaerli and all . . . well . . . we'll have more of a chance going in the opposite direction."

Obviously, embarrassment hadn't been totally culled from them in the cells. With murmurs of thanks, they scampered away.

Retira watched them with a wry smile on his lips. "They're right, you know; Vaerli escaping will be far more important to the Rutilian Guard than the local miscreants."

Coming into the fort, Byre hadn't had the chance to scan his surroundings, so he fell into step behind his father. Retira at least knew a little of the layout of the garrison.

"I hid in the back of a hay wagon," he whispered to Byre. "Not original, but it worked."

"Probably because not many people try to break into one of these places." He shot Retira a sharp glance. "Later on, I expect the full story of how you even knew I was here."

His father pushed him back against the wall only just in time to avoid three guards racing past. The sounds of battle floated through the corridors—the freed prisoners taking whatever revenge they could muster.

"Desperate men like that," Retira said with a grin, "could cause quite a commotion."

Uncomfortable with such grim humor from his father, Byre said nothing. They turned in the opposite direction of the fighting, hoping to find some sort of unguarded exit.

It was hard to keep up with his father. Byre's vision dimmed and twisted as his body, tormented for so long, struggled to repair the damage. Above all, Byre wanted to rest; his legs were leaden, and he barely hung onto the pistol in his hand.

However many soldiers were dealing with the tumult at the front, there were obviously still enough to man the rest of the garrison, for there was a shout behind them. They ran: Byre gasping for breath, Retira urging him on. Climbing a corkscrew set of stairs, Byre nearly collapsed. Only a supreme effort of will and his father's iron grip on his elbow saved him.

They had made a fatal error.

His father swore, making Byre blink in surprise. "What a fool I am, haring about like a numbskull boy." Retira looked around the narrow room that seemed to serve as the garderobe of the Citadel. "I must have taken a wrong turn. I'm sorry."

Byre touched his shoulder. "Never mind, Father. At least we can attend to nature before we die."

They both laughed at that; Byre huffing and wheezing, his father somewhat grimly. Retira wiped the tears from his eye and dragged the one item of furniture, a heavy bench, in front of the door. "At least we'll have some privacy."

Byre peered down the stonework pipe that led to the long drop. "Perhaps we could fit down there . . ."

Banging began behind the door, accompanied by angry shouting, and Retira stroked his gingery moustache. "I'd prefer not to end my days as a plug in the Caisah's drainpipe."

That conjured up some amusing images, but Byre couldn't see the point in pride when their lives were at issue. Wrenching off one of the primitive seats, he gagged at the smell but could see sky beyond. "Maybe there is a ledge," he ventured.

His father peered down the bolt-hole with a sigh. The noise beyond the door was louder now and the timbers wouldn't hold forever. "Shards of Chaos," he swore again, but stripped off his baldric. "If this ends up in a midden pit I'll have your apology." And with that he squeezed down the shaft.

Byre followed after. The stench was beyond belief, while the sludge going up his nose was no better. Yet as a Vaerli he'd had to hide in some awful places, and at least this was a short journey.

He had been right, there was a ledge. Yet as his father caught his arm and pulled him onto it Byre could see it wasn't much better than the garderobe. It was only a piece of crumbling stone and below was a long fall into a chasm. They hugged the wall and inched along, hoping to find a way down. The ledge ended long before it got anywhere near a safe landing spot. Small stones began to crumble under their feet.

Father and son exchanged a glance. The crevice was deep with no vegetation to halt their fall, and the tiny stream that could be seen meandering below was not going to help, either.

"We can't cling here forever, lad." Retira had lost his laughter. "We can at least go back and take a few of the soldiers with us."

"You did plan on this being a rescue rather than assisted suicide, didn't you?"

"I admit, this wasn't quite how I imagined it ending."

Byre closed his eyes. The world was still swimming around him as his body tried to heal itself—it looked like it would not get the chance. Byre tried to find the positives in this situation; the wind was nice and the stone cool on his repairing skin. He listened. He could hear the stream below trickling through the valley and the slow beat in his head—it must have been his heart. Except it was far too slow . . . and far too deep.

As he fell into the moment, his pulse was suddenly not entirely his own; it was the earth itself moving to the demands of the Chaos beneath.

Byre opened his eyelids, which felt as though they were made of lead. "The human malkin is weak here. If we had the First Gift, perhaps Chaos would listen."

His father's expression was one of cautious hope. "I am cut off, Byre. Even if the Harrowing were removed, I could not . . ."

" . . . but you used the First," Byre whispered, so not as to lose the sound of the earth in his head. "I never did. If you could just tell me about it. I know this sounds foolish, but something happened back there in the cells, I think . . . I feel . . ." He stopped, unable to find the words.

Retira's face smoothed as if three hundred years had rolled back. Grasping Byre's hand, he spoke. "Turn yourself inward. Shut away thoughts of the body or mind. Listen with that part of you that none can touch. Hear the land and see the gateway."

Byre didn't understand, but he tried all the same. Closing his eyes once more, he let the complaints of flesh and worries of thought be gone. Instead, he focused on the feeling of stone, earth, and wind. With his father's words leading him, it was remarkably easy to tune himself to them, like they were a familiar song with a rhythm that he had always known.

Behind that rhythm, a gate of light opened in Byre's mind's eye. Beyond was something so marvelous that he didn't care if he never found his body again. He caught a glimpse of the heart of the earth, and it welcomed him. He reached out . . .

The gate snapped shut, closing itself against him, and Byre dropped into his body with a shout.

His father was holding him upright and calling his name somewhat desperately.

"I saw it," Byre gasped. "It was so close, but it wouldn't let me in."

Retira's eyes were full of tears. "You came closer than any of us has in three hundred years. Don't blame yourself. We should go back and face them."

That was when the world shifted. Whatever Byre had seen through the gate, his pleas had been heard.

The valley beneath them moved. The earth shrugged, breaking loose from its slow change and rupturing through the constraints placed on it by the malkin of humans. The earth burst with a rumble and now the stream was transformed to something else. The water roared, smashing down against rocks that had only moments before been caressed by a rivulet.

"You have the way of it, son," Retira said with awe in his voice. "The power of water like the nykur himself."

"Do you think it's safe?" Byre asked, still not sure exactly what he had done.

His father took one look down at the ledge crumbling beneath their feet. "Safer than staying here." His grin was broad and unusual to see on a Vaerli face, even as he leapt from their perch.

Byre had the oddest impression of Retira outlined against the water like a diving bird. It was a joyous image that made him whoop and leap after, well beyond reason. It was, quite simply, magnificent.

CHAPTER ELEVEN
WITCH SIGHT

The story of the Phaerkorn and the Vaerli was one of mutual disinterest. Vaerli blood had nothing that the Blood Witches needed, and since they could take none of that race into their own, they ignored them.

Seldom had their paths crossed, and yet Pelanor had mixed feelings about pitting herself against Talyn the Dark. How would a battle between them go? A tiny fear was gnawing at her. However, another part was angry at being forced to fight her; there was a third even deeper part that wondered with some excitement what would happen.

When Pelanor was released from the tender mercies of the priestesses, she immediately evaporated and slid into the clouds.

The Vaerli had once been more powerful than the Phaerkorn—linked as they were with the powers of this world. Things were different with the Seven Gifts gone, and here she was, hunting one of them. It was an interesting intellectual question: would she be able to crush Talyn the Dark, and what would happen if she did? Would there be war between their people?

She couldn't afford to vacillate. The link between the Hunter and the prey was not an easy thing to find. Pelanor drifted for many long hours, letting her shape be molded by wind and sun and allowing her Blood gifts to search for the mark that could belong to only one creature—the prey of Talyn the Dark. On what felt like the second day, Pelanor found the deathmark buried in the blood of some hapless Manesto.

She condensed herself in a valley not far from where he was sleeping. Looking down at the backs of her shaking hands, she took account of her condition. The blood of Alvick still flowed through her and there was much strength in that, but it could not be relied upon forever. Sooner or later she would have to drink just to survive.

Pelanor fingered the throat of her thin shift and then with a sudden gesture ripped it toward the shoulder. For effect she added scrapes with her own nails, letting a little of Alvick's blood flow. A hastily made plan was all she had.

It was easy, really. The man was sitting tending the last embers of his fire and appeared lost in thought, so Pelanor stood back, watching him from beyond the range of normal human eyesight.

His blood was indeed strong, so powerful he might even make a good *gewalt*. Seldom were there many to be found among the sheep of the rest of his kind, but if Pelanor needed to drink he would be more than adequate.

Summoning up her courage, Pelanor staggered into the firelight and collapsed near his feet. He would only see a tiny, young black woman and never the Witch beyond.

A very long moment passed as she lay there, eyes closed, waiting for the man to move. Perhaps she had misjudged what would happen. If he did something rash, she might well have to kill him.

Then gentle hands lifted her. Letting her limbs hang weightless, she felt herself carried nearer to the fire.

"Where did she come from?" Was he talking to himself? No, she heard a shifting as though someone else was there. It was odd; she had been certain he was alone.

A course blanket of some kind was wrapped around her, and then a faintly warm liquid dribbled into the corner of her mouth.

Her sense of taste was sour to anything but blood, so Pelanor coughed and spluttered. Thus she managed not to allow any of the water down her throat. Finally, she dared to open her eyes, with much fluttering and a little gentle sigh.

Understandably, he was staring at her. What stood behind wasn't. She would never have guessed it, but it was the craggy outline of a Kindred. If she'd had a heartbeat, it would have raced.

The Kindred and the Phaerkorn were not enemies—but neither were they friends. Their eyes could see things that humans could not, and this one could spoil her plans.

"Is she going to be all right?" The man asked it, but there was no reply. Pelanor coughed and fluttered her eyelashes some more, recalling with some relief that only Vaerli could commune with the Kindred.

She sat half upright and pointed at it with a terrified gasp.

"Don't mind him." The man shifted to prop her up. "He's perfectly harmless."

He puttered around with the small pot hanging over the fire. When he offered her stew she managed to slip a little into her mouth, despite the foul taste.

"I'm Finnbarr." He introduced himself easily and without guile, as if he expected everyone he met to be a friend. "Some call me the Fox or Finn. I'm a talespinner from . . . well from everywhere, really." He was waiting for her story.

She so told him one, complete with the odd tear and hiccupping sniffle. Keeping it as brief and sketchy as possible, she said that she was the last remainder of a small village on the edge of the Chaoslands, which the Caisah's men had attacked for housing rebels only days ago.

She had chosen well, it seemed, for Finn's face darkened and he swallowed the story without much question. All the time, though, the Kindred's swirling eyes watched. Undoubtedly, it sensed magic around her and the trailing length of Blood that connected her with Alvick—but since it could not communicate, she had a chance.

The man who called himself Finn could see none of those things, and if he had been forced to guess which race she was of, Phaerkorn would never have been one of them. It was the cleverness of the Blood Council. They let only the palest of their number admit to being Phaerkorn and always made sure they went about heavily cloaked. In the world beyond the White Void they had learned many lessons, and the first had been the distrust of others who did not understand the twelve-mouthed goddess. Better to let the humans think they could tell a Phaerkorn from a "normal" human—better still to never let them find out they drew new members from all races. It meant Finn would never suspect a slight dark girl as a Blood Witch.

"Where are you going?" she asked as innocently as possible.

"South to the Choana's realm. Do you know anything of them?"

She shook her head. It was true she'd heard the name but knew little of their ways. The Choana were a closed society, so the Witches didn't find many converts there.

"The story goes that they roamed the White Void longer than any other race. Their greatest wish was a world of their own, their bards sang epics about it, and they dreamed for centuries. Yet when they came here, they were few in number and much of their magic was left behind. So they went south and tried to re-create the world that they had come from."

"Can . . . can I go with you?"

"What about your people?"

She shook her head and looked at her feet. "I have no one left. I would rather go with you and see things, at least."

Finn looked at her sadly, perhaps feeling his own hurts, but he finally replied, "It is not an easy journey . . ." He paused and tilted his head. "Still, easier than roaming the Chaoslands alone, I suppose . . ."

Pelanor gave him a broad smile with as much emotion in it as she could muster. "Thank you. You won't regret it, I can make myself useful." Her hand crept to his.

Finn smiled but drew away. "Don't thank me until we get there. Get some rest." He huddled down a little distance away.

Pelanor lay back on the dirt, which would have been uncomfortable if she was not what she was, and thought. She hoped Talyn the Dark would appear soon; she didn't want to get to like this man and then have to drink from him. Since leaving the mouth of the goddess she'd found it hard to recall what it was like to even be a human. Pelanor knew she couldn't keep up the pretense for long.

She recalled suddenly, people closed their eyes when asleep. It would be a very long night lying here listening to the sounds. The last thing she saw before "sleeping" was the Kindred's hunched form. Even behind closed eyelids she could feel its regard for the rest of the night.

It was not Talyn's habit to tell the Caisah when she was going, and she certainly was not going to tell him about seeing her father. Indeed, the wound was too fresh for any contemplation. She didn't want to be enemies with her kind, but neither would she listen to them. They had, after all, spent the last three centuries doing nothing to end the Harrowing.

So she set herself more firmly toward her goal, and perhaps with a bit more speed. Returning to her room, she packed a few spare items including a thick fur cloak, just in case Finn had headed into the White North. Food, she took little of: a few dried aromatic spices to add interest to whatever she foraged, some dried fruits, and a bundle of jerked beef. Vaerli knew how to live off the land better than anyone.

Syris' head came up with a resounding snort when she entered the stable. She could hear Faustin's voice in the training yard but didn't go out to see him; Talyn preferred to get away without seeing accusation in the stablemaster's eye.

Taking down her saddle, she examined it carefully. It had been cleaned recently and the cinch strap replaced. Saddling Syris, she led him out into the main courtyard. Only a few early risers were about, the workers of the castle rather than the crowd of fawners that accompanied the Caisah. She wanted to be well away before they surfaced.

Despite all that had happened in the last few days, Talyn's heart lifted. It would be good to be gone from here with nothing but Syris and the Road.

Her prey might have set off cross-country to try to lose her. It was a mistake they often made.

Talyn mounted and rode from V'nae Rae. All through the cobbled streets it was the same; people ducked into the alleyways or cowered against the walls. In the beginning of her term as Hunter she had been hurt by it. The Vaerli were once revered and their company sought. Yet she had made herself, and by association her people, a figure of fear and darkness. Was this what had made them finally decide to act against her? Many great things there were about her people, but if they had one fault it was arrogance. They enjoyed being admired and envied, but Talyn had turned their grace and beauty into something ugly and feared.

These thoughts were not constructive, so she banished them as best she could. Instead there was the hunt to consider.

"Talyn!" The brash yell came near the final gate—just when the Hunter thought she had slipped out of the city, Azrul came galloping up on the biggest bay stallion Talyn had ever seen. She was grinning wildly beneath her winged helmet, and she stank to high heaven. The Vaerli senses were keen, but even humans would have wrinkled their noses at such a heady combination of sweat from Azrul and her mount.

The stallion was snorting and chafing at the bit from Syris' nearness, but Azrul held him leisurely in check with one hand.

"You going out, then?" she asked, shoving back her helmet and pushing her dark red hair back off her face to mop her brow.

"So it would seem," Talyn replied with something close to irony.

"That's a shame. I've just taken my new stallion out for a run." She slapped the stallion's neck amiably. "It would have been interesting to set him against your Syris."

It was rather amusing how the commander always insisted on thinking of the nykur as a normal horse. "That would have been . . . fascinating."

Azrul let out a snort of laughter. "Well maybe not, but he would have given him a moment's worry. I've decided to call him Kaz."

Talyn shook her head and smiled. Kaz was the Caisah's irritating and obstructive Grand Advisor. He and Azrul had a difficult relationship.

"You have a good smile, Hunter—when you care to use it."

Talyn smothered it quickly. "I find seldom cause to, Commander. None of my race does."

A normal person would have dropped the subject, or at least looked ashamed, but not Azrul. "You Vaerli go around with the look of death on you when you are clearly alive. Be happy in that. Find something to smile about!"

Such a comment would have earned Talyn's rage from most people, but she could find no anger for the other woman. It was kindly meant, and Azrul was young and untried. Talyn merely nodded. "The Powers willing, perhaps one day soon we will."

Azrul raised her right hand in the Lady's Kiss. "May the scions see it done."

The two women paused for a moment, comfortable in each other's presence, and for a while having no urge to move on. Talyn was thinking how if she were young again, she would have called Azrul her friend. The pity was that at the moment she could not afford family, or even friends.

"Well, we're moving on tomorrow, anyway," the commander said. "Word just came that there have been some . . . incidents in the east. They're whispering the name of Baraca again, and the Swoop is being sent to calm things down."

It was more likely to knock some heads together, and she guessed it must have been the rebellion her father alluded to. The eastern coast was the most volatile area of Conhaero; it might be a place of small lazy islands and fishing fleets, but somehow they still managed to cause the Caisah trouble. Every time the elusive rebel leader's name was mentioned it seemed the east woke to fruitless struggle. The Hunter had never met this Baraca, and according to the Caisah he was more myth than reality. So it was hard to imagine this rebellion giving the Swoop much difficulty, but nevertheless Talyn warned Azrul to be careful.

"You too, Hunter," she said before ramming her helmet once more on her head. "There is change in the air, though I can't tell if it is for good or ill. Let's hope we both have a chance to meet again for that race."

Then she was off in a cloud of yellow dust, disappearing into Perilous with a loud whoop. Syris pawed the ground and tossed his head.

Talyn could tell he was eager to be off, too. Still, she looked once over her shoulder to where Azrul had gone before urging Syris away.

The normal constraints of horse travel did not apply to her mount, a nykur being a creature of flame and water rather than flesh. The only thing stopping the pair of them crossing the width of Conhaero without pause was her Vaerli nature. Though stronger than latecomers to the land, the Vaerli still needed to heed the call of muscle and sinew.

They rode at a gallop from V'nae Rae. Talyn didn't look back once on her people's home, for already the call of her prey had a strong hold. The land around the castle was thick with signs of habitation: golden fields of wheat and corn, rolling hills peppered with the white backs of sheep, and everywhere thatch-roofed houses huddled together around the Road. All was held tightly together with the malkin of many people. Talyn could remember a time when the lands hereabouts could have been anything from thick woods to icy hilltops. Sometimes it was not a blessing to have lived so long.

Even the Caisah could not command all the land all the time, and soon only the Road remained static. The earth reverted once more to Chaos. Here Talyn let Syris have his head and enter the realm, where he was far more comfortable. The earth blurred and fell away until they rode through only a pattern of changing greens and browns with no discernible texture. Now there was no landscape to impede them. The nykur's chaotic nature guided them eastward.

The first night, she pulled him reluctantly to a stop and made camp on the back of a smooth green hillock. Talyn relied utterly on his senses to alert her to any Chaos creature in the area.

The sun was setting in a shimmer of ruby that rippled on the small lake at the foot of the hill. Lying back, she gnawed on a lump of dried fruit and tried to hone her senses to Finn. However, he was still hundreds of miles away, and Talyn could only feel his presence to the east.

The call of eagles broke her thoughts, and she levered herself up to watch as the Swoop appeared over the horizon. The great dark mass of birds broke from the clouds and spun and circled through the hills before heading east. At their head was the powerful form of the Whitefoam eagle, whose great talons and curved beak flashed through Talyn's vision before streaking past overhead. In its wake trailed a thousand predatory birds singing a song of war and magic that was thrilling to hear.

Talyn sighed. It would have been good to have the power of the Swoop, but even though she was ranked among them she had never taken the vow to the Lady of Wings. That face of the Scion of Right was an attractive one, but her Vaerli nature wouldn't let go of her that easily.

No, she left the majesty of the Swoop to Azrul, and if she felt any envy at her ability to take the form of the White Eagle it was always quickly smothered. The Vaerli Gifts, when she wrestled them back, would be enough for her.

Rolling herself in her blanket, Talyn slept a little under the stars in the cool Chaos night. The weak rays of the early morning woke her, and she saddled up quickly before riding on. The urge to reach her prey drove her hard. For three days she clung to Syris' back like a burr.

In the late afternoon of the third day Talyn was lost in the momentum of travel, feeling all pass around her like water, when old senses lit on a familiar feeling. It felt as though her breath was being tugged from her, in a way that was both exciting and terrifying.

Immediately Talyn called Syris to a stop. Mount and rider appeared abruptly in the middle of a dense forest of singular trees. Few things survived in the Chaos, but one plant had learned to tap into the power of the land and adapt with the flow. The horwey trees could be broad like conifers, spiky like cacti, or flowered like water lilies. They were so much a part of the land that some thought they were in fact Kindred.

Here they resembled a thick forest that the Caisah had planted to the north for his hunting amusement, with trees brought through the White Void, except this place was far more dangerous. Untamed creatures of Chaos made their home here, but it was not these that Talyn had sensed.

The tickle played deliciously on her skin. She slid from Syris' back and wandered farther into the trees out of sheer curiosity.

In the small valley beyond, the cloud was rippling like a curtain through the branches and below Talyn could see a faint sparkle, a dome of light that she knew the significance of.

Since the time of the Conflagration, few Vaerli had seen the Steps of Sacrifice, the *Arohai tuan*. They were carried on the streams of Chaos and could appear anywhere within Conhaero, and though they were the site of great loss to her people they were also held in great reverence.

So soon after seeing her father, could their appearance be a sign? Talyn crunched her way through the leaf-littered floor toward the light, feeling her heart race in her chest.

Shining white-blue with their own brightness, the stairs could have been hacked from ice. Three carved steps lead to a broad, clean dais. They looked harmless, yet here was where the Twelve Families had sacrificed their children and opened the way into the White Void.

Each step was carved with deep letters, the meaning of which had been deliberately erased by the Vaerli who came after. A whole branch of their letter magic had been prohibited so as to prevent any committing the same desperate act—an act that had so many consequences.

Hesitantly, Talyn climbed the steps, each moment expecting to be struck down, but there was nothing save icy stillness and a vague ringing in her senses. Reaching the top of the dais, she looked down. She tried to imagine that moment when the other races had first appeared here, breaking the Vaerli dominance on Conhaero.

"Beautiful, isn't it?" A whisper raised the hairs on the back of her neck.

Talyn spun about, horrified that her before-sense had given no warning.

The woman standing on the other side of the dais could have been her exact mirror image, except for the intricate pattern of tattooed swirls on her face and arms. The words they contained twined on themselves before disappearing under her simple shift.

Talyn swallowed hard on the implication; only one sort of Vaerli wore the *pae atuae* on their skin, and the last of the Seers had died at the Harrowing.

"I did indeed die," the other woman replied to Talyn's thoughts, "but time for us—as you well know, Talyn the Dark—is a flexible thing."

"Putorae?"

"We are much alike, you and I," the Seer said, walking around her, taking her measure. "But then, we are related: third cousins by your mother's line."

"How are you—"

The faintest suggestion of a finger was laid on her lips. "There are many ways open to Seers unknown to others."

"I admit my ignorance," Talyn replied tartly. "You were the last Seer. Your successor was not inducted; none remain to instruct any of us."

Her eyes, dark with stars, were sadly unlike any living Vaerli's. "I know this. Do not think to lecture me, Talyn, not when I have been waiting so long for you here at the site of the beginning of the end."

Talyn looked away while her mind ran with bitter thoughts. "Yes, the place where the Caisah came from."

Putorae shook her head sadly. "Dear lost one, this was not his doing, it was ours. It was here we sealed our own fate. Fearful, we took the innocent lives of our children, and from that moment our future was written."

Now, looking down, Talyn could see a dark pattern forming against the light of the stone: unrecognizable words made clear with ancient blood. There was a lot of it.

"You see it now. Blood does not fade. It was here your grandfather slit the throat of his eldest beloved son, sobbing as he did it, and the other families followed his lead."

Talyn clapped her hands over her ears, aware that the stone was now ringing as if struck, but the sound was in her head, not her ears. Putorae's voice remained.

"We sealed our fate, and the Caisah was merely the instrument—but we can find our way back."

The Steps were suddenly silent and Talyn took her hands away from her ears cautiously. "I'm finding the path for our people," she told the long-dead Seer, and there was pride in her voice.

"You have good intentions, lost child, but you cannot hope to find the road with your eyes shut and your heart closed."

Not another lecture, Talyn almost sighed. It seemed, after centuries of doing things on her own, everyone was now determined to try to drag the reins of her future about.

"You cannot see the world as a Seer does—without the Gifts, none of our race can. Conhaero is not what you think it is. We are not what you think we are."

The knowledge of their origin was lost in the time of the Conflagration. It was something the Vaerli yearned to find out, but it had always been denied. "Tell me then, help me see!" Talyn heard the pleading note in her voice and no longer cared if she sounded weak.

Putorae dropped her eyes. "The time is not now. The Gifts must be recovered before such things may be discovered."

It was always like this, it seemed. Knowledge was held out to Talyn, and then snatched away. Her patience for it was wearing thin.

"You must find Finnbarr called the Fox," Putorae whispered softly. "Bring him to the Salt Plains—only a little magic remains here. I have another self waiting at the Bastion for you. This one has run its course."

She was indeed growing thinner, her body dissolving in gray light; only the lines of her *pae atuae* still showed brightly in the dimness. Talyn held out her hand, willing her to hold form for a few moments longer. "But the Caisah—I am linked to him. I must take the Fox to V'nae Rae for him!"

Putorae's eyes were full of sorrow and stars, but her body was disappearing on the winds of time. "That is up to you to decide. How far the darkness has spread in you I cannot say." And then she unraveled before Talyn's eyes like a broken string of smoke.

The living Vaerli stood there for a moment. A human would have been afforded the luxury of rage or frustration; he might have screamed or howled. Vaerli emotions were ethereal things without the Gifts, and Talyn found it hard to name or express that which she could barely understand.

Should she go to the Salt Plains as Putorae demanded? What sway could a long-dead Seer have over her when her own living father had failed to move her?

She still could not afford to think of such things; first she would find Finn, and then she would decide if she should obey the nefarious Caisah or insubstantial Seer.

CHAPTER TWELVE

RIVER AND SEA

Whatever place the river had been conjured from, it was not a peaceful one. Still, through some happy chance, Byreniko and his father were not smashed to death on the rocks or held under the water by angry currents. Instead, they were washed up on a gentle bank many miles from the torture chambers.

Retira pushed back his graying hair, spat out a mouthful of water, and began laughing. It was infectious, and Byre found himself joining in as they floundered their way to the bank. Once ashore, they found themselves in the soft-dense foliage of a fern forest. Byre had the strange feeling it was welcoming them; offering them a hiding place from those who must surely follow.

For all that, they could not get far without food and rest, especially since the hospitality of the Caisah had left Byre barely capable of movement.

Retira chose a spot in a small clearing, and they made what little meager camp they could. His father was as well provisioned as one could be for two people and had soon made fire in the half-light of a depression amongst the ferns.

Having waited so long to talk on things, it was strange how silence descended on them so completely. Byre found himself watching his father across the flames and trying to decide which of the clamoring questions he should let out first.

In the end, it was Retira who spoke. "I had word that your foster parents were killed, but that you had escaped from the farm. I'm so sorry."

For such an old wound, it still hurt. "They were good people and they loved me as best they could. Talyn did well to find them for me."

"Do not speak of her." There was real anger in his voice. "Or give her no name rather than call her that."

Immortality, once a blessing, could make Vaerli as hard as diamond, and though Byre would have liked to push the point, things were still too fragile for that.

His father stroked his moustache and cleared his throat. "You know, I have a unique perspective since going to the Hill; all my memories have been freed and it feels like a weight has been lifted off me."

Byre didn't know what to say. He had many memories of his own—and many he would have liked to get rid of. When the Harrowing had happened he'd only been a child and his training in the memory Gift minimal, so daily the fear gnawed on him that one day they would break loose, and he would run mad. He tried to imagine what his father had held on to. "It is hard . . . sometimes," he ventured, "to know what is precious and should be kept."

His father nodded. "I retained all of mine. They say that way lies madness, and they are right; to have so much experience is a hard thing. I second-guessed myself a thousand times before coming to find you."

Byre swallowed his misgivings and instead voiced his other question. "How did you know where I was?"

"I have a friend, a friend who dreams. I think you know her . . ." The liquid eyes and the sweet scent of the Sofai filled his mind, and Byre knew he wouldn't discard those memories.

"I do indeed know her. In fact, she helped me, but she remained silent on everything else. What do my dreams mean, for instance?"

Retira poked the fire with a stick with his brow furrowed. He looked so old in the reflected light. The Sixth Gift had been removed with all the others at the Hill, so the outrage of gray in his hair would be followed in due time by wrinkles and decrepitude. The depth of that sacrifice was greater than Byre could comprehend all at once.

His father did not answer his question; instead he stared into the flames, and asked one of his own. "Do you love your people, Byre?"

"I hardly know them." The words tumbled out before he could stop them.

Retira nodded somberly, eyes averted. "That is understandable. Sad, but not unexpected."

Byre shifted uncomfortably. This grim man was not one he recalled from childhood.

"Your sister has chosen the wrong path," Retira said. "I have tried to guide her, but she would not listen, so now you are the only hope for our people. Your journey to the Great Cleft is but the beginning. I came to free you and also to help."

"Did the Sofai reveal something to you?"

"Many things; some I did not want to hear. Yet, going to the Hill has made me realize that living is not everything. Having the certainty of death before you . . . Well, it solidifies many things. The other races do not know what a gift they have in mortality. I have come to wonder if that could be why the Caisah is as mad as he is. Without the certainty of an end, what is a journey?"

His father was talking in riddles, and Byre felt as if he were dancing around the edges of something larger. It was not the Vaerli way to ask questions when the Gifts would have revealed much—and so none of them had learnt the skill.

Retira handed him a slice of jerked beef. "Do not look so worried, my boy. We are together, which is not as good as it might have been, but still better than loneliness in this world. Let me hear your life story. I want to know of those folk who raised you, and all that happened after, good and ill."

Byre stared down at the ground and then began. He spared no detail. To lie, or to try to water down the pain that had been inflicted on him, would have been an insult to his father. He knew they were trying to reach each other with their words, groping like blind and weary wounded toward each other as best they could. So he told him about Syeth and his gentle wife Muri, and if he noticed Retira wince at the joy in his voice for that happy childhood, well, that was part of the honesty, also. He told of the day they'd hidden him in the woods when the mob came to claim the demon Vaerli child, and how later he crawled out in shame to find their tortured bodies hanging from the lintel. Syeth had been sure the mob would leave them be; he'd been strangely innocent and believed in the genuine kindness of people.

From there Byre had little more to share. Only tales of running and hiding, apart from the day he had so nearly rushed into his sister's arms. It was the bottom of despair for both of them. By some mad luck, the person they found that day, out of all Conhaero, was their sibling.

Finally his tale whittled down to this day and place, and the Sofai who had set him on the path. Having found the end of his own tale, Byre asked, "And your life, Father? What has it been since the Harrowing?"

Retira shielded his eyes as if ashamed of his emotion. "Nothing. Life has been nothing for three hundred years . . . just a slow sleep walk, without even oblivion to welcome me. No purpose. No joy."

He stopped for a moment and let the tears flow. Byre still didn't know him, but he didn't need a Gift to feel his terrible pain. Reaching over, he clasped his father to him. They held each other and cried, which might not have been as powerful as the lost Vaerli empathy but was still, as Retira said, better than not having each other.

When they had shed all the tears they had, there was calm.

Retira patted Byre's back and said matter-of-factly, "When your mother died and you were gone, I don't know why I did not look for the flames of death. That was what made it easy to go to the Hill when it was needed. If giving up the Gifts is the price I pay to see my children again, I am happy with the deal."

It was impossible to argue. Byre could see by the look in his father's eye he meant it very deeply—he could only dream of being a parent one day and knowing that feeling for himself. For the first time, he had the faintest of hope that it might happen. The Kindred had offered it.

For a moment, Byre was overcome with fear and sadness, for it was quite possible that his father would not live to see the end of the Harrowing, if it should ever happen. He cleared his throat. "So, how far to the Great Cleft?"

Retira sighed, and looked up into the darkening sky. "Closer than you think. There are those who have their own ways and magic that few know of. Luckily, you are now traveling with such a one."

He shook out a small blanket from his meager pack and handed it to Byre. "For now, you should rest. Your body will heal a lot faster with sleep, and we can afford to wait until then."

"What about you?" The night was drawing in cold amongst the ferns, and his father seemed frail without the protection of the Gifts.

"I will watch," he said, stretching his feet out toward the fire. "I would like to see you sleep. Your mother, no matter how busy she was, always tucked you in and sang—do you remember that?"

Byre wrapped the blanket around himself and found a soft place in the earth to rest his head. He was surely not imagining the pulse of life he could hear under his ear. "I remember," he whispered, even as his eyes closed.

"My voice is not nearly as pretty as hers, but I remember the tune." Retira began to sing, soft and low so that his voice did not travel far among the forest of ferns.

Blessed are the people, sweet and happy we are.
For I am a child of land, it sweeps me into its heart
It carries me next to its skin, and all my troubles are gone.
I whisper my thoughts to the Kin, and they sweep them away
To be born and lost in the flame, where none sleep.

His father's husky voice lulled him to sleep as if he were magically transported back to childhood, and Byre was able to forget, for a moment, everything around them. He drifted to sleep with a smile on his face.

Oriconion had always been a hotbed of resistance. Equo knew the sorry history of this large port on the edge of the Great Lake very well; far from the reaches of Perilous, it had once been the home of people very different from its current inhabitants.

He glanced to his right where Varlesh was stroking his beard and looking down to the tumble of yellow buildings wreathed in ominous smoke. "That can't be a good sign." Away from outsiders Varlesh was not so jovial, his voice dropped to a quieter tone and his gestures became sparer. "They have begun. Damn it all, couldn't they wait for us?"

"Apparently not," Equo replied, "but we are here sooner than we expected to be, thanks to Finn."

"That boy is getting stranger every time we see him. Imagine—a Kindred! What next? Will he be riding a nykur like Talyn the Dark?" Not waiting for a reply, Varlesh stalked down the hill toward the town.

Equo glanced at Si. "Well . . . will he?"

An enigmatic smile crossed his companion's face. "Perhaps—perhaps more." And then he followed after Varlesh. Equo sighed. Sometimes it felt like he was the only one with any brains.

The Swoop would have been dispatched, for the Caisah always reacted the same way. That meant within a day or two there would be more bloodshed in Oriconion.

Still, he followed in the wake of the others, trying to concentrate on the beauty of the town seen from afar—before the ugliness of the reality could be seen. Descending from the hill there was nothing dangerous-looking about it; golden rooftops of the local clay gleamed with the rays of the early morning sun. The fishing boats pulled up on the white sand shores seemed peaceful enough, and in the middle distance could be seen the dark circles of the villages on stilts, which punctuated the blueness of the lake. This web of manmade islands, wetlands, and submerged paths made Oriconion an excellent base for rebellion. The Caisah had tried many times to destroy what the Portree built—but they were a stubborn people.

To the right, set in against the hills were the white-walled, golden-roofed tidy homes of the Manesto. To the left, exposed to the cruel southerly wind, were the huts of the dispossessed Portree, those whose carracks had been broken. These houses looked as if they had been thrown there, made of rubbish and flotsam from the lake.

It had been many years since Equo had lived in one of those homes, but he still recalled it vividly. The Portree were not wealthy or particularly blessed in anything except for their knowledge of the water, but they had taken him, Varlesh, and Si, into their homes when the three men had been hunted by the Caisah. The Portree had risked what little they had for the strangers and for that earned their loyalty.

Equo's musings on those times were cut short. Varlesh had stopped abruptly and was pointing toward the Manesto houses, his face flushed red. "That's new—what by the Wise Crone are they up to?"

Obviously the Manesto were feeling more threatened than ever, for a tall ironwork fence ran between their houses and the huts. The main gate was now on the Manesto side, the Portree's only opened to the lake. A cold shiver ran through Equo, but he grabbed Varlesh's hand and dragged it down. "Don't make a fuss, old man—we don't want to get ourselves killed today."

His companion's eyes bulged, but he nodded curtly. Together they made their way to the stout town gate. Usually there was one wary guard on duty, so it was a sign of definite trouble that half a dozen guards, well-armed and bright-eyed, met them. Equo had to make a hasty explanation that they were here for scholarly study on the Portree history.

The guards laughed at that. "You'll be gone soon, then. They have nothing much to study except how they like the feel of a boot on their neck."

Varlesh's hands clenched into fists.

"Maybe so," Equo replied smoothly, "but it is our mission to find all people's tales before they are lost."

The captain sniffed. "Well there has been some trouble lately, but the Praetor hasn't closed the quarter yet. It's your funeral."

"Let's hope not," Varlesh growled as they moved past the welcoming committee.

"I wonder how Nyree is faring," Equo whispered. "With her working for the Portree in that clinic of hers."

The three exchanged worried looks; it would make an excellent target for the Caisah to crush.

"We best find her fast," Varlesh said. "No time for even an ale."

When he said that, the other two men knew they were in serious trouble, but as they made their way to the heavily guarded gate, Equo knew what he was thinking. Once it had been *they* being persecuted and the Portree their saviors. The question was, could they now return the favor?

On the other side of the gate it was another world; a child with a bony chest was coughing near a beached boat, while a hollow-eyed dog skittered past. It had never been a wealthy place; still, the last time they had been here there had been no obvious hunger, and the streets had been bustling. Equo recalled with melancholy the spice-laden atmosphere and brightly dressed women calling out their catches for the day in the street.

Now the air was full of the scent of decay and despair.

Si's eyes were filling with tears; he always felt things more keenly. Equo could only imagine what he was sensing, and be glad he could not.

Varlesh fiddled idly with the tip of his pipe in his top pocket as if he could not bring himself to go any farther.

"We must find Nyree by nightfall," Equo reminded them.

The clinic was buried among a tangle of narrow streets crowded with leaning houses. They barely saw a single soul along the way. Only a gap-toothed old man huddled on a doorstep rocking himself and humming told them that anyone lived here at all.

It was always the same in times of rebellion; those uninvolved tried to keep out of the way and those involved tried to do the same. It made for very quiet streets most of the time.

The clinic was a low building spreading through what had once been a beautiful flowering garden dedicated to the Bountiful Queen. Even when Nyree had come with her belief in the Kindred, the scion had remained, somehow content with the herb beds and small patches of flowers. Nyree seemed able to coexist with scions, though perhaps that was because she served much the same interests.

The trio went up to the wide-open doorway, and Equo could not help but think how mad that entrance was in a time of conflict. A couple of simply dressed Portree sat on the top step near the door, catching the last rays of the late afternoon sun. Both were young women bearing bandaged limbs and faces mottled by bruises. There was always a hint of oppression about their race, because on both sides of the White Void they had been on the losing side of every war. Still, their beautiful burnished brown faces and liquid eyes remained full of grace. Something about them always suggested oppression was on their terms, as if they could wait it out. The faintest lines of silver tracery on the garments of the slightly older woman indicated she was a *serf army*, mother of the water, which meant she had her own boat, her own crew, and was about as high as a Portree could be expected to go in this world.

Yet, when the three men bowed asking to see the Healer, she smiled shyly and led them herself into the cooler recesses of the house.

All was much as it had been on their last visit, only the beds of injured and sick were more plentiful, but the place smelt airy and nothing of decay seemed in evidence. Nyree always ran her clinic with ruthless efficiency.

Their Portree guide brought them to the only closed door in the building, a smoothed stone that nonetheless glided easily open under her hand. She poked her head around the other side, checking in a quiet voice before opening it wider and ushering them in. A quartet of older Portree women were working over a variety of herbs laid out on a long table before them. Their guide exchanged quick angular-sounding words with them, then she bowed slightly. "My apologies, but the Healer is attending a sick child in the lakeside district. She may be there for some time."

"We must see her," Si whispered to Equo.

The woman's eyes traveled uneasily to him as if she found something disturbing, but she replied evenly, "Rile can take you there." In short order, a lean boy of about ten with the face of a mahogany cherub was summoned and given stern instructions by the *serf army* to take them directly to the Healer.

They left the relative beauty of the clinic and went deeper into the slum. The odd face was seen at the window, but there was the scent of gunpowder in the air and the three men could feel the danger increasing around them.

The huts here were little more than lean-tos and the streets were choked with filth and debris. Still their guide leapt from brick to brick in front of them, chattering away in his own language and apparently unaware of their discomfort.

He deposited them at a hut, much like any of the others; dropping to his knees, he began to draw pictures using a nearby mud puddle.

They entered cautiously to the rather refreshing smell of herbs and unguents, a sure sign that they did indeed have the right place.

Nyree had her back to the door, all her attention centered on a tiny child wrapped in bandages and blankets on a shaky bed in the corner.

In the nature of her kind, she knew they were there but didn't acknowledge them until she was done. Only then did Nyree turn and look at them through her ancient eyes.

She had the same golden-cast skin and small stature of Talyn the Dark, but her eyes were the most translucent, deepest blue. They were the kind of eyes to go mad in, and if they had been filled with stars, as they should have been, Equo could imagine they would have made him drop to his knees. Every time he saw Nyree a little bit more of his heart was lost to her, for she was what the Vaerli should be, not the twisted remains of the Caisah's pet.

Kissing the child lightly on the head, Nyree whispered, "Try to get some sleep, little one."

Her voice was soft and light with the faintest of lilts to it. It sounded exactly the same as the day that she used it to refuse his offer of marriage. Equo felt his insides go hollow just looking at her and thinking of that time. She'd been the one to tend the wounds he received in their flight from the Rutilian Guard. He'd fallen in love with her and all her kindnesses. Still, when he'd proposed she'd gently declined in that unflappable voice of hers. She reminded him that there would be no children from such a union, as Vaerli only bred with Vaerli. She would not deny either of them that chance. No arguments or protestations had swayed her, and her calm rejections hurt more than simply saying she didn't love him.

Varlesh, who knew well enough the whole story, stepped forward. "It's good to see you, lass. Sorry it couldn't be under better circumstances."

She shrugged her shoulders before greeting them effortlessly with a gentle kiss on the cheek, one for each of the trio. "Trouble comes when it will, and all too often here. You are looking thin, Equo. You mustn't let Varlesh get every meal, you know." It was her gentle way of reproof.

He struggled under her kindness; it would have been much easier if she was cruel. His love would have withered long ago if that were the case.

Si clasped her hand, looking deep into those eyes, but whatever passed between them was not sexual, merely the recognition of one deep soul to another.

Nyree broke the look with a light laugh. "You cannot surely have stopped here for merely a social visit." Was it Equo's imagination, or did her gaze linger on him?

Varlesh laughed. "Why, lass, we are here for the rebellion!"

She frowned at that, but gestured them to take a seat on the low wooden bench opposite. Folding her legs, she dropped down elegantly on the dirt. "And what exactly do you hope to achieve, apart from more death? I recall the last rebellion created nothing except orphans and widows."

"The time is ripe," Si said.

Nyree raised an eyebrow. "Indeed, and what makes you think that?"

"Have you not heard the word?" Varlesh clamped his pipe in his teeth, but in deference to the sick child did not light it.

Nyree frowned, so Equo leaned forward. "Everyone can feel it. Something has changed out there in the world. If you had the Gifts, you would see it even better than us."

She pursed her lips and said somewhat tartly, "The stars are in alignment, the tea leaves tell the tale, and the innards of some poor bird give the right signs. Is that right?"

He felt for her; being cut off from her own heritage made such things painful to believe in, but it did not mean other magics did not exist. The world was ready for change, exploding for it, but he didn't know what to say. Si did.

"Kindred are moving, Nyree."

Her hand flew to her lips.

"So you see," Varlesh said tapping the end of his pipe against his teeth, "that is much better than any tea leaves."

"A Kindred appeared to save our friend—right in front of Talyn," Equo went on. "You should have seen her face."

Nyree closed her eyes. "Do not even mention her name, dear friend. Talyn the Dark is no longer numbered among the true Vaerli . . . but, it is as you say . . . a sign."

It was impossible to tell if she would have given her blessing to the rebellion, because at that moment their guide came bursting through the hangings on the front door. His eyes were huge in his head as he threw himself on Nyree, gabbling out words and tugging on her sleeve.

She soothed him with a gentle hand on his face and spoke to him calmly in his own language. The news could not have been good, for when he finally stopped talking she hugged him, and her face was clouded with fear.

"I am sorry, my friends," she said softly, "I think your visit has put you in mortal danger. The Swoop have arrived and are burning the riverside quarter."

They could smell it now, the tang of smoke in the air, distant but threatening.

Equo's mouth went dry, while Varlesh rose to his feet with a roar like an angry bull. "What? By the Pure Maid, they have no right!"

"They think they do. It is retaliation for the uprising in the hills two days ago, which is retaliation by some angry boys here for the killing of a family the week before. It's an ugly and familiar circle." Nyree rocked the sniffling boy. "We are cut off from the clinic, and they are burning their way back to the water."

Equo felt a chill run through him, but Varlesh, as always, moved quicker. Scooping up the child on the bed, he tucked her under one arm as gently as he could. "We shall have to make for the lake, then."

Nyree nodded, but her eyes were full of something Equo suspected was hopelessness. Few people knew the Swoop as well as the denizens of Oriconion.

Si moved forward and took the trembling boy from her while Equo took her hand. "We must hurry."

She nodded and squeezed his fingers, but whatever troubled her she did not say. He could only hope it was not foresight.

CHAPTER THIRTEEN
A LONELY DANCE

Finn was still unaware exactly what advantage it was traveling the Chaoslands with a Kindred. The black-eyed stone form trailed after them—but offered neither comment nor assistance. It was about as much use as a rock.

He and Pelanor followed the far more helpful stars. Finn's fellow traveler was proving to be an easy companion and much better at it than the Kindred. Over the last few days she had become less and less gregarious; she ate very little and sat morosely by the fire. Finn thought that she would at least complain about the lack of decent food and rough sleeping.

They clambered over and through a vast rock-filled world where even a moment's distraction could mean a painful injury and possibly death. It had been hard going even for him, well used to the perils of travel, but his mind had constantly strayed.

It wasn't just the threat of Talyn that haunted Finn; his own dark demons rose to tear at him. He could be leading this young woman into terrible danger, and he was worse than a fool to do it. It was only his own weakness that had let him accept her offer. He really couldn't have stood to be all alone with the shadows of fear.

Worthless. Doomed. Stupid.

The dark abyss was claiming Finn, and he couldn't even warn her.

Then there was Ysel. He'd failed there, too. His clumsy fingers would not find the pattern, and by their third night of rest Finn threw the thread away with a loud curse. Pelanor watched without comment from the other side of the campfire.

She was a neat and tidy girl who seemed to occupy very little space, as though her trim dark body knew exactly where to place itself at any given moment. She said very little, seemingly content, it seemed, to follow where he led. She shared nothing more of her tragedy and ignored his attempts to discuss it.

The Kindred's eyes never left him, and it never strayed beyond a few feet away. Finn ate his meager beans and thought about the tales he had learned at his master's side. Only Vaerli could Name Kindred and it was a very serious event. Naming gave a Kindred permanent form and a power that was rumored to be very great indeed. In his head he ruminated on what its name would be, but he didn't speak it.

Finn sat back, reclaimed his string, trying in equal measures to find the pattern and ignore his two quiet companions.

The night was not still about them. In the dark, the shift of the land could be almost heard: the grinding of rock against stone, the thrust of the mountains, and the complaining groan of the trees forced to change with the land. Only the stars were constant and somehow friendly, so Finn let his eyes wander there.

"Have you met Talyn the Dark?" Pelanor's voice was so unexpected that Finn took a long moment to process what she was asking.

Looking across at her, he tried to judge her interest, but her face was void of expression. Finn was suddenly more aware of the deathmark than ever. "Yes," he muttered.

"What's she like? I have heard lots of stories."

Finn's paranoia choked his throat. It was foolish—she couldn't possibly know that he was Talyn's prey. She was just a girl.

Finn chose his words with care. "She's beautiful in a sort of primal way. You can feel the danger in her, but it draws you in—a bit like dangerous currents in the ocean, if you know what I mean."

A puzzled frown formed on Pelanor's forehead. "I have never seen the sea," she muttered.

Finn shook his head. "Of course you haven't—my apologies." He bent his eyes to the skein of wool on his fingers. "It's hard to explain until you meet her. Hopefully that won't ever happen."

She sighed at this, sounding almost disappointed, but asked no more questions.

The night rolled on to the sounds of the land's shivers and shakes, and Finn found his frustration levels rising at the inability to find the pattern. He had just got to the point where he was going to throw it into the fire when Pelanor cried out.

It was the Kindred; gone was the odd but unassuming birdlike shape of dark gray, replaced instead by an edifice of glowing rock that towered over Pelanor. Finn leapt up and pulled her back. A stench of sulfur was in the air and heat was rolling off it. He looked up into the creature's eyes and saw that the darkness had been replaced with lavalike brilliance. A thousand tales of the danger of the Kindred suddenly sprang into his mind, and Finn cursed himself for ignoring them.

"Quick," he found himself saying while tugging her after him. They ran from the circle of firelight and the creature that had changed so quickly. They forgot bedrolls and food in a hasty effort to save their skin.

Finn found Pelanor outpacing him; however scared he was, she was more so, it seemed. Her fingers slipped from his and he lost her in the dark ahead, despite the moon.

Stopping, Finn caught his breath and turned his head to listen for pursuit. Instead there came a terrifying howl from ahead, rattling the ground and making his heart leap within his chest. "Pelanor!" he called, and began running toward the sound.

His questions were quickly answered. For a second in the moonlight, it looked like a tree had grabbed his young charge. Her body was trapped in flailing long limbs, and then the stench of the thing washed over him.

It was not the Kindred; nothing made of fire and Chaos could smell that terrible. The body was indeed as tall as a small tree, and had no apparent face or eyes. Surrounding it were dozens of long flat "arms," one of which was wrapped tight about his traveling companion. At the top of what might have been the head was a tapered trunk filled with bright teeth. His talespinning gave a name to something of such horror. It was the *Hashani'mort*, a Chaos Devourer, one of the many dangers of this land. They were attracted by magic and thus usually bypassed humans for more tasty prey. Clearly this one had mistaken Pelanor for something she did not have. As Finn's throat tightened, he wondered if perhaps it had been his meddling with the patterns that had drawn its attention.

She was hanging quite still in its grasp, but her face when she peered down at him was more baffled than terrified. She did not scream again, despite the horror of her situation.

His small bow was back at the camp, and he felt an idiot for having left it. Instead Finn blindly pulled from his boot the pair of long knives he always carried there. They were more for hunting than attacking a *Hashani'mort*, but if he stood around much longer there would be nothing left of Pelanor.

The long limbs lashed out at him, surprisingly quick for something that resembled a gray stumpy tree. The razor-sharp appendage whipped at his head, so Finn ducked, rolled, and came up right next to the trunk. The stench this close was thick and thoroughly nasty, and he could barely breathe. He slapped his foot against the side of the main body. Trying not to think about the smell or the way the skin crawled under his hand, Finn climbed the heaving torso as quickly as possible. He kept a good hold on the knives with one hand and breathed through his mouth as best he could.

Finally, he reached the limb that held Pelanor, and she reached out her hand to him. Still she did not cry out, though the *Hashani'mort* was squeezing her tightly, confusedly trying to get the magic from her.

Finn knew he would have to act quickly or choke on his own disgust. Flipping both knives into his left hand, he savagely slashed at the join between limb and torso. None of the tales ever told the whole gruesome story; no one mentioned the consequences when you cut a *Hashani'mort*. The skin ruptured like something rotten, spraying thick brown ichor over its attacker. Luckily he had his mouth closed when it did so, but unluckily he did not have enough time to duck. The vile liquid burned where it landed, and the smell was enough to make him lose his grip.

It was almost a relief to fall the short distance to the ground, but Finn landed hard enough to rattle his teeth. He looked up through blurry eyes, feeling his skin revolt at the coating it had received. All he could see was flames. Surely it was a trick of the ichor, for it seemed like a stream of fire shot over his head and slammed into the *Hashani'mort*.

Finn shook his head to clear it. Whatever it was, there was no doubt it was more effective than he had been; the fire scorched the area around Pelanor and the limb curled back in agony like a plant burned by the sun. She, unlike Finn, managed to drop to her feet like a cat. Amazingly, her face was impassive, as if she had not just had a near-death experience. Her eyes flicked to something behind Finn's head while he tried to clear the ichor from his eyes, worried that he would go blind.

Then there were many hands on him dragging him back, and he could hear Pelanor's voice calling his name. Other voices joined his companion's in a counterpoint to the dreadful howls, but it was an unfamiliar language.

Something cool was wiped across his eyes and suddenly he could see. What he saw was all flame and conflict. Finn blinked—almost disbelieving what his eyes were telling him.

It was the Kindred, tall as the *Hashani'mort*, attacking their attacker. Its skin, once all stone and innocence, now rolled with fire as if lava burned within it. Iron-tipped claws quickly finished off the gray writhing monster. Moments before, it had seemed so terrifying. Now Finn almost felt sorry for it.

A hand touched his shoulder and, wrenching his eyes away from the clash of might before him, he remembered that they were not alone. Five tall, dark warriors were huddled around them. Their simple but brightly patterned loin cloths marked them as Chaos nomads. They were watching the battle too, but their pointing and whispering suggested they were more interested than frightened. One, a man whose high cheekbones were illuminated by Kindred fire, tugged at Finn's sleeve and whispered haltingly, "We go . . ."

Looking at the devastation of smoldering and burning vegetation around them, Finn couldn't help but agree. Even if by some miracle they were not trampled by the two combatants, they could still be caught in minor bush fire.

The leader jerked his head to his men. One of them stepped forward and handed Finn a velvety leaf that, when he rubbed on his skin as they mimed, actually provided relief from the ichor. He then led them away, back toward their camp.

The five of them waited impassively at the edge of the light of the dying campfire, leaning lightly on their spears, while Finn and Pelanor gathered their possessions.

"What was that thing?" she asked finally.

"A *Hashani'mort*. They are drawn by magic and very hard to kill—unless you are a Kindred."

"They are mortal enemies." The leader of their rescuers spoke again, his command of the language somewhat better than it had first appeared. "A Kin will always hunt a *Hashani* for they are one of the few things that can hurt them."

Finn performed a deep bow. "We thank you for your help. I am Finnbarr the Fox and this is Pelanor."

He tipped his head in return, but in the custom of the wandering people did not volunteer his own name. Those who lived in the Chaos were few and knew the danger of naming names too early.

As they gathered their meager gear, Finn whispered to Pelanor, "Do you know this tribe?"

She shot him a puzzled look. "No, why should I?"

It was so odd that he stopped. The tribes of the Chaosland were sparse and relied heavily on each other for survival. She should have known not only their language, but maybe them personally as well.

His silence must have conveyed his surprise, for she ducked her head and muttered, "My father kept me away from strange men." It was hardly an excuse. Then again, it was also hardly the time to argue.

Yet, if Finn's time in the wild had taught him anything, it was that people were seldom what they claimed to be.

A breath of heat fanned over them, and there was the Kindred. The tribesmen seemed unconcerned, watching out of implacable eyes as the massive figure strode toward them, oozing flame. Finn felt a tremor of real fear.

Luckily, it shrank as it approached until there was only a child-sized creature on clawed feet standing next to him, once more the color of stone. Those dark, clear eyes looked up at him, perhaps searching for approval.

Finn knew he was suddenly the center of attention; the tribesmen were muttering in their own tongue to one another. Their leader rubbed his chin, a speculative look on his face. "Is this one Named?"

Finn almost resented the implication. "Of course not!"

The leader nodded. "Good." He turned to his men and spoke firmly in their own tongue. Their conversation faded, but Finn was certain their looks were more suspicious.

"We will take you to Caracel. Many Wise are there." The leader bent and picked up Finn's sleeping roll.

"Who is Caracel?" Pelanor whispered urgently to him as they followed their rescuers into the night.

A chill sensation crept across Finn's skin. With one question she had confirmed her story as a lie. "Not who," he replied as evenly as possible, "what. Caracel is the annual meeting of the all the tribes that walk the Chaos. They trade, marry, and celebrate living another year."

She must have realized her mistake. Anyone who lived in this area would have known that. She whispered an "Oh," and was silent.

Finn couldn't help a well of fear building in his belly. He was suddenly aware that he was surrounded by strangers, none of whom he could trust, and a long way from any kind of aid. As if hearing that thought, the warm head of the Kindred butted against his hip. Perhaps it had meant to be a nuzzle. Finn reached down and absently patted it. Maybe there was one he could trust. Twice now the creature had saved his life, and if that wasn't loyalty he didn't know what was.

However, the creature was not quite the same as it had been. Finn would have sworn there hadn't been a long whiplike tail waving behind the Kindred before. He couldn't guess at the significance of that, but something within him said it was very important indeed.

The trail to her prey had grown very thin, and Talyn's heart was heavier by proportion. Even the land felt like it was betraying her. It had risen up around Syris, and they could not travel at speed through the deep Chaos. Forced to a pace not much more than that of a horse, they were vulnerable to the one present and regular danger of these lands: a Chaos storm. It had been a long time since she had been caught in one of those, and it was an experience she didn't wish to repeat.

It appeared Talyn had no choice. They both felt it begin—a shuddering beneath, rising up through stone and earth from the maelstrom deep below, passing through plant and air and into them. Despite everything, Talyn remained part of this world and she was still touched by its danger.

She found a spot to weather the storm quite near to an aggressively rushing river, slate gray in the half-light just before dawn. Syris tossed his head and those expressionless eyes for once lit up with interest on something other than violence. The nykur were deep-water creatures. Though he had no words, Talyn knew he was desperate to throw himself into it and feel the rush of water against his sides.

"Not yet," she whispered. "Even I need to hide from the storm."

Syris threw his head while daggerlike teeth sliced against one another, utterly contemptuous of such frailty. Still, he remained where he stood while she unbuckled her bedroll from his saddle. Then with a little coaching and a great deal of patience, she got Syris to hunker down on the ground.

Generations of people had tried many ways to survive a Chaos storm; the tribespeople who wandered the land would use trance and the boiled root of the hymnal plant to put themselves beyond the reach of the Chaos. The Vaerli had, before the Harrowing, no fear of the storms thanks to the First Gift, the ability to be one with the land. Now she would simply have to survive the storm as best she could.

Talyn laid the bedroll over Syris' back and clambered in underneath it to rest against his warm green, hairy belly. His sharp hooves could have torn her apart in a second, yet the nykur held back his rage. They had been, since the first day of her conquest, bonded together in trust. Talyn had no fear of him.

She did feel strangely fragile in the face of the approaching storm. She could only hope that with the blanket blocking out all of the outside world, it would be easier to weather the mental chaos.

Curled against Syris, as warm as a baby, Talyn let her eyes drift shut. Beneath her blanket, the world was reduced to the faint algal smell of Syris and the warmth of his hair against her face. Her heart was pounding a little now, nervous in the shadow of the storm.

It did not take long for it to find her. The sensation of heat passed over, making muscles twitch and her eyes fill with colors. Such storms were the product of the Chaos within the land itself, and vented into the outside world they could drive humans mad or suck the life from their bodies. She was used to the storms being violent, rattling bone and muscle; she could recall the last one pressing down on her like a lead weight, crushing her into sand, but this was as gentle as a warm breeze.

It washed through Talyn's mind, blinding her to reality and sensation—taking her away into the past, making her relive it like the present. It was more unwelcome than a host of physical discomforts, but it would not be denied.

The sweaty press of her brother's small form in her back. The scent of fright-ened horse beneath her. The dim outline of her mother leading them onward swimming before her eyes. The salt plain burned around them, and her broth-

er's hands clasped around her waist were starting to hurt. Mother's presence felt uncomfortable too, as if her face was near to a fire.

The things she had seen and felt made her bite her lip in an attempt to hold back tears. The plains were not kind to those who cried. Father had told her that, and yet Father was not here. He had not been one of those burning as they ran from the gathering, which was comforting, but they had not been able to find him in the panic after.

Now there was only Mother—stern, not prone to giving comfort, and mortally wounded herself. She'd admitted all those in a steady voice not long after they had put the Bastion behind them. "I won't be able to get you far, children, so you must be strong."

Mother glanced back, as if she could hear her daughter's fears, except the child knew she couldn't. Nothing but silence now ran between them. Even Byre's childish emotions no longer butted against hers.

She patted her brother's hand, trying to communicate some comfort, but he pulled away. "It hurts," he cried, before subsiding with a sniffle.

Their mother's gaze turned to them at that noise, before searching the horizon—but there was no pursuit. The Caisah had dished out his punishment and there was no need for a chase.

Kourae the Light, the child had heard men whisper Mother's name when she passed. Most beautiful and most powerful of the Vaerli she'd been—not so, now. Her golden skin was burnt and blistered and her hair, which had once brushed the ground, now sat in singed clumps around her head. Only those proud eyes remained as astounding as ever—even without the pricks of light in them. Still she held herself straight: only one arm tucked around her belly and its grievous wound. Leaving a trail of blood for miles, she should have been dead hours ago. Some residual magic still clung to her, but it was failing and death was tucking its fingers about her. Perhaps it was just pride that kept her going, for she alone of all the gathering had raised a sword against the Caisah.

Kourae tripped over her own feet, and only a grip on the horse's bridle held her upright. The girl child managed to stop a strangled cry before it escaped her throat. Mother seldom tolerated weakness.

She was looking up at them, her face gray and limbs shaking, but her voice remained strong. "You know the way from here . . . the village of Annor—you remember it?"

Her daughter nodded as bravely as possible.

"Find some people to take Byre in. If you can make them a good family," *she paused to suck in a ragged breath. "Then go—get away before the Harrowing is complete."*

With that, she released the bridle and turned aside; no long speech, no declarations of love for her children. Vaerli were not used to words communicating what emotion should have.

The girl cried but made neither tears nor sound.

The past spun away, and the storm carried her somewhere else—somewhere warm and dark.

She could hear her own heart beating in her ears and a warm breeze running over her naked skin. It was dark, but she was not afraid because she was not alone. Strong male hands touched her with gentleness and care, and stranger still was the whisper in her mind, the empathic feeling of love. She was crying in awe that she was experiencing how Vaerli loved for the first time. Bodies touched and merged, but minds did too. A vast expanse of fears, secrets and deep passions was laid open to her, as hers was being to him. It was Finnbarr the Fox. Talyn didn't need to see those remarkable eyes; she could feel them locked on her in the darkness. His red-gold hair, she could only feel as silky thickness in her hand. Such intimacy should have terrified her, but she felt only freedom. To know and be known so deeply was horrifying and wonderful.

The Chaos storm could not last forever and the winds of change blew away.

"This one is weak." The voice was deep like a resonant drum. Talyn leapt up and threw the blanket off. Behind her Syris surged to his feet, offering a strong back to what was suddenly a very dangerous situation.

The great opalescent eyes of a griffon were staring down at her, his wings of peacock blue blotting out everything else. The remains of the Chaos storm were scrolling away across the sky in streamers of greens and yellows, and Talyn could feel her own self-confidence going with them. For the griffon was not alone.

Glancing out the corner of one eye she could see a centaur, all muscle and straining strength, and her blood ran cold—for she recognized them.

Of all the Kindred, the Named were the most dangerous. Given names and forms by Vaerli, they had been set free of those bonds by the Harrowing. No more dangerous creatures lived in Conhaero.

She could sense nothing in the before-time. They were completely elemental and not bound to normal rules. Still, she dropped and rolled under Syris' belly, not thinking about anything but escape. She drew her mother's blade and pulled herself in one smooth movement onto the nykur's back. The remnants of the chaos storm were in the ether, but Syris was still faster than any mortal horse. He bolted forward like a bullet from a pistol, needing no urging. The smell of Named Kindred was not to his taste.

Talyn rode him as blindly as a normal human. The before-time meant nothing to the Named and she felt its loss with the pounding of her heart, and the fear that brought sweat to her brow.

So she didn't feel the griffon's dive at her. The faintest breeze told her a second too late, and then there was only the sudden red-hot pain as its claws locked around her. She cried out, fingers reaching for Syris but finding only air as she was carried from his back.

The world twisted and turned. Talyn got dizzying glimpses of the ground, but she managed to hold onto her blade. The pain was an amazing—an excruciating—wake-up call to the realities of flesh that she had ignored most of her life. This was how her victims felt, all the agony and the helplessness.

She was let fall, and this time her numbed fingers dropped her sword. It was useless anyway. She was too sore and bloodied to do anything more in that instant than roll over and groan. The griffon's claws had cut through bone and sinew. The Third Gift would take hours to heal the damage: if she lived that long.

The centaur danced closer; he was a golden, well-muscled creature, his equine part a bright chestnut, his human a swarthy male with curling black hair and eyes that brimmed flame.

"I know this one." His voice was deep like ancient caverns and his vambrace-sized hooves edged closer to Talyn.

"Drynis Alorn," she muttered, wiping blood from her eyes. Even among the Vaerli there were few that Named Kindred, for there was danger and power in such a doing. She recalled now her uncle's wife Mallor had the making of the centaur, though she did not know the fate of his Namer. However, there was one thing she was sure of. "You were imprisoned along with the rest of the Named. How did you escape?" Locking away the Named had been the last action of the Vaerli.

The fiery pits of his eyes burned brighter. "It was a crime that has been corrected, pitiful remnant of the Vaerli." His great fist closed around her shoulder, dragging her upright to meet his gaze. Talyn caught her breath at the pain the mistreatment caused. "The Named now walk the earth once more, and soon we shall not be alone."

She glared at him, wondering what he could mean. The sundering of the Gifts meant there could be no constraints on the Named now, and that could only spell trouble for everyone. Her eyes wandered to the blade, lying not far off.

Drynis laughed and gave her a little shake. Holding her aloft like some prize, he thundered, "Dare you try your mettle against me, little one?"

"Enough," the griffon's voice interrupted the centaur's delight. "We have not the time for this. Kill her, eat if you will, but do not make us late."

"Why eat one bitter Vaerli when sweeter meats await?" Drynis dropped her to the ground. "Besides, our masters may well want to question her."

Talyn heard the words and was surprised. The Named had no masters except those who Named them. With the Harrowing, though, such bounds meant nothing.

Unfortunately, she could not afford the time to find out. Thrusting the pain of her wounds away, she surged upright, powering her legs with her remaining strength. She reached the blade in the sand as the centaur and griffon argued. It felt much better to have her hand wrapped around the hilt. She swayed slightly on her feet but kept her weight balanced evenly, ready for them this time. They would attack together, but they would also learn she was no easy victory.

The inhuman eyes blinked and the centaur's golden face creased with a broad smile full of sharp white teeth. "The little one thinks it has claws. Much has changed since your time; you don't even know that it's over, do you?"

The griffon beat his wings, making the sand swirl, and Talyn had to steady herself as best she could. "Time is short, Drynis. The Caracel begins and we must feed."

The centaur stepped closer, and those huge hooves struck the earth with intense menace. "You are right, my friend. Our Lords command and we must obey—but I will bring a gift."

Talyn readied herself. This would end quickly. Her only thought was of the Golden Puzzle and how everything she had strived for would end.

He moved no closer. Instead he raised his hands and those eyes burned brighter. "In the name of Chaos."

Every nerve suddenly exploded. Lightning flashed inside Talyn's head as the agony of a thousand Vaerli leapt to life inside her. She had wished fervently for the Second Gift, the empathy she only dimly remembered. Now, it was abruptly turned against her. Unlike the flash from her brother, this was from all her kin. Every little bit of anger, fear, and hurt found a place inside her. The Gift was turned against her, and she screamed—finally taken by that which she had never expected. The world dissolved into terror, and when darkness finally took her it was a kind of relief.

CHAPTER FOURTEEN

A LOST SONG

If there was one comfort that remained to Equo, it was Nyree's hand in his as they struggled through the sea of angry and desperate people toward the port. Several times he had thought he'd lost Si, Varlesh, and the children they carried. Yet somehow they kept together—even through the sweat of fear and the atmosphere of panic.

It was not just emotion that clouded the air, but also smoke blowing toward the lake. Depending on how the wind blew, they were either choked by it, or slightly revived by the competing breeze coming off the water.

Above, the great circling birds of prey of the Swoop provided a terror-inducing presence. They had once been the harbingers of the Scion of Right but were now used by the Caisah as a weapon of fear and destruction.

Nyree spared a glance up, and a flicker of horror passed across her brow. She must have seen them in better times.

Together with Si and Varlesh, Equo locked arms and tried to push the crowd toward the shoreline.

Nyree raised her voice. "To the water, my friends—we must get to the water if we want to live!"

Those immediately around them calmed a little hearing her familiar voice, but there were too many terrified people for them all to take notice. Folk who would have made rational decisions only minutes ago were reduced to primal creatures driven by smoke and fear.

"Crone's hairy whiskers, keep to the main streets," Varlesh yelled in Equo's ear as they were pushed and pulled in the swelling mob. He jerked his head to where some people had been funneled into the smaller alleyways, and it was immediately apparent the fire would find them before they could free themselves. Varlesh caught a glimpse of tears running down Nyree's face—but they were not of fear, they were of grief. Luckily, the mob prevented her from going back, or he suspected she would have.

They made it to the jetty, where there was even more panic, for the Swoop had set fire to the boats. The Portree owned very little, but these vessels were their livelihood and how they measured family, and now everything, from the smallest coracle to the twin-masted fishing vessels, was in flames. The Swoop circled above, watching their handiwork, like beautiful vultures.

Nothing remained to any of the people here; given the choice between a fiery death and the water, they chose the water. Many leapt off the collection of jetties and piers, while others rushed through the sand to the waves. The lake was their natural home and now they were swarming toward it, wading out into the sucking mud, and carrying their children on their backs. Indeed, several carracks seemed not that far away.

Equo moved forward to join them, but Si held out a restraining hand before he got very far.

The Caisah had many creatures, not only in the skies, but also under the water. A terrified woman who had been the first into the lake was the first to cry out. Her scream was high pitched, horrified and disbelieving. She raised a hand as if waving to those on shore, and disappeared under the water. Then she reappeared a moment later, hysterically calling for help. The waves frothed with blood when she went down a second time. She did not reappear.

Now the water became as panicked as the land; people splashed about, screaming, unsure where they should go. It was perfectly horrific, just the way the Caisah liked things. Those who miraculously survived this day would never forget it—and would remember not to challenge him again.

The crowd was in danger of breaking the pier. Equo's small group, tightly huddled together, were close to being pushed into the heaving water or being trampled under the feet of those still on land.

Nyree grabbed hold of Equo. He held onto her fingers, knowing they would likely not survive long. The two children clutched them, almost beyond terror.

"Well, I for one will not die like this," Varlesh bellowed, cutting through the screams and shouts with real anger. "We show what we can do now, or lose everything!"

Equo reached out with his other hand to catch hold of Si's, then he in turn reached out and grabbed Varlesh. The sensation of Nyree's fingers vanished— there was only the line of men. The sound and horror of the world faded into a muffled drone which seemed as insignificant as a bee in the flowers. It was a kind of bliss to fall into their old ways.

They had not done this for many years, perhaps generations of other people. In the back of Equo's mind was the certain knowledge that performing a Union right now would bring the Caisah's attention. But these people could not die today while they watched.

Varlesh let the hum begin in his chest, a tuneful throaty noise that passed along to Equo. In his throat he gave it shape and form, a melody was traced through it. Then onto Si it went and it was his mouth that let it out into the world. It was a joyous sound; for though they had not practiced the song for an ancient time, it was still as fresh and beautiful as from the first day. The Union erupted from Si's throat, a rain of exquisite music sweeter even than the Vaerli's *maie atuae*. For indeed it was their people who had taught Nyree's the greatest joy in music. His people were bards: the only true bards.

Even if there were dire consequences, it felt like bliss to hear the Union raining about them. The people were stopping. Even those in the water could not hold onto panic when the music washed over them. Through them it passed, speaking of the fragility of flesh but also of its beauty and its wonder. Few words there were in the Union, yet those that there were spoke of the triumph of hope and determination over loss and weakness.

The body is the glass through which we see the world.

Si's song brought the mob to a halt. They listened, swaying. Their cheeks, to a person, wet with tears.

Nyree clutched the children to her and wept without sound. Her eyes were raised to the sky but what she saw there she did not share. The Union would be hard on her most of all, with the loss of the Second Gift.

Equo looked up too, seeing the Swoop flutter in strangely disarrayed patterns as the song reached them. Peregrines, falcons, and vultures squawked and cried their piercing cries. From high above a thick powerful form with great hooked talons dived down in a mass of screaming feathers. But even the Whitefoam eagle's magic could not break the Union. Instead, Azrul the Commander of the Swoop shed her avian form in a flutter of white light and there before them was the scion of the Lady of Wings.

Equo could see a certain raw-boned youthful beauty in her face. The Union showed them everything. It pulled back the pretensions people liked to build around them and displayed the communality that all creatures of flesh shared. She was blinking the huge burnished gold eyes of the eagle she'd been and swaying slightly to the sound pouring from Si's mouth. As the music went on, the gold gave way to brown in her eyes.

Varlesh tugged at Equo's arm, gesturing out to the lake but voicing nothing to break the Union. Equo nodded affirmation.

His companion's chest filled with another note: deeper and more powerful, a stirring sound that rattled the bones. He passed it on to Equo, who threaded it with the melody of command, the call of the Union to flesh to obey. Then Si took it and gave it words of gentle demand.

The waters heaved and bent as the previously deadly bodies with their silvery leather backs rose to the surface, forming a bridge across the waves. The backs of the killers would lead them across the harbor beyond the rocks, to where the fire could not reach.

The three men, singing the Union between them, led the way, stepping easily on broad wet backs. Below them beat the hearts of predators, but the Union held.

The people by the lake followed eagerly after, willing to accept the hand of salvation even if it did come in an unexpected shape. Parents hoisted their children high and carried them nervously over the strange bridge. Friends and neighbors helped each other cross, faces full of fear and joy.

Nyree came last, her eyes glazed and thoughtful, and her feet sure on the backs of monsters. She stepped down next to Equo on the sandy shore opposite the harbor and looked back. The captain of the Swoop was a small figure from here, but she did not move. Azrul the Whitefoam eagle for once did not know what to do. Si let the Union fade. The music filtered away on the wind. The people sighed, released from its hold, suddenly aware of what had just happened. It was very few to have saved from the whole city, hundreds rather than thousands.

The creatures of the deep, the dark demons of the waves who had been summoned for other purposes than that of the Union, sank back into the water and disappeared.

Azrul, too, was released. Leaping into the air, she was enveloped in a blaze of white light, becoming once more the powerful form of the eagle. Her call when it came was somehow both defiant and mournful. The charcoal gray cloud of the rest of the Swoop condensed around her. Then she was gone, flying to her master, disappearing back into the smoke above the city.

The trio of men stood a little apart, but still Varlesh drew the others farther away from Nyree, his eyes somber as stones. "Azrul will tell him, even if he didn't feel our magics."

Equo nodded, feeling the euphoria of the Union wearing off. "But, what will he do is the question . . ."

Varlesh rubbed his eyes wearily. "He most likely suspected the Ahouri were not dead, but this time he has proof. He's losing interest in the Vaerli, and now he will think we started the rebellion. What do you *think* he will do?"

They stared bleakly at each other. Si took their hands. "It was time. It was the right time for us."

It wouldn't make death any easier, but Equo smiled. "It was good to sing the Union again."

"Aye." Varlesh chuckled. "Good to know that it is still there and we haven't totally forgotten."

Equo looked down at their hands: Varlesh's thick and broad, marred with calluses; his own long and tapered with fingers made for music or writing; and Si's soft as a child.

"We will endure," Si reminded them. "As before."

"Yes." Equo relaxed a little. "We are still well protected. He may search all he likes. He will find no trace of our people."

"Equo?" Nyree's voice interrupted their reverie. They jumped and danced apart. Outsiders sometimes mistook their odd relationship for something else entirely. But the Vaerli obviously had more concerns on her mind. "I need to talk to you."

He stepped away, making what he hoped was a warning expression to Si and Varlesh while Nyree's back was turned.

He was expecting a thousand questions, or at least a comment or two on the unexpected magic they had just performed. Instead she led him toward the water's edge and pulled up the edge of her sleeve. "What do you think of that?"

On the delicate underside of her wrist was a faint blue line of the flowing text of the Vaerli. It twirled a short distance down where the veins disappeared under her shirt. He couldn't help running a fingertip along that line and shivered at the feeling of her soft skin. "It's very pretty."

"I suppose it may be, but it wasn't there this morning. And in fact, though I can't be sure, I think it wasn't there until you sang." There was real fear in her voice.

"You know what it means, then?"

She sighed, tugging down her sleeve, and dropped her eyes away from his. "There were always two Seers of the Vaerli, one made, one born. I was to be the made one, the *Hysthshai*, for my generation. I was the apprentice of Putorae . . ."

"The one killed by the Caisah?"

"The very same: the last of the seers. I had not yet begun to receive the *pae atuae*, the word magic that all the *Hysthshai* are marked with. But I had studied by her side for all of my childhood. I was ready." She sighed heavily. "But Putorae was killed, the born seer was not revealed, and the *pae atuae* did not appear. Then we had more concerns than the lack of seers."

Equo wanted to hold her and offer some meager comfort against the pain which was obviously resurfacing. For a second his hand hovered above her turned back, but he lowered it awkwardly. "We have to help these people right now, Nyree." He reminded her of her duty instead.

"But that is it," she replied quietly. "Putorae saw many things in the future and I was the one to learn them all. In the few weeks before she went to the Caisah, she was troubled by these visions. Today you made one of them come to pass, the revelation of the Ahouri."

Equo's throat went dry. He hadn't really expected Nyree not to know, she was both ancient and well educated.

She had turned while he was standing there stunned and now she was holding him fast with her peerless eyes.

"There were things Putorae knew," she said. "Things not all Vaerli did. She told me of our greatest horror, and it does not wear the Caisah's face. I cannot say more, but I fear that if this vision has appeared, it heralds that the rest may come to pass also."

The tone of her voice, an odd dark look, and Equo suddenly realized she suspected him of something sinister. He pulled back, disturbed that she did not perceive the truth of his nature.

"There is a group of fishing crannog to the north," he replied gruffly. "We should get everyone there before dark. From there the rebels will be able to get them to safety."

He went back to Si and Varlesh and thought hard on what she had said.

The Caisah's wrath would be more than enough to deal with for now—they certainly didn't need anything darker or more mysterious than that.

Byre and his father rested. The earth moving beneath them was a soothing lullaby. He woke with a start to the sun's rays piercing through the canopy of rustling ferns.

His father was seated, just as he had been before, but his head was dropped against his chest, and a faint snore rumbled through the clearing.

They had spent the last few days hiding from Rutilian Guard as they swept through the Chaoslands. Normally the guard stayed on the Road but something drove them deep into land that was both dangerous and unknown.

Even Byre and Retira, with their experience, found the going hard. A Vaerli after the Harrowing was almost in as much peril as any other person in the Chaoslands. Creatures whose entire purpose was to hunt and eat prowled the inner lands. Even those that lived on plants could still pose a threat. The towering bulk of a thramorn had almost crushed them in their sleep while on her late-night feeding expedition. With the constant changing landscape, animals could not afford to wait for their food to wither and die, and many existed without sleep. The thramorn had no more noticed their camp than a person noticed a worm. Intent on scrounging as many tasty fern fronds as possible, her large foot had only barely missed Byre. A thramorn, for all its bulk, was as silent as a cat. With so many predators it had to be.

Though it had been frightening, Retira was not angry. He simply pointed out that both of them should have noticed the trees stripped by the river and been on watch. It was a basic mistake that he took the blame for, claiming the joy of traveling with his son had temporarily blinded him. His relaxed and jovial manner was something Byre remembered. It had always been their mother who had been the disciplinarian. She would not have been so forgiving.

Retira led Byre farther into the forest, pointing out where the land was already heaving itself upward. Within a week it would most likely be a mountain pass. He might have cut himself off completely from the Vaerli and their Gifts, but he still had a thousand years of experience of the wild. The land sense had been an invaluable tool, he conceded to Byre, yet he argued it had made Vaerli lazy. With the feeling of land in their heads they had not really needed to look more deeply at it.

"Have you noticed the changes in the tempo of the earth?" he asked.

Byre shrugged. "I have not spent so much time in the Chaoslands. With no one to teach me the ways . . ." He stopped, too embarrassed to go on.

"No one would expect you to remember. But I have spent much time wandering . . . perhaps more than is healthy. There is a change in the rhythm of the land. Places which raged are now silent, and the more placid areas are now so dangerous even I dare not go there. It has been happening gradually, but it is easy to see if you have the lifetime of our people. Still, I do not know why."

The images of seething fire suddenly washed over Byre. He hadn't realized it consciously before, but the place of his dream was definitely underground. Could the lurking creature be a Kindred, or something even more menacing?

"What I do know," Retira went on, not noticing his son's abrupt discomfort, "is that you must get to the Great Cleft soon. The Choana say it is open only for a few days in the year."

Such knowledge was not a Vaerli thing. They might be masters of the earth, but they never ventured beneath. Byre caught himself from asking how his father knew such a thing, for the World Builders were known for their utter secretiveness. Even the Blood Witches had marginal contact with the other peoples of Conhaero, but the Choana had disappeared into the icy wastes. Only the broken bodies of those who sought them out told that they even still existed. They were dumped on the edge of the frozen plain, with warnings against further incursions carved into their chests. Even the Caisah did not bother them as long as they showed no signs of challenging him for power.

It mattered little how his father got his information. If it were true, then they might as well turn back now. Byre stated the obvious, though. "We cannot get there in time."

Retira tapped the side of his nose and grinned. "Not by normal means. Even your sister's nykur could not manage it, but the old still have a trick or two to teach."

Byre had learnt much of the Vaerli lore at his mother's knee. Even so, he couldn't imagine what his father was talking about. But there was no persuading an explanation past his father's smiling lips. He wanted to keep his secrets.

The following morning they packed up camp without Retira saying anything more. Used to silences and secrets in equal measure, Byre followed him down to the newly sprung river two hours' walk from their sleeping place. The heady taste of the Gifts had been withdrawn from him, and so the land gave none of Retira's mysteries away.

His father took out a small flute chased with silver but no word magics, and blew three sharp notes upon it. The earth rumbled and it was not the gentle easing of a Kindred from beneath. Instead it was a ripping sound, as if the very fabric of the soil was being torn. Byre winced in sympathy.

What emerged was deep green, as large as one of the Caisah's carriages, and smelt musty like something kept too long in the dark. It took him a moment to recognize the protuberance as the stem of some massive plant.

Cautiously he touched the pod. It was warm under his hand and soft like flesh, but when he pushed harder it felt like steel was buried beneath. "What is it?" he asked his grinning father.

Retira blew another note on his flute, a descending one that sent shivers through the plant. It sprung apart, revealing a glossy cream interior like fine silk, and the smell changed to one of heady glory. It was as if a monster had shed its skin and become a butterfly. Byre did not know what to make of it.

Even more alarmingly, Retira tucked away his flute and actually stepped into the pod. He reclined in the smooth interior and patted a spot near him. "The Choana did not disappear, Byre, not at all; they have been beneath us all along. I found a place with them, and thanks to that you will not have to suffer the rigors of further travel. Come in."

Byre paused at the entry of the pod. The curled lips were twitching, and he knew very well that they would close as soon as he was in. He had never suffered from a fear of being shut in, but he couldn't get the imagery of being swallowed out of his head.

Retira held out his hand. "I said it was safe. Don't you trust me?"

Now was not the time to point out how long they had been separated or to make some snappy comment about his father's mental health. It was a simple choice of go forward or fail. Not having anything to lose but his life, Byre stepped into the pod.

It closed around him with a sound almost like a sigh. It should have been dark, but there was a strange green-white light coming from the walls. It cast his father's face in alien, odd angles.

Byre gingerly took a spot next to him. As the pod lurched, he found himself grabbing reflexively for a handhold but there was none. Apparently it wasn't needed, though, for the surface he was sitting on was somehow attached to him.

"Don't worry," Retira said. "Once we set off, the pod will move remarkably smoothly."

"What is it . . . this thing, anyway?"

"Just what it seems. The Choana have the way of making growing things do their bidding—plants, that is, not animals. That is forbidden."

For a second, Byre imagined what masters of matter could do if let loose on unsuspecting creatures. If they chose to, they could create nightmares. He said nothing, but swallowed his fears. He had put his trust in his father, and if he lost faith now he might as well have been left in the Caisah's cell.

"Now I'm going to get some rest." Retira yawned. "The pod will take some time to get back to its root. Nothing will endanger you here." And with that he turned over and, nestling into the interior, dropped to sleep.

Byre could do no such thing. The whole motion was unnatural and even though he was sure it was a plant, he still didn't trust it. And if he didn't trust the method of travel, could he really trust his father?

It was a hard thing to think about because the memories of his life before the Harrowing were his most cherished. But the toughened part of him that had lived his life since then realized he knew nothing of his father, really. Byre had the chilling worry that he was being led into danger, cynically tethered by his emotions.

He should ask. He should wake Retira and simply demand to know how they came to be traveling in this strange conveyance of Choana making. He should be brave enough to reveal his concerns.

Byre wasn't. The memories got in the way and he didn't know how to get past them. He had already lost three parents. So he closed his eyes and tried not to think about those questions.

The Sofai slipped into that space. It was far easier to think of her dark eyes and soft voice than closer problems. But there were questions there, too— what had she got him into?

CHAPTER FIFTEEN

A WITCH ALONE

Pelanor hung close to Finn. She definitely did not like the smell of these men that they had fallen in with—even less than that of her first traveling companion. They reeked of wildness and masculinity that put her further on edge.

Her nerves were wrecked—for she was hungry, deeply ferociously hungry. It made her stomach cramp and her eyes feel disconnected from her body. Every muscle was aching, her mouth dry, and suddenly she was beginning to remember what pain was.

Pelanor longed for Alvick, her mate, and her Blood. His gift would fill the need within her, ease the great hunger, and hold her back from the Dark Gate.

However, if she could not have Alvick then others could stand in his place.

Even now, walking behind Finn, she fantasized about lunging forward and burying her mouth around his flesh. His skin would part beneath her teeth and there would be relief from the dragging agony of the Hunger.

She could not—it was part of the test. So she managed to stay her hand . . . for now, at least.

Day was just beginning to shake itself out of the desert ahead, over the heads of their traveling companions. Pelanor swallowed. The sun was a burning blood red.

She closed her eyes for a moment, trying to get that delicious imagery out of her head.

"Are you all right, Pelanor?" Finn had dropped back and put his hand on her shoulder, concerned for a weak mortal woman in the desert.

"Not really," she replied softly. "I mean, can we trust these people?" If only she could get him alone, maybe there was a chance she could satisfy the Hunger a little.

"After saving us last night?" He glanced at her with some humor. "Would you prefer we trust the *Hashani'mort*? You tell me, you're from the tribes."

Her lie had been discovered, and it was obvious that he was a lost cause.

Although she assumed Finn was a jovial-enough fellow to mortals, to her he was simply irritating. She feared if she opened her mouth she would say something biting that would reveal herself. Still her lips twitched, aching to let out something.

"I'm glad you think it's funny." Finn gave her a gentle shove, but she didn't tell him that it was no giggle she'd suppressed.

They walked for three hours, until the waves of heat rippled over the baking rocks. Finn was sweating, but neither Pelanor nor their guides complained.

Looking back over one shoulder she observed the one thing that did make her uncomfortable: the Kindred was watching her.

Blood Witches didn't exactly fear the Kindred—once passed through the mouth of the goddess, fear was supposed to be a mere memory. It was more that they were uncertain of them. Their magic was too different, too alien, and far removed from that of Blood to really be comprehended. Also, they saw things. Undoubtedly this Kindred could see through her lies and knew what she was.

So Pelanor struggled to understand it as well. In the back of her mind was the possibility that if she had to eliminate Finn it might well attack her. She narrowed her eyes. The tail was new, as Finn had pointed out. Though she knew nothing about their magics she wondered on its implications. The Kindred were awesome allies, able to call on their powers of fire and Chaos at any time, and if cornered even the earth itself could be their ally. Would her Blood magics be enough to counter such a threat?

Soon, though, there was no time to think about things as they crested the last hump of sand and rock. Before them was Caracel.

In the great ochre valley below was spread a sprawling mass of tents, bawling livestock, and more humanity than Pelanor had ever cared to see. The noise and the smells were offensive to her highly tuned senses.

"Amazing, isn't it?" Finn was by her side once more, a bright note in his voice. "All the Chaos tribes meet here once a year to trade, arrange marriages, dance, and compete. See there." He raised one finger and pointed down into the center of the throng. "There's a large oasis here. It moves every year, but the tribes always find it."

Much like a leech will find a vein, she thought to herself, but she was not fooled by his innocent remarks. "I know all that," she snapped, "I've lived among them all my life." Pelanor would not fall so easily into such an obvious trap.

Then she decided to ignore him for a while. Let him think what he would, he was not her prey and counted little in the scheme of things.

They were led down into the Caracel, and Pelanor had to steel herself before entering the stinking caldron of humanity. All around there was sound: the screeches of gap-toothed women, the squalls of angry infants, and the barking of unattended dogs.

She felt buffeted by it, lost without Alvick to hold her into reality, and washed away in a sea of humanity. Forgetting her previous decision, she grabbed Finn's arm, looking for something to hold her steady. It felt like every eye was on her, each one hostile. Were they aware of her hidden teeth? Some said sheep could sense the wolf.

Even a Blood Witch might not stand against a mob. Amongst her kind there were plenty of warning tales of Witches who had been exposed and then reviled by humans; people who could not possibly understand the twelve-mouthed goddess and the bargain made with Blood.

The tribesmen might be laughing and enjoying themselves at the moment, but whisper the word *Phaerkorn* and they would find anger quickly enough. The sooner she was face-to-face with her prey, the sooner she could be away with her mission completed.

Finn was looking at her strangely so her feelings must have somehow crept onto her face. She wiped away whatever disgust was there and tried her best to put on the mask of humanity.

As they followed their guides deeper into the tent-strewn chaos, he began peering around, looking through all the tribespeople with all their different costumes and headgear. After a moment Pelanor realized what he was doing: looking for her tribe, trying to match her costume with others.

The clothes she had stolen at random in her flight south, and she didn't need to be put in the position of trying to explain to their owner who she was.

She tugged cautiously on Finn's sleeve, trying to make herself as pitiful and beautiful as possible. "You know, I'm afraid we will see my tribe."

Then she had to embroider herself another lie about a forced marriage, an angry chief, and her own flight through the Chaoslands.

"Well," Finn said with a pat on her back, "I thought there was more that you weren't telling me. You don't have to be afraid."

Biting back a reply, she tried to imagine herself elsewhere at that moment. *Alvick would have his throat thrown back, offering the gift of his blood. She would reach down . . .*

The tribesman's voice interrupted her delightful reverie.

"This is our *yahma*." Their guide gestured to a tent the color of sand. Seated outside was an old woman as gap-toothed and rotten as any they had seen on the way here. She was a folded, stinking pile of never-washed clothing with only old bones propping them up.

Pelanor shuddered. The old were the worst of all humans. They reeked of everything the Blood Witches fought against. Unfortunately, they also saw more than the young—something she didn't need right now. The *yahma* looked at her, and Pelanor knew there was nothing that escaped this old woman. She might be near the Dark Gate, but she had learned much on her way there.

Having reached the most exalted position of any tribesperson, the *yahma* was the ultimate judge of her people. She chose the way they traveled, the waterholes that might be relied upon to still be there, and which couples deserved the protection and sanction of marriage. It was the role of the woman in the Chaoslands to carry the name forward, to guarantee the continuation of the tribe. It was the reason that many Blood Witches often hid in their number. Men herded their cattle and hunted what game they could find, while women sat in sheltered tents and dreamed whatever the Chaos storms brought.

This woman, sitting in front of her simple tent, had probably seen at least three generations of her menfolk burnt in the Chaoslands. Her eyes, deep and black, were staring at these new people in Caracel with sternness and wariness. Danger could come in pleasing shapes in these lands.

She was chewing a long-stemmed and battered pipe, which she continued doing with some concentration for a while. Finally she took it out. "More trouble, Hacel?" Her voice was cracked and bent like a piece of leather left out in the sun.

Their guide had not given up his name. As far as Pelanor knew, Hacel meant wanderer in their tongue, so she'd given nothing away even then.

"They were lost in the dust, *yahma*," he bent over one knee until his thick crop of hair nearly dropped into the sand. "Also they were pursued by a *Hashani'mort* and protected by this." He stepped aside, and the shifting small form of the Kindred was revealed. The *yahma* popped her pipe back into her mouth and chewed on it reflectively. The whole group seemed to hold its breath, waiting for a pronouncement. Even Pelanor, who cultivated little interest in humanity's doings, was curious what this old crone of the desert would make of the Kindred.

Whatever her conclusions were, the *yahma* kept them to herself. She waved the pipe, dismissing them. "They have the freedom of Caracel. Let them walk where they will."

Finn grinned broadly at Pelanor. It was a curious thing about humans, how much they cared about the company of their fellows. A Blood Witch needed no other than her Union—they were a perfect couple, insular and independent.

So it was strange that Finn took her out into the madness of Caracel and insisted she enjoy. Certainly there were many things to see that she had never even heard of. An initiate was kept apart from the world, learning the Blood code and history of her kind. Caracel was so full of life that after her distaste had worn off, Pelanor found herself entranced and curious.

Apart from trade, the main business of Caracel was marriage—which was another alien concept. The mechanics, at least, she could appreciate. It was an incredibly colorful event, and it was the men who were the most involved. Each put an inordinate amount of care into the costume, for this was his only chance to impress a woman from another tribe.

Pelanor and Finn paused at a circle of tents where a group of men were preparing. The small triangles of brightly woven cloth hung from their hips, front and back. They greased their hair with yellow mud until it stood up in great spikes, and painted ochre stripes and swirls onto their faces.

Curious despite herself, Pelanor trailed the dancers as they took to the area set aside for the attracting of a mate. Here they stood for hours, hooting and leaping in a long line, accompanied only by the deep throb of a drum. Despite not understanding the words, their rhythmic song still managed to reach her. The beat was close to that she had heard near the Dark Gate, and could still hear if she concentrated on her link with Alvick. It was the sound of life, of blood and sex.

The women arrived just before dusk, dressed in lengths of thin linen. They were chattering like excited teenagers, which was pretty much what they were. They stood quietly by while the men began to whoop in time with the rhythm. They leapt, called, and flashed their garishly painted faces at the women.

Whatever this was meant to convey, it seemed to work. Women in twos and threes stepped forward and made their choice, leading the grinning men away.

Naturally, there would be sex waiting for them in the dark, a clumsy human trait that only attempted to be what the Union was. It could only ever be an echo.

Pelanor managed not to snort her amusement.

By the looks of him, Finn was thinking on that which waited for them in the night. But he was a human male and vulnerable like that. She was very grateful that Alvick was beyond all that nonsense.

Finn wasn't looking at her, but she didn't want to get into that particular sticky situation so she tugged imperiously on his sleeve.

"I'm tired, I need to rest."

For an instant he looked confused, like she'd said something wrong. "Very well, we'll go back to our *yahma*'s tent."

They trudged back and every step Pelanor found herself thinking of blood: the taste of it, the rich iron smell of it, the thickness of it on the tongue.

She could feel her strength to resist the urge dwindling. So when they got back to the camp, she threw herself on the ground, wrapped a blanket around herself, and drifted into that half world of memory. At least there she could savor remembrance of Alvick's flavor and not be tempted by the humanity around her.

Talyn the Dark had better hurry to her prey soon, or there might not be much left of it.

Finn watched Pelanor drift off to sleep and was grateful for it. She had spent the entire day with a face that made anyone seeing it flinch. She was suddenly so full of anger, and he had no idea why. If he had had to guess, he would have paid good money that she would enjoy being among her own people, perhaps even run off back to them. Instead, she stuck close to him.

Which was not what he wanted—far too many things occupied his brain. He could not spare any worry for a troubled teenager. Now that she was asleep, Finn levered himself up from the sand and quietly snuck back to the tent at the center of their group. The old woman was perched on the worn stone outside the opening. He'd almost expected that.

Her face cracked open in that toothless and harmless smile. "I wondered how long it would take you to shake off that Jaeckcel." It was the word for a nasty human-shaped Named Kindred—rumored to drink the souls out of men in the midst of a Chaos storm.

"Ah, she's not that bad," Finn replied.

The old woman sucked on her gums noisily to show her disagreement, but didn't say anything.

Finn put on his most winning smile before sitting next to the *yahma*, but below her rock so that her head was above his. She was not just some old woman, but someone who had more wisdom and experience than he did. The best stories always resided in the minds of the old.

Her dark eyes glittered with amusement. "The only time the young are polite is when they need something . . ."

"You know many things, wise *yahma*. Perhaps you can tell me why a Kindred has taken shape and is following me?"

She looked down at her brown fingers, folding them almost nervously on each other. "The Kin do not bother us, child. We are not their people."

"Surely you know something of them?"

She smiled. "Not even as much as you. I can give no answers when they are to be found inside your own head."

Finn sighed. He had not really expected much, but something in the old woman's eyes had tempted him to try.

"Don't be sad now, boy." Her fingers touched his shoulder lightly. "There are many ways and times to find the truth. Just remember, the Vaerli do not have all the gifts. Your quest, I think, is only just beginning."

"You don't understand. My tribe doesn't have anything to do with the Kindred—not like the Vaerli."

She cocked her head, while her smile said she didn't really believe him. "Of course you do, boy. Do you think it chose you by chance?"

Finn's stomach clenched. "I don't know what you are talking about."

The *yahma* was not looking at him now, but rather at something over his shoulder. Her face had gone remarkably pale, and the cheeriness had drained from her eyes. Even before he turned around, Finn could feel a burning heat on his back; one that flared too quickly to be the campfire.

The nykur stood tossing its head, outlined against the white glow of the moons. Its presence was full of such danger and majesty that Finn felt his throat tighten. He could not deny its beauty; the play of powerful muscles under rippling green hair and the glint of starlight off its terrible sharp teeth. All this had made the *yahma* freeze with horror.

Finn found himself getting to his feet, drawn by some dark attraction toward it. He reached out with one hand as if to seize this vision of fire. The *yahma*'s choked cry was very far away. He walked calmly to the creature.

Finn found himself there, touching the nykur, and there was no mistaking it—it was Talyn the Dark's mount. That green hair looked fine as silk, but as he pulled back his fingers he found there was a bite to it; his skin was cut and bleeding.

So much heat was coming off the creature, like it was a furnace. One thing was sure, Finn thought to himself: on cold nights, Talyn would need nothing more than this creature.

Yet the nykur offered him no actual violence. It snorted and turned to look over its shoulder at him.

Behind him the *yahma* was talking, fast, and high pitched. Finn wasn't listening. Syris was actually leaning toward him, liking his touch.

Finn was lost in the eye of the nykur. Then there was a sensation of more heat and pressure, as if something nearby had suddenly and violently exploded.

He heard the *yahma* scream, and whipped around only quickly enough to see her being dragged off into the darkness. He moved, but the nykur was faster, placing his large body in the way.

The night was no longer a friendly place, for there was the sound of something massive flapping overhead. Terrified screams followed, and the loud brays of panicking camels split the sky.

"Pelanor!" Finn called, ducking under the nykur's curved neck and dashing back to where she had been lying next to the fire.

However, the world had gone mad in those last few seconds, and the whole of Caracel had leapt to life and terror. Finn called her name again. Dust was choking everything and the monstrous cries from above periodically dived down, though Finn still couldn't see what they were. Everywhere was the scent of blood, which only served to panic the revelers all the more.

Then something warm pressed against his right side. It appeared that the Kindred had not deserted him after all. Those swirling lava eyes were at a different height. The creature was small no more, but in this madness its new bulk was comforting.

"I can't do anything," Finn yelled to it, not quite sure what he was expecting.

The echoing rattle of unseen wings made him duck, but this was followed by a thump as something landed nearby.

The Kindred tensed—if that was possible for a creature seemingly made out of stone.

The heap unfolded itself to be revealed as Talyn the Dark.

She was bleeding, but in the light of the guttering campfires, a thousand tales of exquisite women sprung into Finn's mind. Talyn had beauty like a blade. *I know you*, Finn thought to her, *I remember you.*

Whatever he thought, Talyn was only concerned with survival. The nykur appeared out of the smoke to stand at her shoulder. Finn was incapable of comprehending how she had got there. She pressed her hand against the beast. "Good to see you." The comment was not directed at Finn.

She vaulted onto the green back and looked down at him. It was a trick of hers, he realized—trying to fool him into thinking she had not noticed him at all. Her eyes gave away much that she did not allow her face to, a flicker of fear and a moment of indecision. "Ah, my prey." She smiled at him and then held out her hand.

Finn looked about; there was more blood on the sand, and the images of horror around were burning their way into his memory. Death had come to the Caracel, but not by Talyn the Dark's hand. Yet she could stop it.

Finn put his hand behind his back and stepped away a little. "Help them."

No one but the Caisah had ever commanded a Vaerli. Talyn flicked back her head as though he'd slapped her. "I cannot." She kneed Syris closer.

"In the name of honor, Talyn the Dark, there are women and children here!" He backed farther away.

She blinked, opened her mouth, considered another moment, and then decided a glare was all he deserved.

"Would it help if I begged?" He wouldn't be like her and let pride stop him from helping. "They are dying . . ."

She sighed. It was a tiny sound among all the chaos around them. "Even I cannot stand against the Named. Besides, they will follow us. I am their prey like you are mine."

How could anyone take Talyn the Dark as their victim? Snapped out of his reverie, Finn felt a warm pressure against his back; the Kindred that had been following him since Perilous was now pushing him toward the Hunter. The deep wells of its eyes had somehow appropriated an emotion: concern. This creature had fought for him, and he trusted it.

So he took Talyn's hand and let himself be pulled on to Syris to sit behind her. The nykur jogged sideways but did not throw him. Finn spent an uncomfortable second not knowing where to put his hands, until he finally settled on the only sensible place: about the Hunter's waist. She flinched like her mount, but there was no retaliation and for the time being he got to keep his extremities.

Finn looked back to the Kindred, but he only caught a glimpse of its retreating back. In the half-light he could have sworn it was covered by wings.

"You have curious companions," Talyn said.

"You're right, there." Finn recognized something familiar about a hunched figure not far away, silhouetted against the burning tents. "Pelanor!" he called.

When she looked up, he at first thought she was injured, for her hands and cheeks were wet with blood. Then he realized how completely he had been fooled. Her eyes blazed golden and the figure beneath her was not somebody she'd been helping, but rather someone she had been drinking from.

She was Phaerkorn, a Blood Witch, and despite the horror he was fascinated. Few had lived to see one feeding, and Pelanor was far from how the tales said they looked.

Her body radiated power; the blood she had just drunk must have added to it.

"Talyn the Dark." She held out her hand toward the Hunter, and her voice was filled with dark longing. "Your blood is mine."

Pelanor leapt toward them, her fingers seeming long and deadly. Her whole person was transformed from the girl Finn had known.

Finn felt Talyn tense in front of him, every muscle in her body thrumming with Vaerli strength. "Not this night, Witch." And then his hands were grasping nothing.

Talyn stepped into the before-time, easily leaving behind the confusion of the last few days. It was a relief to move into the fray.

The Witch was full of blood and confidence in herself—and it would be good to change some of those things. The Witch launched herself at Talyn, leaping high in the air—sharp fingers angling for the Hunter's neck. She batted them aside in a fluid movement but still did not draw her sword. An idea was forming in her mind, even as her body moved to the steps of battle. A Phaerkorn might be swift, but not faster than an irate Vaerli. They traded lightning blows, a blur of motion no mortal eye could follow.

The Witch was small and light, but her strikes were as if from an iron club. Despite the situation, Talyn was impressed. That little pause was all the Witch required. The Phaerkorn slipped beneath her guard and wrapped her strong little fingers around the Hunter's throat. A normal mortal would have gasped for air, but the Vaerli were made of stronger stuff and had little need for such things.

She backhanded the Witch off, feeling her fingernails rake over her skin, while she snarled her outrage. The idea now became a hard pebble within Talyn's mind, so she stepped closer into the fray.

Serious now, she blocked the Witch's blows and dealt a left hook to her chin that even to a Phaerkorn was disorienting. She staggered back, shook her head, and a line of blood ran out of the corner of her mouth. With a quick lick she reclaimed the precious liquid and leapt forward again.

Now the Hunter ducked beneath the Phaerkorn's reaching hands and caught her attacker round the waist. She was very light, and Talyn used that momentum to swing her around and down into the ground with a crash.

Dropping into the now, she pinned the screaming Witch into the ground. Crouching over the Phaerkorn, she used her palms and her knees to keep her there.

The Named would be on them soon. Talyn cocked her head, listening to the sounds of panic. "Why?" she shouted into the face of her hissing and raging attacker. "We are not enemies."

"Your people want you dead," she screamed through drawn lips. "I cannot go back without your blood."

Apparently her Vaerli kin had not had enough courage to sacrifice themselves, in the end. She laughed. "You shall never have it, Witch."

The Phaerkorn tested her strength once more before sagging back. "Then it will be my Alvick and I who die."

A shame to waste such talent: it was not this child's fault that the Vaerli had bought her first Blood. She was trapped in her place as much as Talyn was in hers. The Hunter felt the unfamiliar tug of rebellion and that one idea niggling in the back of her head.

Pulling the Witch upright, she set herself on a path that might offer salvation for both of them. "Your name is Pelanor?"

"Yes." The Phaerkorn's eyes narrowed, undoubtedly wondering what new madness this was.

"Then here is a Pact for us, Pelanor. The first Pact between our peoples, and it must needs be a quick one. I will give you the Blood you need to earn your right to live, but in return you must find my brother and keep him safe. Do you agree?"

Pelanor frowned as if she did not see the peril of their situation—as if she could not hear the Named finishing their terrible work at Caracel.

"Do you agree? Quickly!"

Witch and Vaerli looked at each other. There were eye to eye, and for a moment bared to each other as only killers can be. "Yes," Pelanor said.

It was simply done, but done right. Talyn felt the act drop into place like one of the Caisah's golden pieces. "Very well then," she said, swiftly pulling back her hair from her neck. "Take your price and the Pact is sealed."

Neither did the witch hesitate. Her mouth bit where the Vaerli offered and, unlike previous injuries Talyn had suffered, this struck deep. The Phaerkorn had latched on like a panther at her prey. Talyn reeled, dropping to her knees with Pelanor still drinking from her neck. Her eyes swam as life was dragged in great sucks from her. It was warm, and everything seemed to fade to red insignificance.

Pelanor could have drained her dry—so when she stopped, it was surprising. Talyn looked up into her close face. Only the lingering ruby at the corner of her mouth hinted at what had passed between them. Pelanor lifted her up. "Our deal is sealed, Hunter. I will find and protect your brother, never fear." Then she dissolved into mist and blew away.

Only automatic reflexes got Talyn back onto Syris' back. Her prey's arms actually seemed to help her. Still not feeling herself, Talyn called for the nykur to ride.

Luckily, Syris was less drained than she. He leapt forward with a nykur's boundless power.

Her senses were returning, and just in time as well.

"Ware above!" Finn called, and Talyn leaned forward, burying her face into the sharp hair of Syris' surging neck. A second later her prey threw himself down across the Hunter's back. Out of the corner of one eye, Talyn glimpsed the huge claws grasping nothing.

The Hunter pushed Finn back with one hand and with the other aimed her pistol at the griffon's back. The snap of gunpowder made Finn grab her hard, but they rode on through the cloud of smoke. No cry of alarm sounded from her intended target, so she knew she hadn't hit.

Syris plunged nervously, spinning in a panting circle. The world went suddenly silent, all cries and screams stifled beyond the circle the nykur was describing.

"Let's ride," Finn said into Talyn's ear.

"Even Syris cannot outrun the Named."

She heard Finn's breath catch, and imagined he knew the tales of the creatures better than most.

Talyn looked up. Her Vaerli sight saw beyond the darkness, but she chose not to share with him the circling predators she saw there. Then something else moved at the edge of her vision. "Your friends are varied, and they seem to have bought us time," she whispered to Finn. The Kindred were moving, but she would not give him the satisfaction of knowing that.

Taking what they had been given, Talyn wheeled the nykur around under them and urged him away. This night had been full indeed, but if they lived to see dawn she would be pleasantly surprised.

CHAPTER SIXTEEN

A WITCHING GIFT

Pelanor's tears were hot.

The Phaerkorn never cried. It was a sign of weakness, and it only meant loss of the precious Gift. The young witch mopped vainly at the blood running down her cheeks in long streaks. Her mentors would have been angered at such a display.

She was covered in blood; the rich iron smell filled her, and yet she had never felt so small and foolish. It had been good to take it—fulfilling and amazing—but she had not won it with her strength, and she was in a new Pact now. It was perhaps the first between Vaerli and Phaerkorn, but it meant she was not free to return to Alvick. It was a painful to think that he would assume she'd abandoned him.

She looked up to where the sun was just rising out of the sand. A time of change was upon everyone beneath that sun, and perhaps this was her chance to become something more than a Witch. A seed of ambition, carefully hidden from the Council, began to unfold. The rank of Blood Mother had been long filled by the Witch known only as the Mouth, and yet her *gewalt* was dying . . .

Pelanor realized if she went back, the Council would make use of her like any other new Witch. Thanks to Talyn there was another option. The blood she now carried in her veins gave her a measure of the Vaerli power, and thus finding Byre would be no difficulty. Who knew what opportunities could arise from there?

Whispering a word of comfort to the wind that might well reach Alvick's ear, Pelanor once more dissolved to mist.

The stumbling trail of horrified survivors reached the southern crannogs by dawn the next day. The collection of round, perfectly symmetrical islands were crowded with little houses and nestled in amongst protective marshlands. Their inhabitants emerged from their huts, lowered pontoons and bridges, and ran wailing toward them. Everyone seemed to find some relative in the crowd—but there was none for the three men.

Equo knew the fighting would soon find its way here and it would be just as fierce as that in Oriconion. The crannog villagers had several boats tied up, evidence that the Rutilian Guard had not been here yet.

He had little hope for any of them, but he kept these thoughts to himself. Varlesh and Si, though, were people he could never hide anything from. One glance between them and they knew this foolish escapade would conclude soon enough.

It would be a sorry end to a fabulous tale, and it was one that would die with them. None of their people would be able to sing the Passing Ode for them.

"What now?" Varlesh watched the city folk and villagers, seeing the comfort they were bringing to each other—even if it couldn't last.

Si, meanwhile, was walking among them, soaking in the feelings, letting the raw run of emotion swell his powers.

"The Ahouri were long allies of the Vaerli." With no one within earshot, Nyree finally spoke. "So why would you hide yourself from me?"

Varlesh shared a long look with Equo before patting him on the back and moving toward the village's firelight.

"It was the only way to remain hidden," Equo replied with a sigh. "The Caisah condemned us. We did the only thing we could to survive—we Shattered our form."

At last she saw, her eyes drifting past him, to where the other parts of his being were moving away. "Just like your scion, the Trifold Spirit. Is that where the inspiration came from?"

"Yes," he muttered. "Though we did not all become Maid, Mother, and Crone."

Nyree did not laugh. "I never even guessed."

Equo couldn't help a little laugh. "We did well, then, if it was concealed even from a Vaerli Seer."

Her mouth twisted wryly. "I was but an apprentice, and such a thing hadn't been known to be possible."

"Many of us died when we broke ourselves apart, but without it the Caisah would find us easily."

"And now you have trumpeted your existence to him."

"I am afraid so."

Nyree ran a hand through her hair while looking, for the first time since he had known her, uncertain. "I wonder if he knows of this, as well." She held out the inside of her right arm, revealing that the tiny threading that had been apparent before, had grown. Now the whole length of her limb was filled with the delicate tracery of blue wording.

She looked up with fear in her eyes. Clamping his palm over the design, Equo pulled her to him for what he hoped was a comforting embrace. He had no words that would not seem false platitudes. Instead, he guided her away to break bread with the villagers.

Over a small bonfire, the villagers and the newcomers huddled together. A hunchbacked young man fetched his *trylan*, the one-cord instrument usually used at happier gatherings, and began to plunk away a bittersweet tune on it.

With its desolate twang to act as counterpoint, the Portree headwoman began talking about the rebellion that had started farther down the lake. The whole shoreline had been stripped of able-bodied folk as men and women trekked into the mountains to join the uprising. Equo supposed it would be guerilla warfare again.

Leaning forward, the old woman's dark eyes reflected the torchlight. "They say that Baraca has returned."

Equo felt his stomach tip over. Every time they'd heard that name it was trouble. Baraca was a byword for rebellion, that was for sure, but he was also an enigmatic storm crow. Twenty years before, it had been mention of him that had signaled the previous terrible uprising.

The headwoman patted the young girl at her side. "My granddaughter, Isi, will set off with our young folk to join the muster in the hills tomorrow. It is a very great confidence to know the place of the gathering."

Varlesh glanced across at Equo. All three of them, even Si, understood what this meant. Baraca would gather his forces in secret and then strike out for the Caisah's one weakness: the Road. With enough destruction, the malkin would not be enough to hold it firm against Chaos. Even the Caisah could not magic his troops into an area without the Road.

Then they would hope the Caisah himself would come down to fight. Baraca had said it many times before. Equo recalled that impassive face, weathered like stone, telling them calmly that if only they could weaken the Caisah, then others would rise. It hadn't worked last time, but Baraca was not a man to give up easily.

Varlesh was busy pulling a fish bone out from his teeth. Flicking it into the fire, he got up with a sad groan. "Good luck to him, I say, and who knows, maybe twenty years has taught him something. I'm off to sleep."

Eventually they all shuffled off to rest, leaving the headwoman and her granddaughter to share last-minute confidences as the embers of the fire began to die.

Varlesh and Si, feeling Equo's restlessness, found their own shelter away from his. Equo lay in the coracle he had been given to sleep in, knowing that by saving the townsfolk the three men had effectively opened a locked box of misery for themselves.

None of them could remember exactly what it had been like when they had been one person. It was a subject they danced around. An unvoiced wound.

Like the Vaerli, the Ahouri were a condemned race, but even more deeply affected than the original inhabitants. They'd been blown apart by the very powers that had made them enemies of the Caisah. No one knew if they could ever reforge themselves into the once-powerful Form Bards.

Equo had not thought about it for a very long time, and yet change was in the air. Perhaps Si was right—now could be their moment, as well. Finally, he fell into a restless and troubled sleep.

Sometime just before dawn, Varlesh walked to the boat. His feet were quiet but his nearing presence woke Equo instantly. "Don't think too much on it, boyo."

He chuckled at his other's humor. "I'm as old as you, Varlesh, or don't you remember? And besides, this is what I do . . . think."

"If we all stuck to what the Shattering had done to us, it would have been a boring couple of centuries."

"But we still conform. You act, I think, and Si—he just is."

"He is our soul and our magic, maybe even our conscience."

"It doesn't matter." Equo pulled himself out of the coracle, working out the kinks in his neck as best he could. "We'll still die apart, and probably sooner than later."

Varlesh twiddled his pipe in his fingertips. "You have been thinking too much, and not enough, as well. Why do you think the song came back to us now and not before?"

Equo was just about to reply when Si appeared at his shoulder.

"Quiet," Si commanded, being much more direct than was usual. The air had stilled. Even the slapping of the waves somehow sounded distant and the calls of the marsh birds were totally gone.

"I think they've found us!" Equo turned and frantically waved to Nyree, whom he could see sitting outside one of the huts. She only waved back cheerily.

"Don't frighten her, lad." Varlesh turned his eyes toward the sky. "It is us they come for—not them."

Varlesh had never been a great reader of the pitiless. It didn't matter to the Caisah that the villagers were mostly the young and old. They had defied him.

The Swoop came diving from amongst the clouds like a rain of beating wings and sharp beaks.

With a sharp oath, Varlesh drew his long hunting knives and charged back up the beach to where the first of the birds were beginning to flicker into women. Following, Equo drew his short sword, though his heart was bleak indeed. No force apart from the Kindred themselves could compare to the might of the Swoop.

Once employed in the name of the Lady of Wings, they had become something far less forgiving in the hands of the Caisah. The women were all unnaturally young and unnaturally strong. They appeared from the mist of their bird forms clad in the sky-blue armor of their scion with steel blades of icy purity. Their faces reflected no emotion as they flung down their enemies and dispatched them, man, woman, and child. Everywhere was panic. Equo glimpsed the headwoman fighting with her granddaughter in the shadow of their crannog house—but could not reach her.

Varlesh roared like a mad bear and charged a group bent on dealing the last blow to an old woman cowering on the sand before them. They blew away from him in a cloud of feathers and condensed with chill focus. For one so large, Varlesh moved with graceful economy. Catching two ringing blows on the edge of his blade, he danced farther away, daring them to follow. They did, eyes gleaming with anger that anyone would dare to threaten them. Varlesh backed away a little, jaw tight with concentration, muscles bunching in readiness. The one on his right darted in, her long blade flashing, but she was too confident. He had seen the stroke long before it arrived. Ducking under it, Varlesh scooped up a piece of net discarded by one of the villagers and gave the woman a thump on her rear with it as he passed by. She squawked in protest—dignity offended more than anything.

Equo shook his head. Sometimes Varlesh did not know when to joke and when to be in deadly earnest. These were not the type of women to play games with. One might have been overconfident, but the others had learned from her mistake. A third had joined the circle, ready to attack Varlesh from the rear.

With a little prayer, Equo realized he had to join this particular battle. His skill was not with a blade, yet he could hardly stand by and watch part of himself be killed. He had hoped to somehow land in front of this newcomer, but his ham-fisted attempt at a rescue suddenly turned into a tussle as he landed instead on her back.

It was like grabbing a wildcat. Women of the Swoop were no more used to be manhandled than they were being patted on the rear with a net. Knocked over, Equo found himself rolling about on the ground, trying to stop the woman getting up and running him through for his impudence. He tasted dust and every part of his body was battered, but he hung on grimly, knowing it would end quickly if he did not.

A fierce high note broke through the sounds of battle, the sound of Si calling up their power. The Swoop stilled—blades hung unused, cries lodged in their throat, all violence frozen. Equo opened his mouth and quickly sang the counterpoint even as he heard Varlesh drop his sword and do the same. Si's song might hold them a little while, but they needed the full strength of the Union. If there was one thing the Ahouri knew, it was the magic of shape, and that was what Si had called. Equo smiled around the music pouring from his mouth, wondering if it would work.

The Lady of Wings would never have allowed them to meddle with what was hers. The Caisah's power, however, was of Conhaero. He commandeered the Swoop to its loss.

The Union wrapped itself around the women, breaking and dividing the threads that held their bird shapes in check.

The magics resisted, trying to hold true to their nature, but this was the real strength of the Union. The Vaerli had the Chaos. The Ahouri had Shape. With heightened senses the three men saw the strands of power unravel abruptly, as if the strings were suddenly cut.

The air was suddenly full of birds, screaming, flapping, and clawing their way into the sky in indignation. Feathers of all colors fluttered in the air. The smell was sharp and bitter.

Varlesh yelled in delight, while waving his hands. "Get out of here, you blighted creatures! Flee!"

Si was smarter still. He darted forward with a piece of his jacket wrapped about his arm and snatched the great white eagle out of the air, just as she broke in fright. He snapped her up like a glorious chicken flying the coop. His hands clenched tightly around those mighty talons. Si held her, flapping and screaming, away from his body, least she tear him apart.

"A binding," Varlesh yelled, rushing forward, the sound already in his mouth.

Equo took his hand, giving the melody throat, before reaching out to touch Si lightly on the back of the neck. It was he who whispered the thread of magic to the screaming bird that was Azrul, captain of the Swoop.

The eagle ceased to struggle, hanging limp in Si's hold, with wings arched down to hang in the dirt. The great curved beak panted open as the avian tongue vibrated with panic.

Equo felt a great sadness run through him. The scion's emissary should not be reduced to such a situation. He took the eagle from Si, letting her gain a foothold on the shredded coat. She offered no resistance, probably horrified to find herself trapped within the shape of the eagle. He got Varlesh to tear a strip of cloth and tie it around the eagle's eyes.

"It does seem a little cruel to keep her so," he commented.

Varlesh snorted into his whiskers. "With her as hostage we might be able to keep the Swoop away for a time, and she's much easier to control like this."

"I don't think Si meant to keep her as a surety."

They could have argued further, but the headwoman of the village came rushing over to them. Her flamboyant orange turban was stained dark with her own blood, yet she did not appear to notice the head wound that caused it.

"Isi," she gasped, grabbing hold of Varlesh's arm as her long knife dropped to the sand.

"Is she hurt?" Equo waved urgently to get Nyree's attention.

"No, no," the headwoman sobbed. "They took her. They said she would tell them where the gathering was, or they would drop her from the sky."

Nyree had run over just in time to hear the end of the conversation. Everyone craned their heads back, scanning the cloud of retreating birds. It was true. They'd been so consumed with getting the eagle caged that they had not noticed the slight shape of the girl borne aloft by the Swoop.

The Vaerli woman wrapped her arm around the distraught headwoman's shoulders. "Will she tell them?"

Barely were the words out of her mouth when they saw the girl fall: a small struggling shadow against the pale clouds. The crowd drew in its collective breath, but did not cry out until she had crashed into the forest below.

The headwoman tilted her head proudly upright while tears carved their way down her cheeks. "She did not."

The Swoop banked abruptly southwards. The headwoman looked away sadly, and she offered only choked words. "Baraca's gathering is to the south at Lake Quene. Isi was young. She must have been very afraid." She looked up, her expression clenched with hate. "They still let her fall."

Equo suddenly realized that everyone was looking at them. Varlesh pulled him aside, while Si trailed in their wake.

"Baraca's rebellion will be over before it starts," Varlesh whispered. "Who knows how many Portree youngsters like that girl will be killed."

Equo nodded. "Perhaps we have a song to warn Baraca, or maybe get us there before them."

The three of them wracked their brains but came up with very little. They had forgotten many of the songs, while others were beyond their current range. The High Songs were required now, and those were still lost to them.

"No," Equo said, raking his hands through his hair, "there is nothing to get us there before the birds."

"Maybe not for you." Nyree was looking at them from under darkened brows, her hands clenched at her side. "I will not let any more children be killed if I can help it. How long have we got?"

Equo did some quick mental calculation. "Quene is at least three weeks away by foot, a week or more even by river, but the birds will get there faster."

"They will need to find the warm air currents up over the mountains," Varlesh reminded him.

"So," Equo sighed. "Unless you have some way of getting us there by tomorrow evening, it will be too late."

"In that case," Nyree said, taking the still-trembling eagle from Si, "I will lead you through the White Void to warn the rebels."

"You can't do that," Equo gasped, just as his companions raised their own voices in protest. "It is far too dangerous!"

"Oh really?" She smiled sweetly. "I can go back to the sanctuary and continue as if nothing has happened, can I? Sleep on happily while all those poor Portree are massacred?"

They all blinked at her sudden display of anger.

"Good then," she snapped, gathering up her skirts. "I will decide what I will and will not risk. Now follow me."

Just like that, the Vaerli took charge. Equo didn't know what to expect of the White Void, but if Nyree's pale, strained look was anything to go by, it would be at least an unforgettable experience.

Byre dreamed of his sister. He saw the shadows around her as she walked away from the light. He called out to her, nightmare making his voice thin and tiny. She glanced back once and he realized her face was that of a Kindred stretched in horror.

He called out her name—her true name that she could no longer claim—and chased after her, but the darkness would not let him. His outstretched fingers ran right through her as though one of them were made of smoke. Hot tears were running down his face as he yelled her name, even as she receded into the darkness.

He woke with a gasp into his father's angry face. "Even in your sleep, you must not call that name."

Byre bit back his own anger. Talyn had done many terrible things, so he understood the place she'd been driven to. Surely her name was still something she could come back to, but even though Retira was his father, he hadn't earned a window into Byre's thoughts yet.

"Where are we?" he asked instead.

The sternness drifted from his father's face, and Retira pointed to the top of their pod. It was glowing a soft green, as though held up to a bright light. "Nearly there."

Byre fingered his fighting stick and thought of his sister again. It was strange that she had come to him in such a place and at such a time. He had dreamed more in the last few months than he had in all his life—well, as far as he could recall. Being *nemohira*, his memory was selective.

If his father was keeping all his memories, the consequences could be grave. He looked at his father, searching for the signs of insanity, but Retira was only smiling slightly. It was not the mad grin it should have been. "I had to, there had to be one who remembered it all; someone to hold all the history within them. It has been a most . . . enlightening experience learning how to read expressions rather than thoughts."

Byre blurted out, "Why would you try and remember everything? That is a path to madness."

"Vaerli are not . . . well, they are not all that they might be. We chose to forget those things that we should have remembered."

He was teetering on the edge of revelation. Byre could see his father was making a choice, to speak or to refrain. He knew he was being judged.

"Tell me."

Retira looked away. "Perhaps it is better that you do not know your people, my son. Perhaps that is your blessing."

"I want to know them! I'm not one of them until I do."

The decision was made behind his father's eyes. "Then my silence is your best protection."

Byre would have spoken, tried to draw him back, but the pod lurched to a stop and the moment was lost. Retira got to his feet as the top of the pod peeled back, and Byre followed him. "Welcome to Achelon," his father said, and stepped aside so that Byre could take it all in.

Many secretive peoples had come to Conhaero from the White Void. When the Vaerli called, those that had answered had been races and religions pursued or persecuted in their own world. So it was natural that those lesser in number than the Manesto chose to hide. The Phaerkorn with their blood rites were easy to fear, but the Choana who called themselves World Builders were less well known. They had quickly taken themselves to the long white wastes of Conhaero. Centuries of foolish adventurers died blue and frozen trying to reach them.

It was strange indeed, then, that as Byre stepped out into their world he was suddenly hot and drenched in sweat. He climbed from the pod out onto a surface of polished black stone and looked up into the roof of the earth. After so long in half-light he was dazzled, which was totally confusing, until he realized the ceiling was lit with clusters of gleaming crystals.

Once his eyes adjusted, he took the rest in. The vast cavern was almost totally covered by a sprawling plant mass of which their pod was part. It looped and curled around boulder and rock to hold aloft the vaulted ceiling. Carved into every portion of its thick trunk were houses, doors, and windows, while long suspended gangways linked them all. They stood out from the plant that gave them form, brightly painted and cheerfully human among all the greenery.

No snow or ice could reach this place, and looking around, Byre could only marvel at the scale and beauty of the work. At this the lowest level, he could also see pods, much like their own, lying quiet and still. It was obvious that the inhabitants of Achelon were not nearly as isolated as the rest of the world imagined.

"The Choana like to travel." Retira was scanning the row of doors at the level on which they stood.

Byre now understood why they were called World Builders. The temperature was balmy, the faint light of the rock crystals was nearly as bright as that of the sun, and the Caisah had never been here. He was still turning about trying to take it all in, when a woman emerged from one of those doors and ran toward his father.

Byre's stick came up, ready to knock back her attack, but Retira caught his hand. The woman, wrapped in purple silks, threw herself into his father's arms. It was strange with the memory of Mother overlaying it. Byre stepped back in confusion.

The woman was tall and had to bend her blonde head to kiss Retira. She was laughing, as well. They spoke quickly in a strange language and hugged easily.

It was an awkward moment, no doubt of that. Yet if his father had found happiness with another woman, he would be churlish to be angry. Three hundred years was long enough to mourn, even for a Vaerli.

Retira pulled away and spun the woman around. "Forgive me Byre, this is Moyan. Moyan this . . . this is my son."

Byre found himself embraced with great vigor, and Moyan kissed him on both cheeks. Up close she was beautiful, not in the Vaerli way, flawless and untouched, but in the way of mortals. Her blue eyes were surrounded with a fine web of lines; her hair was gray at the temple but still thick and heavy. She must laugh often, for the history of each one was written on her face. Byre had read that many Vaerli despised the signs of age, but memories of his foster mother made them beautiful to him.

Moyan turned to Retira, her voice husky with emotion. "I am so glad you found him—but what about your daughter?"

He shook his head sadly.

Byre gritted his teeth, mindless to the words of consolation the woman murmured to his father. He turned his mind from anger and instead examined the rows of houses that towered above him. It was a large place, bigger than Perilous certainly, and thus any of the known cities in Conhaero. Yet it brought no warmth to him, as a haven from the Caisah should have. Perhaps it was the silence. Apart from the woman's constant stream of words, there was no other sound in the whole place. A great city such as this should have echoed with the noise of many.

Nothing stirred and no people could be seen along any of the balconies.

"Is this a ghost town?" he asked Moyan, as his skin began to crawl.

"It is the festival of Souls," Moyan replied evenly. "Families will spend the next few days indoors. Come home, Retira, it is not wise to be out."

The mention of "home" reminded him he still knew nothing of Retira's life since the Harrowing.

Byre cleared his throat. "Why is that?"

The woman exchanged a look with his father. "The earth lets forth the souls of the dead."

"The Great Cleft opens," Retira said holding his gaze steadily, "and you may enter."

The smile froze on Moyan's face and her fingers tightened on his father's shoulder.

"It's all right darling," Retira murmured.

Her eyes were wide and somehow desperate. "You know what it is then—the Cleft? You can't let him go there!" She gestured wildly, as if to suggest they might as well climb into another of the strange pods and leave.

Retira's face sagged and he passed a weary hand over his face. "I am sorry, Byre. I should have told you sooner; the Cleft is the place we call Ellyria's Gate."

The overwhelming fear from his dreams rose up all around him. Byre took a step back. Even in a land of chaos there were places, special and sacred places, which stood still. V'nae Rae and the Bastion were the most well known, but there were others, some that had never even been seen by Vaerli. The stories of Ellyria's trials were the first tales whispered to children, and the Gate was where she stepped from the mortal world into the realm of the Kindred.

His father was talking, his voice soothing, but the words were lost on Byre. It all made sense, the pain, the glimpses of Kindred, and the fire that had haunted his dreams.

"You can see it now." Retira's hand rested heavily on Byre's shoulder. "Another as innocent and brave as Ellyria must go to the Kindred—must offer himself up for trial if the Gifts are ever to be returned to us."

Byre laughed aloud. It was terrible irony that he had only just escaped one torture to be thrown into another. Only, the fires of the Kindred would be worse—far worse than anything humanity could dream up.

He shook off his father's hand. "You rescued me for this? Your own son a sacrifice to creatures you are too afraid to face yourself!" How the Sofai must have laughed after he had left her caravan—the sacrificial lamb having to find its own way to the altar.

"No," Retira's voice shook. "Do not say that. If I could, I would have given myself to that place decades ago—but I cannot. The sacrifice must also be one from the line of Ellyria, and it was your mother who was of that blood."

Moyan shot Retira a disgusted look. "You used me for this? Is this the only reason you claimed to love me, to get access to the Cleft?" She shot them both a withering look, and spinning on her heel, ran back to the houses.

Byre took a deep breath while watching his father trying to conceal his tears. Looking down at his boots in a confused mixture of rage and embarrassment, he tried to let his thoughts get beyond the pain he had seen in his vision.

One fact remained that did help: Ellyria had survived. Despite the pain of the Kindred's tests, she had triumphed, winning the Gifts for her people. Concentrating on that fact, keeping it before him like a good-luck talisman, Byre rested his hand on his father's shoulder.

They bleakly stared at each other for a while. Byre broke first, hugging his father hard. He noticed something else. Retira was thin, lighter than he remembered, and so much smaller too. It could not all be childish recollection. Whatever Byre had to suffer, his father had already given up more. He'd given up any chance of reunion with his people and his children by shedding the Gifts. He had even cut loose the ties of immortality and would die soon enough, perhaps never seeing the ending of the Harrowing.

Compared to that mighty sacrifice, Byre's chance to take the trials was insignificant.

"Forgive me, Father," he whispered, pulling back and holding Retira at arm's length. "I spoke rashly. I know you would have done this if you could."

"If there was another way . . ."

"Ellyria survived, Father. She triumphed, and I will gladly attempt the same."

His father smiled grimly, but Byre wondered if he was thinking the very thing he was. Ellyria was a hero. Byre barely even knew his own race. He hugged his son tight until Byre could feel nothing but the warmth of his arms.

Retira spoke into his ear. "When the way opens, I will show you to the place, Byreniko. I will wait for you there until you emerge."

Byre clutched his father and hoped that he could believe him. Neither was ashamed of the tears on their cheeks.

"Come then," Retira said gruffly. "Let me soothe Moyan's feelings, and then we can get some rest."

Byre turned to follow him, but just as he did a cool breeze touched his face. It was strange; it had no place in this vast cavern, surely. He couldn't understand it, yet his head felt clearer than it had for weeks and somehow a smile was on his lips.

Then the mist came pouring down from the rock above, enveloping him like a cloud. Though he called out, somehow he knew Retira would not hear.

A face formed in the mist, dark and beautiful, with sloe eyes and a curved mouth in which he could see the faintest of tipped teeth. The body that gradually resolved from the mist was tall, dark, and spare. The woman smiled and spoke softly. "Do not go with your father."

"Who are you?" he asked, noticing how she very much resembled the

Sofai in beauty and age. However, there was something else that made him think they had met before.

"You already know." The mist was condensing, somehow adding to her solidity. Stepping forward she took his hand. "Part of her is in me, and that means I am part of you as well."

"My sister." Her skin was warm against his, warmer than it should have been. Byre could feel the reaction it provoked in his own. He closed his eyes at the joy of it and images flashed through his brain, a blue-eyed man who made her heart leap, a floor that seemed to be made of gold flickering like flame, and a Blood Witch who fought for her prize. Anger and determination boiled through him, and he knew it was not his. His strength was nothing compared to his sister's; it burned hot enough to consume.

With a gasp Byre pulled his hand away from the Witch he now knew was called Pelanor. "She sent you to save me." It was a wonder that any thought of family still survived in the pit of pain and rage his sister had become.

The Witch was staring at him. "You have similar eyes, but yours are full of something else . . . is it light? You must not die; it is the agreement Talyn and I made."

The kindness in her voice was unexpected and strange from a Blood Witch. He thought of his sister's face and that one brief moment when they had sought each other out. He recalled the broken bodies of his foster parents hung out to rot for the crime of taking in a Vaerli child. He remembered the moments in the torture cell when he had touched for a second the Gifts of his people, and felt all their despair and agony wash over him.

Like every creature that drew breath, Byre did not want to die, but neither did he want to go back to the existence of nothingness where he floated through his life and it was always so hard. If there were a way to find his people again, to talk to them, to hold their hands, then he would risk his immortality for it. He didn't know what the Phaerkorn saw in his eyes, but it was not hopelessness anymore.

Byre shook his head, looking toward the passage his father had disappeared down. Talyn still cared, which was good for her, but what he had learned from Retira meant he could not care about his own safety any more than Ellyria had.

The Blood Witch had made a Pact with his sister, and he would be unable to get past her if it came to that; no Vaerli without the Gifts could. So he took the chance of taking the Witch's hands in his own. They were warm with Talyn's blood. "I can't leave my father now . . . not when we are so close. Surely you have someone you would not abandon?"

He squeezed her fingertips, praying she knew what he meant. Pelanor's smooth brow furrowed and the corner of one of her teeth bit her lip. Byre was certain he was about to end up face down on the cold stone floor, but then she laughed. "You obviously have more winning ways than your sister. You do remind me of someone most precious. Go, I will watch."

He didn't know what she meant, or what she would do at the Cleft. It was just another complication, thanks to his sister. One he really didn't need.

CHAPTER SEVENTEEN
OLD LOVE

Finn was staring at her, and it was quite unnerving. But Talyn was not about to tell him that.

The fact was, most breathing prisoners avoided looking at her. Finnbarr the Fox, though, watched her: sometimes out of the corner of one eye, sometimes brazenly over the fire as they traveled north toward the Bastion.

Perhaps the problem was that he didn't fully realize he was her prisoner. Maybe he thought that she'd saved him from the Named for some heroic purpose. Or maybe he was just full of foolish romantic notions—thinking he could influence her after that kiss.

Talyn put him right on that score on the second day. "I'm taking you directly to the Caisah as soon as we've been to the Bastion."

"I thought you were supposed to take me straight to Perilous." Right then, Talyn knew how much trouble he really was. Finnbarr the Fox was grinning. No one had ever talked to her like this. She should have stepped over the fire and backhanded his smile into the sand. That's what she should have done.

The sad reality was, she was weak. Whenever Finn's hands touched Talyn, or his breath tickled her neck as they rode, her skin warmed. The Hunter could only be glad he couldn't see the blood rush to her cheeks.

Talyn did not reply but glared at him menacingly. He looked back steadily.

Finn was a hard man to resist because his charm was the subtle kind that did not assault directly. A small smile, a little laugh, and somehow she could feel herself defusing. It was so strange—this gentle a man in a world of violence. Talyn had never met the like before.

Even now, with bitter words lying between them, there was no vinegar in his voice or accusation in those eyes.

Talyn flung the remains of her too-hard bread into the fire and tried not to think about what it might mean.

Finn shrugged and took out the curious length of string he'd been playing with for days.

Although he plainly expected no justification from her, Talyn still found herself giving some. "There is a place I must visit before I hand you over—the Bastion. I have business to attend."

He stared at her over the fire. "You're taking me there? It's sacred to the Vaerli. Only they can walk the Salt."

It was annoying to be told her own people's history. "I must go, therefore you must go."

She'd made a mistake. Finn was frowning; he knew that as the Caisah's Hunter she'd never failed to deliver her bounty.

"Don't worry," Talyn snapped. "I will still get you to V'nae Rae."

She turned away, rolled into her blankets, and pretended to sleep. Not long after, she heard Finn curl up. She lay there listening to his breathing for what felt like hours before finding any rest herself.

It took another day riding fast into the Chaos before they reached the edge of the Salt Plains, and from there all speed ceased. Even a nykur like Syris could not blur into the plains.

It was the second most sacred site to the Vaerli, gifted to them by the Kindred as eternal. From its outmost limits, it was four days of arduous walking and a journey Talyn had never imagined making again.

She slipped down from Syris' back and looked calmly over the gleaming white plain where she had last seen her mother. The wind blew hard and sharp from the innermost reaches, and somewhere out there many bones would be gleaming on the Salt.

Finn drew a ragged breath and shaded his eyes to see past the glare. However, there was nothing to see—only a desolate expanse of white, cracked and pitted.

"Once," Talyn found herself speaking, "you would have never been able to set foot on that plain. To even touch it was to endure painful death for anyone not Vaerli . . . but the Caisah crossed it and the power was broken. Now anyone can walk the Salt."

"Not anyone. Even now it doesn't look that friendly."

"It isn't. You'd be blind within a day unprotected." She tore off the ragged hem of her tunic and held it out to him. "Bind your eyes with this. You should still be able to see enough to manage, but hopefully the glare won't wreck your vision."

"I'm sure the Caisah will appreciate that." He trusted her, taking the fabric without question. "You will still have to lead me."

Talyn dropped her eyes before Finn did. "There are other things on the plain, too." She pressed one of his hunting knives into his hand. "Just in case."

"You're only letting me have this because you're arrogant enough to think I am no danger, but what happens when you are asleep?"

"Vaerli sleep little, but lightly," she said with a smile, "and besides, even with my eyes closed I can bring you down."

Most men would have grumbled at that, their honor pricked, but Finn simply shrugged and put the knife into his boot without further comment.

"We leave Syris here." She was already removing the slim saddlebags from the nykur's back. "Some things on the Salt are drawn to his kind, and we don't need the attention."

Syris smashed his foot contemptuously into the fringes of the Salt, making her laugh. Rubbing his cheek, Talyn blew gently into his nostrils, sharing breath, reassuring him. As always, there was no need for words between them; he would wait until the sun burned out of the sky for her to return.

With that somewhat melancholy thought, Talyn turned and nudged Finnbarr the Fox out into the white plain.

Her Vaerli eyes darkened and adjusted, narrowing to tiny slits, adapting to the conditions as her kind always had.

The walk to Bastion was a test in itself. It was always taken on foot and was always hard. It was traditional to travel without food, thus exposing the Vaerli to the elements, bringing their usual proud nature low. Reaching the Bastion was supposed to be a humbling experience, but looking at Finn, she just hoped this time to make it alive. Before the Harrowing, crossing the plain was tiring but not dangerous when the Seven Gifts protected the Vaerli. Times had changed.

The first day was the worst. Nothing rose against the horizon to break the monotony; there was only the thick white glare and a remorseless sky of blue. Talyn could already feel parts of her beginning to burn away under it. If it were not for the ever-constant need to lead Finn, she might have even enjoyed the sensation.

The truth of the matter was, with his eyes bound, he was reliant on the Hunter. In fact, even if his eyes were as well equipped as her own, he would still have been at her mercy. Only her people's memory could lead them through the featureless white.

At first she was callous and let Finn trail stumbling in her wake. His feet caught on the cracked earth and he fell, cursing, several times. Each time Talyn did not pause, though she listened to hear his complaints. None came.

The fifth time she swung around in exasperation and pulled Finn to his feet. He clenched his fingers tightly on hers. "I apologize. I don't make a very good blind person."

Talyn caught the twitch of a smile in the corner of his lips, and despite her annoyance she could only admire a man who, while being a prisoner, blindfolded and in deadly peril, could still find something amusing in the situation.

"I doubt if I was in your place I would be laughing," she said.

He tugged the protective cloth down farther about his eyes. "I don't know, mistress Vaerli. When you're at the bottom, sometimes the only comfort is a little laughter."

She suspected he was trying to tell her something about her own situation, but she let him get away with it for now. Instead, Talyn pulled him closer. "Well, much as it amuses me to see you fall every three steps, it will slow us down." Tucking his hand into her sword belt, she challenged him, "Keep pace with me, or I'll drag you on your belly all the way to the Bastion."

And Finn did, matching her stride for stride so easily that she almost was tempted to break into a run just to test him. What was even stranger was that he decided to talk to her.

Undaunted by neither her silence nor her reputation, Finn began to tell her stories. He recited tales of her own people—which was an uncomfortable sensation. She'd not heard those tales for three hundred years, and never from a person not Vaerli. After she got over her irritation, it was soothing to hear stories of the Pact, the Kindred, and the Seers of the past. When he got to the tale of the Harrowing, Talyn drew the line. "Not that story . . . not here."

He didn't comment, instead telling her his own tale. Slowly she was drawn into Finn's past, his world of stories and hope and frustration. He opened up his experiences, that of a mortal man in the Caisah's domain. He took her into the frightened underbelly of inns and farms, where people were uncertain and terrified of the land they lived in. She could smell their sweat and hear their

HUNTER AND FOX ✿ PHILIPPA BALLANTINE

cries when the Chaos storms roared. He also talked about the hope: not just hope for them, hope for her own people too.

"You . . . you have met other Vaerli?" Talyn found her throat was tight about the words.

"Yes. I wanted to find out their stories. Everyone says they are a proud race, short on words. I think since the Harrowing they have changed—for they seemed eager enough to share them with me."

"There is no law against it," she whispered.

"I'm glad. It was good to hear their tales."

Talyn cleared her throat. "How did they look?"

"Haunted and very sad; like they are waiting for something but don't know what."

"You would know that better than I. In fact I have not seen a Vaerli in centuries . . . except . . ." She caught herself before she could tell Finn about seeing her brother or her father.

Under the blindfold it was hard to read his expression. He quickly filled in the awkward gap, pattering out stories of his childhood by the sea, miles of slippery seaweed and rock pools, seahorses and adventures on boats. It sounded idyllic and rather unreal.

Reality, though, had its own way of intruding; not all the guardians of the Bastion slept during the day. The perfect white salt began to ripple, almost imperceptibly at first. Talyn halted, eyes scanning the surface, straining all her senses. At her side, Finn was still talking, unaware under his blindfold of anything untoward.

"Quiet!" Talyn clamped down on his arm. Immediately he was silent, tilting his head and trying to hear what had got her attention.

It was no sound. It was a tickling sensation on the back of the neck, the faintest of tremors up through the soles of her boots. Her mind raced, recalling all the guardians and weighing up which it could possibly be.

The Salt exploded around them with an almighty bang. White spears as tall as a man erupted from the ground. A dozen or so surrounded them both in a threatening semicircle.

Finn had pushed his blindfold off and was squinting around him. The salt pillars shuddered, thin streams pouring off them, revealing faces of pure white malevolence carved like ancient warding masks. They were all teeth and rolling eyes.

Feeling rather than seeing Finn reach for that dagger in his boot, Talyn stayed his hand. "Don't move. They are the Old Souls of the Vaerli, ancestor-spirits, they are only here to see me. They won't attack one of their own. Stay near. It will be all right."

The talespinner shifted close until his length was pressed against her and his breath was right on her ear. Taking his hand, Talyn drew him toward a path between the pillars. Barely had they taken a step before the gap was closed by another springing up there. The snarling faces turned toward them.

"Tell me again they know you," Finn whispered with an edge of urgency.

Talyn was genuinely surprised. She was Vaerli, and they were meant to be guardians of the Salt. They should not have barred her way. None of her people's stories explained this, nor told her what to do next.

The faintest of tremors warned her just a moment before they would have been killed. Pushing Finn away, Talyn stepped back, but only enough to allow the sharp spear to pass in front of her toes. Drawing her pistol, she blew the face into a stinging rain of salt.

The rest of the pillars dropped, collapsing with the sound of thousands of crystals and a distant ominous rumble.

"Move," she yelled and pulled Finn to his feet.

"But they're gone . . ." He staggered, for the ground was beginning to shake strongly enough for even the fool of a talespinner to feel.

If she'd been by herself, Talyn knew there would have been little danger. Her reflexes could have kept her ahead of the emerging pillars. It might have even been fun. Yet she wasn't—and left alone, Finn would have been dead in an instant.

They ran hard, ducking and rolling according to Talyn's before-sense. Her throat became raw from yelling directions at the hapless man, her eyes stung with salt, and she was suddenly soaked in sweat under her armor. If she let go of his arm, things would be much easier.

However, that would be failure. Talyn couldn't spare a second to glance at Finn, too busy listening to her Gift and trying to keep them both alive.

Unbelievably, Talyn saw a rocky outcrop rising from the plain. It stood out against the horizon and offered hope against all reason. She could be fairly sure it had not been there the last time she came this way, and absolutely positive it hadn't been there a few moments before.

Talyn hesitated for a heartbeat, trying to find a path, and tugged too slowly on Finn. A pillar speared up and the talespinner was suddenly down, while ruby blood stained the Salt in shocking contrast. Finn was going to be impaled as another rumbled up from below.

Forced to dive atop him, she rolled desperately to the left. Finn yelled into her ear a mangled expletive.

She ignored him, tumbling them both narrowly past more pillars. Then, pulling Finn to his feet and tugging his arm over her shoulder, she dragged him the rest of the way to the relative safety of the outcrop.

The pillars for a moment danced like white daggers across the surface of the plain, almost in frustration, before subsiding out of sight. Convinced that at least for now they were not in danger, Talyn dropped Finn onto one of the rocks.

After his initial shock, he'd stopped yelling and instead had turned very pale. For once, he was silent.

"A pity I wasn't fast enough." Talyn got down on one knee and proceeded to cut the leather of his pants from his injured leg.

"If that's an apology, I accept," Finn muttered through clenched teeth.

"I confess I am not much practiced at using my Gift to help others."

"Not much call for it in your line of work."

Suppressing a twitch in her mouth, Talyn probed gently around the wound on his leg. It was a real mess. A sharpened length of salt did not cut like a blade, it ripped like rock. Finn's wound was on his inner calf, as long as her forearm and encrusted with salt crystals.

"I bet that hurts. Salting wounds is sometimes used as torture."

His lips were clenched and very white. So there was nothing for it; tearing up one of her spare shirts and wetting it with some of their precious water, she cleaned and bound it as best she could. "A pity the Third Gift is still denied me." A touch of healing for him would have been easier on them both.

"Yes, I'll have to take that oversight up with the Caisah when I see him." Finn shifted himself on the rock, trying to get comfortable.

Talyn sat back on her haunches and looked at him. His eyes were streaming and every inch of exposed skin was red and painful from friction, with unforgiving salt or burns from the sun. He was going to be difficult to move, and even harder to keep alive.

Going to the edge of their fortunate island of stone, she looked out over the salt flat and considered her options. If she left him here, she would probably make it. The pillars were not insurmountable with the Sixth Gift, but he would surely die even if she left him water. But then, perhaps she had been foolish to think the guardians would not be affronted by bringing a stranger to the plain.

If he died she could still get her bounty. It was all perfectly logical.

Talyn rubbed the back of her neck, shifting uncomfortably. No, it would be better to keep him alive. But how? If they stayed here, they'd both eventually die.

"Reached any conclusions?" Finn's voice sounded steadier. Talyn stayed quiet, not willing to risk letting him know her thoughts.

"I'd be all right if you left me some water."

She went back and sat next to him, making a show of reloading her pistol. "You'd be dead within a few days, and rather unpleasantly."

"It's nice to know you'd want to share dying with me."

Talyn laughed despite herself. "We can wait and see how attractive I find that. Perhaps the guardians will lose interest in us. Whatever happens, I'll outlast you; this is my world, remember."

"This is the longest conversation we've had since the Caisah's party. I should have known death would bring out the best in you." Finn shifted his leg and again grew pale under his tanned skin.

"You're not really the stoic type, are you?" She primed and charged the pistol before ramming it and laying it at her side.

"Expecting those pillars to come up here?" Finn asked, casting a wary eye on the Salt around them.

"Not that," she replied, leaning back on the rock for a bit of sun, "but there is an ill vibration in the air. I think there are more than just guardians about the Salt today."

Finn didn't reply, just took off his jacket and lay down under it to protect him from the painful rays of the sun. She was amazed how quickly he was able to go to sleep. Talyn, though, couldn't so easily escape her worries.

This was a Vaerli place; nothing here should trouble her. Yet immediately she had been challenged. Only now did she recall the words of the Kindred who had saved Finn at Perilous. If they truly did consider the Pact broken beyond all fixing, then the world would become far more dangerous indeed. It was even possible that another Conflagration could be in the offering, as it had hinted.

The Salt crackled as if disturbed, and a feeling of horror rose up the back of her throat. With a start, Talyn leapt up, clutching up the pistol and cocking it. She roused Finn with the tip of her boot.

A gray haze had obscured the horizon to the north, the direction of the Bastion, and it seemed to be moving closer.

Finn climbed unsteadily to his feet as she wordlessly handed him his second knife. It would be nothing against a guardian, but it was important he not panic. Talyn was grateful he asked no questions, for truthfully her own throat had suddenly become very dry.

The silence in the plain had grown thicker as if a storm was approaching. The air crackled with electricity and both their hair was rising to its command.

Finally the mist halted its advance twenty paces from their island. Shapes moved within, but Talyn could sense nothing else from the Seventh Gift. The before-world was just as shrouded. Still, there was foreboding in the air, making her spine run with shivers and her heart race.

She felt Finn hobble closer to her side; there was strange comfort in that.

Slowly something began to gather in the mist. It was human-formed but not large, and the head was covered in what appeared to be a massive hood. Even as it stepped closer, to the very edge of their rock, Talyn could make out no details of its face. The body was a woman's—only as tall as hers but narrower in hip and breast. It wore a thin white shift that seemed to be part of the mist it had come from.

"Talyn the Dark, you trespass on land no longer yours." The voice from the unseen face was light but bounced oddly in the ears, as if many other voices were whispering a moment behind it. Could this be some sort of Named creature left idle to wander the plain?

"The land belongs to none now that the Vaerli have abandoned it," Talyn replied curtly.

Whatever the creature was, it ignored her reply. "If you give us the Wrong Man, we may allow you to go." The unseen eyes turned toward Finn.

He flinched and took a step back, as if that regard was too weighty to bear.

Talyn frowned. "Wrong or not, he is my prey. Find your own."

"Why, thank you for that," Finn whispered sharply.

"You are blind if you do not see what is in front of you, child of fools."

Talyn surged forward a few paces, before recognizing the creature was trying to goad her out onto the Salt. She didn't need to justify her parents to this thing, but honor was another matter. She raised the pistol and fired it straight at the concealed head. The bullet flew true, but the woman was not there. She had stepped aside in the before-time. So this was what it was like to be on the other side of the Gifts—not a pleasant feeling. Talyn had no time to dwell on the hows or maybes.

The hood was cast back, and the true nature of the creature was revealed.

It could have been her cousin or aunt. The golden-brown skin and dark hair were true Vaerli, but the woman-creature before them was twisted in terrifying ways.

Talyn had seen much in her time, but even she took a step back.

The beautiful face of the woman stared calmly back at her, surrounded by a ring of squirming malformed heads that seemed very like to Kindred shapes. They snapped and snarled around her neck, alternately bulging and retreating in what was obviously agony. She took no notice, eyes fixed on the Hunter in icy calm.

"Do you know us, Talyn?" she asked, and each word was whispered in a circular fashion by the corona of heads.

It was the fault of the Fifth Gift. Though the Hunter couldn't recall seeing any such thing, a shadow lingered in the back of her mind, the memory of recollection. It was elusive and maddening because she badly wanted to know what she was facing. The word "us" made Talyn feel like her head was spinning.

She had almost forgotten about Finn. He rested his hand on her back—a bit too much familiarity, but for once she was glad of human contact.

"What is that?" His voice held no fear, just a boundless talespinner's curiosity.

It was not Talyn who answered. The woman, still wrapped in the mist, held out her hand to him. "Come with us, Finnbarr, and we will reveal all to you."

Even though she was not its target, Talyn felt the woman's power dragging at Finn. With an amazing show of fortitude, he turned away from it.

Putting his hand on her shoulder, he took a few ragged breaths before glancing up with a grin. "Why doesn't she come get me, then?"

It was a good question. It certainly seemed an unremarkable piece of rock, and yet it had appeared suddenly in the nick of time to save them. The earth was the domain of the Kindred.

Stepping around Finn, Talyn glared back with as much conviction as she could muster. "Come claim him, then."

The unearthly necklace of Kindred howled, but the woman barely blinked. "You may live to regret that, little cousin." With that, she stepped back into the haze and was gone as if swallowed. The mist slipped away from them like a ribbon being reeled in from somewhere, taking its mysteries and menace with it.

"I think I'd rather just cook up on this rock like a piece of bacon, first," Finn said with a slight waver in his voice.

"Or I could blow your head off right now, if you'd prefer," Talyn offered.

He glanced at her sideways. "I hope you aren't serious."

Reholstering her pistol, Talyn dropped to a crouch and once more scanned the horizon. "Not now, but give me a few days and we'll see."

Finn laughed and sat down with her.

Let him think it was a joke, but the worrying facts were she had no idea what they were facing. A creature with power, that much was obvious, but why such an interest in Finn? Putorae also wanted him at the Bastion, and she had not forgotten the Kindred that had saved him. Talyn was also beginning to wonder if the Caisah's bounty was not solely because of the performance at the dance. For someone who was supposed to be merely an annoying tale-spinner, Finn was attracting interest from a lot of quarters.

Talyn had the disturbing feeling that something momentous was happening to which she was only a bystander.

Still, Talyn kicked herself for not sticking to the plan. If she had, right now she would be collecting another golden piece, that much closer to lifting the Harrowing. Everything had been going much better before she had heard the name Finnbarr the Fox.

With a deep sigh of frustration, she reloaded her pistol once more and tried not to look in his direction.

CHAPTER EIGHTEEN

THE BOUND EAGLE

Traveling with Nyree would have been a pleasant thing—if it were not for the constant fear of the Swoop and the ever-present screeching of their leader. Apparently, eagles were not meant to be kept in cages and bounced around like luggage.

Equo could feel those metallic, golden eyes boring into his back as he followed Nyree up the slope of the hill. The sound of avian revenge was a constant rasping cry, while she attempted to batter her way out of the willow cage the Portree had supplied.

"I can't say I blame Azrul," Nyree said with a sigh. "If I had wings, I could not bear it either."

"Better her in a cage than us," Varlesh called from the rear where he was trying to maneuver their borrowed donkey up the track. The creature was almost as stubborn as Varlesh.

Equo rubbed his sore head and tried to think of something else to discuss. "How much farther until we can Travel, Nyree?"

She paused and wiped her brow. "The Threads of the White Void are tricky things, but if we can find one, we should be able to reach Baraca in an instant."

"Anything to get out of this damn forest," Varlesh muttered, casting a concerned eye around at the thick trees they had been tramping through.

It was true—their surroundings did have an unhealthy feel to them. The branches swung low and were almost always in their faces, while the trees rose so high that it was at times hard to tell if it was night or day.

It was the silence, though, that brought everyone's nerves to the breaking point. It felt as though they were the only living things in the woods. Nothing much stirred in a Chaos forest, but when it did it meant danger. Still, it was near the point where Equo would have been glad of something to break the quiet.

"The White is near. I can feel a Thread nearby," Nyree said in a whisper.

"A handy way to travel." Equo edged closer so his voice would not get too far.

The Vaerli's eyes were unreadable as she looked up at him. "Using them was forbidden by the Pact. They travel through the realm of Chaos, and that was one thing the Kindred would not allow."

Varlesh coughed, not very discreetly. "I hate to stand in the way of us getting where we're going faster—but aren't we worried about annoying the Kindred?"

Nyree waved her hand as if dismissing them like a flock of moths. "Since the Harrowing, they seldom dwell near the surface. We should be all right."

Varlesh exchanged a sharp look with Equo; they both recalled a far more recent meeting with a Kindred. "I do not like the sound of 'should,'" Varlesh grumbled.

Nyree smiled one of her secret smiles. "There are no certainties in life, friend."

Azrul screamed, flapping her wings against the cage, making all of them jump.

The forest got darker and quieter the farther they went in. Equo found sweat was crawling down the back of his neck. After a time even Azrul kept her peace, watching them out of baleful golden eyes.

"Not far now," Nyree kept whispering under her breath. At first Equo wasn't worried about that, but the farther they went on, the more she said it. Each time her voice became softer and somehow more fervent.

She pushed ahead of them just as they broke through into a small clearing. It looked like nothing more than that, but she immediately stumbled and fell into the greenery.

The men all rushed forward. Equo reached her first. Her eyelids were fluttering and her whole body was covered in sweat as if she were on fire.

"What is it?" Varlesh dropped to his side.

"I don't know." Equo brushed her hair back. Now her skin felt strange under his hand, almost as if it was moving. Blue writing began sliding over her body, writhing and scrambling its way up from under her clothing. It was like watching a snake slither across something very precious; it made his own skin crawl.

It transformed Nyree as they watched. It made her familiar face exotic and strange, but it took away none of her beauty. He recalled what she had said, but could not imagine why she was suddenly being claimed by a seerdom that had remained quiet for hundreds of years.

"We need a camp," Si said softly.

While Equo watched, the other two quickly arranged a fire and their camp rolls.

"I don't like pitching here." Varlesh stood at his shoulder. "I cannot see this Thread she spoke of, but the feel of this place . . . it is disturbing."

"I agree," Equo said, "but we don't know what is happening to Nyree. Maybe she needs to be here."

They made their friend as comfortable as possible, wrapping her in blankets and pillowing her head against the ground. Then the sun went down, limiting their visibility and making them even more uncomfortable.

About the same time as the sun disappeared, Nyree's eyes flicked open, staring into nothingness, and she began to scream. The sound was horrible. He could discern words mixed in with animal cries of pain—but in the Vaerli tongue which he did not know.

Equo felt completely helpless. He could only hold her down to prevent her harming herself as she thrashed around, yelling. It sounded like her throat would break. Varlesh paced with fingers jammed in his ears, while Si crouched nearby watching with interest but seemingly unconcerned.

The words on her skin were burning and shifting as if seeking some particular form.

"Perhaps the Union can help," Equo yelled over the screams.

"Her magic," Si's voice pierced the noise. "Hers alone."

Varlesh looked as though someone was pouring hot lead in his ear. "Perhaps if we just gagged her," he suggested.

When it came to it, none of them could bring themselves to—so they got no sleep at all. Instead, they took turns watching as Nyree cried out in words they couldn't understand and pain they couldn't relieve.

The thought was not far from any of the three's mind that the horrors of the Chaoslands could be drawn to the clearing. Whether it was some divine providence or just good luck, they made it through to the dawn.

Somehow, with the rising of the sun Nyree dropped back, limp, alive, and breathing, but unable to be roused. In exhaustion the others slept, wrapped around each other in a heap to keep warm.

Equo woke with someone's foot under his ribs. His first thought was Nyree, but when he glanced, over she was sleeping. The Seer's face looked very different carved with strange blue Vaerli words.

"She rests easy now, but I heard her call." An unfamiliar voice broke the morning stillness.

Equo gazed bleary-eyed up at this new woman standing over him.

She could have killed all of them while they slept, for looking around it was apparent that even Si had not heard her approach. His two companions were still slumbering.

Climbing cautiously to his feet, Equo examined their visitor. She was shrouded in a cloak of deep purple like the night sky just before the dawn. The face beneath was stern, but a carving of mellow brown beauty. She was far taller than he. Equo looked around, but this newcomer seemed to have neither companions nor pack. She simply stood there as if she'd been summoned forth from the Chaos.

Those dark eyes narrowed on him. "I see you, Ahouri, do you see me?"

At his back he heard Si and Varlesh stand, taking positions around him. No form on Conhaero could be hidden from them.

"We see you, Phaerkorn," Si said.

"There is no blood for you here," Varlesh growled.

The Witch smiled with a flicker of brilliant white teeth. "You are supposed to know the truth of all forms, so surely you can see I am not hunting you?"

Equo moved nervously to a spot in front of Nyree. "Depends on how desperate you are."

She sighed and perched herself on the log. "Then let me ease your mind. I have recently drunk from my *gewalt* long and deep. I need nothing from your veins."

"Then why are you here?" Equo tried to remember where he had put his long hunting knife in the chaos of the night before.

"Once, your kind and mine were friends of a sort." The Witch seemed uninspired to move.

"Not friends—allies perhaps, in order to survive the White Void."

She inclined her head. "Our Twelve-Mouthed Goddess and your Trifold Spirit worked well together. Had they not, neither of our races would have survived. Now we must again trust each other." She gestured to the still form of Nyree, whose eyelids fluttered like trapped butterflies.

Equo drew his blade. "You may not have her."

The Witch sighed. "So quick to judge! The Ahouri are much changed. I do not seek Vaerli blood or anything else. I merely came because she called."

"Explain yourself, woman," Varlesh muttered, tugging on his whiskers. "The Phaerkorn have not gotten any more sensible with time."

"One of our number is missing." The Witch's face flickered with a real and deep emotion. "On her first Blood, what is more! She has made the kill and yet she has not returned, and the one she hunted was Talyn the Dark."

For once, even Varlesh was wordless. Equo knew the rites to create a Blood Witch were long, arduous, and often fatal. Not many survived them, and everyone who made it was loved. He could imagine the lengths they would go to in order to find their kin. As for killing Talyn—he would want to see the body before believing it.

"I am her matron, the one who brought her out from the sheep of normal kind, so I feel more . . . responsibility than most. I must find her." She paused, looking down at her perfect curled hands. "I flew in the clouds, a whisper on the air, until I heard this Vaerli say something which drew me here." The Witch leaned forward and peered with narrowed eyes at the *pae atuae* that had now run its course over Nyree's face.

As if on cue, the Vaerli sighed heavily and her eyelids flickered open. Whatever change had happened was not just on her skin. Those dark eyes were now filled with tiny motes of light. Other races had been afraid of the Vaerli before the Harrowing; many had looked at those stars and fallen in love. They said those lights drew out a person's soul and chained it. Fortunately, it was already too late for him.

The Blood Witch fell back, as surprised as any of them. "A real *Hysthshai*—surely a sign to gladden the hearts of your people, Seer."

Nyree got to her feet with a little assistance. "Not just the Vaerli. I saw many things in the darkness—including your people. We are all bound together, and it seems events are rushing toward us in ways I had not dreamed before."

"You Saw something?" Equo asked.

"I Saw many things, dear heart, most of which I cannot understand. It has been a long time since I sat at Putorae's knee." Nyree staggered and leaned against him. "I'm afraid, though. Afraid of what I saw in the shadows."

"The girl needs some rest." Varlesh poked Si into helping him get a decent campfire and breakfast. Azrul, silent since the previous night, shrieked once more from her cage.

Nyree sat down next to the Witch and asked Equo politely to help his companions. The two conversed in low tones, and being excluded definitely distressed him.

"Women's business." Varlesh nudged him. "A Seer must chose carefully what to divulge to whom and when. They can cause untold damage otherwise, so don't take it personally."

"I'm not." Equo sniffed, but then squirmed underneath a disbelieving look. "Dammit, you know me too well."

Leaving the women to it, they soon had a fire going and a reasonable breakfast cooked: wild mushrooms, slices of cured ham, and tack bread fried in the grease.

"Now that is what I call worth getting up for!" Varlesh licked his lips.

"Disgusting . . ." The Blood Witch was pale under her brown skin.

Nyree stood at her elbow, appearing a lot healthier and alert. "Iola will be traveling with us."

"The more the merrier," Equo muttered under his breath, feeling completely shut out of the decision-making process. Despite having excellent hearing, neither Vaerli nor Phaerkorn made a comment.

"Just please don't try to feed me." Their new companion looked away. "Cooked blood smells terrible."

Varlesh shrugged and handed Nyree a plate. "All the more for us."

The Witch drifted off while they ate. Equo watched cautiously until she was gone. "Can we really trust the Phaerkorn?" he whispered.

"They have kept to themselves and have no dealings with the Caisah—we cannot say that about many folk." Nyree chased a mushroom round her tin plate.

It was not an answer, and Equo was worried she had slipped into that annoying trait of seers, evasiveness. He leaned forward earnestly. "But why is she here? Do you think we cannot protect you?"

"It's not about that. I need her help to open a path. Vaerli magic is not what it once was."

At the admission, Equo felt his stomach clench.

"We must reach Baraca today, or it will be too late." Having finished her meal, Nyree handed Varlesh back the plate. The subject was obviously closed. The other three shared a look.

"Did it hurt?" Si leaned across and touched her face where the *pae atuae* had made its trails of hidden words.

She looked surprised—as if for a moment she had quite forgotten what he meant. "No, not really, but it doesn't feel quite like my own skin yet."

Si stared hard at her for a moment before wolfing down the last of his mushrooms.

The others remained silent, but Equo caught Si's eyes across the tiny fire. In his mind was the uncomfortable thought that the last time Si had spoken such a great deal, bad things had happened after. Si was closer to the wildness that had once been the Ahouri's nature. Being Shattered had changed Equo's own perception, but there were things Si sensed that the others could not. Unfortunately, he did not have the ability to tell them directly—Varlesh was the talker.

Nyree knew little of what passed between the three of them. Having finished her food, she set about braiding back her hair in a businesslike fashion. "I will require a little time to open a path for us."

Hearing a trace of concern in her voice, Equo was moved to ask, "Is it dangerous?"

"Anything to do with the White Void is risky. It touches Conhaero in many places, but each opening has its own particular dangers."

They packed up and quenched the fire in silence, watched over by Azrul. The eagle no longer battered her cage; instead her attention seemed locked on Nyree. She shifted uneasily on her perch and tucked her white wings tightly about her as if sensing an oncoming storm.

Unnerved though he might be, Finn still managed to feel tired. They had spent a difficult morning watching the Salt. His eyes burned and every part of his body ached in sympathy. Talyn had used her jacket and a pile of rocks to at least make him a shelter to keep the sun off. He'd thanked her for the thoughtful gesture and asked if she would like to share the shade. The stare he got in return threatened to cool even the salt plain completely.

"There is room enough for one only," she said, "and a Vaerli doesn't hide from the sun—or anything else."

For a moment Finn contemplated asking her if she was afraid to be near him, but somewhere in the progress of the last few days he'd learned a little restraint. The idea of being kicked off onto the Salt had little appeal.

Instead, he dozed fitfully beneath the small shelter and watched Talyn out of the corner of one eye. She was crouched not far off, leaning back on her haunches, pistol resting on the ground close by and sword lying across her thighs. Everything about her was alert and those dark eyes never stopped scanning. It gave Finn the illusion that someone was watching out for him. He wasn't quite foolish enough to think it was any more than that.

Finn passed his time watching her. He liked doing that. Her face had stern beauty, but it was nothing like the wonder it had been when she laughed. Little chance of that now.

Finn's eyes drooped as the heat washed over him. His body felt far away, with only his mind floating in the whiteness.

"She would slit your throat in an instant if the Caisah commanded it." The quiet voice reached him from a nearby dream—or perhaps it was his unconscious.

Talyn was beginning to like him, he was sure.

"What about that poor boy?"

Ysel. Guilt washed over him suddenly—with everything that had happened since Perilous he had almost forgotten the child. All Finn's attempts to make the pattern had failed.

"Don't you want to help him?"

He did, he needed to—but here he was stuck on the salt plain.

"All things are possible." Suddenly the whiteness was not so calm. It was pulling at him. He felt stretched as though every inch of his skin was being flayed alive. He called out Talyn's name. This no longer felt like a dream. He caught a glimpse of her dark hair, a suggestion of hands grazing his arm, and he suddenly knew with dread certainty that it wasn't a dream.

He fell for a long time through the white with the echo of laughter around him. Fear made his heart race and his ears roar. Finn yelled against the blankness of it all until there was no other sound to the world than that.

Then he began to discern patterns in the whiteness, fluctuations that reminded him of the patterns he'd once woven with his fingers. He grasped this suggestion of sanity. Raising his hands to them, he let his mind blend into the lines as they had before. A curious calmness drifted over him, until there was nothing but the patterns and the shifting light.

They resolved themselves into a woman's face and, though the light passed through it, he could still tell it was the face of a Vaerli woman. It wasn't Talyn, though. This face had none of the warring emotions and barely-held dark passions. Instead it was a face of deep peace that made even this frightening in-between place seem safe. Finn smiled—or at least he felt as though he was smiling, even though he was no longer sure he had a face.

"We meet again!" the woman's voice rang through the light.

He was incapable of answering. Perhaps his throat was in the same place as his face.

"You don't remember anything of me, I know that. However, a child knows his mother all the same."

He should have been shocked, horrified, or denied it. Yet a deep core of his being recognized an echo of his own features in her. Blood knows blood. A warmth and peace emanated from her, and a deep sorrow that washed over him.

"You have escaped them this once, my son, but they will come for you again. Remember when the storm is the darkest and blinds you, I will be there. You have my blood in you. Hold tight to it and do not forget your mother."

The light was burning brighter now and whatever strange world he had slipped into was letting go of him. He had the fleeting impression of lips on his forehead and the scent of flowers, and then his body materialized around his senses.

Finn felt an iron grip on his upper arm, more real than anything else. It pulled with a persistence that could not be denied. By sheer pressure of will, Talyn the Dark pulled him back into the real world. He fell into it with a gasp, to find himself lying across her: heart pounding, face-to-face. For the briefest of moments he could have sworn he saw stars in that gaze.

He wanted to tell her how beautiful she was and how much he had missed her despite everything, but the words would not come. It was a real first for him.

"You are no feather," Talyn finally said, rolling him off her with a huff.

"I'm sorry," he stammered leaping to his feet. Was he imagining a blush on her cheek as well? "What just happened?"

"They tried to take you. Somehow they opened the White Void and were pulling you through."

"To where?"

"That I cannot say—but nowhere pleasant, I would think."

Remembering the woman with the ring of heads, Finn shivered. "In that case, thank you."

"I would hold onto your appreciation. I don't know if I have the strength to do it again. My powers, unlike theirs, have their limits." It was the first time Talyn had shown real concern, and the slight crack in her voice made Finn even more nervous.

A light remark, something to break the tension would have been his usual response—this time though he could find nothing. He sat back down under the makeshift shelter and waited.

It didn't take long. She came and sat down next to him, folding her arms around her legs. Finn was aware how close she was—the smell of leather mingling with the strange, spicy scent of her hair and an almost palpable heat against his arm. "What happened to the Kindred that saved you at Perilous?"

That one caught him unawares. He shifted uncomfortably. "Why do you ask that?"

Talyn whirled about and glared at him. "Because there is more to you, Finnbarr the Fox, than meets the eye! A Kindred saved you, the Caisah wants you, and I was told to bring you here by an apparition."

The last one made him blink. "What?"

She only smiled enigmatically and wouldn't explain.

He feigned disinterest and shrugged. "I'm nothing special." He hoped his small gift would make her drop the subject.

"I'll be the judge of that." Her eyes narrowed dangerously. "Now tell me about the Kindred."

"It left me or lost me . . . I can't tell which . . . back at the Caracel."

She considered that for a while, lowering her eyes and seemingly consulting some interior knowledge. "I doubt that. Kindred can develop very fierce attachments. For one to intervene seems to say there is more to you."

"Well," Finn murmured, breaking her gaze with difficulty, "you must be wrong, because it isn't here now."

"The connection remains." She fiddled with the Caisah's pistol. "I think you should call it."

For a moment he couldn't quite believe what Talyn had said, but despite that he could only ask, "How?"

She held out her hand, and after a hesitation he took it. Talyn shook her head. "I never would have thought . . ."

Daringly, Finn squeezed her fingers. "You'd be holding hands with me?"

She laughed, a short, sharp, surprising sound. "No, never would have thought I'd be showing someone not a Vaerli how to do this. Never mind. Close your eyes. Think of the Kindred."

Doing so gave Finn an intense moment of vertigo similar to the feeling of the pattern in the cat's cradle. He could feel Talyn, not just the warmth of her hands but also her presence. She burned through his senses. Finn could smell her and feel her behind his eyes. It felt as though if he reached out, he could crawl inside her head. Her thoughts were not so very far from his . . .

Call for it! Her voice crawled up his spine, reminding him of the task at hand. *Think of the last time you saw it. Think of it coming to you.*

Finn had a hard time recalling what it looked like. It had a tail and wings, but it seemed to have been more . . .

The connection was suddenly broken, and Talyn was throwing his hands away from hers with a shout. "What have you done?" She looked simultaneously horrified and delighted.

Finn blinked, still stunned by the abrupt breaking of the connection. "What?"

Talyn leapt to her feet and now scanned the sky. "You Named him, you idiot—you Named a Kindred!" The delight had faded away quickly. Now she seemed just very, very angry.

"I don't understand."

She dragged him up and pointed back in the direction they had come. Finn didn't understand until he saw the shape of dark wings flying toward them like a spear of darkness against the shocking blue of the sky.

"What . . ." his voice dried up on him. "What is that?"

Talyn growled, "Save me from mad fools! You have summoned something you do not even know the Name of, but it was you who gave it to him!"

Finn felt his stomach drop away. He'd studied at the Master Talespinner's knee. He knew the tales of the Named Kindred. The shape in the sky was drawing closer, and with it a power almost unrivaled in Conhaero.

"Now, foolish man, you will see the power of the Named." Talyn, in a frightening gesture of surrender, sheathed her sword and turned toward the shadow.

CHAPTER NINETEEN

A LOST DANCE

The White Void. Equo looked over his shoulder at Varlesh and Si. Though their people had come through it long ago, it had not lost any of its mystery and danger. Songs of the passing had been lost, along with all their other memories when they were sundered. Still, some deep racial memory made him uneasy.

Shortly after morning, Nyree had asked them to build up the fire and take their places cross-legged around it. Then, as unashamed as only a Vaerli could be, she stripped off her tunic until all she wore was a chased-silver necklace. Equo watched her with a dry throat as she unbound her dark hair. It did nothing to hide her golden-skinned beauty or make him any more comfortable.

He tried to concentrate on the necklace. She must have worn it beneath her clothes all this time. It was an intricate creation—as all Vaerli art was. The swirling silver arms of the World Tree held a small vial of a dark substance. It was very beautiful; nestled there between her breasts, beating with her heart . . .

Equo looked away. Varlesh nudged him hard, so he dared to look back. Now Nyree raised the vial to her lips. A vague shimmer seemed to run down that beautiful form, then she began to dance. Circling the fire with strange shuffling steps, Nyree sang wordlessly. Her voice rose, finding impossibly beautiful notes. A powerful rhythm ran through the song described by the beat of her bare feet on the earth.

Before long, the rest of the group found themselves clapping along with it. Time seemed to flow oddly. Eventually, Equo's hands stung from the clapping and his eyes from the smoke. The whole world seemed to be encompassed by that circle. Reality blurred to nothing. Only the sound and the dance remained.

How long had Nyree been moving? That long black hair was stuck to her body with sweat, and her eyes were fixed to a point beyond any sight. The rest of them swayed to her rhythm, pounded out the circle with her in their heads.

As the pace changed, rising faster and faster, Nyree held out her hand to the Blood Witch. She joined the dance. The two women swung around each other, pounding feet and hands. Finally, as the song rose to a climax, the Witch tore her hand open with her own fangs. Nyree abruptly dropped to her knees as Iola placed her bloody palm against the Vaerli's chest.

She threw up her arms so that the firelight ran down the blue tattooed lines as if they were filling up with something. She called out, the first words in what must have been hours. "I accept!"

The air bent and shifted as white light burst forth from the spot where Nyree stood.

Few things in the world surprised Equo, but he was not of the Vaerli and had no knowledge of the White Void. It spilled out into reality with the power of all nature unleashed. The roar and the fury of it ruptured the trance that Nyree had built—knocking the others to the ground. Through his fingers, Equo peered out into the pure whirlwind of the space between worlds, the agony of which his ancestors had dared to reach this place. It tore at him with its beauty and its peril.

Only Nyree had remained on her feet, staring into that rift. Her dark nakedness was a shadow against its brightness, while her hair streamed in a wild corona. Squinting against the light, Equo saw her help the Blood Witch up. She screamed something into Iola's ear, something that she had to repeat twice. The other woman nodded and then turned away from the Void, running hard to escape its pull. She disappeared into the frantically waving forest.

He had no time to question Nyree about what she had said, for she was now calling to them.

She seemed so fragile, but she was Vaerli, and so they placed themselves in her keeping. Varlesh, pulling the shocked donkey after him by sheer physical strength, went first.

The light took them up and fluttered around the space they had been. The other men followed. Silence beat on Equo's ears painfully until he gave up his own scream unto the Void. The weight was too much, and he was sure they would all be shattered into thousands of pieces.

Then they were through on the other side, blinking and dazed. Varlesh was throwing up into the scrub, while Si gazed about in a dazzled awe. A wave of nausea washed over Equo, and he had to lean against their pack animal for a moment.

"Are we there?" Varlesh asked weakly, standing up and wiping his mouth.

Nyree commandeered a new bundle of clothes from the stunned creature and pulled them on quickly. Equo noticed how her hands were shaking. "Indeed. We are only minutes from the mesa cave."

The surroundings were thankfully not those weird tilted trees, but blasted scrublands.

"Is this the Chaoslands?" Equo asked Nyree, keeping his eyes averted as she dressed.

Lacing up her bodice, she nodded. "The very edge, though. I can feel the Road in the distance, so the mesa cave is not that far."

Varlesh was nervously watching the sky. "Crone's whiskers, we're cutting it close."

Si was solemnly patting the twitching nose of the still-trembling donkey. "Wings, meet their match."

"Here's hoping you're right," Equo said, and pulled the hood of his cloak up as a warm wind began to whip over the hills.

They trailed after Nyree in silence. Watching her closely, Equo noticed that she was not moving as quickly as usual. Now and then, she would stop to wearily push her dark hair out of her eyes. So coming through the White Void had not been without its toll. He would not cheapen her choice by saying anything, though.

Cresting a small rise, the group could see down the rest of the blasted landscape. A broad valley opened up, at the end of which was a huge tabletop rock formation. While this dark red lump of stone was interesting, Equo found his attention drawn to the tent city that had sprung up around it.

"Must be half the Portree tribe down there," Varlesh, still puffing slightly from their ascent, gasped. "By the Crone's whiskers, if the Swoop finds them . . ."

Nyree was already running down the slope with one hand holding her skirts above her knees. The three men exchanged a glance, but if the Vaerli could abandon her pride, then so could they. The donkey protested, but soon all of them were dashing down the hill. Despite the ridiculous nature of the moment, Equo found he enjoyed the run; he stretched his legs, the air raced through his throat, and the wind pressed against his face.

They all staggered to a halt when they reached the valley floor. Varlesh bent over with his hands on his knees. "That wasn't fair—the damn donkey slowed me down!"

Before they could have an argument on just who had won their impromptu race, Equo looked up and realized they were surrounded by young Portree— all armed and all looking less than hospitable.

Before things could turn really ugly, the crowd parted and the tall, burly figure of Baraca strode toward them. The man looked very different from the young, angry Manesto Equo remembered. Time had battered the rebel leader; his forked beard was now pure white, his face profoundly weather-beaten, and most obvious of all was the patch over his right eye. Yet despite all that, he was still taller than anyone else in the crowd, and with arms thick with great cords of muscle. Such a distinctive person could never go into any town unrecognized, but then life in the wild had always been his choice.

Looking them up and down, Baraca took extra interest in Nyree's new tattooed arms. "Welcome to my secret gathering place, Seer." The rebel's face might not be pretty, but his voice was a deep, handsome baritone.

Varlesh bristled. "And what about us, you old bear? Are we welcome?"

The two large men glared at each other like angry combatants, making fake feints at each other, before roaring and embracing. Varlesh had always got on best with the rebel.

"Lost something, I see," he shouted. "Lucky for you that we're out there keeping an eye on you.

While he began to tell the rebel why they were all here, Nyree slipped up to Equo. "There's something different about him, don't you think?"

"Not really; the same old Baraca. He's a bit older and the eye patch is new."

"He is here," Si whispered, taking a hesitant step forward, "and now the wings are too. All is in place."

From the cage on the donkey's back, the eagle screamed, though from delight or fear was impossible to tell. Nyree and Equo turned their faces to the sky. Si was right; out from the clouds were coming the black mass of the Swoop. Dropping down out of the light Equo saw death coming on silent wings.

The warm thermal winds of the mountains had betrayed them, and now there was nothing left to do but fight at Baraca's side.

A Kindred had not been Named since the Harrowing. It was an indisputable fact that Talyn knew. It was also indisputable that it had been done, and by someone not Vaerli.

Glancing across at Finn, she realized that he really didn't understand. As a talespinner he knew the stories, yet he could never understand the raw power of the Kindred and what it truly meant to harness that. Finn was listening to the approach of beating wings, and he had no idea he was a walking impossibility.

Yet, how beautiful he was in that moment before realization hit: bright and fresh and totally unaware of his power. He was so wide open to the world, as she couldn't remember being even when she was a child.

Locked away behind that guileless smile were mysteries she hadn't spotted. The Caisah had perhaps seen deeper into her bounty than she'd given him credit for. Whoever or whatever he was, Finn was an undoubted power to contend with.

The light was being bent now as the Kindred he had Named made its true presence felt. It smashed the air above them, and for a long moment Talyn could not bring herself to look up. If she did, everything would immediately change.

For Talyn, awe had been removed from her life, just like real joy. She'd been a walking ghost all this time, and as long as her eyes stayed down she would not have to face the certainty; she could continue to lie to herself.

However, even a stalwart Vaerli has curiosity, and when she did finally join Finn in staring up at what he had wrought, it was everything and more.

For, Finn had not just been content in Naming a simple being. He had given it a quite specific and powerful name.

He couldn't have known what he did, or the price that would have to be paid later. Perhaps something in the flame of this Kindred called out for greatness and he'd only voiced what he sensed. It was a Name that only two in the past had dared to give. The second had failed in his conviction, knowing what power he was trying to bind, and his torments were Vaerli legend. The other was Ellyria herself, but such bravery was only to be expected of her.

Tears poured down Talyn's cheeks as she stared up at Finn's dragon, and unconsciously her hand caught at his. Such beauty tore away all concerns for safety and life. It pierced through Talyn until it felt as though death was a worthy sacrifice to see such a thing.

Now she understood why no dragon had flown the skies of Conhaero for generations; it was simply too much.

Sunlight streamed off polished golden sides, the air thrummed with the power of its wings, and the eyes of darkest magic stared down at them. Such intelligence and joy beamed from those opal eyes. He was unlike any scaly reptile or any other creature she had ever seen. He was larger than the great ships of the Portree and darkened the Salt with his billowing shadow.

Every line was smooth and beautiful like some exquisite drawing by a master artist. The dragon turned his proud head gracefully down toward them.

Talyn finally remembered to breathe. Her body suddenly seemed very small and insignificant. "Oh, Finn . . ." Those were the only words she could find. She might have been angry a moment ago, but somehow the dragon had taken her emotions.

"I cannot have done this . . ." Finn's voice was shaky.

The dragon dropped closer, until they were almost blinded by the light shining off its crystal belly.

Talyn squeezed Finn's hand. "Tell him his name, quickly, the name you thought of for him in your heart of hearts. The Name you called him forth with!"

"Name?" Finn stammered. "I never Named it."

The dragon's eyes flashed like twin suns.

"How did you call it to you just now, it must have been with a name!"

Finn worked his mouth several times before managing to get out, "Wahirangi CloudLord."

It was not the name a Vaerli would have chosen, but it was apt from a talespinner. It appeared the newly made dragon was not displeased—for it didn't kill them on the spot. He sighed, a sound like many distant bells, and settled down in front of them.

"Talyn the Dark," said the creature in a voice so warm and deep that she wanted to run immediately to it and be loved. "Only now do you really begin to see why this little one was so important."

"You, too, have risen in importance, since you were in my head," she replied as evenly as possible, while trying to keep her tone deferential. She might be a Vaerli, but they were a penny a dozen compared to dragons.

Wahirangi's chuckle was like warm treacle. "I will confess that my change in circumstance is a surprise to me as well. Perhaps almost as much as to Finn himself . . ."

"You . . ." Finn paused and ran his eyes up and down the great length of gleaming dragon. "I can't be responsible for you!"

"So say you, but it doesn't negate the fact that you did indeed give me a Name; something that I never expected to have. The change is," the dragon gave a shake of its head, sending salt flying, "invigorating."

"But I don't know Kindred magic," Finn protested. "How could I do this, when I have no idea how?"

"This may be revealed—with time." Wahirangi raised one golden curved claw. "There are layers of secrets on you, Finnbarr. I could sense their depths from my moment within you."

"Yes, yes," Talyn said impatiently, "he is a mystery on a mystery. So now you can save him by getting us off the Salt."

"I agree." The dragon lifted his head, smelling the wind. "Things have woken here, more than just I. It is best I take you from this place immediately."

He held out one iridescent front leg, and they clambered cautiously up to sit in front of his shoulder blades. Beneath Talyn's hands, Wahirangi's skin was not at all a scaly reptile's. Instead, it was very warm and smooth like the most beautifully well-oiled and supple leather. Despite herself, Talyn stroked the hide. No, she corrected herself, it was even finer than that, more like the strongest silk covering steel.

Finn positioned himself behind her and, as when he'd ridden Syris, struggled to find a place to put his hands.

She guided them to her waist. "You best hang on. This Kindred may not yet have learned to be a dragon."

"I would not let you fall!" Wahirangi tossed his head and let out a snort.

Talyn had to remind herself that their lives were now in his hands, and it was not the best time to argue. With a surge of muscle the dragon leapt into the air, the great wings snapped open, and suddenly they were flying. It was a moment of amazement and beauty.

Talyn found herself grinning even as the wind battered her face and her stomach lurched. From here they could see everything, even if at this precise moment "everything" was the vast white of the Salt.

"Truly incredible," Finn shouted into her ear. "I must tell this tale. No one can have seen such a sight."

"None but Ellyria herself and the Swoop," she replied, "but if you tell it do you think anyone would believe you?" Behind her he was blissfully silent.

"Where shall we go?" Wahirangi's query rumbled through them as he circled higher.

Talyn had forgotten all about her mission for a brief time. Thinking on it now made her realize some difficult truths. It was unlikely that Wahirangi would surrender Finn to the Caisah. It made collecting her bounty all the more problematic.

Ellyria's dragon had been, in legend, both clever and resolute. He'd been a mighty adversary, so there was no reason not to imagine that this one was any different. Even with Syris at her side she would be no match for a dragon. It would require cunning and daring to collect her bounty now. Still there was a little time until she would have to make that decision.

"We need to find the Bastion entrance," she yelled to Wahirangi. It was galling when the dragon curled his head back to look to Finn for confirmation. She felt his nod against her shoulder blade and her teeth clenched.

The dragon climbed higher, making her ears pop and her stomach lurch, but from this greater height they had a better chance to spot the doorway. It should be a slight mound in the expanse of the Salt.

"It will take me a little time to find it," Wahirangi roared. "I have yet to get used to these new senses."

"No hurry," Finn yelled back, "I could fly all day." He gave an almighty whoop of delight as if he was a child.

Still, Talyn knew what he meant. It was beautiful: nothing but the brilliant blue sky and the wind. Up here not even the Caisah could reach her.

As Wahirangi circled the Salt, Finn put his mouth close to her ear. "It has been bothering me for days, Talyn, but you really don't remember me, do you?"

"Should I?"

"It wasn't that long ago, even for me . . ." His voice was muffled, but she couldn't ignore the melancholy in it.

"Time is a funny thing," Talyn murmured, not about to explain the constraints of immortality to him.

"We have met before. More than met," his fingers brushed the top of her ear, gently pushing her hair behind its curve. It was an intimate gesture.

"I do love you, Talyn the Dark." He held her face and looked right into her eyes. "Reject it if you want. It won't change."

How could she stand against such honesty? He was not lying. He knew full well what she was and had done. She thought for a moment of the little girl with the golden voice, and what sort of woman she would she have become. Would he have loved her if she was that person? Or did he only love her for her shadows?

Looking into the eyes of her love, Talyn realized he accepted all of her: dark and light, past and present. It was something she had not expected, to be loved in such a way.

It should not be. Vaerli should love only Vaerli. Manesto only Manesto. It was the way she had been raised, and by keeping to brief sexual encounters she had managed to avoid moments like these.

Finn had been a mistake, and falling in love with him was certainly not in her plans. That didn't change a thing. Her blood rushed at his touch and all reason seemed to flee before him.

With a long-held-in sigh, Talyn launched herself forward, banging against his mouth. Tasting iron, she flinched back. Finn was laughing and grinning through a cut lip.

"I'm so sorry!" Talyn stroked his face. "I am new to this. I just . . ."

"It's all right." He took her hand gently in his own. "It is only a little blood, and I have plenty to spare."

He leaned forward and kissed her, gently this time, showing her how. He tasted of blood and sweat, and she thought irreverently of the Phaerkorn and their rites.

"Shall you be my gewalt?" *Talyn asked lightly.*

"That would not be such a bad fate." Finn's fingers traced the edge of her face before running gently through her hair.

CHAPTER NINETEEN A LOST DANCE
247

Lights flashed in front of Talyn's eyes. It was impossible. She was *nemohira*, yet Finn had somehow managed to bring back a memory she had chosen to forget. He had broken the discipline. He was more dangerous than she'd thought.

The foolish thing was he didn't even know he had done it. He was still talking—unaware of the confusion he had caused. "I thought you would never forget me or those weeks by the sea."

If Talyn was not careful, he could drive more up from the depths of memory, and such recollection could well bring on madness.

So she had to stop him. "I did not forget by chance. I chose to forget. I am *nemohira*, which means I select those memories that are important. The rest I discard." Her voice was chill even to her own ear.

"You chose to forget me?" She didn't need to turn to know Finn's face would be full of hurt. "I thought perhaps you were playing a game with me at the masque . . . even later . . ."

"Well, I was not," Talyn said shortly. "If I had needed to remember those things, then I would have. They were obviously not important enough."

She did not voice the other choice—the one she realized immediately. Her forgotten self could have discarded those times with Finn to forget love and to be able to go on with her mission. It was what she would do. It was what she had done.

He was wounded by that, for his body stiffened against her, and his hands that had lain with such surety on her waist were now held clumsily. It explained much. Her past self had loved Finn enough to drive out his fear of her. It was why he had dared to meet her eye and why he had been unafraid even when she bound his eyes.

It would have been nice to remember making love to him, to recall the feeling of his skin against hers, but obviously that memory would have been linked to all the others. She'd been wise enough to discard them all.

"Memory is illusion," she reminded herself, "and my cause the only reality."

"That isn't why you forgot. You thought I was a weakness. You think of me as soft, but there are many ways to be both good and strong in this world. You rely too much on just strength."

Talyn said nothing. What was there to say to the truth?

Wahirangi began to spiral down, his sharp eyes having finally spotted the faintest circle of white against white.

The last time Talyn had been this close to the Bastion, there had been much more color on the Salt.

All the Vaerli came to the gathering, where leaders were chosen and sacred rituals performed. It was a duty to meet at the Bastion every tenth year. The place had been full of children. Talyn recalled laughing and chasing Byre around the camp, breathless with excitement and full of sugared treats the adults gave away easily. Practitioners of all the Vaerli arts made the air alive with the beauty of stories, song, and dance.

These memories Talyn had kept. They maintained her determination and kept her vengeance hot. "Take us down there," she commanded.

Wahirangi did not drop immediately. Only when Finn leaned forward and asked did the dragon fold his wings and dive. They landed as lightly as a cat on the Salt, and the dragon made no more noise than a feline.

Slipping quickly off his back, Talyn took a look around the spot where she had last seen her tribe. It couldn't have been quieter. It was exactly the thing it had become—a graveyard.

However, they were not the only ones here. Talyn's heart raced faster as she bent to the Salt.

"Not alone, then." Finn was at her side and apparently he knew tracks also. "The steps of a small woman." They shared a knowing look.

That was another problem. She suddenly realized past-Talyn would have known these things about him. Finn had the advantage over her. What had she shared with him in the night? What secrets and plans?

The world had certainly turned upside down in the last few weeks, and people being at the Bastion was the least of it.

"Probably grave robbers." Talyn got up and brushed salt from her knee. "Let's see how they like a live Vaerli."

He smiled faintly at that. "Do you want me to come with you?"

Talyn eyed Wahirangi, who was watching all this with a dragon-sized interest. It would indeed be better to get Finn away from the creature. She sighed and pretended annoyance. "Very well, since you won't be the first."

She led the way down the steps and into the depths of the Bastion. Finn trailed behind. It was not as if there were statues to loom over him or doors of knotted gold to blind his eyes, but there was the aura of the place. The

Harrowing had not changed it. It was cooler below, but still the air seemed close. The mind somehow heard sounds even if the ear did not.

Finn dropped back so that Talyn was forced to retrace her steps. He was standing before the Promise Stone, the oldest piece of *pae atuae* the Vaerli had ever written, the very first.

"I understand this," Finn said, his fingers hovering over the ancient words.

Talyn had ceased to be surprised by the talespinner—that he should know a language reserved for her people was the least of his miracles this day. She was surprised when he actually spoke the words of the Pact in the Vaerli tongue, as faultlessly as if born to it. Emotion choked Talyn, and for a minute she feared she might cry right there in front of him. She hadn't heard the Pact words spoken in her native language for three hundred years.

Finn turned to her. "They forgot the last two stanzas."

She wouldn't tell him that they hadn't wanted to recall those terrible warnings; they only wanted to remember how great they were. "Come, it is not far now," she said softly.

CHAPTER TWENTY

FEATHERS AND FLAMES

The Swoop dropped out of the clouds like a long-lost god's revenge. Equo looked up at the cloud of eagles, falcons, and buzzards spinning above their heads, and wondered at how death could come in such a magnificent shape.

"Crone's whiskers," Varlesh hissed, dragging Si by his elbow, "we need a Song, and now!"

Si pulled his arm free, suddenly very determined. "The wings are not ours to touch."

Equo glanced across at Baraca. For a rebel leader, he was showing no signs of fear as the Caisah's enforcers swooped closer, merely watching out of his one good eye the dance of the birds above.

His Portree compatriots did not run or scatter. A few muttered and clutched tighter to their pikes, but there was no sign of fear on their faces. They were not surprised, Equo realized with a start.

"You expected them," Equo blurted out. "You knew they were coming."

Baraca did not answer him immediately, but the corners of his stern lips lifted just a little. Something was, as Nyree had already suggested, different about the rebel, and it was not merely age or the loss of his eye. Equo couldn't put it down to anything physical. The man had always been brusque and sure of himself, but he still should have been worried by the sudden appearance of the Swoop.

In the cage the White Eagle screamed again, but it was not as loud or demanding as it had been. In fact, it sounded almost mournful.

Sheathing the sword he'd drawn at the approach of the newcomers, Baraca strode over to the nervously shifting donkey. Before anyone could cry out, he'd wrenched open the cage door. Equo's shout of dismay dried to nothing on his lips; the eagle, instead of leaping skyward to her Swoop, clenched her talons around the rebel's muscular forearm. She drew blood, but did not sink them as deep as she might.

It wasn't his vision; there was a faint aura of light around the rebel. Equo blinked.

"I don't believe it," Nyree gasped, taking an involuntary step back. "That cannot be!"

The fear in her voice chilled Equo, but he didn't have the opportunity to ask what she meant, for the birds dived at them.

Materializing as the woman warriors in their azure armor, he fully expected them to begin lying about with their swords. However, their stern faces were softened by confusion; some cocked their heads and looked about as if sensing something on the wind they recognized but did not believe.

Baraca turned to Varlesh, Equo, and Si. "I think it is time you returned this young lady's form to her."

"By the Maid's backside, we will not!" Varlesh's face was flushed red under his beard.

"Do as he says," Nyree whispered. Her tattooed hand was pressed to her head in pain, shielding her eyes as if the light was too bright. Something in Baraca's look promised everything would be all right. It didn't seem foolish to believe that, even though it had been a long time since Equo really felt it.

"Yes!" Si's hands were clenched at his side. "As he says."

Varlesh shook his head but began to sing. The low rumble echoed through his chest, Equo easily gave it form, and then their third opened his throat and formed words from their song, words that unbound what they had tied.

The eagle keened, raising its great wings to the sky before tumbling into the shape of the leader of the Swoop. Everyone seemed to hold their breath as she got to her feet. Azrul, still in her armor, unfolded herself and released a great sigh. Her breastplate was dented, and when she removed her helmet, shaking out her hair, her face was drawn and tired. Equo noticed again how young she was—very young indeed to be the cat's-paw of the Caisah.

She turned and looked at Baraca. For an instant they all expected combat, then with a creak of armor she bent her knee to the ground and dropped her head to her chest in front of the rebel leader. The gasp of shock that passed through her Swoop compatriots was loud and shocked. Equo stared in just as much disbelief at the cascade of Azrul's honey-colored hair that obscured her face.

Her voice, when it came from under it, was youthful but determined. "I surrender into your care the Swoop of the Lady of Wings, and ask for absolution for its deeds."

"Azrul!" One of the women, tall with an intricately braided head of copper hair, stepped from their ranks. "What are you doing? We are sworn to the Caisah."

Their leader looked up for a second at the stone-faced Baraca before shooting her reply back over her shoulder. "No, not sworn: shackled. Nephai, you forget that we owe allegiance only to the Lady herself."

Before the other woman could reply, Azrul had spun about and got to her feet in one smooth movement. "If you disagree then it is within your rights to challenge for the right to lead the Swoop."

Equo waited for the two warriors to begin combat. The tense moment ticked on, but the red-haired woman could not hold her commander's gaze for long. With a slight bow of her head she stepped back, but the rows of her fellows shook like birds rearranging their feathers.

Azrul, tall with the confidence of youth, turned to Baraca. "Do as you promised, then."

Nyree was suddenly at Equo's side. She burrowed in against him, and in surprise he wrapped his arm around her shuddering form. "I knew this would happen," she whispered mournfully, an apology for something he didn't yet understand.

The suggestion of light around the rebel leader grew stronger, as if a thousand pieces of multicolored glass were directing their beams at him. Abruptly, Baraca lifted his eye patch and the essence of the Void captured there burned out of the hole: it was unmistakable.

The world was outlined by the white light of the Void. It poured forth from the place where Baraca's eye had once been. It streamed through the air of Conhaero with a scream that hovered on the edge of what the ear could make out. Standing in its path, only Azrul remained upright. Everyone else, the Portree and the Swoop, staggered back. The Void was unbearably close.

Equo thought of the Trifold Spirit in that light, the person who'd been swallowed up by something indefinably "other" so that his people could reach Conhaero. It was the color of madness and Equo understood that the friend they'd once known was gone. Baraca had become more than human. He was now a scion, the first to arise in many, many centuries.

Above the howling Void, the rebel leader's voice called out in a language Equo did not recognize. Then the light snapped away and the world let out its held breath.

Azrul was wiping tears from her eyes with the back of her hand. Baraca was standing as he had before, but now that light which he'd kept hidden flickered around his shoulders, a reminder of the power he commanded. His eye patch was still closed and its power shuttered.

"A scion," Varlesh's voice was cracked and hoarse. "A real scion like the old days. Baraca . . ."

"What is your real name?" Nyree asked, and her tone was somewhat sharp.

"One-eyed Baraca will serve well enough for now," he said simply.

Equo had always wondered about the scions. They had been long gone from Conhaero when he'd been born into it, but people's passion for them had not waned. They were not the old gods of the places before Conhaero, but some part of the mortal soul needed divinity.

Yet their old friend's shoulders were bowed and his expression weary. He might carry the spark of something greater, but it looked a burden and not part of his nature.

"So what have you done, One-eyed Baraca?" Nyree took a step forward while everyone was, in fact, taking one back. "I know, even if they do not. These fools will think you offer hope, but all you are is the beginning of the end."

Azrul tucked her helmet under her arm and stared as the Vaerli Seer became visibly irate. "He has freed us from the Caisah, and my Swoop is indebted to him."

Nyree rounded on her, now. "Foolish Manesto-child, as always your people tread on matters that they do not understand. Did you not think there was a reason that the scions left Conhaero?"

She shrugged. "They just did, no one knows why."

"That is a lie!" Nyree's *pae atuae* were beginning to shift on her skin. "They told their followers they could not risk staying. The first sign that Putorae saw of the next Conflagration was the presence of the scions."

"What do you mean, Nyree?" Varlesh's frown of confusion was deep indeed.

The Seer took Equo's hands. "The return of the scions is the sign that the end is near. The burning my people have feared, the disaster that they risked damnation to prevent, cannot be far behind."

"Vaerli superstition," Baraca rumbled. "I am here to free Conhaero of its oppressor. The world needs the scions again."

The *pae atuae* began to glow, slithering on her arms and face, but when she turned to Equo he saw with horror that she was crying through black eyes: those Vaerli eyes which were full of stars. "It is all coming true, dear one. Everything I saw, everything that Putorae feared is happening. Now I understand what it really means to be a Seer; to see everything and be able to stop nothing."

"You're not saying Baraca is doing something wrong, are you?" Varlesh asked softly.

"Not by himself, no, but the return of the scion is the first sign," Nyree said with a ragged sigh, "the first sign of the new Conflagration. Our problems are so much more than merely the Caisah."

"Rebellion and now flame," Varlesh rumbled, casting a look at the other parts of his being. "Can nothing ever be just simple?"

It was an eerie place—this city under the earth—and the hovering presence of his inherited Blood Witch did not make Byre feel any better. So he passed two nights in the home of his father's woman as on-edge as he had ever been. Moyan avoided him, though he could feel her simmering concern with every gesture and glance. She tried to be kind to him but was obviously still very angry with his father.

However, he was aware that it was not just the three of them in the small house. His suspicions were confirmed when, in the still dark of the second night, Pelanor materialized at the foot of his bed. Byre gave no sign he'd woken but opened his eyes just wide enough to see her. A Manesto couldn't have distinguished her ebony skin in the shadows, but he could. Watching her, keeping his breathing regular, he admired the strong line of her face and the thick curl of her hair at the nape of her neck. Vaerli were supposed to be uninterested sexually in other races—part of being unable to breed with them, he supposed. Yet those heightened senses, as far as he was concerned, made that very difficult.

Perhaps it was also the danger. The Phaerkorn had almost as many dark legends attached to them as his people.

"Brother of Talyn," Pelanor whispered, fixing him with her dark eyes, "you are no good at keeping still." The smallest tips of her canine teeth pressed against her lips. Byre did indeed twitch.

He coughed uncomfortably. "I can't sleep."

"That I can see . . ." She cast an arch look at his rumpled sheets. "Are you perhaps worried about this task your father has set you?"

Women of all races made Byre terribly uncomfortable if he found them attractive—so now he knew he was blushing. Pulling himself up in the bed got him a little away from her. "Not at all."

Pelanor cocked her head and smoothed the edge of the bed. "It is more than likely a path to your death, and since I am sworn to protect you, I should stop you going."

It would have been easy to take that opportunity, to nod and say that was just fine. He could have pretended that he didn't have a choice, but life as a Vaerli had taught him to take the hard road. Instead, he leaned across and grabbed her arm. It was warm, and that had to be from his sister's blood.

This closeness brought the room to life. Even secondhand, touching another Vaerli was a joy he had never expected to feel again. The vague tickle of empathy alerted his senses, but he ignored it. "You agreed to keep me safe—not to prevent me from doing anything."

Pelanor frowned. "How did you know . . ."

"Like my sister, I am not without some tricks. Do you think you could really stop me if it came to it?"

He caught a flash of discomfort from her. Shaking off his hand, she pursed her lips and stared at him, considering perhaps how to react. The second of empathy had passed as he waited anxiously for her to decide. Whatever had happened between Pelanor and his sister he could not tell, but he was sure he was not yet as powerful as the Hunter. He hoped the Blood Witch didn't know that.

She sighed dramatically. "By the goddess' third mouth, you are a fool!"

"We have no divinities in Conhaero," Byre said without thinking. "They were lost in the White Void. Your 'goddess' is merely another scion."

Pelanor gave him a sharp look out of her lustrous eyes. "Surely there are few who would dare split hairs with a Phaerkorn on that particular matter," she observed tartly.

Byre shrugged, though his body thrilled with the hint of danger in her voice, but after a moment she gave a short little laugh.

"Just to be clear," Pelanor continued as she got off the bed, "I think I probably could indeed stop you, but you are right; I only agreed to keep you safe."

"Then you won't interfere tomorrow?"

"Interfere, no," her whisper caressed his ear even as her body faded to gray and evaporated into the warm air of the bedroom, "but I will definitely be keeping an eye on you."

Byre dropped back into a hot and restless sleep, never far from the knowledge that she was still in the room with him.

Retira woke him the next morning with a gentle pat on the shoulder. "It used to be tradition for a Vaerli going into battle to watch the sunrise with his kin, to see the new day and know that not all is darkness. Down here, though . . ."

Byre quelled his own rising fear as best he could. "I don't need to see the sun, Father. I have seen enough of its rises and falls. Instead, I'd like to see the world of the Kindred."

Moyan watched them go, her arms folded over her chest, and said nothing. After days cooped up in the little house, Byre thought it would have been good to go outside. He was wrong.

This city was not a welcoming one. Byre and Retira passed beneath marble archways and corridors carved from the very rock of the earth—they were very beautiful, yet everywhere doorways and windows were shut against them. No one was on the streets. A city this large should not be so quiet. Whatever the festival meant, he didn't like it.

They passed through cavernous gardens lit with a curious yellow light that came from the very walls, and fruits and plants that Byre vaguely recognized grew under its light, though distorted in frightening ways.

Yet it was the complete lack of people that sent shivers up his spine. Every corner they turned, he expected to run across some pale-skinned group of people, or find a child playing with a ball in a courtyard. But nothing happened. The air was so still and warm that Byre found he was happy to follow his father at such a hectic pace. If he had his way, they would have been sprinting, such was the air of menace and desolation around them.

It was obviously worrying Retira, too.

"This is not usual then?" Byre dared to ask.

"It is the festival," was the unconvincing answer. "Not much farther now." He forged ahead like a drowning man sighting land.

Byre kept pace with his father but couldn't help looking behind them. The people were still somewhere here—it was as if they were lurking behind doors with breaths held. The thought of the Witch was now somewhat comforting. Pelanor's ethereal presence was at his back, and her disembodied voice echoed in his ear, "Quickly." So she, too, sensed something was not right.

The corridors changed. The dwellings disappeared, and it became one seamless black, hot tunnel that angled sharply down. Sweat began to run down Byre's neck, and his clothes suddenly felt very heavy indeed. Even more uncomfortable was the thought that this was just a taste of the Kindred's fires.

They came to a huge set of doors, and Retira stopped before them. Bound in gold and platinum and decorated in unfathomable symbols, they were an impressive obstacle with no handles or mechanism.

Byre reached out and cautiously touched them. They burned under his fingertips briefly before swinging open. Like everything in Achelon, there was no sound.

They shared a wary glance.

"We could go back," Byre offered, but his words faded. They both knew it was not a real option. "Perhaps there is another way in . . ."

"There isn't," Retira replied. "The Gates are at the very back of the room, and this is the only entrance."

"Then we go on. Our lives are through this door, or not at all."

His father nodded with a face grim and set. "Forward, then."

The room they stepped into was a rough-carved cavern, but Byre did not have much of a chance to observe it.

Immediately his sister was there, not physically but inside his head. The Second Gift came whirling back, only more powerful than he had ever experienced it. Byre could feel her walking in his shadow even if she couldn't feel him in hers.

He stopped following their father and paused to let the beauty of it wash over him. She had changed; one taste of her mind in the chamber of torture had revealed that, but now he had a chance to see just how much.

Byre could have wept at the dark corners and narrowed corridors of his sister's mind. She was not the child she had been, nor the person she might have turned into. She was battered, bruised, and surrounded by failure.

Through curiously doubled vision, Byre walked on. He would say nothing to their father; he'd made his feelings known about Talyn. Also, it would be cruel to mention the return of his Second Gift when such pathways were forever blocked to Retira.

The sacred room was stark, beautiful, and carved from the dark-gray stone of the earth. It eerily counterbalanced the flickers of vision Byre got from Talyn. She was in the pale glory of the Bastion, and it too was deep in the earth.

It couldn't be just fate that brought both of them to these places at the same time. But he could sense no awareness from his sister, and the Second Gift felt curiously stunted. It was a one-way connection. The Kindred certainly had a strange sense of humor, to give so much but keep the best bit in reserve.

"Are you all right, son?" Retira held out his hand as if Byre was a child once more.

Even though he wasn't, he smiled and nodded. The double vision and the intrusion of Talyn's thoughts made him feel that if he blinked at the wrong moment, everything would shatter like glass.

Byre's eyes drifted to the elaborate hangings that were the only decoration in this chill chamber. His father was talking and gesturing to the huge granite slab at the very end of the room, but Byre's concentration kept shifting to the iridescent embroideries. He could hear the whispering of the Kindred beyond the granite, but he was sure they weren't the only beings in the room.

"Byre?" His father turned again and stepped toward him. It seemed very slow, as if he were battling against unseen winds. The air was thick, and his head felt as if it were not set on his body properly. The hangings around them were different in his vision. In one version they were merely decoration. In the other he observed a corner being twitched aside. Byre saw the muzzle of the blunderbuss and the explosion of shrapnel that would follow. His body moved, even if his mind could not work out what was happening.

Catching his father around the waist, he had him on the ground before the second reality could happen. A heartbeat after they both hit the floor, the gun roared and the air was alive with tiny, deadly missiles. His father's face was a curious mixture of horror and delight. "The Seventh Gift, it has returned to you!"

It was the only explanation. It should be impossible, as Byre had never reached the right age to get the Gifts before the Harrowing, but even as he thought about using them again they seemed to slip away. It was a strange Gift indeed to leave him at the moment it was most needed.

Neither of them had time for further conversation. The elegant hangings were ripped down and two dozen Rutilian Guard swarmed out. Retira and Byre scrambled to get out of their reach and climbed frantically up rows of carved seating. Suddenly, it was all about survival, when only moments before it had been something else.

Then Byre glanced back over his shoulder—just for a second. Everything changed.

It was the Caisah; Byre had never seen their tormentor, but it could be no other. He was tall, dressed in shining armor and actually smiling. While the guard swarmed after the two men, the Caisah jerked a woman with her hands bound out from behind the curtain—as pleased as a street magician with his trick.

At his son's side, Retira gasped. The effect of seeing both the Caisah and Moyan like that must have been quite the shock. As they watched, the tyrant grasped her around the throat and casually lifted her off her feet. She hung limply, tears streaming down her face, while the sounds of her choking echoed around the room.

Retira shot Byre a look of desperate anger. "Your sister's master! I wonder how far she can be behind?"

He touched his father's shoulder. "She is not with him, so there is hope."

"Come down from there!" The Caisah beckoned and threw down Moyan as if she were no more than a child's toy. His troops rolled her body out from under his feet as he stepped closer.

Byre judged the distance to the stone gates. It was too far to run. Even if he outdistanced the Rutilian Guard, he wouldn't be able to avoid the Caisah's magics. His only chance lay in the mercurial unpredictability of the leader himself.

Talyn's memory was still leaking through him, and the snatches he gathered told him there might still be a way. The Caisah's arrogance could be used to gain them time, at least. Taking hold of his father's elbow, he helped him to his feet. Both of them walked back down as confidently as they could.

The guards looked unconcerned as two Vaerli approached their lord. No one demanded Byre's stick, so assured were they of their master's power, but they did look very surprised when Pelanor materialized out of the air to stand at Byre's side.

"Ah yes, I was wondering when you would show yourself, little Witch." The Caisah waved one finger at her admonishingly. "Remember what happened last time we met, and behave yourself."

Retira blinked in minor confusion, but Pelanor made no reply.

The tyrant turned his attention to Byre. "You . . . I know you from somewhere . . ."

Straightening his shoulders, Byre replied. "I am Talyn the Dark's brother. We met briefly on the day you took her."

A slight smile at that, as if it were a treasured memory. "Are you perhaps angry I didn't take you instead? Still, I saved your life as well, so maybe you'll forgive me."

Retira was squeezing Byre's shoulder, reminding him of his duty, or perhaps warning of the dangers of conversation with the Caisah. Despite everything, he was capable of being charming and there was something intriguing about him—a being like Vaerli, but not.

"And you," the man-not-man continued, his stare shifting to Retira. "We have met as well."

"There were many of us at the Bastion that day."

The gaze dropped away, and the Caisah passed his hand over his face. When he spoke again it was in a far less confident voice. "I remember you all. A terrible thing. Terrible."

Suddenly Byre understood. The Caisah was like one of the madmen that gave up the memory disciplines. The weight of so much time and recollection was driving him as insane as any Vaerli with the same affliction. Despite himself, Byre darted a look at his father. He and the Caisah shared more than just Talyn.

Byre pitied him then—despite everything he had done to the Vaerli. Living with memory was never an easy thing, and must be even more so with the weight of so many horrors.

"So you should, too." Retira angled his body toward the Caisah and shot his son a look of desperation that surely meant something. The older

Vaerli pushed in closer. "You're a murderer and an oath breaker, coming to our Bastion and using the name of our Seer to gain entry like a thief." His voice boomed in the chamber, and even though he was much shorter than the Caisah he managed to somehow to look down his nose at him.

It wasn't the best tactic, for their captor only smiled. "You know why I came. It is you who broke the Pact!"

At his back, Byre felt Pelanor draw closer, her presence a chill to his right. The words should have been important to him—his father and the Caisah were, after all, arguing about the most infamous day in Vaerli history, one that he had only seen the aftermath of. Yet, realizing what Retira was doing, Byre tried to edge closer to the Kindred's door. Pelanor drifted with him.

They were as silent and as subtle as possible. Luckily, the Rutilian Guard were hovering around Retira as he blustered and roared at the fuming Caisah. They could see no danger in the silent Vaerli and the tall, dark woman at his side.

"Then why did you have to take my daughter?" A silence fell and even Byre paused. He couldn't help but hear the break in Retira's voice.

"You know why," the Caisah replied, his voice cool. "You know what you did when you . . ." His gaze flicked up and observed Byre. Whatever revelation he had been about to utter he swallowed it. His gaze hardened, and Talyn's memory told that this was a very bad thing. "Come here," the Caisah commanded, used no doubt to obedience from his Vaerli Hunter.

That was the exact moment when chaos erupted.

"Run," Retira yelled, throwing himself upon the Caisah. The guards' first reaction was to protect their liege, and the way to the door was suddenly free. Pelanor disappeared into the air, wrapping her chill presence about Byre. He turned to obey his father.

He didn't see what terrible power the Caisah called on, yet the world seemed to twist and bang against his ears. Then he saw his father sailing past him, thrown through the air like a broken leaf. Retira hit the door hard, and the room reverberated to the sound of his breaking bones.

Byre ran—but this time to his father. He didn't care about the door anymore, or his foolish quest. All he cared about was holding Retira, trying to stop the blood and trying to keep the life in him. It was awful and ugly, and he'd seen it hundreds of times before, though it had never been his own father.

He could hear the Caisah's footsteps and feel the menace of his presence hanging over them. Father and son shared a look through blood and tears that would be their very last.

"Put him down," the Caisah spoke. "Come with me and join your sister. You don't need to die as well."

"No," Byre spoke softly for Retira. He wanted his father to know that he wasn't giving up.

Retira's life was burbling away, washing out his mouth, but he struggled to say something. "I disobeyed." He clutched hold of Byre's sleeve. "The decision was made to forget it . . . but I did not . . ."

"Forget what?" Byre leaned closer.

"The fires . . . you must make sure they do not die . . . we're failing . . . we're . . ." Retira gurgled and then jerked in his son's arms. He breathed his final breath and was still.

The power of the Caisah was gathering. Byre could feel it tightening around him, stealing the breath from his lungs and squeezing every bone in his body. Pelanor dropped back into her body with a half-scream, forced by the tyrant's strength to give up her magic. She crumpled to the floor, elegant even while in agony. Her mahogany eyes locked with Byre's in understanding.

His father was gone. All was emptiness and pointlessness. Soon enough he would follow. Was this why the Sofai had sent him—to die for the Caisah as his sister lived for him? The breath was being taken from his body, and his throat constricted on nothing.

Chill broke through the darkness, soft breath entered his mouth. Byre sucked in a great joyous gasp as life returned to his starved body. He was not seeing things, there was indeed another woman standing above them, between Pelanor and he on the floor. Byre scrambled across to his Blood Witch and helped her up.

She made to embrace this new arrival. "Matron Iola!" Then she stopped, her hands inches from the other Witch.

The newcomer was as beautiful as Pelanor, though there was the faintest hint of silver in her hair. She had her palms raised flat between herself and the Caisah, but Byre could see that she was shaking.

Glancing across at the Caisah, he saw that the tyrant was frozen in place. The only sign of his concentration was a slight frown on his brow. The Witch, though, was muttering under her breath.

Pelanor bit the corner of her lip and bowed her head. "She Who Stands at the Gate, aid my matron. Give her strength."

It was a battle of wills then, and a smarter person would have taken that opportunity to run; however, curiosity and a strange instant loyalty held him in place. Besides, barely had the thought crossed Byre's mind than whatever power she had gained from her scion ran out. The world darkened for an instant, becoming somehow shapeless and terrifying. The implosion of power threw all four of them apart.

Pelanor and Byre found themselves sliding across the uneven floor with Iola. Across the room, the Caisah lay in a crumpled heap. The Rutilian Guards looked for a moment stock-still in horror.

Pelanor moved faster, helping her matron up. Byre felt the symmetry of her actions in an instant, and part of him already knew the outcome.

The Blood Witch was a shriveled remainder of previous form: pale gray and withered. Pelanor ripped open her palm with her own teeth and pressed the oozing wound to her matron's mouth. Iola waved it away. "Too late, little daughter . . ."

"Why?" Pelanor's voice was torn with emotion as trails of blood oozed from the corners of her eyes.

"The *Hysthshai*, she told me I could save you. Two must die for two to live, she said . . ." These last words were a rattle and then Iola turned her face away and disappeared into nothingness for the last time.

Byre took Pelanor's hands, as she seemed ready to rend her own flesh in grief. Across the room the Caisah was rising, not in the slow, awkward manner of one badly wounded, but in the quick movements of someone very annoyed.

"It has to be now, Pelanor," Byre whispered.

Her eyes, when they met his, were wells of despair and abruptly found determination. This was now more than a Pact.

Together they ran to the rough-hewn door, and together their hands pressed against it. Wonders of wonders, there were two hand-sized gaps within inches of each other; each perfectly sized for the Blood Witch and the Vaerli.

The feeling of before-thoughts lingered in Byre's mind, as if he were only taking the steps already laid out for him. The cavern shook. Looking back over one shoulder, Byre saw the Rutilians get knocked off their feet, while their master remained erect, staring with undisguised longing at the wall which was ripping itself open like curtains on a stage.

The Cleft was opening, and beyond was flame in which shadows moved. The heat blasted Byre, until he thought his flesh would melt from him. It was mesmerizing, with the shapes of Kindred dancing in the fires, alien forms which promised so much, both knowledge and pain.

Pelanor, the gift from his cursed sister, took his hand, and a wave of cool passed over him. "The first Witch to see the Kindred," she murmured to herself. "They will have to make me Mouth now . . ."

Within, the flames resolved into the rocky outline of the guardians; this Kindred had eyes of black obsidian and a body of running lava. For a moment it looked on Pelanor and Byre, but then it fixed on the Caisah, who had moved forward a few paces as if entranced.

"No closer, Eagle King, broken bird." The Kindred's voice was surprisingly light for a creature of the earth, but the sound of it was almost painful to hear in its purity. "The time has not yet come; our agreement has not yet run its course."

The tyrant straightened. "Not yet, you say. Have I not waited long enough? Have I not done as agreed?"

"You will know when it is enough and complete." The Kindred grew from man-sized to twice that height in an instant, as if to emphasize this point. "The boy is now within our realm, you could not prevent it, as it was bought with blood. Go back until your time."

Never before had Byre imagined that the Caisah could be humbled, yet there it was. The mightiest man in all of Conhaero stared into the flames once, before nodding and turning away.

Byre would have watched him go, but the Kindred filled his vision until he could think of nothing else. Like an owl eyeing a mouse, the creature peered at Byre and Pelanor.

"You have many questions, Kin." Its voice seemed gentler somehow. "They will be answered in time, if you may first answer this for me: do you wish to go on?"

"I thought . . . that is, I thought it was my duty."

"Duty is indeed a powerful motivator amongst those ground-walkers, but you may not follow Ellyria's path for that reason alone. If you purely enter to undergo the trials, it is not enough."

Byre felt Pelanor's hand squeeze his. "I think it is asking what you want for yourself?" she whispered.

Closing his eyes, he considered. His urge to go on, to find the dream that had set him on this task, had that been purely for a people he hadn't felt his own for three hundred years? Was even his dead father enough of a reason to step in the flames and take up Ellyria's burden?

With a sigh, he opened his eyes and looked up at the burning Kindred. "Not for those things alone. I want to know who I am. I want to know who my people are, and our past."

It was hard to tell if this was an acceptable answer. The head cocked and looked at Pelanor. "And you, little Witch-child, there is no blood in our realm for you."

Her chin tilted upwards. "Perhaps not, but I still have plenty of curiosity myself. Besides," she said, shooting a glance sideways at Byre, "a Pact is a Pact."

"Very well then, the flames await. Enter." The Kindred drew back.

Heat was now all around them, but Pelanor's chill presence softened the entrance. Byre smiled. He could hear music in the earth, like he remembered from childhood. Hand in hand, Witch and Vaerli went forward, stepping into the world of the Kindred to find what secrets it held.

CHAPTER TWENTY-ONE

POISON FROM THE PAST

Talyn the Dark did not pause or glance behind to see if he was actually following. Finn could hear her breathing, fast and low as if she had run a great distance—which was perhaps in a sense true. She was not the only one.

If the vision of the woman claiming to be his mother was correct, then the Bastion was his heritage as well. What of his father—was he Vaerli too? He had to be—but then shouldn't he look like one of them? He didn't have the dark hair and skin . . .

Finn couldn't think straight with his head full of so many questions. Nothing in his form or thought proclaimed him Vaerli, and he was not sure if he wanted anything to do with their perilous Gifts either.

So he said nothing to Talyn of what might be; he would not try to claim something he was not yet sure of. That could wait until the moment she dragged him before the Caisah to get her bounty, because if there was one thing Finn was sure of now, it was that she would complete her mission, dragon or no dragon.

Ahead the walls of salt curved away into unfathomable distance, but Talyn had stopped and put out her hand to steady herself against one. Concerned, Finn broke into a jog just as she began to scream. Before he could catch up, her whole body jerked and then she toppled over.

Finn yelled her true name, the one she wouldn't recall he knew. No reaction. Dropping to his knees, he gathered her up. Talyn was twitching so much he feared for her.

"Byreniko!" Her brother's name was torn from her throat.

Finn whispered her own into her hair as dread cramped his gut. For a long terrible time there was no answer, then Talyn's body twitched and her eyes flew open.

"He's gone." She licked her dry lips before speaking again, "I heard a shout. A cry of victory or pain, I couldn't tell . . . and then all was emptiness."

Finn didn't let go, wondering if she had heard her true name from his mouth. When Talyn didn't pull away, he thought of leaning in and kissing her, but her fingertips were on his lips. He had no idea how they got there. The Vaerli before-time was a cruel Gift indeed.

Talyn smiled and got out of his embrace with spare elegance. She walked away before reminding him, "I don't remember how it was to love you, Finn."

Talyn was striding ahead of him, which was impressive considering her legs were much shorter than his. Then she was gone, not waiting to see if he followed.

Perhaps she was right. It was memory of love that had got him into this dangerous situation, and could still end with torture and death at the hands of the Caisah.

Finn paused for a moment to examine one of the beautiful murals that decorated the walls. This first panel, painted the most intense shade of malachite, was marred by a series of shadows. It didn't take his talespinner's mind to work out they were the terrifying outlines of people contorted in agony. The Harrowing had happened here, he reminded himself. This place was soaked in blood and ash even after all this time.

He trailed his hand along the panel, feeling the indentations that had once been living beings. The next frieze caught him enthralled. It was a beautiful dark-haired woman standing poised, looking out into the world as if behind a thin sheet of glass. The trail of *pae atuae* on her skin pointed her out as the Made Seer.

Curious at how such a lifelike image had been created, Finn touched her outline. A snap of electricity leapt from the wall to his fingertips, and the world contracted.

The woman who had saved him shook her head and looked out at him with star-filled eyes, not quite real but not quite dead either.

He heard his name called and looked over his shoulder to catch the strangest sight: Talyn with her mouth open on his name. Her eyes were wide with shock, but frozen in place like an insect in amber.

In the chilly corridor, the only things that seemed capable of movement were himself and the apparition from the wall.

"Mother?" Finn realized he had not called anyone that for many years. "What have you done?"

She sighed. Whatever portion of herself she'd left here was very slight—

mostly gray—illusion. The talespinner part of him understood she had placed a tiny slice of herself aside in time. He'd learnt plenty of stories about such things: lovers who got to leave a last message, angry villains who wanted to spit out one final angry curse, or long-lost parents saying good-bye.

They all made good stories, but this was his mother—and she was smiling at him. Unfortunately, there was nothing to hug; his outstretched hand didn't even feel a chill when it passed through her.

"I wish that too, my son. I have put us between-time," she said softly, "a place that even the Caisah's Hunter cannot reach."

"You are Vaerli . . . that means I am Vaerli?"

"Part of you is . . ." She made a gesture that might have touched his face if she was corporeal.

"And your name?"

"Putorae."

Finn's stomach lurched. That could not be true. Putorae had been the last Seer of the Vaerli, and had died just before the Harrowing. Yet she had the markings of the Seer and her powers were rumored to be greater than even a normal Vaerli. A thousand questions burned in Finn.

Her beautiful face creased with sorrow. "I know there is more than I can possibly tell you. This form only has so much power in it, not enough to tell the whole tale. It has been waiting a long time for you."

It was grossly unfair. He above all people should have a proper story, and there was obviously a complicated one to be revealed.

"I have other slivers of my former self seeded along the way. You and your brother will have to find them."

He had a brother! Shock chased all other thoughts from his head.

Unseen winds began to tug at her form, pulling her apart like tenuous mist. "Go back to your dragon, the one you have Named. He will take you to your brother and there will be more answers there, I promise."

"But Talyn, she is . . ." Finn stopped, unsure what he was actually going to say.

His mother, his real long-lost mother, gave him a deep hard look.

She didn't need to say anything. He had a chance to make it right, a chance to understand his own past. He looked back to where Talyn the Dark was standing, hand opened toward him.

It was not concern that marked her face, but rather the vision of her prey slipping away. It said it all. She'd chosen to forget him and all they'd shared. Only an idiot would keep chasing a phantom, and he might be many things, but an idiot was not one of them.

He would take the advice of another phantom; this one at least loved him. "Poor Talyn is lost to us," the shade of Putorae, last Seer of the Vaerli reminded him. "Go quickly and find your brother, my beautiful son."

So Finn had to make a choice. It had all seemed a simple plan to foment rebellion, so he'd never imagined he would be in this position. He had to abandon his dreams of Talyn the Dark throwing her arms around him and remembering their love. He just had to accept she'd chosen to forget.

"You're right," he whispered. "Sometimes when you fight for someone you don't always win. In stories maybe that happens—but not in the real world."

Finn would keep his memory of Talyn but release the dreams he'd nurtured. He needed answers—and she had none for him. While the ghost of his mother held the Hunter locked between-time, Finnbarr the Fox turned on his heel, back the way he had come to find his own destiny. Behind he left the hopes of his past.

Talyn pressed her hand against the now-vacant mural. She'd never had Vaerli powers used against her, least of all by one long dead. Finn had been there, hand touching to the frieze, and the Hunter had only enough time to recognize the face materializing in the wall before the trap closed on her.

Putorae had played the Hunter for the fool, using her own vain loyalties to the Vaerli against her. When the bubble in outside-time faded, only Finn's tracks remained, back the way they'd come. Dimly she'd caught the noise of the great Kindred dragon's wings leaving her to ruin.

It was worse than merely having lost her prey. Somehow Putorae had severed the bond between them; it was as dead as the Bastion itself. Talyn the Hunter now had no way of tracking Finn. Nothing to offer the Caisah. Alone, the Hunter sank to her knees with a sob.

Over the sound of her own tears she heard the whispers of fabric dragging in the sand. The woman's head and all those extra ones were hidden under a large hood. Leaning against the curve of the tunnel, Talyn wondered if she was imagining compassion in that gaze. Wordlessly, she beckoned Talyn toward her, before turning and walking away.

The Hunter had no other purpose, and it mattered little if she was killed at this point. If she fled there were only two fates possible: death by her people's hand, or death by the Caisah's will. Rather than make that decision, Talyn climbed to her feet and followed.

They came down into the gathering place. This was the great white and empty cavern where the Council had met to discuss business. It was also where the Harrowing had begun. The woman with her hood up seemed almost normal. "This is the last road for you, Talyn the Dark."

She was right. All paths from the Bastion would end in the same place. Talyn should have saved the briefest recollection of being loved for a moment of desperation like this. Empty of fear or rage, she walked over to the other woman. She knew those eyes of bright stars; they could only be Vaerli.

"Why did you call me a fool?" she asked, sounding petulant even to her own ears. Funny how here at the end, pride was the emotion that remained intact.

"Not a fool, a child of fools." The woman grinned. Talyn didn't flinch when the woman touched her; let flames take them both.

Nothing.

Looking up at the normal Vaerli face underneath the dusty hood, Talyn felt herself break. "It's impossible," she gasped.

The other smiled tenderly. "We have no fear of the Harrowing. It cannot touch the Last Believers. We could teach it to you as well . . . if you choose."

Tears were now running down Talyn's face. Words she'd never shared with another came bubbling out. "I've journeyed all this time with only my destination in mind, and I've never noticed where I stepped or whom I trampled on to get there. Looking back now, I wonder if there is a way back for me. Is it possible, do you think?"

The Vaerli smiled. "I have walked that path, and I know for such as we there is no going back. For Talyn the Dark, there is only going forward, because now you too are a Breaker of Oaths."

"I know. I have failed the Caisah and my own people."

The abomination's face softened into kindness as she held out a hand to Talyn. "To go forward you need to understand the now. Let me show you."

What other alternative did she have? The other's hand was hot like that of a Kindred, but it felt to incredibly good to feel Vaerli skin on hers. It was a thrill she'd never expected to have again.

The woman led her silently deep into the cavern, through another dark passageway. They emerged, and there they were standing in the Golden Puzzle Room at V'nae Rae. Talyn looked about, sure her mouth was agape. They must have passed along one of the Threads of the Void, yet there had been no sensation at all. Every story she'd ever heard told of the horrors of using such a thing. Whoever the woman was, it was obvious she was a mistress of the Void to have passed through so simply.

It seemed like an age to Talyn since she had stood in this very spot, fitting the latest piece into place. She looked down at the puzzle spread out and gleaming in the sun. Bending, she caressed the leading edge, trying to recall every dark moment that had led to each piece.

"A valiant effort," her new friend said—her constant companions whispered in her wake, "but don't you see how you have been fooled all this time?"

She cast her hand out in a sweeping gesture while the Kindred halo howled in accompaniment. The puzzle twisted; its pieces shuddering to reveal what the Caisah had always promised but dangled out of her reach.

It was a picture, a huge sprawling image, and Talyn recognized it at once; the last Seer of the Vaerli, dark, beautiful, and smiling softly. Putorae.

So it had been a cruel joke all along. The Caisah had broken their Pact and played with her all this time. This was not the answer to the Harrowing! It was all a sham.

Talyn had placed her trust in oaths and pacts and magic; standing right in front of her was the proof that such things could be cruelly false. With a howl of primal despair she lashed out at the Golden Puzzle. Kicking and screaming, she broke it apart in a whirlwind of frustration that washed over her and consumed all thought.

The feeling eventually drained away, leaving a panting Talyn looking down at the shattered and scattered pieces—bits of her past she could never put back together.

So engrossed was she in what she'd done that she didn't notice the doors swing open. For an instant the Caisah and his Hunter stared at each other in mutual shock. Out of the corner of her eye Talyn realized that her new friend had faded back into nothingness.

The tyrant was the first to recover. She saw the flicker of his expression change, as if he'd been about to say something and then changed his mind. As always, his thoughts flew faster than hers.

Smoothly shutting the door behind him, he took in the shattered remains of the puzzle. Then stepping over them, he spoke softly, "So, where is your prey, my Hunter?"

It was ridiculous. He could see what she'd done, so he must have known she'd discovered his trick, yet here he was calmly asking for her side of the bargain.

Ignoring his question, she glared at him. "You are a liar and an oath breaker of the highest order!"

He raised his eyebrows as if it was trifling matter. "On the contrary, I fully intended to give you the answer you wanted. It seems it is you who is the oath breaker."

Talyn was lost to all reason. Dipping into the before-time, she drew her pistol and shot at her tyrant's forehead. If only it could have been that easy.

The Caisah flinched out of the way, though how he could have seen it coming was incomprehensible. Throwing aside the weapon he'd given her with a scream of frustration, Talyn drew her mother's sword and dashed across the room. Three hundred years of desperate hatred and loss had built up and now spilled over the edge of her control.

The tyrant, seeing all this, withdrew his own sword. He blocked her first wild swings easily. Talyn managed to rein in her anger, instead slipping into the before-time. He was there, as impossible as that was, parrying her blows, riposting so swiftly that she found herself forced back; at least he was having to defend himself.

Now as coolness stole over her rage, she wondered how this was going to end. In all the time the Caisah had been in power there had been many attempts on his life; some covert, some as blatant as this.

Knowing all this, Talyn understood she had only one chance. Throwing caution to the wind, she abandoned all conventions of swordplay and stopped thinking about what she was going to do. Instead she just let her body do it. It was a desperate measure to fool the before-time.

Instead of parrying his downward strike, Talyn stepped into the stroke. The blade smashed into her collarbone with all the power of his arm behind it. The pain was blinding as muscle and bone were sliced and pierced by the sword.

She had a momentary impression of his eyebrows shooting up in shock. His blade was caught in her flesh, which was struggling to manage the sudden flow of blood and repair what she'd allowed to be injured. Ignoring the agony by blind determination, she used her undamaged shoulder and her forward momentum to thrust him back on the wall.

Talyn had managed to surprise the Caisah—an unusual experience for him. Hearing the air get knocked out of his lungs, she didn't take the time to revel in it. Arching back against him like a lover in the throes of passion, she thrust forward with her mother's curved blade as hard as she could. The sword carved through the Caisah's shoulder and was buried in the wall behind him. The vibration of it piercing stone went through Talyn's injured collarbone so that she cried out with him.

It must have been a while since the Caisah had experienced real pain. She was more used to it than he was. So that made two surprises for him in a very short space of time. She'd have to take satisfaction from that, at least.

While he was coming to terms with this new reality, she yanked her narrow knife free and nailed him through the other shoulder in a similar fashion. She could have tried to slit his throat, or sever his head, but she knew the stories, knew it wouldn't work.

He screamed again, but it was a sound he was having fun with. When he looked up, Talyn saw that he was actually laughing.

Shaking and realizing with horror that she was crying, she asked him the one question that had consumed her. "Who are you?"

They were closer than they ever had been—even while dancing at the masque.

"You want an answer, my hawk? You spend so much time looking for answers. I am afraid it is almost pathetic."

She didn't care about her pride now. "I need to know," Talyn pleaded, as if he could be reached with desperation.

He looked down at her hands clenched on his jacket, and sighed. "I am the leader that never should have been—the broken bird."

She followed his gaze over her shoulder to where the large golden eagle statue spread its wings over the window. Strange how she'd never noticed before that under the eagle's claws was a rough edge, as though something had been broken off. More riddles and lies.

Turning back to him, she howled in frustration once again. It didn't matter; she was going to rip his head off just to see if the stories were true.

That was when the Caisah flexed his power. The air gathered around her and the Hunter was flung backwards against the wall. Trailing blood from her collarbone, she heard her ribs snap when she smashed into the unforgiving stone.

So they were both pinned on opposite walls: one by steel, one by magic. However, she was sobbing in anger. He was laughing.

Finally the Caisah's true face was revealed. It wasn't the calm one she'd always seen; instead it was one of complete madness.

The Hunter could feel the Caisah's Pact dissolving around her. It was as though her skin was being stripped from her and she howled at the unfairness of it.

At that moment, the woman walked out of the air to stand at her side. The Caisah, where he was pinned to the wall, didn't even take any notice; perhaps he couldn't see her at all.

"You cannot kill him," the woman whispered, wiping the blood from Talyn's eyes, "not yet, that is."

The Hunter grasped her with her one good hand. "Tell me you can help me! Tell me you can stop him!"

"You know in your heart of hearts that we can. Let us show you the right path; there is still hope for our kind. Come with us." The Caisah's power was subsiding about her.

None of what she'd believed in mattered. She was an empty vessel, worth nothing to anyone—least of all herself. Beyond words, she took the hand offered to her. The woman was Vaerli, the closest thing to kin she would ever know now. Perhaps they were more her family than her own had been for centuries.

The woman guided her away from the Puzzle Room, the still-laughing Caisah, and the past she had wasted on him.

Let the Caisah rage, Syris mourn, and the Vaerli search in vain for her, she would not come to V'nae Rae again. Talyn's last thought before she left was bitter indeed.

So many gifts . . . and I wasted all of them.

ABOUT THE AUTHOR

PHILIPPA BALLANTINE is the coauthor of the Ministry of Peculiar Occurrences series with Tee Morris. Ballantine also wrote the Books of the Order series: *Geist*, *Spectyr*, and the forthcoming *Wrayth* and *Harbinger*. Her works have won both a Sir Julius Vogel Award and an Airship Award. Although she was a citizen of New Zealand, love brought her to Virginia, where she currently resides with her family, including five cats. Naturally, because she is a trained librarian, she's addicted to the smell of old books.

http://www.pjballantine.com/
https://www.facebook.com/pjballantine
@PhilippaJane